Outcast Child

Kitty Neale

An Orion paperback

First published in Great Britain in 2005
by Orion
This paperback edition published in 2006
by Orion Books Ltd,
Orion House, 5 Upper St Martin's Lane,
London WC2H 9EA

A CIP catalogue record for this book is
available from the British Library.

Typeset by Deltatype Ltd,
Birkenhead, Merseyside

Printed and bound in Great Britain by
Clays Ltd, St Ives plc

The Orion Publishing Group's policy is to use papers that
are natural, renewable and recyclable products and
made from wood grown in sustainable forests. The logging
and manufacturing processes are expected to conform to
the environmental regulations of the country of origin.

www.orionbooks.co.uk

Henry closed his eyes, overwhelmed by the emotions that ripped through him. Molly's baby had been born late at night on the day that Judith had been killed. One life beginning, and one ending. *Oh Judith, Judith, you can't be dead, you can't*, he agonised, still unable to accept his loss. Every time he heard a woman's voice in the house he wished it were hers, and sometimes he actually thought he could smell the flowery perfume that she loved. Alone in their bedroom he would pull her clothes from the wardrobe, holding them tightly to him and drinking in her aroma. During the day he tried to hold his grief inside for his daughter's sake, but as the funeral drew closer it was becoming impossible.

'Have they caught the driver yet?' Phyllis asked, breaking into his thought.

Kitty Neale was born and raised in Battersea, South London. This solid background gives credence to her second novel, which is set in and around that area during the fifties. Her working life was varied; from shop assistant, secretary to the British Tourist Authority and then manager of a busy doctors' practice. In 1987 she moved to Surrey with her husband and two children. It is here that she took up writing. *Outcast Child* is her latest novel in Orion paperback; her latest novel in hardback, *The Empty Hearth*, is also available from Orion.

By Kitty Neale

The Empty Hearth
Outcast Child
A Cuckoo in Candle Lane

This book is dedicated to my daughter,
Samantha Munro Hurren.
She is my angel, my inspiration and my best friend.
'Sam, this one's for you darling'.

With thanks to my husband Jim for all his patience and support. Not to mention the many cups of tea. 'Love you, darling.'

Chapter One

Clapham, South London, 1954

Daisy Bacon dashed out of her street door, pausing momentarily on the steps as she glanced up and down the street. There was no sign of Sean or Patrick Carson, and with a sigh of relief she ran across the road to Susan Watson's house. With a loaf of bread clutched to her chest she rang the bell, and after a few minutes her friend appeared.

'Hello, Daisy,' she said, her freckled face lighting up.

'Hello, how's your mum?'

Susan brushed a strand of wispy, honey-coloured hair to one side, and heaving a sigh she beckoned Daisy inside. 'She's a bit better, but the baby keeps wailing all the time. Mum says she ain't got enough milk and it'll 'ave to go on the bottle. I hope that does the trick 'cos I'm fed up with hearing it screaming,' and with a small sad smile she added, 'I wish I was an only child like you.'

Daisy threw her friend what she hoped was a sympathetic glance. Yes, she was an only child, yet she envied her friend and wished that she too had lots of brothers and sisters.

They climbed the dank dark staircase with the wallpaper peeling off the walls, and as Susan led her into their small flat Daisy's ears were immediately assailed by the hiccuping sobs of a crying baby. The kitchen-cum-living room looked as though it was crammed to the rafters and Daisy felt a surge of guilt. How could she be jealous of her friend? The large family lived in just three rooms and she knew that Susan slept in a bed with several of her siblings. Two of the children were sitting at the table; their eyes avidly fixed on the loaf of bread that Daisy still held clutched to her chest.

'Mum sent me across with this,' she said, holding it out.

'That's kind of her,' Susan's mother said, the baby quiet now as she turned slightly in the threadbare fireside chair.

Daisy's breath caught in her throat and she hastily averted her eyes from the sight of Mrs Watson's thin pendulous breast on which the baby sucked frantically. The poor woman looked as white as a sheet and her eyes were ringed with tiredness.

'Have you decided on a name yet?' Daisy asked.

'No, but I was thinking of calling him William. It's a lovely name, but I expect it would get shortened to Willy.'

There was a hoot of laughter as the older child began to chant, '*Willy Watson . . . Willy Watson.*'

'Shut up!' Peggy Watson shouted. 'Susan, give them some of that bread, but not too much 'cos the others will want some when they come in, and mind you leave a bit for yer dad.'

Daisy had rarely been in the Watsons' flat. She and Susan played mostly outside, but now she watched in amazement at the deft way her friend handled the bread-knife. Susan seemed older somehow as she bustled round taking care of her siblings, and Daisy began to realise how different their home lives were. With a small strained smile, she said, 'I had better go now. Are you coming back to school tomorrow, Susan?'

'No, but if Mum's up to managing on her own I'll be back on Monday.'

'I'll be fine once this one's on the bottle,' Peggy Watson said. 'I just need a bit of sleep, that's all.'

'Yeah, and some decent grub inside you too,' Susan snapped.

'Now then, it ain't your dad's fault that he got laid off. Things will pick up when he gets another job.'

'I hope he gets one soon, 'cos you need more than just bread to build you up, Mum,' Susan commented as she handed a slice to her mother.

Daisy, upset by the sight of the children cramming bread into their mouths as though they were starving, blurted a hasty goodbye.

Susan went to follow but her mother's voice kept her rooted. 'Don't leave that knife where the children can get hold of it, yer silly cow!'

Turning hastily Daisy called, 'It's all right, I can see myself out,' and feeling a surge of pity for her friend she made her way home.

'What's the matter, darling?' Judith Bacon asked as her daughter came in. 'You look awfully sad.'

'I feel sorry for Susan, and the rest of the family. Honestly, Mummy, if you hadn't sent that loaf across I don't think they would have had anything to eat.'

Judith gazed at Daisy, her eyes soft. In some ways her daughter was in ignorance of the ways of the world. As an only child they had cherished and sheltered her, but now she was growing up and the blinkers were coming off. Judith knew that they were lucky, owning this large four-storey house, and Henry her husband had a good position in a shipping office. The job was well paid and Daisy had never known the poverty that others suffered. 'Things will get better for them when Susan's father finds another job,' she said gently, unconsciously echoing Peggy Watson's words.

'But how will they cope until then? Oh, I just wish we could do something,' Daisy cried, her eyes moist with unshed tears.

Reaching out, Judith gathered her daughter into her arms, and although Daisy was twelve years old, she wished she could protect her for ever from the harsh realities of life. 'Listen, darling, I've made a big pot of beef stew and dumplings for dinner and I'm sure there will be plenty left over. If you like you can take it across to the Watsons later.'

'Oh thanks, Mummy,' Daisy said as she leaned back to gaze up at her mother's face.

Giving her daughter a last reassuring squeeze Judith released her, unaware that Daisy's kind personality was a reflection of her own. Daisy took after her in looks too, with short brown hair and vivid blue eyes.

As Judith began to prepare the vegetables her heart was heavy. Daisy didn't know it yet, but it seemed likely that the Watsons were going to be rehoused. Susan hadn't been around to hear her mother saying that she was expecting a visit from the Housing Officer, and with yet another child she hoped to be given larger accommodation. Judith shook her head sadly, wondering how long it would be before they moved, and with no other girls of her own age living in the street, she knew her daughter was going to be heartbroken.

Chapter Two

It was a week later and Judith was sitting at the table watching her husband as he meticulously buttered a slice of toast. Henry Bacon was a quiet and taciturn man who sometimes found it difficult to show his emotions, but she loved him dearly. She knew that many people thought him standoffish, but his reserve hid a basic shyness. When Judith thought about Peggy Watson's husband she counted her blessings. Billy Watson was a drunkard and a bully, and there had been many occasions when his wife had sported a black eye. And now there was another mouth to feed, she thought sadly as she pictured the thin, undernourished baby. Oh it wasn't fair, it really wasn't. Why was it that some woman could have one baby after another, while she . . .

'Are you all right, dear?'

Judith forced a smile. 'Yes, of course. I was just thinking about the Watsons. Daisy is going to be awfully upset if they move.'

'She'll adjust, and she's got other friends.'

'Yes, but none that live nearby. I wonder now if we did the right thing in sending her across the common to St Catherine's. Maybe she should have gone to the local school.'

'Both Daisy and Susan wanted to go to St Catherine's. It's an all-girls' school with a wonderful reputation, and if you remember we decided it was a good choice.'

'Yes, I know, but she's going to be lost without her, Henry.'

'Stop worrying, Daisy will be fine. Now I had best be off or I'll be late,' Henry said as he rose to his feet.

Judith followed him into the hall where he picked up his briefcase from the hall-stand. At the same time, Daisy came running down the stairs, tucking her blouse into her grey pleated skirt.

'Bye, Daddy,' she called, running forward.

Henry leaned down and kissed her on the cheek, then turned and did the same to Judith. 'Bye, girls,' he said, smiling as he left the house.

Soon after that, Daisy left for school and Judith was alone in the house. Once again her thoughts turned to babies as she began her daily chores. It wasn't just Peggy Watson. Even her best friend and neighbour Molly Carson was heavily pregnant, and knowing how much Daisy would have loved a brother or sister, she felt again the desolation of her miscarriages.

Later that day, deciding that there was just enough time for a cup of tea and a chat before Daisy came home from school, Judith decided to pop next door to see Molly. As she left the house she gazed up at the sky, appreciating the touch of warmth that March had heralded in. Spring was always her favourite time of the year and she loved it when the bulbs bloomed in the garden, bright yellow daffodils, mixed with the soft blue of forget-me-nots.

Judith stepped down to Molly's basement, and when her friend opened the door she was unable to resist smiling. As usual, Molly's clothes looked like they had been thrown on haphazardly. She was large in pregnancy and the bulk of her tummy caused her grey flared skirt to rise up at the front, revealing an inch of frayed nylon petticoat. Her dark greasy hair was pulled back into an untidy bun, but her brown eyes twinkled as she ushered Judith inside.

'Sure, you're a sight for sore eyes, Judith. Come on in and I'll put the kettle on. By the way,' she added, 'I saw Peggy earlier and she's looking more like her old self.'

'Yes she is, and I'm glad that Susan's back at school. It doesn't seem right that the girl was kept at home, yet I know that Peggy couldn't have managed without her.' With a small frown Judith then asked, 'Did she say anything about being rehoused?'

'Only that she's expecting to hear from the Council soon. 'Tis about time they did something for the family, they're packed like sardines in that tiny flat. Oh, and Billy Watson's finally got himself some labouring work on a building site at Clapham Junction. Mind you, if he doesn't stop drinking it won't last any longer than his last job.'

As Judith watched Molly preparing the tea she was suddenly struck by an awful thought. Molly already had three sons, and now with another baby on the way, would she want to move too? With just this basement room, scullery and two bedrooms on the first floor it was almost as cramped as the Watsons'. The Irishwoman had moved here six years ago, and Judith would miss her terribly if she went.

'Molly, will you be asking for a bigger place too?' she blurted out.

'Well now, I can't say I haven't thought about it. But even if we were given a larger flat, we would never get such a big garden. I would hate to live in one of those high-rise places that the Council are building now, and Paddy would be lost without his pigeons. No, Judith, I think we'll stay put.' She laughed then, adding, 'Where else would we get a garden big enough for the pigeon loft?'

Judith heaved a sigh of relief, unable to imagine life in Fitzwilliam Street without Molly. When she herself had first moved to the area the tall, four-storey houses had looked affluent and imposing, with steps leading up to the front doors and large bay windows. Gradually though, most of the properties had been converted into flats. Since then there had been further changes and now many of the flats had been turned into bedsits, the tenants transient, staying for a short while before moving on again.

Smiling now at her friend, Judith picked up her tea, thinking about the lovely vegetables that Molly's husband grew and passed around not only to her, but also to other neighbours in the street. They were a lovely couple, always cheerful despite not being very well off. Paddy's job as a maintenance man in a local engineering factory wasn't well paid, but with what he grew in the garden, along with Molly's thriftiness, they always ate well. Both had pronounced Irish accents, despite coming to London over twenty years ago, and though all the boys had been born here, they too had a slight inflection when they spoke.

The two women chatted for a while, and then glancing at the clock on the mantelpiece, Judith rose to her feet. 'I had better be off, Molly. Daisy will be home soon.'

Nodding, Molly followed her out, and as both women climbed the steps to street level they saw Phyllis Tate advancing towards them, her thin face pinched in anger as she called, 'Molly, them bleedin' kids of yours 'ave broken me window.'

'What! How did they do that?'

'They was playing football in the street again. It ain't right, Molly. Why don't you make them play on the common?'

'Phyllis, I've told them time and time again not to play ball in the street. Are you sure it was my boys?'

'Of course I am. I ain't blind you know, and now the little buggers 'ave done a runner. What are you gonna do about it, Molly Carson?' Phyllis asked, hands on hips and her stance stiff.

'If it was my boys I'll flay them,' Molly said, her round plump face suffusing with colour.

'Yeah, but what about me window?'

'Don't worry, I'll get Paddy to replace the glass for you.'

'Humph! Are you sure your husband knows how to do it?'

'Of course he does,' Molly said, her eyes now sweeping the street for her sons, but it was Daisy and Susan that came around the corner. 'Here's your daughter, Judith, and I envy you, so I do. I wish I had girls instead of my little hooligans. Still, you never know,' she grinned, patting her stomach.

Judith smiled as Daisy came running toward her, knowing that Molly didn't mean a word of it. She loved her boys and was fiercely protective of them.

'Mum, can I play outside with Susan until dinner's ready?' Daisy asked as she reached her side.

'Yes, but go inside and change out of your uniform first.'

'Oh, Mum!'

'Don't argue, Daisy, and I'm sure Susan has to change too.'

With a rueful grin at her friend they separated, Susan running across the road to her house, shouting, 'Get your skipping rope, Daisy.'

The three women remained standing on the pavement, all eyes peeled for Molly's sons, and in no time Judith saw her daughter running out of their house again, waving at Susan who had reappeared too. She smiled at them briefly, but was distracted when she saw the Carson boys turning the corner. They were walking along sheepishly, and seeing the three women watching them they stopped short, their eyes wide with fear.

'Sean! Patrick! Get yourselves here!' Molly bawled.

At that moment Judith heard the sound of screeching tyres and turned swiftly. In one heartstopping second she saw her daughter skipping in the middle of the road, chanting a rhyme, oblivious to the speeding car as it advanced towards her. It wasn't slowing down! Why wasn't it slowing down? It would hit her! It would hit Daisy!

Judith dashed into the road, her face white with fear as she screamed, *'Look out, Daisy! Look out!'*

Unable at first to comprehend what was happening as her friend suddenly dived from her side, Molly now watched in horror as Judith ran straight into the path of an oncoming car. No! Oh God, no! Rooted to the spot she saw Judith shove Daisy in the back, the child flying into the kerb. Then almost immediately there was a sickening thud as the car hit Judith . . . her scream of agony dreadful to hear as she was tossed into the air like a rag doll.

For a moment Molly's legs refused to move, but as the car roared off she suddenly sprang to life, running to where her friend lay. Seeing the blood oozing from Judith's body she was unable to stifle a scream, but then Daisy flung herself down beside her mother, wailing like a wounded animal. Fighting her nausea, Molly cried, 'Daisy, come away, darling,' as she tried to pull the child from the awful sight.

Daisy's eyes were stricken as she looked up at her, and Molly was horrified to see that her hands were covered in her mother's blood. She leaned forward, grasping Daisy under her arms, but as she tried once again to pull her to her feet, the child fought wildly. 'Help me,' Molly gasped, looking around frantically at the crowd that had formed.

Phyllis came to her side, her breath ragged. 'I went to the phone box on the corner and called an ambulance. Is she . . . ?'

Unable to hear the rest of the sentence, Molly fought the blackness that threatened to engulf her as a pain ripped through her stomach. She looked again at her dearest friend's broken and battered body and knew, without shadow of doubt, that Judith was dead.

Chapter Three

'I've given your daughter another thorough examination, Mr Bacon, and I still can't find anything physically wrong with her,' the doctor said. Then patting Daisy on the head he turned to Henry, adding quietly, 'I'd like to talk to you outside.'

Henry followed the doctor onto the landing, and closing Daisy's bedroom door behind him, he asked anxiously, 'What's wrong with my daughter?'

'She's still in shock, which isn't surprising under the circumstances. The fact that she can't talk is psychosomatic, and I'm sure that with time she will eventually regain her voice.'

'Eventually!' Henry exclaimed. 'But she hasn't spoken for two weeks. How much longer are you talking about? Days . . . months?'

'There's no way of knowing. However, if you feel it would help I could refer her to a specialist.'

'A specialist! But I thought you said there was nothing physically wrong with her.'

'Humph.' The doctor cleared his throat. 'I was referring to a psychiatrist, Mr Bacon.'

'Do you really think that's necessary?' Henry asked, his face white.

'I'm not sure if it will help at the moment, and perhaps we should wait to see how your daughter is in another few weeks. I feel sure that with gentleness and patience she will recover.'

Nodding his agreement, Henry escorted the doctor out. As he opened the street door he found Phyllis Tate mounting the front steps, a dish wrapped in a tea towel in her arms. 'I've made you a nice shepherds pie,' she said, pushing past them into the hall. 'I'll just open a tin of peas to go with it.'

Henry's smile was strained as he bade the doctor goodbye and followed Phyllis into the kitchen. The neighbours had been marvellous, but sometimes he felt like screaming. He wanted to be alone. There was the funeral to face tomorrow, and as the time drew nearer he needed to give vent to the feelings that were like a hard knot of pain in his chest.

Phyllis, in the process of opening the tin of peas, turned briefly to look at him, saying, 'Molly's fine now and her baby boy is so bonny. You would never believe he came a month early when you see the size of him. She's on her feet again and insisting on coming to Judith's funeral.'

Henry closed his eyes, overwhelmed by the emotions that ripped through him. Molly's baby had been born late at night on the day that Judith had been killed. One life beginning, and one ending. *Oh Judith, Judith, you can't be dead, you can't,* he agonised, still unable to accept his loss. Every time he heard a woman's voice in the house he wished it were hers, and sometimes he actually thought he could smell the flowery perfume that she loved. Alone in their bedroom he would pull her clothes from the wardrobe, holding them tightly to him and drinking in her aroma. During the day he tried to hold his grief inside for his daughter's sake, but as the funeral drew closer it was becoming impossible.

'Have they caught the driver yet?' Phyllis asked, breaking into his thought.

Henry struggled to compose himself, but now found anger rising again; anger that he tried to fight against, but that threatened to consume him. Shaking his head he said, 'No, not yet, but I hope they do soon. God, if I ever get my hands on the person responsible for killing my wife I'll kill them! *Kill them!*' he yelled, spittle flying out of his mouth. He felt a tug on his arm and spun around, shocked when he saw his daughter standing behind him, and unaware that his voice sounded sharp, he said, 'Daisy, I didn't know you were there.'

*

Daisy turned swiftly and ran back upstairs to her bedroom. He was so angry; her dad was so angry. Filled with both fear and remorse, she flung herself on her bed, clutching the pillow to her chest.

Never before had she felt so lost and alone, unable to believe that she would never see her mother again. *Oh Mum, Mum*, her mind screamed. *I'm sorry, I'm sorry.*

The bedroom door opened and her father came into the room. He would hate her . . . hate her if he knew. The bed dipped as he sat down, and as she looked at him, her eyes wide with nerves, he leaned forward and scooped her into his arms.

Daisy felt herself being rocked back and forth, her father's arms tight around her. She heard a strangling sound, and then he began to sob, his body shaking.

'I'm sorry, darling, I didn't mean to snap,' he gasped.

Her own eyes filled with tears, but they refused to fall. *Why can't I cry? Why can't I cry too?*

There was a knock at the front door, voices, footsteps on the stairs, and her father rose hastily to his feet, surreptitiously wiping his eyes.

Molly Carson stood on the threshold, a soft smile that was tinged with sadness on her face. 'Hello, darlin',' she said. 'I've brought someone to meet you.'

She advanced towards the bed, cupping a bundle, which she placed gently in Daisy's arms. 'Meet Francis,' she said, pulling back the shawl.

Daisy gazed in wonder at the baby's face. His eyes were closed and she could see tiny blue veins in his eyelids. He had a little puckered mouth, a tiny nose, and as the shawl fell further back she saw a slick of black hair. She felt a lump in her throat, and for the first time since her mother's death a tear rolled silently down her cheek, followed by another that dripped off her chin and onto the baby's face.

'That's it, darlin',' Molly murmured, taking Francis from her arms. 'Tears are the best medicine.' She handed the baby to Phyllis, who had followed her into the room, and then sat down on the bed, holding Daisy closely to her ample bosom.

Despite the tears Daisy was still unable to speak and on the day of her mother's funeral she sank back into her shell where nobody could reach her.

Gradually the pattern of her life changed, and now after school she went to Molly's until her father came home from work. Susan Watson still walked to and from school with her, but the only way they could communicate was by Daisy writing on a pad, which she constantly carried with her. She knew it made Susan impatient at times, and now that she couldn't bear to play in the street after school, they were gradually drifting apart.

The blow came four weeks later when there was a knock on the door at about six in the evening. Her father answered it, and Daisy was surprised when he led Susan into the sitting room.

'I've got something to tell you,' she said.

Daisy nodded, her eyes puzzled.

'Me mum got a letter from the Council. They've given us a house in Balham.'

You're moving? Daisy scribbled on her pad.

'Yes, next week. Don't look like that, Daisy, we can still be friends.'

She wrote rapidly again. *School?*

Susan, who by now was used to Daisy's cryptic notes, knew immediately what her friend meant. 'I'll have to change schools.'

Daisy stared at her friend, unable to believe what she was hearing, but before she could write anything, Susan said, 'I can't stop. I've got to keep an eye on the kids 'cos me mum is all in a dither and is starting to pack our things already.'

Blinking away the tears that were filling her eyes, Daisy walked with Susan to the door and after seeing her out she rejoined her father in the sitting room.

'Don't look so sad, darling, you've got lots of other friends,' Henry said.

Flopping onto a chair, Daisy shook her head. Her father was so wrong. She didn't have lots of friends. The other girls at school had been kind at first, but as the weeks went by they slowly began to drift away. She didn't blame them. Why would anyone want to be friends with her? And anyway, after what she had done, it was no more than she deserved.

The following week, after Susan and her family moved out of Fitzwilliam Street, Daisy had to walk home from school on her own. At first she didn't mind. It was easier to be alone, not to have to worry about trying to communicate by writing on her pad all the time. But by the end of the third week her nerves were jumping. Now, when she was walking home from school, Molly's sons Patrick and Sean took every opportunity to torment her. They seemed to resent it that she went to their house after school, but unable to bully her in front of their mother they took to ambushing her on the Common.

Still grieving and unable to cope with their teasing, Daisy took to comfort eating. Molly baked cakes three times a week, and now made an extra batch for Daisy and her father. When she gave them to her to take home, Daisy would sneak them up to her room, and at night when unhappiness gnawed at her stomach she would cram the cakes one after another into her mouth.

'Look, it's Porky Pig,' Patrick jeered as Daisy walked home from the sweetshop on Saturday.

Her heart sank. She tried to skirt around them, but every time she moved they moved with her, blocking her path.

'Come on, give us a grunt, Porky!' Sean cried, howling with laughter.

'Leave her alone!'

Daisy spun around, relieved to see Molly's eldest son, Liam. He was sixteen and at work, but on the rare occasions that she saw him he was always kind to her. He had black hair and wonderful emerald-green eyes, which were now blazing with anger. 'Get indoors the pair of you, and I'll have a word with Mam about your behaviour.'

Without a word the boys ran off, and smiling gratefully, Daisy gazed up at Liam.

'Take no notice of them, darlin', they're just a pair of silly kids. You come and see me if they give you any more trouble — all right?' he added.

Daisy nodded, and after giving her a little wink, Liam walked away.

It was then that Daisy's hero worship was born, and for many nights as she lay in bed stuffing cakes, she would think of Liam and of how he had helped her. In her imagination he became her handsome knight in shining armour, riding to her rescue on a huge black horse.

Chapter Four

Vera Tucker looked at her measly wage packet with disgust. How would she ever be able to save enough money to get her son back? At this rate it would take years.

In despair she flung herself onto the bed in her tiny room. It felt as if a part of her was missing and her arms ached to hold her baby again. Georgie was only four months old and he needed her, needed his mother. Hate for Lennie Talbot rose in her chest. He had taken their son and thrown her out, and she was helpless against him. Maybe she should have told him the truth – told him why she wouldn't sleep with him any more. No, he would have gone mad. Yet what had happened wasn't his fault, or hers – the truth lay in the past. God, if only she hadn't got mixed up with him in the first place. It was hopeless – how could she fight the biggest gangster in the area?

Oh my baby, my baby, she thought, tears stinging her eyes. Money . . . if she only had money, then she could somehow snatch Georgie back and go abroad where Lennie would never be able to find them.

There was a knock on her door, and fighting her tears she rose from the bed. Guessing that it was her landlady, she grabbed her wage packet and counted out the rent money. Olive Cole insisted that it was paid on the dot, and in the three weeks that Vera had lived in this bedsit she had come to despise her landlady. The woman was a sloven and a gossip, and Vera avoided her as much as possible. Heaving a sigh she opened the door, the money in her hand.

'Hello, Miss Tucker. How are you? I haven't had a chance to talk to you all week.'

'I'm fine, thank you,' Vera said, her voice dismissive as she held out the money.

'Thank you, and have you got your rent book?'

Blast, I forgot it, Vera thought as she turned back into her room. It was the opportunity Olive Cole was waiting for and she followed in behind her.

Searching frantically, Vera found the book behind the small make-up mirror on her dresser, noticing that after quickly scanning the room, her landlady was now staring avidly out of the window, looking down at the street below.

'How's your job going at the hospital? You're a receptionist, aren't you?' she asked.

'Yes,' Vera said shortly, fed up with the way that Olive Cole questioned her at every opportunity.

Crossing the room she handed the landlady her rent book, annoyed that instead of filling it in she continued to look out of the window. 'Oh look, there's Mr Bacon,' she said. 'It was a terrible tragedy when his wife was killed, and now he's been left to bring up his daughter on his own.'

Vera looked without interest at the car that had drawn up opposite, but then Mrs Cole spoke again and her ears pricked up. 'Mind you, he's comfortably off you know. He owns the house and he's got a very good job. He's the manager of a shipping office. Yes, Mr Bacon is quite affluent and he gave his wife a lovely send-off. She had a beautiful mahogany coffin with brass handles.'

Normally Vera was sickened by Mrs Cole's gossip. She seemed to know about everything that went on in the street, and what she didn't know, she made it her business to find out. Trying to hide her interest, Vera asked, 'How did his wife die?'

'Oh, it was terrible, terrible,' she said, turning to Vera. 'She pushed her daughter out of the way of a speeding car, but was unable to save herself.'

'Really?' Vera said. 'How awful. When did it happen?'

'It was only three months ago,' Mrs Cole said, going on to describe the accident in vivid detail.

When the woman finally stopped speaking, Vera said, 'The poor man, but I expect he's got a large family to help him with his daughter.'

'Oh no. He's only got one relative. A sister that lives somewhere in Hampshire, and as far as I know he doesn't see much of her.'

Vera had no idea how Mrs Cole knew so much about the man, but for once was glad to listen to her gossip. An idea was forming, an idea that could solve all her problems, but one that would take a lot of careful planning.

Four weeks later Vera was ready to put her plan into action. She had bleached her dark brown hair to a soft honey blonde, and wearing a smart suit she strolled down the street carrying a bag of shopping. After watching Henry Bacon's movements carefully she knew that he was a man of habit. He arrived home at exactly the same time every day, his movements like clockwork, and now as his car drew into the kerb she was almost by his side.

'Oh,' she cried, pretending to trip, and as she fell her bag of shopping spilled onto the pavement.

Just as she had hoped, Henry Bacon rushed to her side, and leaning down to grasp her elbow he helped her to stand up. 'Are you all right?' he asked.

'Yes, I think so, and thank you so much,' Vera told him. 'Oh dear, my shopping,' she said in dismay. Then taking a step forward she cried, 'Ouch!' as she bent to clutch her ankle.

'Here, let me,' he said, rushing forward to pick up her groceries, and after stuffing them hurriedly into the bag he returned to her side. 'You may have sprained your ankle. Have you got far to go?' he asked, his face creased with concern.

'No, I only live on the other side of the road,' Vera said, and looking at him helplessly again she took another step forward, crying out in pain as she forced tears into her eyes.

'Please, let me help you,' Henry said.

Vera lowered her eyes, hiding her triumph. It was working
. . . her plan was working.

Chapter Five

Henry stood in front of the hall mirror, straightening his tie. He still couldn't believe it, couldn't believe that a beautiful woman like Vera could be interested in him. He thought back to that time seven weeks ago when she had literally fallen at his feet, and still found that his memory was hazy about how they had ended up going out together. Her ankle had turned out to be just slightly twisted, and she had thanked him profusely for his help. He had vague memories of the conversation somehow turning to food, and the next thing he knew Vera was accepting his invitation to go out to dinner.

At first he had been wracked with guilt. How could he be attracted to another woman when Judith had been dead for less than six months? But Vera was wonderful, and if he could have likened her to anyone it would be the film star Lana Turner. She was always so refined and smartly dressed. At first he had been a little in awe of her sophistication, but she had been so understanding of his problems with Daisy, and had insisted that rather than hurt the child, they should keep their meetings secret.

They now went out together twice a week, and to cover this Henry told Daisy that he had joined a chess club. He didn't like lying to his daughter, but didn't think she would be able to cope with the truth – that and the fact that he didn't want his business bandied around the street. It had been hard enough asking Phyllis Tate to babysit and he was sure she was suspicious about his outings, but so far she hadn't probed any further.

Finding Daisy beside him he smiled at his daughter. 'I'm off now, darling. Are you sure you'll be all right with Mrs Tate?'

Her eyes were wide as she looked up at him, but she gave a small nod.

'Right, I'll just put my head around the door to say goodbye to her. Be a good girl, Daisy.'

Having driven to their meeting place, Henry got out of the car and scanned the street, pleased to see Vera coming towards him. He leaned forward, kissing her lightly on the cheek and then opened the passenger door. 'Hop in, I've booked a table for dinner.'

'Oh lovely,' she said, giving him one of her wonderful warm smiles.

'You look beautiful,' Henry told her, admiring her silver-grey suit with the jacket nipped in at the waist.

'Thank you, and I must say that you look very smart.'

They looked at each other, suddenly bursting into a fit of giggles as Henry was unable to resist saying, 'We sound like a mutual admiration society.'

Reaching the restaurant Henry held out a chair for Vera, and when she was settled he sat opposite her at the table laid for two. The waiter brought the menu and once they had ordered, Vera took out her cigarettes. After lighting up she blew a cloud of smoke into the air, and then asked, 'Did Daisy like her birthday present, Henry?'

He frowned. His daughter's birthday last week had been a strain for both of them. Judith had always made a special tea and baked a cake, adding another candle each year. This time there had been little to mark the occasion, and it served as a poignant reminder of how things used to be. Now, pushing thoughts of Judith to one side, he said, 'Yes, she liked the charm bracelet. Thank you for helping me to choose it.'

'Oh, it was nothing, and I enjoyed our little shopping expedition. Did you take Daisy to see the specialist on Thursday?'

Henry smiled, pleased that she remembered. 'Yes, but he couldn't add anything to what our doctor has already said. He too feels sure that Daisy's symptoms are psychosomatic, and that with patience she will regain her voice.'

'The poor child,' Vera said sympathetically as their first course arrived, and after the waiter had placed the bowls of soup on the table, she added, 'I wish I could do something to help her.'

Henry lowered his head, and as he picked up his spoon his thoughts were racing. Every time he looked at Vera his heart leaped, and at first, feeling disloyal to Judith he had fought his feelings. But should he? Surely Judith would want him to be happy? There was his daughter to consider too. Daisy needed a woman in her life, someone to be there when she came home from school, someone to care for her. Oh, he knew no one could ever replace Judith, but Vera was a wonderful person and he was sure that she would be a perfect stepmother.

'You're very quiet, darling, is something wrong?' Vera asked, reaching out and placing her hand over his.

'No, I'm fine,' he told her, and at the look in her eyes he wondered if he dare reveal his feelings. Was it possible that she felt the same? No, surely it was too soon?

'Are you sure you're all right?' she asked.

Henry smiled, and hearing her concern gave him the courage to speak. 'Vera, I know we've only known each other for less than two months, but in that time you have come to mean a great deal to me.'

'You mean a lot to me too, Henry.'

'I think we should stop meeting in secret, Vera, and I would like to introduce you to my daughter.'

'Oh, are you sure, darling? It might upset her to know that you're seeing someone and I wouldn't want to cause her any more pain.'

God, she was wonderful, Henry thought again, so kind and caring. He leaned forward and whispered, 'Vera, I think I'm in love with you.'

'Oh Henry,' she whispered, her eyes shining. 'I love you too.'

Daisy stared at the woman her father had brought in, surprised when she came to kneel in front of her.

'Hello. I know your name is Daisy and your father has told me all about you. My name is Vera, and I hope we can be friends.'

The woman's smile was warm and Daisy thought she was beautiful. She had wonderful honey-coloured hair and soft grey eyes. Daisy's brows creased. She was sure she had seen Vera before — her face was familiar. But where?

'You look puzzled, darling. What is it?' Vera asked softly.

Picking up her pad, Daisy scribbled on it.

'Yes, you probably have seen me. I live right opposite you, and my hair wasn't always this colour. I'm afraid I'm rather vain, and I fancied a change. Do you like it?'

Daisy found herself warming to Vera. Yes, she did like her blonde hair, and smiling she nodded her head.

'Your father and I have become good friends, Daisy. I hope you don't mind.'

Surprised, Daisy looked up at her father. Why should she mind? She noticed that his face was flushed, but couldn't understand why and returning her attention to Vera, she wrote on her pad, *No, I don't mind*.

'That's wonderful, and I'm sure we'll all have lots of fun together,' Vera cried, her smile wide.

Four weeks later, Daisy's father drew her onto his knee. His eyes were bright and after giving her a hug, he said, 'I've got something to tell you, darling. Now, you know that I loved your mummy very much, and no one can ever take her place. But you see I've come to care for Vera, and you seem to like her too. Am I right?'

Daisy nodded, but at her father's next words she reared up, her eyes wide.

'I've asked Vera to marry me, and she has agreed. Won't it be wonderful to be a family again, darling?'

Daisy's thoughts churned. She missed her mother so much and hated the emptiness of the house now. Her mother always sang as she worked, and when not singing she listened to music on the wireless. Since her death the house was always so quiet, almost as if it had died with her.

But now Daddy was saying that he was going to marry Vera, and that would mean that she would come to live with them.

24

Daisy screwed up her eyes, trying to imagine what it would be like. Vera was pretty and kind, and it was nice to see her father laughing again. A thought struck her, and leaning forward Daisy grabbed her pad. Writing rapidly she asked, *Will I have to call her Mummy?*

'No, of course not, darling. Judith was your mummy and always will be.'

When are you getting married?

'Well, this might come as a surprise, darling, but we're getting married in three weeks' time.'

Chapter Six

'I think it's indecent, so I do,' Molly said indignantly.

'Now then, 'tis none of our business,' Paddy told her.

'But Judith only died eight months ago.'

'Molly, what the man does is no concern of ours. Surely you don't begrudge him a bit of happiness?'

Francis began to bang his spoon on the arm of his highchair, baby food scattering all over the floor. Molly swooped him up into her arms, and wiping his face with a damp cloth, she said, 'Of course I want Henry to be happy, but 'tis Daisy I'm worried about. Have you seen the woman he's marrying? She looks like something out of a fashion magazine.'

Paddy laughed. 'Oh, 'tis jealousy that's eating you, is it, Molly Carson?'

'No, it isn't!' she said sharply. 'But Olive Cole said that she had seen Vera Tucker's shenanigans, and is sure that the woman set out to trap Henry. I'll tell you something else, Paddy; she dyed her hair blonde just before she met him. Now why did she do that?'

'Begod, woman, how should I know? Lots of women dye their hair, and it's not a crime surely?'

'Well, it's very funny if you ask me.'

'Does this mean we're not going to the party tonight?'

'No, of course not. Mind you, I think the wedding's a bit strange too – just the two of them going off to get married in the Register Office this morning, and not even Daisy going with them.'

Paddy heaved a sigh. 'Molly, I've told you, 'tis none of our business. Now drop the subject will you, because I'm fed up with hearing about Henry Bacon.'

Molly cast her husband a dark look, and putting Francis back into his highchair she filled a bucket with water. As she began to wash the kitchen floor her lips were clamped tightly together. It didn't matter what Paddy said, she was unhappy about the goings-on next door. Judith had been her best friend and she felt it her duty to watch out for Daisy – and by God, that is just what she intended to do.

'How do you do, Mrs Carson,' Vera said imperiously, her head held high.

'There's no need to be so formal. Call me Molly.'

'Oh, I don't think so. I am sure you must realise that you and I have nothing in common.' Vera held her breath. For her plan to work she had to alienate these neighbours. There must be no interference, no nosing into her business.

'What do you mean, we have nothing in common?' Molly cried, rearing up with indignation. 'Do you think you're too good for the likes of us, is that it? Well, let me tell you I was great friends with the first Mrs Bacon, and Judith was a lovely woman. Since she died I've been looking after Daisy after school, and I'm very fond of the girl.'

'Mrs Carson, now that Henry and I are married there will be no need for you to look after Daisy. I am sure my husband appreciates all you have done for him and will see that you receive sufficient remuneration.'

At that moment Henry walked to their side, saying, 'Ah, I see you've met our neighbour, darling,' as he put an arm around Vera's waist.

'Yes, and I was just telling Mrs Carson that there will be no need for her to look after Daisy now. She has been marvellous, Henry, and I am sure you appreciate all her help.'

Molly's jaw dropped. Vera had changed like a chameleon and was now all sweetness and light. 'But . . . but . . .' she spluttered.

'Yes, Vera's right, Molly – you have been wonderful and I don't know how to thank you.'

'Henry, darling, would you get me another drink, please,' Vera said, handing him her empty glass. As he walked away, she smiled sardonically at Molly. 'If you'll excuse me, Mrs Carson, I must talk to my other guests.'

Vera made her way across to another woman who showed signs of being interfering. Phyllis Tate was munching on a ham sandwich and smiled widely as she approached, revealing a mouth crammed full of partly-chewed bread.

'Hello, ducks. Congratulations on your marriage. Henry Bacon is a fine man.'

'Yes, I know, Mrs Tate.'

'Call me Phyllis, dearie.'

'No, I don't think so. We are unlikely to become friends and I hate informality.'

Phyllis Tate gasped, staring at Vera as though struck dumb.

'Enjoy the party,' Vera said as she walked away, hiding a smile. Well, that was two of the busybodies dealt with, and that only left Olive Cole. There were no other people in Fitzwilliam Street that she had to worry about, and any who tried to ingratiate themselves with her, she would deal with. However, Olive Cole was her main concern and as yet she hadn't thought of a way to thwart the woman. Luckily Henry couldn't stand her either, so it was unlikely that she would ever be invited to their home.

As she walked across the room Vera heaved a sigh. She hated what she was going to do, but thinking of her son a surge of pain shot through her. Georgie was already nine months old and the time was passing so quickly. Oh my baby, she agonised, fighting the tears as her resolve hardened. Yes, she planned to steal Henry's money, but what choice did she have? She would do anything – anything – to get her son back. Without Georgie, her life meant nothing.

Chapter Seven

Six weeks later, Vera was almost going out of her mind. She had searched everywhere, but was unable to find any evidence that her husband was affluent, and cursed the fact that she had listened to Olive Cole's gossip. To test the water she had coaxed Henry into buying new furniture for the living room, and he had done so with little resistance. And though he wasn't mean with the housekeeping money, there was still little left over at the end of the week. Last week on Christmas Day he had been very generous, and she had been thrilled with the set of pearls he had given her. Daisy, too, had many presents to open, and even though subdued she was thrilled with her gifts. Christ, it must have cost him a pretty penny so he must have savings – he must, she thought frantically.

Having found the key, she was now going through his desk, carefully pulling out documents to ensure that she put them back in the same order. There were old bills, the deeds to the house and evidence that he had life insurance, but no bank statements. Finding nothing, Vera slammed the bureau with frustration, and after locking it she stomped back to their bedroom. Replacing the key in Henry's dresser where she had found it, she ground her teeth. Where else could she look?

Glancing at the clock on the bedside table, she grimaced. If she didn't get a move on she'd be late, and in a few more hours Daisy would be home from school.

Oh Georgie, Georgie, her heart cried as her thoughts turned to her son. The only news she got of him was when she secretly met her cousin Betty Clarke who was still working in the club.

Though Betty rarely saw Georgie, she was at least able to tell her that he was well.

Standing up she moved to the dressing-table, and after applying a fresh coat of lipstick she put on her suit jacket before hurrying out of the house.

'How is he? Have you seen him?' Vera asked eagerly.

'I've got something to tell you,' Betty said, looking quickly around the café to make sure no one was in earshot.

'Is it about Georgie?'

'Yes, and you'll never guess what, Vera. Lennie has asked me to look after him.'

'No!'

'Yes. Apparently he's finished with his latest floozy.'

Vera sat back in her chair, amazed at this turn of events. 'But why has he asked *you* to look after him?'

'I dunno, but I said yes. Perhaps he's decided that Georgie needs someone permanent in his life, instead of one tart after another.'

'Are you sure that he only wants you to look after George? Knowing Lennie's appetites you might find yourself in his bed.'

'I don't think I'm his type, thank God. No, he made it plain that all he cares about is that Georgie gets well cared for.'

A thought struck Vera and she smiled with delight. 'Betty, do you know what this means? I'll be able to see Georgie now.'

'Oh, I dunno about that. If Lennie found out he'd kill us both.'

'But why should he find out? You could bring Georgie to see me in Fitzwilliam Street. It's out of the way, and out of his manor.'

Betty gazed back at Vera, and as though unable to resist the appeal in her cousin's eyes, she said, 'All right, but I'm not risking it very often. How about once a fortnight?'

Vera looked down at the tea that had gone cold in her cup. It was better than nothing, and maybe she could work on Betty, eventually persuading her to come more often. 'When do you start looking after him?'

'Tomorrow.'

'Betty, please, you have no idea how much I miss my son. I know it's a lot to ask, but would you bring him to see me as soon as possible?'

'Give me a few days, Vera. I'll need to test the water and work out the best time. It will have to be when I'm sure that Lennie is going to be away all day, and that will probably be when he's at a race meeting.'

Vera's smile was beatific as she whispered, 'Oh, I can't wait, it's wonderful. I'm actually going to see my son.'

Vera had to wait two weeks before Betty came, and now she was hopping with excitement. When the bell rang she flew to the door, her eyes widening in amazement when she saw Georgie. Oh God, he was so beautiful, with dark curly hair and big brown eyes. She stepped forward in eagerness and pulled him out of Betty's arms. For a moment he looked startled, but as she smiled at him, her face brimming with love, he reached out a hand and touched her on the cheek. Unbidden, tears welled in Vera's eyes. This was her son and she clutched him fiercely, never wanting to let him go again.

It was Betty who broke the spell. 'Are you gonna let me get over the doorstep, Vera?'

'Oh yes, sorry. Come into the kitchen and I'll put the kettle on.'

'I think I'd better make the tea,' Betty said. 'You sit down with Georgie.'

Vera didn't need telling twice, and with her son perched on her lap she gazed at him in wonderment. She had secreted a teddy bear wrapped in blue paper by the side of her chair, and reaching down for it she placed it in George's arms. Betty put a cup of tea in front of her, but she hardly noticed. Her whole attention was focused on her little boy as he pulled at the paper with chubby hands.

Vera heard a noise and stiffened. It sounded like the front door, but before she had time to react, Daisy was standing on the threshold of the kitchen, her eyes wide as she looked at George sitting on her lap.

'What are you doing here? You're supposed to be at school,' Vera snapped.

Daisy wrote on her pad. *Sick, teacher sent me home.*

'Well, you look all right to me.'

Dragging her eyes from the baby, Daisy scribbled on her pad again and handed it to the woman who sat opposite Vera. *What is your baby's name?*

'Bless you, ducks. He ain't mine . . . he's Vera's.'

Vera jumped to her feet, her face red. 'You stupid cow, Betty! Now you've really dropped me in it. Nobody knows about Georgie, I told you that!' The baby began to scream and Vera fought to regain her composure. Christ, what was she going to do now? If Daisy told her father about Georgie it would ruin everything. 'Betty, you'll have to go. I need to think – to sort something out, and quickly.'

'Yeah, all right,' she said, taking Georgie from Vera's arms.

'Look, I'm sorry for shouting, but you have no idea what a mess I'm in now. I know you said you would only bring him once a fortnight, but please, I'm begging you: will you bring him again next week?'

Frowning, Betty hesitated, but then said, 'Yeah, all right.'

'Oh thank you, thank you,' Vera said, dashing the tears from her eyes, and leaning forward she kissed George, her heart breaking that she had seen him for such a short time. Blast Daisy, and now she had to somehow sort her out before Henry came home.

Closing the door behind her cousin, Vera returned to the kitchen and found Daisy sitting on a chair, her expression showing her bewilderment. Pacing the floor Vera began to think frantically. Somehow she had to keep the girl quiet. The fact that she couldn't talk didn't help because there was nothing to stop her writing on her pad. Something began to niggle in Vera's mind. Yes, Daisy couldn't talk, but why?

She closed her eyes, trying to recall everything Olive Cole had told her about the accident, and fishing for answers she said, 'Daisy, it was awful that your mother died saving you.' The lie slipped easily from her lips as she added, 'I saw the accident, and if your mummy hadn't had to push you out of the way she wouldn't have been hit by that car.'

The child's face blanched with fear. What was it? What was she so frightened of, Vera wondered. 'It was naughty of you to play in the road. Didn't your mother tell you how dangerous that is?'

Daisy picked up her pad, her pencil racing across the page and with a frantic appeal on her face she held it out. *I didn't mean it. Please don't tell my daddy.*

Oh, so that's it, Vera thought. No wonder Daisy was mute. She obviously thought she had been the cause of her mother's death.

'Your father would be very angry if he knew about this, Daisy.'

Jumping to her feet Daisy flew to Vera's side, pulling at her sleeve as she shook her head. 'All right, I won't tell him, but on one condition. You must never ever tell him about Betty and my baby. Do you understand?

Daisy nodded, her head bobbing up and down rapidly.

'Right, now go to your room.'

Vera followed as Daisy left the kitchen and she watched her climbing the stairs. Would it work? Would her threat ensure the child's silence? She crossed the hall and went into the sitting room, wringing her hands in agitation. Yes, Daisy might keep quiet, but for how long?

As her thoughts raged, something twisted in Vera's mind. Damn the girl! If Daisy hadn't come home early she could have spent more time with her son. Resentment turned to hate as Vera realised that from now on she would be living on a knife-edge until she got hold of Henry's money. If only she could find out if his savings were in a current account. If they were, she could learn how to forge his signature, enabling her to transfer money to her own account. Then as soon as the money was in place she could do a runner.

Chapter Eight

Daisy dawdled home from school. She was still missing her friend Susan, but in the midst of the huge and unwelcome changes that had taken place in her life, the Watsons' move to Balham no longer seemed such a huge event. She sometimes wondered if she would ever see Susan again but now as she turned into Fitzwilliam Road, her thoughts turned to her step-mother and she dreaded facing the woman. Vera had changed so much towards her in the last eight weeks, but only when they were alone. When her father was at home she wasn't so bad, and now when Daisy got the chance she would sneak down to Molly's for a little while after school, eking out the time until her father came home from work. She frowned, unable to understand why Vera was so cruel to her. She wished she could tell her father, but knew it was impossible.

As Daisy turned into Fitzwilliam Street her stomach rumbled and she hoped Molly had done some baking. Her stepmother was trying to make her lose weight and there were never any cakes in the house, but when she went to Molly's there were always fruit buns or coconut pyramids on offer. She would eat one or two, then stuff another few in her blazer pocket to eat when she was in bed.

Daisy was unlucky. As she drew near to her house she saw Vera looking out of the window, gesturing for her to come indoors. Her heart sinking, she climbed the steps, scared of what she might have to face.

'Just look at you,' Vera started as she came into the hall. 'How dare you show me up by coming home in such a state.'

Daisy's stomach lurched and she crossed her legs frantically.

Her stepmother's mouth tightened. 'Well – what have you got to say for yourself?'

Shaking her head, Daisy lowered her eyes, flinching when she noticed the scuffs on her shoes.

'Answer me, child!' Vera snapped, grabbing Daisy by the shoulders and shaking her violently. 'I said answer me!'

She could feel her stepmother's long nails digging like claws through her blazer as she was jerked back and forth like a rag doll. But just when Daisy thought the assault was never going to end, she was released, and feeling the wall against her back, she slumped against it.

'Now speak! Do you hear me – *speak*!' Vera screamed, her steel-grey eyes unblinking as she loomed over her, like a predator fixed on its prey.

With her mouth opening and closing like a fish floundering out of water, Daisy tried. But no sounds issued from her throat, and she shook her head helplessly.

'Huh, you should be on the stage with your acting talents. But pretending that you can't speak won't wash with me, my girl. So either you explain yourself or I'll punish you – and you know what that means, don't you?'

Daisy shrank in fear. *No!* her thoughts screamed. *No, don't put me in there!* She stared up at Vera, her eyes begging a frantic appeal.

'It's no good looking at me like that. It's your own fault,' Vera said. 'All you've got to do is to talk, but you won't, will you?' And grabbing Daisy's arm, her grip vice-like, she dragged her across the hall.

Daisy tried to hold it, she clenched tightly, but it was no good: as soon as the cupboard door came into view it happened – pouring down her legs and soaking her socks.

'You filthy, filthy child! Just look at my lino!' Then, her face flaming with anger, Vera yanked open the small door under the stairs, shoving Daisy forcibly inside. 'You can sit in your own stink too, my girl,' she snapped as the door was slammed shut.

It was dark, so dark, and Daisy scratched frenziedly at the rough wood, feeling her nails splintering. She wanted to shout, scream, but despite trying she couldn't make a sound. Her cries came instead as frantic thoughts, inside her head. *Turn the light on! Oh please, turn the light on!* There was the sound of Vera's footsteps going upstairs and she followed the noise with her eyes, jumping in terror as something brushed against her face. Spider – there was a spider! Her arms flailing wildly, she sank down in the narrow space, and bringing her knees up, she curled into a tight ball.

She had tried to stay clean, but it was no good. Patrick and Sean had been hiding, just waiting for her to pass. In her haste to get away she had fallen over and knew – as soon as she saw the state of her clothes – she would be in trouble. She had scrambled up, feverishly trying to brush the wet mud off her skirt while the boys stood watching, laughing gleefully.

Now, shivering with fear, Daisy lifted her head, peering into an inky blackness that was thick, and dense, the smell of her own urine stinging her nostrils. *Dad!* she screamed inwardly. *Dad, get me out of here!* But there was just silence – utter silence.

She retreated then – back into the past. To a time when she had been happy, a time when her mother was alive. In her imagination Daisy could feel the comfort of her mum's arm as she nestled against her soft, warm body, remembering for a while how happy they had been as a kaleidoscope of memories flashed into her mind. The seaside, yes, that had been a wonderful day. When together they had buried her dad in the sand, giggling together as they pretended to run away – leaving him there, with just his head visible.

Head. Oh no! She shouldn't have thought about a head! Daisy tried to fight it, screwing her eyelids tightly together and desperately trying to dispel the image. It was no good, and despite her efforts the picture forced its way to the front of her mind.

Blood, so much blood, pouring from her mother's head and forming a pool in the road. Daisy saw her own hands then, stained bright red as she tried to cover the gaping wound. People, she was surrounded by people, and someone was trying to pull her away.

She couldn't bear it any more, couldn't stand the awful memories, and leaning forward she began to bang her forehead against the cupboard door, silent words shouting loudly inside her head in time with the blows. *Let me out – let me out – let me out!*

Another thought suddenly flew into her mind. Count, go on, count! It's worked before and Vera can't keep you in here for ever. She always makes sure you have a bath before your dad comes home from work. So go on, count.

One – two – three – four – five. She had reached one thousand seven hundred before the door opened.

'Right, I hope you've learned your lesson,' Vera said.

Blinking her eyes in the light, Daisy stepped out of the cupboard, her limbs stiff from being crouched in such a small place. Looking up she nodded her head, praying that she wouldn't receive any more punishment.

Her stepmother wrinkled her nose. 'God, you stink. Go upstairs immediately and have a bath, and when you come down you can lay the table for dinner. Well, don't just stand there, child! Get a move on!'

Scrambling upstairs and into the bathroom, Daisy turned on the taps, and when the bath was nearly full she quickly undressed, sinking with a sigh into the water. The blissful warmth eased the stiffness in her limbs, but she knew she would have to be quick. Vera would start shouting again if she lingered. Yet just for a few minutes she allowed herself the luxury of relaxing in the soft, warm water. Her wash was then hurried, and all she had time to do after getting dressed, was to drag a comb through her towel-dried hair.

As Daisy returned downstairs to lay the dining-room table, she glanced at the hall clock, relieved to see that it was nearly five-thirty. There would be no more punishment now. Her father was due home.

Chapter Nine

At six-thirty in the evening the family were sitting round the dining-room table eating a meal of steak and kidney pie, the rich pungent aroma drifting into their nostrils as they dug into the pastry.

'How many times have I got to tell you, Daisy? Elbows off the table, please,' Vera said.

Henry Bacon frowned. His daughter obeyed her stepmother automatically, and didn't even raise her head as she ate avidly, the food rapidly disappearing off her plate. 'How was school today, Daisy?' he asked gently.

Her striking blue eyes rose to meet his. Eyes that would be beautiful if they weren't surrounded by so much flesh – eyes that reminded him so much of his first wife. Daisy's mouth opened and shut, but as usual, there was no sound. She was so plump now, with fat cheeks and a double chin, and so different from the happy child she had been when her mother was alive. He smiled reassuringly, trying to give her some encouragement, but then heard his wife's shrill voice.

'Answer your father, Daisy,' she ordered.

He stiffened at her tone. 'No, it's all right. Daisy will talk when she's ready, and you know that it can't be forced, Vera.'

'You're too soft on her, Henry. It's about time she snapped out of it.'

'Have you forgotten what she's been through? The doctor said we must be patient.'

'Huh – *doctor*,' Vera bristled. 'He's a quack. In my opinion she does it to get your attention, and you pander to her.' She rose abruptly from her seat and walked over to the fireplace, taking her cigarettes and lighter from the mantelpiece. With quick nervous movements she opened the packet and placed a cigarette between her tight lips. Impatiently flicking the lighter she lifted the flame to the cigarette and inhaled deeply before blowing a thick cloud of smoke towards the ceiling.

Henry watched Vera's actions and sighed heavily. He was beginning to think he had made a dreadful mistake in marrying her. Yet Vera had been wonderful during the first two months of their marriage, and they were happy. Now though, she had changed. She had become hard and obsessively jealous, and he was at a loss to understand why.

Vera ground her cigarette into an ashtray, and walking back to the table, began to gather the plates together. 'I'll get the pudding,' she said brusquely, before leaving the room.

As the door swung shut behind her, Henry reached across and touched his daughter's hand. 'Are you all right, sweetheart?' he asked.

Daisy's short brown hair bobbed as she nodded, but her eyes held the same appeal. God, he thought, even with all that weight she was like a thirteen-year-old version of her mother. The memories flooded back, and once again he felt the desolation of Judith's death. It was almost a year ago now, and a year that had brought so many changes.

Still with his hand over Daisy's, Henry wondered if she would ever get over the shock of seeing her mother killed? It must have been a horrific scene, and Molly had told him how Daisy had knelt by Judith's side, trying to stem the blood that flowed from her battered body.

Vera came back into the room then, abruptly breaking into his thoughts as she slapped a bowl onto the table. 'Apple pie and custard,' she told him. 'And I don't think Daisy should have any. She's far too fat as it is.'

Henry saw the disappointment on his daughter's face, and though he knew Vera was right, he gave in, pushing his pudding across to Daisy, saying, 'I don't think it will hurt just this once. I've had enough to eat anyway.'

Daisy clasped a podgy hand around the bowl, leaning over it defensively as though she expected it to be snatched away. She then began to shovel the pie into her mouth, cheeks bulging like a hamster, and hardly finishing one spoonful before she shoved another in.

'Stop eating like that at once! My God, Daisy Bacon, you're aptly named. Just look at you – bolting your food like a pig at its trough.'

'That's enough, Vera. I won't have you talking to her like that.'

'I'm sorry, Henry, but I really am at the end of my tether. You've no idea what I have to put up with, and what chance have I got with her if you keep countermanding everything I try to do?' His wife then sank onto a chair, looking at him with tear-filled eyes.

Oh no, Henry thought, not the tears again! He couldn't stand the tears. 'Come on, dear,' he said, his voice placatory. 'Let's not argue. Can't we have just one meal in peace?'

Vera sniffed pathetically. 'I do the best I can, and it's not easy, you know. I'm trying to put Daisy on a diet, but she fights me every step of the way.'

'All right, my dear, I'm sorry. I acted without thinking and it won't happen again.' Sighing, Henry folded his napkin, another innovation of Vera's. Her snobbery was something else he found difficult. She somehow thought they were a cut above the neighbours and spoke of them derisively.

Henry had to bite his tongue when Vera berated Molly Carson – soon finding out that to jump in and defend her just made matters worse. His wife's jealousy would rise to fever pitch – though how she could be jealous of plump, blowsy Molly, he didn't know.

'If you've finished I'll clear the table,' Vera said, sniffing pathetically again.

'Yes, thank you, dear. The dinner was delicious,' he told her, hating the way he had to butter up to her moods. 'I'll go into the sitting room now to have a look at the evening paper. Would you like to join me, Daisy?'

'No, Henry. She must help me with the clearing up – then she can join you.'

He nodded slowly. 'Very well, Vera,' and throwing a guilty glance at his daughter, he quietly left the dining room.

Henry sat on a fireside chair, his eyes flicking distastefully around the room. Vera had insisted on completely refurbishing it when they married, saying that she couldn't be expected to live with his first wife's memories. He had been so besotted with her at the time that he had agreed, though it had cost him a pretty penny.

The comfortable three-piece suite he and Judith had saved for so diligently had been sold, replaced by a cream sofa with dark, highly polished wooden arms, and chairs to match. He shifted uncomfortably, still missing the comfort of his old wing-chair. Vera said the room was modern and smart, but to him the pale blue walls and deep blue carpet looked cold and clinical. A drop-leaf mahogany table stood under the window with an ugly aspidistra in the centre, blocking out the light. The bow-fronted drinks cabinet was also dark mahogany, with glass doors displaying various bottles of spirits that he soon found out he wasn't meant to drink.

Henry shivered. The room felt chilly, but thankfully there was a low fire burning in the grate. Bending forward he gave it a quick poke to liven it up, then picking up the evening paper he shook it out impatiently, annoyed with himself for dwelling on the past again.

After about fifteen minutes the door opened, and as his daughter came slowly into the room, Henry smiled at her, holding out his arms. She threw a quick look over her shoulder and then scampered across the floor, flinging herself into his arms and laying her head on his chest.

Heaving her onto his lap Henry laid his head on top of hers, inhaling the clean scent of shampoo. He didn't speak, and berated himself. How would Daisy learn to talk again if he didn't encourage her? Yet somehow her silence was soothing after listening to Vera's shrill voice.

They sat quietly like this for some minutes, but then the door opened again and Vera came in, a curl of derision on her lips as she said, 'Don't you think she's a bit big for sitting on your lap, Henry?'

Daisy scrambled away, her eyes wide as she looked at her stepmother.

Henry frowned. The child seemed frightened. Was Vera too strict a disciplinarian? Did she show his daughter any love and affection? His fears were allayed when Vera crossed to the sideboard, and opening one of the drawers, she pulled out a game.

'Come on, Daisy,' she said. 'We'll have a game of snakes and ladders before you go to bed. What about you, Henry? Would you like to play too?'

They played several rounds, until Vera said it was time for Daisy to go to bed. She went without protest, giving him a quick kiss on the cheek before leaving the room.

Once he and Vera were alone, Henry switched on the radio. Time passed with only sporadic conversation between them as she sat opposite, sewing the hem of a skirt.

'Henry, I don't know why you won't discuss our financial affairs. Surely as your wife I have a right to know,' Vera said, breaking the silence.

Not again, Henry thought. Judith had never questioned his handling of their finances. He paid all the bills, gave her housekeeping money along with a clothing allowance, and he was thrifty in saving for their future. Vera must think him incapable because soon after their marriage she began to constantly harp about money. 'Vera, I've told you before that you don't need to concern yourself. I save diligently and I have adequate life insurance. You have nothing to worry about.'

'But . . .'

'There is nothing more to discuss,' he said, his voice sharp.

Vera's lips were tight as she returned to her sewing, then letting out a long sigh she yawned.

Henry found his own mouth widening too. Glancing at the clock and seeing that it was after ten o'clock he rose to his feet, saying, 'I think I'll turn in.'

42

'All right. I'll just lay the table for breakfast, then I'll be up.'

Henry had just settled into bed, and was removing his glasses to place on the bedside table, when Vera came into the room.

'You're not too tired, are you, darling?' she asked, as she began to undress.

He tensed, knowing what was coming. He didn't want to make love to Vera; somehow with the anniversary of Judith's death on his mind it didn't seem right. The two women were as different as chalk and cheese. With Judith their lovemaking had been quiet and tender, and they always cuddled up together afterwards, falling asleep in each other's arms.

It had been a shock when he had made love to Vera, and at first he had found her passion exciting. There was no softness, no tenderness – just a frenzied animal-like coupling that sometimes felt more like hate than love. He would be left bleeding and sore where Vera's fingernails had raked his back or chest. She devoured him, overwhelmed him, and when it was over she would just turn over and go to sleep, like a satiated cat. But not tonight, he couldn't face it tonight. 'Well, I am rather tired tonight, dear,' he told her, but as she came naked to the bed and climbed astride him – Henry knew he would be unable to resist.

Vera turned on her side, her lips curled with distaste. Henry found her irresistible, and stupidly thought she enjoyed their lovemaking. But it was anger that had fuelled her tonight, anger that he refused to talk to her about his finances. She had driven her claws into him in frustration, knowing he would now be bruised and sore. Blast him – blast the man.

The sound of Henry snoring made Vera shudder and she turned over impatiently to look at him. In the moonlight his face was relaxed in sleep and she stared at his features: mousy brown hair, already receding, a loose mouth, wide and slack, and he had long, slightly bucked, front teeth. His nose was thin, and reaching out she pinched it. Thankfully the action stopped Henry's snores, and with a snort he turned on his side.

Vera was almost asleep when she heard the bedroom door

open, and with the light behind her Daisy stood silhouetted on the threshold, gesturing frantically.

'What do you want?' Vera hissed. 'Don't you know that you're supposed to knock before coming in here?'

The child ignored her and as she stepped into the room, Vera impatiently switched on her bedside light, feeling Henry beginning to stir beside her. Raising her fingers to her lips and throwing back the blankets, she rushed to Daisy's side, ushering her back onto the landing and shutting the bedroom door behind them. 'Now, what is it?' she asked, noting Daisy's terrified expression.

White-faced, and eyes wide with fear, Daisy pointed to her pyjamas.

Vera looked at the stain, her eyes narrowing. 'Well, well, started your monthlies, have you? Come on then, I suppose I'll have to show you what to do,' and indicating that Daisy should follow, she walked along the landing to the bathroom.

Opening the mirror-fronted cabinet and taking out a package, Vera said, 'Right, miss. You wear one of these, and make sure you change it regularly.'

Daisy just stared at her, a look of bewilderment on her face, and Vera sighed with exasperation as she bent down. 'Stupid bloody child,' she complained as she fumbled impatiently with the sanitary belt. 'There, all done, and I suppose you know what this means, don't you?'

Once again Daisy just gawked at her.

'Oh, for God's sake! Don't tell me I've got to explain all that too!' Vera rubbed her forehead impatiently. 'No, I'm blowed if I will. It isn't my responsibility,' then smirking, she added, 'I tell you what, I'll give you the same advice as my mother gave me. Stay away from boys!'

Seeing the expression on Daisy's face, she laughed softly. 'Yes, that's confused you, hasn't it? But it's good advice, my girl, and I should know. Yes, you stay away from boys. Now get some clean pyjama trousers on, and go back to bed.'

Turning on her heels, Vera went back to her own room, already berating herself for being so insensitive. When she was cruel to Daisy she hated herself afterwards, but somehow she was unable to stop. She knew she shouldn't have put Daisy in the cupboard today, but every time she looked at the girl, fear and frustration rose to the surface. Her nerves were at screaming pitch, wondering how much longer she could keep the child quiet. She had to keep up the threat – had to instill it in Daisy that her father would hate her if he found out about the accident. It was rubbish of course, but the girl didn't know that.

Vera climbed into bed, and shivering she pulled the blankets up to her shoulders. Damn it, she had to get hold of Henry's money. She should be looking after her own son instead of acting the part of a mother to Daisy. Already she had missed being with George for his first birthday, missed his first steps. God, she wished she could spoil Georgie like Henry spoiled his daughter. He treated Daisy like a china doll, and Vera couldn't help comparing it to her own childhood. All she had known was grinding poverty, and her father hadn't shown her any love. No, all she had known was cruelty.

When Daisy returned to her room, the sharp stabbing pains in her stomach made her wince. She'd been so frightened when she saw the blood and had run to Vera in terror. For once her stepmother's matter-of-fact attitude had calmed her, though she still didn't understand what was wrong. Monthlies, Vera had called them. What did she mean? Was she going to have this illness for a whole month? And boys – Vera had told her to stay away from boys. Did that mean it was catching, like chicken pox?

She climbed into bed, drawing her knees up to ease the pain, her thoughts turning once again to her stepmother's cruelty. Why did Vera punish her so much? What had she done to upset her?

Oh Mum, Daisy thought, clenching her eyes to stem the tears that were threatening. *If only you were here. If only you hadn't died.* Her heart thumped. Vera knew! Vera knew the truth about the accident. She remembered her father's anger – remembered how he had said that he would kill the person responsible for his wife's death. She shivered, terrified at the thought of her father finding out.

45

Chapter Ten

Daisy must have fallen asleep, but had no memory of it, and awoke to see weak sunlight shining through the window. She squirmed uncomfortably, rubbing her gritty eyes as she heard her father's voice.

'Daisy, come on. Breakfast's nearly ready.'

After rushing to the bathroom, grimacing as she got ready, Daisy made her way downstairs. Glad that at last, the pain in her stomach had eased.

'Here you are, Vera's made you a nice boiled egg. Would you like me to cut your bread into soldiers?' her father asked as she took a seat at the table.

'For goodness sake, Henry, she's not a baby,' Vera said. 'Now then, Daisy, did you change your sanitary towel this morning as I told you?'

Daisy saw her father blanch and her eyes widened. Did she have to stay away from him too? Could he catch it? She pushed back her chair, but Vera's voice kept her rooted.

'Yes, that's surprised you, hasn't it, Henry. You treat her like a child, but she'll be fourteen in five months and is late starting her periods.'

Daisy turned to look at her father, but as their eyes met he lowered his head, his face red as he tapped the top of his egg with a teaspoon and meticulously began to peel away the brown shell. 'I don't think this is a subject for the breakfast table, Vera,' he gently admonished.

The meal was eaten in almost complete silence after that. Her father usually chatted to her, but this morning he was quiet,

46

though Daisy was aware that he covertly glanced across at her from time to time. For once she had no appetite and ate her food half-heartedly, glad when at last the meal was over.

After helping Vera to clear up, Daisy wandered back upstairs to her bedroom, and approaching the window saw the Carson boys tumbling up the basement steps next door. Perhaps if it's safe for me to go near him, Molly will let me take the baby for a walk, she thought, smiling as she pictured little Francis, who in a very short time had become Frank to everyone. He was a beautiful baby. Blue-eyed and chubby-cheeked, with dark hair that stood up like a brush, he had a ready smile for anyone who paid him the slightest attention.

Flicking off her slippers and putting on her shoes, Daisy made her way downstairs, her writing pad clutched in her hand. Finding her father in the sitting room she wrote rapidly, asking him if she could go round to Molly's.

'Yes, all right, Daisy,' he said, still trying to avoid eye-contact. 'But be back home in time for lunch.'

Her tread heavy, Daisy stepped down to the basement and knocked on Molly's door.

'Well, Daisy, 'tis you,' Molly said, standing on the threshold and wiping her hands on her grubby apron. 'Come on in. You'll have to excuse the mess though. Frank is into everything these days – he's a little divil.'

Daisy wrote rapidly on her pad, asking if it was safe to go in with her illness?

'What illness is this?' Molly asked, her eyes puzzled, and as she read the girl's words she added, 'of course you can come in. Why would having your monthlies stop you?'

Scribbling quickly again, Daisy held it out for Molly to read.

'No, of course it's not catching. What on earth makes you think that?' she asked.

When Molly read the answer to her question, she sighed heavily. 'That woman needs shooting,' she mumbled. 'You and I need to have a little crack.'

The kitchen was cosy and welcoming as Daisy stepped inside,

wrinkling her nose appreciatively at the delicious smell of baking. A large fruitcake stood on the kitchen table and at the sight of it her mouth watered.

'Ah, I see you're looking at my cake, Daisy. I'd offer you a slice, but I've yet to ice it.'

Daisy reluctantly dragged her eyes away and held up her hands in a gesture to indicate that she understood.

'Oh, 'tis a shame that you still can't speak, but you will one day, I'm sure. Your poor mammy. She would be heartbroken to see you in such a state.'

Daisy, feeling tears beginning to form, screwed up her eyes in an effort to fight them, still unable to bear it when anyone talked about her mother.

Molly reached out a large chubby hand and, gripping Daisy's chin, she raised her face until their eyes locked. 'Listen, love, if ever you need me I'm here, and I want you to remember that. I'm not deaf, you know, and I've heard that one's voice shouting at you through these walls. There's many a time I've thought to have a word with your father, but himself tells me to mind my own business.' She released Daisy's chin. 'Now, about your monthlies. No, it isn't catching, and that one should have explained it to you instead of leaving you in ignorance like this.'

Daisy, her face now flaming with embarrassment, listened to Molly as she told her what was happening to her body – her eyes growing wide.

'Now, if you've any more worries, just come and see me, and . . .' Molly was interrupted as the back door opened and Paddy, her husband, stepped into the room, one of his prized racing pigeons cupped gently in his hands, and Frank clutching on to his trousers.

'Molly, will you take a look at Bridget for me? She looks a bit off-colour and . . . Why, hello, Daisy. How are you, darlin'?'

'Paddy, get that bird out of my kitchen!' Molly cried.

'But . . .'

'No buts, Paddy. I've told you before – they're vermin, and I'll not have them inside my house.'

'You're a hard woman, Molly Carson,' he complained, turning

to look at Daisy and adding, 'Well, I'm sorry I can't stay to have a crack with you, but as you can see I'm being chased out again. Sure, you'd never believe I was the man of the house, would you? Now Molly, if I can't bring Bridget in, will you come out into the yard and take a look at her?'

'Oh, I suppose so. Daisy, will you keep an eye on Frank for me?'

She wrote rapidly on her pad.

'Yes, sweetheart, of course you can take him for a walk. I'll be glad to have him out from under my feet and it'll give me a chance to ice the cake.' Molly made a dive for Frankie, grabbing him as he toddled around. 'He's like lightning, Daisy, and I'm still amazed that he started walking so early.' Puffing heavily, she stuffed him hastily into his pushchair before he had time to protest.

Paddy, still cupping the pigeon carefully in his hands, hurried out again while Molly added a hat and scarf to Frank's outfit. 'There, me laddo. Now you behave yourself,' she admonished, pushing her son's arms through his reins.

Daisy couldn't help smiling at the sight of Frank struggling to free himself, his chubby legs kicking frantically.

'Make sure he stays strapped in, Daisy, or he'll be out of there like a shot.'

Daisy wrote on her pad again.

'Yes, once you get to the Common he can walk, but don't let him go on the big swings or the roundabout and hold him tightly on the slide.'

Daisy nodded, wheeling the pushchair to the door. Holding the handles tightly as Molly grasped the footrest, they carried baby and pram up the steps.

'I'll see you in an hour or so,' Molly said, leaning forward to give Frank a kiss. 'And be a good boy for Daisy,' she admonished, with a small wag of her finger.

Molly watched Daisy as she walked down the street, thinking that she looked to have put on more weight. God, how she missed Judith, and it had been so hard to put on a cheerful front for

Daisy. The cake was for Frank's first birthday on Thursday, but instead of it being a happy day, Molly was dreading it. How could she ever forget that it was also the day that Judith had died?

She remained on the pavement until Daisy turned the corner. Then, sensing that she was being watched, her eyes flicked to next door's bay window where she saw Vera peeping out from behind the net curtains. Molly tossed her head, and swinging round she marched back down to the basement, her spine stiff. She knew that Vera looked down her nose at her, and she couldn't stand the woman. There was a calculating hardness in her eyes that made Molly's skin crawl. When Vera had married Henry, despite her reservations, she had tried to make the woman welcome, but her friendly overtures had been rebuffed. Since then they had never spoken, but just lately she had noticed a change in Daisy. The child seemed to be a bundle of nerves. Was Vera mistreating her?

'Paddy, I'm going to have a word with Henry Bacon about Daisy,' she said, stepping into the back yard.

'Molly, keep your nose out of it. He won't thank you for interfering, and the child looks fine.'

'But . . .'

'Leave it, Molly,' Paddy interrupted. 'Now here, have a look at Bridget for me.'

Molly took the bird's warm body into her cupped hands and gently stroked the soft feathers, feeling the pigeon's frantic heartbeats vibrating in her palm. She lifted her hands, gazing into the bird's eyes, then tutted impatiently. 'Paddy, she looks all right. Anyway, why ask *me* to look at her? You know more about the pigeons than I do.'

'But they always seem better after you've held them. You have a soothing touch. Now, are you sure she's all right? I think she looks a bit peaky.'

'It's just that my hands are warm, Paddy, whereas yours are always cold. She's fine, I tell you. 'Tis all in your imagination as usual. Honestly, you're like a mother hen with the birds.' She chuckled as she handed the pigeon back. 'Mother hen! Yes, that's you, Paddy. Perhaps you should keep chickens instead.'

'I can't race chickens, Molly.'

'No, but at least I'd get a supply of eggs,' she retorted, her head lifting at the sound of raised voices coming from next door. 'See, they're at it again. Poor Henry, I think it was the worst thing he ever did, taking up with the likes of Vera.'

'You shouldn't have let Daisy go next door, Henry. That woman's a bad influence on the child.'

'I've told you before, Vera. There's nothing wrong with Molly. She's got a heart of gold and is very fond of Daisy.'

'Huh, she's a slut! I bet her house is filthy – and have you seen the state of her children? I wouldn't be surprised if they're crawling with fleas.'

'Oh, for goodness sake, Vera. They're boys and no different from the other children in the street. Molly does her best, and it can't be easy for her having only the basement kitchen and just two bedrooms on the first floor to house them all in.' His eyes narrowed as he looked at Vera. 'Unlike us, she hasn't got a bathroom either. How would you like to drag a tin bath into the kitchen every week?'

Vera turned away from the look on Henry's face. Oh, I know all about tin baths, she thought. In fact, having a basement and two bedrooms would have seemed like luxury to her when she was a child.

Forcing tears into her eyes she turned to Henry again, crying dramatically. 'You always undermine everything I try to do! I'm doing my best to turn your daughter into a respectable young woman, but you let her associate with riff-raff.'

'Vera, calm down,' Henry said. 'Molly isn't riff-raff, and Daisy won't come to any harm by going round to see her.'

Walking over to the fireplace Vera threw herself onto a chair, and crossing her legs, she swung her foot impatiently. 'Very well, Henry, have it your way, but don't blame me when your daughter turns out to be like all the other hooligans in the street. You seem to forget that Daisy is growing up now and needs to start acting like a young lady.'

'My daughter is still a child and what she needs is love and affection. All *you* seem to do lately is to snap at her, and it has got to stop.'

Seething, Vera bit hard on her bottom lip, fighting to contain her temper. She knew the strain of trying to keep Daisy quiet was getting to her, and if she didn't pull herself together she could ruin everything. Oh, if only she didn't have to look after the girl. It was then that she was struck by a thought, and taking a deep breath, said, 'Do you know, Henry, it might be a good idea to think about sending Daisy to stay with your sister in Hampshire. The schools are much better out of London, and after all, I'm sure you want the best for her.'

'No, Vera, I won't send her away. Anyway, how on earth do you think Daisy would manage at a new school? St Catherine's has been marvellous. They know her history and have made allowances for her.'

'Yes, dear – but have you thought of the effect it must have on her, seeing the exact spot where her mother was killed every day? I'm sure there would be more chance of Daisy regaining her voice if she had a change of scenery. It might be just what she needs.'

Henry ran a hand over his face, moving across the room to sit opposite her. 'You may have a point, but I really don't like the idea of sending her away.'

'I know, darling. But as I said – it must be terrible for her to be constantly reminded of her mother's death.'

'Hmm, maybe you're right,' he answered, yet still with a trace of doubt in his voice. 'I'll have a talk with Daisy later to see how she feels about it, but I won't force her to go against her will.'

Talk to her, Vera thought. How does he think he's going to do that? And anyway, I'll make sure she listens to me first. All I've got to do is to make my usual threat and there is no way the girl will refuse to go.

When Daisy reached Clapham Common and was some distance from the busy road, she released Frank from the confines of the pushchair, but kept a tight hold on his reins. He toddled forward, chubby legs wobbly on the uneven grass, only to be jerked to a halt as he reached the end of the straps. Dropping down with a plop on his bottom, his lower lip stuck out belligerently, and his woolly bobble hat slipped down over one eye. Daisy, trying to manoeuvre the pram with one hand, and holding the reins with the other, squatted down by his side, pointing to the playground. In a flash he was up again, and together they rushed forward.

She sat Frank in a bucket swing, making sure the wooden bar was fixed firmly across his tummy. Then, standing behind him, she pushed gently, smiling as he squealed with delight. But he soon became bored and was itching to go on the slide, his chubby fingers pointing as the swing came to a stop. It was as she was carefully removing Frank from the swing that his brothers approached, and Daisy's heart sank.

'Well, look who it is! Daisy Bacon, or should I say, Porky Pig?' Sean said, a wide grin on his face.

Ignoring him, Daisy lifted Frank into her arms and made her way across to the slide, where he wriggled like an eel to be put down.

'What's the matter, cat got your tongue?' Patrick, the younger of the two, sneered sarcastically. 'Come on, Porky, you know you can do it. Say *oink, oink*,' he urged, putting his index finger under his nose and pushing it up, giving his impersonation of a pig.

Her shoulders stiff, and still with her back to them, Daisy steadied Frank as he climbed the stairs of the small slide, holding him carefully as he reached the top.

'Hey, Frankie boy,' Sean called, running round to the other side. 'You don't want to go on there, it's for babies. Come on, I'll take you on the big slide.'

Daisy tried to hold on to him, but Sean, six months older than her, and a head taller, grabbed Frank and swung him away. He put him down onto the ground and like lightning Frank was off, heading for the big slide, with Sean ambling along behind him.

Her legs felt rooted, but at last Daisy reacted, rushing across the grass and stumbling in her haste to reach the child.

Everything then seemed to happen in slow motion. Daisy saw Frank toddling behind the big swings. He was too close, much too close, she thought, watching two girls swinging almost to the top of the bars. One of them was descending just as Frank was passing, and as the swing arched back it caught him, sending him flying up into the air.

Daisy screamed. She flew across the playground, and reaching him she knelt at his side. 'Frankie, Frankie,' she called, her voice coming out in a strange croak. It was like her nightmare all over again; Frank's head was oozing blood, just like her mother's. He didn't move, and she was too frightened to touch him. 'Get help! For God's sake, Sean, get some help!' she cried hoarsely, just as she heard a faint groan.

A lady came running up to them, and bending down began to examine Frank. 'It's all right, I'm a nurse,' she said reassuringly.

Daisy held her breath as she watched, gasping with relief when Frank suddenly struggled to sit up. 'Is he all right?' she asked anxiously.

'Yes, I think so. I know it appears to be a lot of blood, but it's only a small cut and looks worse than it is. Still, he should see a doctor, just to make sure. Do you live far from here?'

'We live in Fitzwilliam Street and it's only about a five-minute walk,' Daisy answered. And it was then that the realisation hit her. She was talking. Her voice was back! 'I can talk, I can talk!' she cried.

The lady shot her a puzzled glance but as Frankie whimpered she turned her attention back to him, running her hands over his legs and arms. Looking reassured, she said, 'I think we can risk taking him home. I'll carry him if you'll show me the way.'

'I'll just get his pushchair,' Daisy told her, glaring at Sean and Patrick who were standing side by side, staring wide-eyed and white-faced at Frank.

She turned to get the pram just as Liam, Molly's eldest son, came pounding across the grass, his football boots tied together by the laces and hanging around his neck. Daisy felt her face flame; Liam always had that effect on her. His jet-black hair was in wild disarray and his green eyes were wide with anxiety.

'What's happened to Frank?' he shouted breathlessly as he skidded to a halt.

'He got hit by a swing, Liam,' eleven-year-old Patrick cried, a hint of tears in his eyes.

'How?' he snapped, turning to look at Daisy accusingly.

'It was Sean's fault,' Patrick told him, his fear making him forget his loyalty to his brother.

''Twasn't my fault. 'Twasn't!' Sean shouted. 'He . . . he ran off.'

'Look, we need to get him home, and I suggest you sort this out later,' the nurse told them, lifting Frank gently from the ground and cradling him in her arms. 'Now come on, show me the way.'

They trooped in a procession across the Common; the nurse in front with Liam by her side, and behind them, Sean and Patrick, both quiet. Then last of all Daisy, pushing the empty pushchair. It was awful that Frank was hurt, but she was unable to contain her excitement. She had got her voice back, and now in disbelief she kept testing it, talking to herself as she followed the others. 'I can talk. Wait till I tell my dad.'

At last they reached Fitzwilliam Street, and it was Liam who was first down the steps, calling to his mother as he opened the door.

'Oh God,' Molly cried, as soon as she saw Frank in the arms of the nurse. 'What's happened to my baby?'

'He's had a nasty bang on the head, and though I think he's all right, it might be a good idea to get your doctor to have a look at him,' the nurse told her, handing the child into Molly's arms.

'Liam, run down to Dr Taylor and tell him what's happened,' Molly ordered, immediately taking charge. Then turning to the nurse she added, 'Thank you for bringing him home.'

'It was no trouble, I'm just glad that I was passing. It may have been better to call an ambulance, but as he wasn't unconscious I thought it would be quicker to bring him here.'

Frank clung to his mother, making sobbing little hiccups, while Molly supporting his head crooned, 'There, there, darlin', Mammy's here.'

'Look, if you can manage, I must go. My shift is due to start in half an hour,' the nurse said.

Molly looked up, her manner distracted as she said, 'Yes, I'll be fine, and thank you again for your help.'

As soon as the nurse left, Molly looked from Daisy to her sons. 'How did this happen?' she demanded.

'Frank got hit by a swing,' Daisy told her.

'Daisy, you spoke!' Molly exclaimed.

'Yes, my voice has come back,' she told her, unable to help smiling.

'I can't believe it, Daisy. Oh, 'tis wonderful. When did it come back?'

'It was when Francis was hit by the swing. I think I screamed, and then just after that I found I could talk.'

'Begod! It must have been the shock, but I still don't understand how Francis hurt his head.'

Daisy quickly lowered her eyes. If she split on Sean he would make her life even more of a misery, but she was saved from answering when Patrick piped up, 'It was Sean, Mammy. He took Frank from the little slide and he ran off.'

'Did he now! And what were you doing at the swings? You were supposed to be watching Liam playing football.'

'I didn't mean it, Mammy,' Sean cried, and Daisy was amazed to see her tormentor break down in tears.

'Patrick, go and get your Dadda,' Molly ordered. 'And Daisy, it might be better if you go on home now. Don't look at me like that, sweetheart. I'm not blaming you for what happened, but me laddo here needs to be punished, and 'twould be better if you weren't here to see it.'

Daisy gave Molly a small smile, then after a quick glance at Sean, hurried out. She had only just reached the top of the steps when she heard Paddy's roar, and as much as she hated Sean, Daisy couldn't help feeling a little sorry for him.

Daisy ran indoors, anxious to find her father. She glanced in the sitting room, but finding it empty, she made her way to the garden. He was there, bending over the front of a border, deadheading a row of early daffodils.

She couldn't wait to see his face and approached him quietly. 'Are we going out for a run in the car today, Daddy?'

'In about half an hour, dear.' His head suddenly snapped round, his jaw dropping as he gazed up at her. 'Daisy! Daisy, you spoke!'

'Yes, Dad. My voice came back,' she grinned.

'How? When?' he asked, his voice high as he jumped to his feet.

Daisy told him what had happened, squealing when he grabbed her and swung her round and round, his face alight with happiness. When they came to a stop, gasping and out of breath, he asked, 'Is Francis all right?'

'I think so, Dad. Liam has gone to get Dr Taylor.'

'I'm sorry Francis was hurt, but so glad that you've got your voice back.' Then squeezing her gently he added, 'Come on, let's go and tell Vera. She's going to be so thrilled.'

Henry and Daisy rushed into the sitting room, both beaming with excitement.

'Vera, Vera, it's wonderful! Daisy has got her voice back!'

Vera forced a smile, yet was inwardly seething. Just when she had almost convinced Henry to send her away, the child had regained her voice. 'That's marvellous, Henry. Say something, Daisy.'

Daisy cleared her throat and then said nervously, 'Hello, Vera.'

'Goodness, it seems so strange to hear you talking. When did this happen?'

She listened as Daisy went on to explain how she had regained her voice, and then unable to bear the happiness on their faces, Vera walked across to the window. Standing with her arms folded she saw dark clouds beginning to cast a thick grey blanket across the sky – a sky that matched her mood. 'It's threatening to rain,' she said disconsolately.

'Oh dear, what a shame. I won't be able to finish sorting out the bulbs, and I had better put the secateurs back into the shed. Sorry to rush off, Daisy, and we must do something to celebrate that you can talk again. Vera, how about we all go out to dinner tonight?'

Vera gave a wan smile. 'Yes, that would be nice.' When she heard the door close behind Henry, she turned to look at Daisy, her expression stern. 'You may have your voice back, my girl, but you had better remember to keep your mouth shut.'

Daisy stared back at her, and then without answering, she ran from the room.

Vera crossed to the fireplace and snatched her cigarettes from the mantelpiece, her shoulders slumping. She couldn't stand this much longer, she just couldn't. She had tried everything but still couldn't get access to Henry's money, and deep down she knew she was running out of time.

Chapter Eleven

After tea, Daisy helped Vera to clear the table and then went into the sitting room. 'Dad, can I go round to Molly's to see how Frank is?' she asked.

'Yes, of course, dear,' he answered.

Vera came into the room, her eyebrows raised, but Daisy scampered out before she had a chance to intervene.

As she closed the street door behind her, Daisy stood on the outside steps, looking down onto the street. She was surprised to see Patrick sitting on the kerb, his feet in the gutter and his head drooping despondently. Rushing quickly to his side, she asked, 'What's the matter? Is it Frankie?'

He looked up, his face streaked with dirt and his grey eyes shadowed. 'No, Frank's all right.'

'Oh, thank goodness,' she said, heaving a sigh of relief.

Patrick sniffed loudly, cuffing his nose with the back of his hand. 'Sean's mad at me, and 'tis all your fault,' he accused.

'But why? Why is Sean mad at you?'

''Cos I snitched on him and he got a lathering from Dadda.'

'Well, you can't blame me for that. It was his fault that Frank got hurt,' Daisy protested.

Patrick scowled, then suddenly jumped up, shoving her violently with his hands. 'Go away, you fat cow!' he shouted.

'*Patrick!*' the voice was loud from behind them.

They both spun round, Daisy blushing when she saw Liam.

'Leave her alone and get indoors. Mam wants you,' he ordered.

'Thanks,' she murmured as soon as Patrick ran down his

basement steps. 'I . . . I was just popping round to find out how Frank is.'

'He's fine,' Liam said. 'Mam told me that you have your voice back, and it sounds strange to hear you talking again.'

Daisy smiled, then at the sound of approaching footsteps they both turned as Sandra Reynolds reached their side, a wide smile on her face.

'Hello, darling,' she said, grabbing hold of Liam's arm. 'What film are we going to see then?' And they both walked off, so wrapped up in each other that they completely ignored Daisy.

She watched them enviously, admiring Sandra's trim figure in her pencil skirt and tight sweater, clinched in at her small waist with a wide elastic belt.

Liam suddenly turned as though on an afterthought and called over his shoulder, 'Bye, Daisy.'

'I think that fat kid's got a crush on you, Liam,' Sandra said, her laughter shrill as they moved out of earshot.

Daisy was unable to hear Liam's reply, and with her face flaming with humiliation she walked slowly down the basement steps, tapping lightly on the door.

'Come on in, darlin',' Molly invited, standing aside.

As Daisy walked into the kitchen she saw Sean sitting at the table. Their eyes met and he glared at her angrily. He was the odd one out of Molly's children, with auburn hair, very fair skin, and a sprinkling of freckles across his nose. His eyes, a deeper shade of blue than baby Frank's, were icy and accusing as he rose abruptly from his seat, stalking out of the room.

'Take no notice of him, Daisy, he's in a sulk. Paddy gave him a good lathering, but 'tis no more than he deserved.'

'He wasn't to know that Frank would get hurt. It was just an accident, Molly.'

'Well, that's as maybe, but from what Patrick told me, it could have been worse. It sounds like Sean was showing off and playing the big man as usual.'

She was surprised at Molly's insight into her son's character. Yes, Sean *was* a show-off, but strangely only when he had his brother Patrick in tow. On the rare occasions when she bumped into him alone, he didn't torment her. 'I saw Liam outside, Molly. He said Frank's fine.'

'Yes, he's as right as ninepence. He's got a nasty big bump on his head and is a bit bruised, but he was soon bouncing back again and up to mischief as usual. He's in the garden with Paddy if you want to see him.'

Daisy nodded, then grimaced impatiently. She still wasn't quite used to being able to talk again, and found that on occasions she would just nod or shake her head when asked a question.

'I bet your dadda's glad that you've got your voice back,' Molly said, walking out into the garden with her. ''Tis wonderful to hear you talking again.'

'Yes, he's thrilled,' Daisy told her as they passed the pigeon loft and stepped onto the lawn.

Frank was well wrapped up and sitting on the grass, his chubby legs out in front of him, frowning in concentration as he tried to turn the pages of a rag book.

Paddy was vigorously digging a border, the fork going deep into the soil. A short, stocky man, he was red-faced now with exertion, and seemed unaware of them until Molly swooped Frankie up and into her arms, showering her son with wet kisses. Frank tried to squirm his head away, and chuckling Molly said, 'I'll take him in for his bath now, Paddy.'

'All right. I'll be in soon.'

When they returned to the kitchen, Daisy watched as Molly filled the large, square Belfast sink with water. 'He won't fit in here for much longer,' she said, testing the temperature with her elbow. 'He's growing so fast now and will soon be joining his brothers in the tin bath.'

Daisy smiled as Molly stripped Francis down to his birthday suit and plonked him in the water where he squealed with delight, banging on the surface with his hands and soaking his mother in the process. 'You little divil,' she laughed, rubbing a hand across her wet face.

'I'd better go, Molly. I only popped round to see how he is,' Daisy said, unable to help herself giggling at Frankie's antics.

'As you can see, he's fine. So stop worrying.'

Sean came back into the room then, deliberately knocking Daisy with his elbow as he passed. Molly, with her back towards them, saw nothing; Daisy's gasp covered by Frankie's squeals as he splashed in the water.

As Daisy climbed the steps to her own front door, her heart was sinking. She had to go to school in the morning, and knowing Sean would be waiting for her on the way home, she dreaded it.

Vera heard Daisy as she came in and tensed, her nerves on edge every time the girl went to see Molly. Now that she had regained her voice Vera's fear was mounting. What did they talk about? Did they discuss Daisy's mother? With the anniversary of her death coming up it was possible. Vera squirmed in her chair. The hold she had over Daisy was tenuous, and if the girl came to realise that she had *not* caused her mother's death, it would be the end of everything.

Vera's thoughts shifted to her son. At least she had something to look forward to. Betty was bringing George to see her tomorrow, but the visits seemed so short and it broke her heart every time they left. Why had life been so cruel to her? She had never known love before having Georgie, and when she had first held him in her arms it felt as though her heart would burst with happiness. Without her son it felt like a part of her was missing, and the agony when Betty took him back to Lennie was tearing her apart.

Chapter Twelve

'Vera, I've got something to tell you,' Betty said as she watched her cousin frolicking on the floor with George.

'Come on then, spit it out,' Vera said, still smiling softly.

'Lennie's got a new girlfriend.'

'Huh! Well, that doesn't surprise me.'

'Yeah, but I think he's serious about this one, and he's moving her in. That's not all. He . . . he said that after a month or two, when Georgie has got used to her, I won't be needed any more.'

'What! No!' Vera cried. 'But you told me you were going to look after him permanently.'

'I know, and that's what Lennie told me. But now he says I've got to go back to working in the club. Oh Vera, I don't think I can stand it.'

Vera jumped to her feet, her face white. 'But this means I won't be able to see him any more. No, no,' she gasped, and bending down she swooped her son into her arms, clutching him fiercely against her chest.

George struggled, and with tears in his eyes he held out his arms to Betty. 'Mmm . . . Mumm,' he cried, his face bright red.

'He called you Mum!' Vera said, shock evident on her face. 'Did you teach him how to do that?'

'No, of course not. Don't be daft, it just sounds like he's saying Mum.'

This was the last straw, Vera thought, tears filling her eyes. My own son doesn't know who I am, and will end up calling another woman Mummy. As George continued to struggle in her arms, she reluctantly gave him to Betty, and with angry movements she pulled out a chair. Her distress mounted when she saw the way her son snuggled up to her cousin and she closed her eyes. It wasn't fair, it wasn't. All she had were these short visits once a fortnight, and now even this was being taken away. Lennie couldn't do this to her, he just couldn't.

The breath left Vera's body and she slumped forward. God, she had to get money, *had* to – it was the only way. Oh, if only Henry had a fatal car accident or something, at least then she would get his life insurance.

'Vera, what am I gonna do?' Betty wailed. 'I don't want to work in the club again. I can't stand the thought of it.'

'Well, leave then,' she snapped.

'You know I can't do that. Lennie never lets his girls go.'

Vera was hardly listening to Betty. Something was forming in her mind, something so horrendous that at first she pushed it away. But the idea persisted, and in her desperation she finally decided that she had no choice.

'Sit down, Betty. I've got an idea . . .'

'But you can't! You can't do that!' Betty cried, her eyes wide after listening to Vera's plans.

'I can, and I will.'

'But what about Henry's daughter?'

'I'll have to get her out of the way. There must be no witnesses.'

'But how are you gonna do that?'

'Oh, I don't know. Give me time to think things through, Betty. I just need to know that once Daisy's gone you'll come here with George.'

'If Lennie finds us, he'll kill us, Vera.'

'As long as we lay low we should be all right for some time. We aren't in his manor here, and with local shops at the bottom of the road we won't have to venture far.'

Vera saw Betty shiver, her fear evident, so in a cajoling manner she said, 'Think about it, love. You won't have to work in the club again, and honestly, you'll be safe here. Please, Betty, I've got to get my son back. Surely you understand that, and once I've got the money we can go away – far away – where Lennie will never be able to find us.'

Betty stared back at her. 'Gawd, Vera, if you had told Lennie the truth in the first place, none of this would have happened.'

'Don't be silly, I couldn't tell him! If I had, he would have made me have an abortion. You don't know Lennie. He adored his mother and put her on a pedestal. To him Lena Talbot was like a queen, a perfect woman amongst all the tarts. If I had destroyed his illusions I dread to think how he would have reacted. Not only that, Betty, his reputation means everything to him, and he would do anything to protect it. You've seen his temper, seen what he's capable of, and if he thought anyone else knew about it, he would probably kill them to keep it quiet.'

'Gawd, I wish you hadn't told me now.'

'I know, but I was in such a state when I found out and needed to confide in someone. You were the only person I could trust and I knew you'd keep your mouth shut.'

Betty continued to stare at Vera, her face white, and with a shudder she said, 'Well, I ain't likely to spread something like that around.'

'I know, and thanks. Now will you come here with George?'

'I dunno, Vera. What you're gonna do sounds awful, and what if you get caught?'

'You won't be implicated. It's me that's doing it, so you have nothing to fear. If you say no, then somehow I'll have to get my son back without you, but by then you'll be back on the game.'

Betty gulped, her head lowering. Then heaving a sigh she finally said, 'All right, I'll do it.'

After reluctantly saying goodbye to George, Vera saw her cousin out, her mind still churning. There was so little time and she had to get rid of Daisy quickly. If only she could get the girl sent to her aunt's in Hampshire – but how? Henry would never let her go. He adored the girl and treated her like a baby. Baby – that's it! Vera thought. Yes, that was how she would get rid of her.

Chapter Thirteen

On Saturday the sun was shining but it added little warmth as Daisy stood gazing at the view. They were on the top of Box Hill in Surrey, one of her father's favourite places. Daisy looked at the fields set out like a patchwork quilt in varying shades of green, separated by the dark outline of hedges – and in the far distance a church steeple. There was a road too, cutting through the countryside, the cars on it looking the size of Matchbox toys. Sighing, she watched a bird as it soared across the sky, wishing that she too could stretch her wings and fly. One of Daisy's pet hates was to see birds in cages. Whenever she passed the pet shop she always had an irresistible urge to run in and open all the cage doors, to release the poor trapped creatures so they could fly free, as they were meant to.

It was so quiet, the only sounds coming from the soft hum of bees buzzing amongst the wild flowers, and the gentle rustle of a breeze dancing through the new growth of leaves on a tree. Daisy turned as her father's voice broke the silence.

'It's lovely up here, isn't it, Vera?'

'Yes, the countryside is beautiful,' she answered distantly. Then, her glance embracing them both, she smiled softly, saying, 'I've got something to tell you.'

'Have you?' Henry said, a puzzled look crossing his face.

Vera hesitated, her eyes sweeping the landscape before she said, 'Well, I hope you'll be as happy as I am. You see, I'm going to have a baby.'

There was a stunned silence as both Daisy and her father

66

gawked at Vera in amazement. A baby, Daisy thought. Vera was going to have a baby!

The frozen tableau broke as Henry threw his arms around Vera. 'Oh, that's wonderful, darling!' he cried.

'Henry, let me go, we're in public!' she snapped, lifting her hand to tidy her hair.

Daisy glanced around; there was nobody in sight.

Looking deflated her father said, 'Sorry, darling, I'm just so thrilled. Oh, I hope it's a boy. I've always wanted a son.'

'Well, I can't guarantee that,' Vera answered with a slight smile on her lips.

Daisy hung her head. A son, her father had always wanted a son. She hadn't known that. What about her? Did that mean he didn't want her?

As though sensitive to her feelings she felt the touch of her father's hand. 'Isn't it wonderful news, Daisy,' he said. 'I've got a beautiful daughter, and now I might have a son too.'

'Can we go home now, Henry? I've got an awful backache,' Vera said.

'Yes, of course. You must rest, my dear.'

As they picked their way through the long grass, Vera groaned and Henry was immediately at her side. 'Are you all right?' he asked worriedly.

'I'm just so tired,' she said as they reached the car.

Henry opened the door, solicitously helping Vera inside, and once she was settled comfortably they started their journey home.

'I hope you're happy about this baby, Daisy,' Vera said. 'Of course, I expect you'll find it a bit difficult, adjusting to not being an only child.'

'Oh, I'm sure she's pleased,' her father said, not giving her a chance to answer.

Daisy gave a small smile. Yes, she was pleased; it would be nice to have a baby brother or sister. She heard Vera groan again, and the car swerved a little as her father turned to look at her anxiously.

'Are you all right, darling?' he asked.

'It's just my back, but I'm sure it's nothing to worry about,' Vera gasped.

'As soon as we arrive home you can have a rest. Daisy and I will cook supper.'

Later that evening, Vera sank onto her bed, a small smile on her face. What an idiot Henry is, she thought. Still, it was nice being pampered. He was treating her like a china doll; putting cushions behind her back when she sat down, and rushing to make her cups of tea. It was certainly a lot more pleasurable than the last time.

It had been a good idea to pretend that she was pregnant, especially now that she had seen Henry's reaction to the news. He was overly protective of her, and she was sure that her plan to get rid of Daisy would work. All she had to do was to time it right – and bingo!

'Here you are, darling,' Henry said, as he carefully carried a tray into the room. 'I've washed up the supper things, and told Daisy to get ready for bed. All *you* have to do is relax and have a nice rest. Maybe I should call the doctor out?' he added worriedly.

'No, I feel much better now,' Vera told him, hiding a smile. He was so easy to fool. She had pretended to feel unwell, and he had behaved exactly as she expected – cosseting her like a hothouse flower. I'll give it just two weeks, she thought, and during that time I will let Henry think that this is a difficult pregnancy. Then if all goes well, and I get rid of Daisy, I can put the next stage of my plan into action.

Chapter Fourteen

It was two weeks later, during the Easter holidays, and Daisy was sitting at Molly's table bouncing Frank up and down on her lap. She winced when he grabbed a handful of her hair, and he gurgled with delight at the expression on her face.

'Let go of Daisy's hair, you little divil,' Molly chuckled. 'Here, give him to me, love. Now tell me, how's that one's pregnancy coming along?'

Daisy rose reluctantly to her feet. 'Vera still isn't well, and I must go now. I've made the beds, but she wants me to do some hoovering and dusting.'

Molly clicked her tongue. 'You seem to be doing an awful lot of housework, Daisy.'

'I know, but Vera is tired all the time and Dad's really worried about her.'

'Your poor mammy lost two babies before you came along, so 'tis no surprise that he's nervous.'

'Lost babies? My mum lost babies! I didn't know that!'

'Oh dear, me and my big mouth. I'm sorry, love, you've gone as white as a sheet. I really shouldn't have mentioned it.'

Before Daisy could respond there was the sound of boots clattering down the steps. The door was thrown open and Molly's sons burst into the room. 'There's a fair coming to Clapham Common on Saturday,' Patrick said, his face alive with excitement. 'Can we go, Mammy? Can we?' he appealed.

'What's *she* doing here?' Sean scowled, his eyes on Daisy.

'That's enough of that, me laddo. 'Tis up to me who comes into this house. Take no notice of him, Daisy,' Molly added, putting Frank down onto the floor. 'Now get yourself out of me sight, Sean. You're becoming far too big for your boots lately, and I'm going to ask your father to sort you out once and for all.'

Daisy made hastily for the door. If Sean got into trouble he would take it out on her as usual. 'I'll see you later,' she called, not waiting for a response.

When she reached her own front door she hesitated, reluctant to go inside. Vera kept insisting that she was jealous of the baby. She had tried to protest, telling her father that she was looking forward to having a brother or sister, but he didn't believe her. Her stepmother had seen to that.

'Hello,' she said, nervously stepping into the kitchen.

'It's about time you showed your face, Daisy. I want the hoovering and dusting done before your father gets home.'

'Yes, all right,' she said, hurrying to get the cleaner out of the downstairs cupboard.

Lugging it upstairs, Daisy started on the bedrooms, dusting the furniture in each room as she went along, beads of perspiration evident on her brow by the time she had finished. In the hall she glanced at the flight of stairs that led up to the fourth floor, glad that the rooms up there were only used for storage and didn't need cleaning too. Breathing heavily with exertion she returned downstairs to start on the living room.

'Hurry up!' Vera said, coming to check on her progress. 'Your father had an appointment at the dentist this afternoon and he will be home early. You'll have to leave the basement until tomorrow now, and when you've finished in here you can lay the table for dinner.'

'Yes, all right,' Daisy murmured.

She finished quickly, putting the hoover away before rushing into the kitchen and grabbing a pile of cutlery from the drawer. In the dining room Daisy had just unfolded the tablecloth when she heard the front door opening, and throwing the cloth hastily onto the table she rushed into the hall. 'Daddy!' she exclaimed, throwing her arms around his waist.

'She doesn't deserve to be cuddled, Henry,' Vera said as she stepped from the kitchen, surveying the scene.

'Oh, and why is that?' he asked.

'I'm so dreadfully tired, Henry, but it's a battle to get Daisy to do the simplest thing. I only asked her to lay the table and she started to sulk.'

'I'm surprised at you, Daisy. You know your stepmother isn't feeling well and it wouldn't hurt you to help her – especially when it comes to the heavier household chores.'

Daisy stared up at her father, shaking her head dolefully. She wanted to tell him the truth, but Vera had told her to keep her mouth shut and she was too scared to disobey.

'I've told you, Henry, she resents the fact that I'm pregnant,' Vera wailed, her eyes flooding with tears.

'Go and finish laying the table, Daisy,' he snapped, turning away from her and rushing to take Vera into his arms. 'I'm so sorry, my dear. I can't believe that my daughter is acting like this and I'm ashamed of her, I really am. Come on now, calm down. You really mustn't upset yourself like this. I'll have a talk with Daisy later and try to sort this out, once and for all.'

'No, it's all right, Henry,' Vera said, sniffing pathetically. 'Daisy's just a kid and perhaps it's natural for her to be jealous. After all, she's been an only child for so long and I'm sure she'll be all right when she's adapted to the idea.'

Daisy, her own eyes full of tears now, rushed back into the dining room. Why was Vera telling lies? Her father hated her now, she knew he did. Picking up the cutlery and wiping her wet face with the back of her hand, she laid the knives and forks into three place settings. The task completed she crossed to the window, looking dejectedly into the street.

'If you've finished that, Daisy, go and wash your hands,' Vera said, stepping into the room.

She nodded, quietly leaving the room. With one foot on the stairs Daisy jumped when Vera's voice rose from behind her. 'Oh, what a wicked thing to say!' her stepmother screamed.

Bewildered, Daisy turned, just as her father shot out of the sitting room. 'What is it? What's the matter?' he cried.

'She . . . she said . . .' Vera wailed, throwing herself into his arms.

'What did Daisy say?' Henry urged, his face white as he held her.

'Your daughter said she wishes the baby was dead,' Vera sobbed.

For the first time in her life Daisy was afraid of her father. His face was suffused with rage as he stepped towards her, his hand raised. 'I didn't say it, I didn't!' she cried, stepping back hastily.

He stopped in his tracks; taking deep gulps of air to quell his anger. 'Go to your room!' he finally shouted. 'I'll talk to you later!'

Daisy ran then, taking the stairs two at a time and slamming her bedroom door behind her.

Vera heaved a sigh. It was all going according to plan. Henry was convinced that she was having a difficult pregnancy and was terrified she would miscarry. Soon she would put her final move into action.

She sipped the tea that Henry had insisted on making for her, then groaned delicately as she made to stand up. 'I had better dish our dinner up, or it'll be ruined,' she gasped.

'Sit down, dear, I'll see to it,' he told her.

'Thank you, darling. There's a casserole in the oven and the vegetables are ready, but are you sure you can manage?'

'Of course I can.'

'I've made an apple pie for pudding. I know it's Daisy's favourite, and because she's been so good with her diet I thought I'd give her a little treat.'

'Oh, that was kind of you, dear. Though with the way my daughter's been behaving, I'm not sure that she deserves it.'

Henry walked into the kitchen, his brow creased. Poor Vera, she was trying her best, but Daisy was making life very difficult for her. Since announcing her pregnancy he had noticed the change in Vera, finding that she had turned back to the soft and caring woman he had married. Perhaps that had been the problem – perhaps she had just been broody.

Reaching down, he took the casserole out of the oven, the rich aroma filling the kitchen. As he drained the potatoes his thoughts were distracted; he was unable to understand why his daughter was being so difficult. He had expected her to be thrilled about the baby, but instead she was unreasonably jealous. Henry's mouth tightened. How could Daisy say such a thing? How could she say that she wished the baby were dead?

He tipped the cabbage into a colander, sadly remembering the devastation he and Judith had suffered when she had miscarried. God, he thought, don't let it happen again! Vera was already having a difficult pregnancy and Daisy's attitude wasn't helping. This jealousy had to be sorted out once and for all, and he would have to give his daughter a good talking to. Perhaps she needed some sort of reassurance that she wasn't being supplanted by the new baby, and he would do his best to give her that. But despite that, Daisy had to be made to understand that he wouldn't tolerate any more bad behaviour.

Once Henry had left the room, Vera waited for about five or six minutes before making her way to the kitchen, and as she passed the stairs she gazed at them momentarily. She had waited until the first day of her period, which was always heavy, and now this would be the final phase of her plan to get rid of Daisy.

'I'm just going up to the bathroom, Henry. If you're nearly ready, I'll tell Daisy to come down for dinner.'

'Yes, all right,' he answered, turning to give her a strained smile. 'I'll have a talk with her after we've eaten.'

Feigning concern, she said, 'Don't be too hard on her, darling. I'm sure she didn't mean what she said.'

After going to the bathroom Vera opened Daisy's bedroom door. 'Come on,' she said, poking her head into the room. 'Dinner is ready.'

Daisy slowly slid off the bed, her dress riding up to show huge fat thighs, and Vera shook her head. She really had tried to help Daisy to lose some weight, but despite her efforts, the girl was as fat as ever. 'Hurry up,' she snapped, her nerves making her temper flare again. Then, making sure that Daisy was behind her, she walked along the landing. Reaching the top of the stairs, she paused. Timing – all it needed was good timing, but she had to get it just right.

Slowly Vera began to descend, and when almost at the bottom she cast a quick glance over her shoulder. Yes, Daisy was about halfway down. *Now*, she thought. *Do it now!*

Taking a deep breath, her mouth wide, she screamed loudly as she pitched forward, pretending to fall. Then, grabbing the banister, she sank carefully onto the floor.

Seconds, it had only taken seconds, but Henry's reaction must have been instantaneous as he appeared at her side. 'Vera, Vera, are you all right!' he cried.

'Oh Henry,' she groaned. 'It was Daisy. She . . . she pushed me. Call the doctor! Please, call the doctor. I might lose the baby,' she wailed.

'Get out of my sight!' Henry roared as he glared up at his daughter. Then, not waiting to see if she obeyed, his voice loud in agitation, he begged, 'Vera, are you in pain? Can you stand up?'

'No, I don't think so,' she moaned.

Henry carefully picked her up and carried her into the sitting room where, after placing her gently onto the sofa, he rushed to the telephone. 'I'll ring for an ambulance,' he said, voice shaking.

'No, Henry! Please, call Dr Taylor . . . he can be here in minutes,' Vera begged. Yes, and he's a silly old duffer too, she thought.

Vera submitted to the examination, glad when it was over.

'You say you were pregnant, Mrs Bacon. How far along were you?'

'About four weeks,' Vera said, glad that Henry was out of earshot.

'Well, I'm not at all sure that you were pregnant, Mrs Bacon, but if you were I'm afraid you have lost the baby.'

'Oh no!' Vera wailed, forcing tears into her eyes.

'I'll just have a word with your husband,' the doctor said, opening the sitting-room door.

Vera, dabbing delicately at her eyes, held her breath as Henry came rushing into the room, his face creased with concern.

'I don't think there's any need to send your wife to hospital, Mr Bacon. I'm not sure that she . . .'

'Oh Henry. I've lost the baby!' Vera wailed, desperate to stop the doctor from letting the cat out of the bag. When he tried to speak again, she wailed louder, trying to sound hysterical.

'Can't you do something!' Henry cried, his eyes frantic as he took her in his arms.

'I'll give your wife a sedative, Mr Bacon, and then she should stay in bed for a few days with her legs raised up on pillows. If you are worried at any time, then please ring the surgery.'

Vera saw the anguish on Henry's face and as he stood up, his shoulders were slumped. 'Thank you, Doctor. I'll see that she rests. In fact, I've some holidays due so I'll take a few days off.'

'Yes, good idea,' he answered, administering a sedative.

After showing the doctor out, Henry returned hurriedly to the sitting room, his face still white with anxiety. Vera whispered tearfully, 'Would you help me upstairs, dear? I don't think I can manage on my own.'

'Of course you can't,' he said rushing to her side and lifting her into his arms.

Once settled into bed, Vera said, 'I didn't tell Dr Taylor that Daisy had pushed me, Henry. I told him I tripped.'

'I just can't believe it of her, Vera. My God, she could have killed you!'

'She killed our baby, Henry. Oh, she must hate me to do such a thing!'

His mouth tightened, and his eyes darkened with anger. 'I knew she was jealous – but to push you down the stairs . . .'

'I . . . I'm frightened, Henry.'

'Oh, my dear, please don't be frightened. I'll see that she never does such a thing again.'

'But you won't be here all the time, Henry. Please, please,' she cried, 'can you send her away until I recover? She could go to your sister in Hampshire.'

'I don't know, Vera. My sister runs a little shop on her own and she has a retarded daughter to look after too.'

'*Please!* I don't think I could bear to look at Daisy at the moment. She . . . she killed my baby.'

Vera looked at Henry as he began to pace the room. The sedative was taking effect and she was fighting to keep her eyes open. He walked over to the window, staring at the street below, then finally turned to face her. 'All right, Vera, I'll go and give my sister a ring.'

Vera's eyes closed. It had worked, her plan had worked! She would have to prolong the time it took for her to recover, and she had to convince Henry that she needed some help in the house. That accomplished, she could move Betty and Georgie in.

Chapter Fifteen

Daisy's eyes were like those of a wild animal caught in car headlights, as transfixed she stared at her father. Send her away! He was going to send her away! His words rang in her head. Auntie Edna in Hampshire! She was being sent to Aunt Edna's in Hampshire. Dimly she had memories of the little village, a holiday there when she was about ten or eleven. But that was when her mother was alive. Since then Daisy had only seen her aunt once, and that was at the funeral.

Her thoughts raced, remembering her Cousin Lizzie. She was strange, a little odd, and though three years older than her, she had seemed childlike. Daisy had vague memories of a day out on the beach, Lizzie with them; her cotton dress tucked in her knickers as she turned cartwheels, frolicking like a small child in the sand.

'Daisy, are you listening to me?'

'What? Yes . . . no . . .' Daisy floundered. 'But I don't want to go, Daddy. Why are you sending me away?'

'I would have thought that was obvious,' he said coldly.

'Let me stay here, please.'

'No, Daisy. As I've explained, your behaviour has been disgraceful, and you have given me no choice. We will be driving down to Puddleton tomorrow, and you will stay with your aunt until Vera has recovered.'

Daisy threw her father a look of anguish before dashing out of the room. She ran blindly along the hall and wrenched open the front door, ignoring her father's shout as she burst outside.

Acting on instinct she fled down Molly's basement steps and banged frantically on her door.

'What is it? What's the matter?' Molly asked as Daisy barged past her into the kitchen, her breath coming in gasps.

'He's sending me away!' she cried.

'Calm down, darlin'. Is it your father you're talking about?'

There was another knock on the door and Molly tutted impatiently as she went to open it. 'Henry, come in,' she invited, her voice high with surprise.

'I saw Daisy rushing in here. I'm afraid there's been a bit of upset, Molly, and I've come to take her home.'

'No, I'm not coming!' Daisy shouted, her voice rising hysterically.

'Henry, sit down,' Molly ordered. 'You too, Daisy.'

'No, Molly,' he said bluntly. 'I don't want to get you involved in this. It's a family matter.'

'Now look here. Daisy ran to me and all she has said so far is that you're sending her away. Is this true?'

'She's only going to her aunt's in Hampshire for a while.'

'But why?'

'Molly, I appreciate all you've done for us, but this is none of your business. I have good reason for sending Daisy away and I haven't taken this decision lightly. Now if you'll excuse me – I'll take her home.'

'I'm not happy about this, Henry. It doesn't make sense and I can't think of any good reason why Daisy is being sent to her aunt's.'

'Molly, I don't want to fall out with you, but I must ask you not to interfere,' he said curtly.

'When is she going, Henry?'

'Tomorrow. Now come on, Daisy, say goodbye.'

Daisy rushed up to Molly, throwing her arms around her waist and burying her head in her bosom. She wanted to say goodbye but found she couldn't speak; her throat was constricted with emotion.

Molly squeezed her tightly and then planted a kiss on her

cheek, but just as she was about to say something Henry forestalled her, snapping impatiently, 'Come on, Daisy.'

'Bye Molly,' she managed to croak before following her father outside. Reaching the top of the basement steps Daisy threw him a stricken look, and then hurried home ahead of him, making straight for her room. She had thought things would be wonderful when her voice came back, but what was the point of talking? No matter what she said, her father didn't believe her.

Daisy shivered as she sat on the bed, her hands clenched between her knees, dreading going to her aunt's.

Vera was still in bed the next morning, so it was just Daisy and her father sitting at the kitchen table eating their breakfast. The atmosphere was tense, and as her father pushed his plate to one side he broached the subject again.

'Daisy, we need to talk. When you pushed Vera down the stairs you caused her to lose the baby, and not only that, you could have seriously hurt her. Now I know you were jealous, but that's no excuse. What on earth possessed you to do such a thing?'

Unable to defend herself, she hung her head.

'Answer me, Daisy. I just don't understand your behaviour. What's got into you lately?'

Staring at her father across the table, Daisy was determined not to speak, yet seeing the censure in his eyes she was unable to stop herself from blurting out, 'I didn't do it . . . I didn't! Vera's telling lies, Daddy!'

'Vera fell because you pushed her, Daisy, and it's no good trying to deny it.'

'But I didn't,' she insisted again. 'She must have tripped. Please, you've got to believe me. I wouldn't try to hurt her, or the baby.'

Her father studied her face, his eyes puzzled. Then abruptly pushing his chair back he stood up, and with a sharp intake of breath he said, 'Right, I think we had better sort this out. Come on, we'll go and talk to Vera.'

Daisy's heart began to thump wildly. If Vera thought she'd

been telling tales she would carry out her threat. No, that mustn't happen! Shaking her head frantically, she cried, 'No, Daddy! Please, don't talk to Vera!'

He sat down again, a dreadful look of sadness passing over his face. 'So you did push her then?' he asked quietly.

Oh God. What choice did she have? Her father thinking she had tried to harm Vera was bad enough. But even worse was the thought of what he would do if he found out the truth about the accident. She couldn't risk Vera telling him – she just couldn't. And hating what she had to do, Daisy slowly nodded her head.

'Go and finish packing. We are leaving for Puddleton in about an hour, and I suggest that you apologise to Vera. She might be up to seeing you this morning,' he said coldly.

Choking with emotion, Daisy went upstairs, and after knocking tentatively on Vera's door, she stepped quietly into the room. 'Daddy said I should apologise to you, but . . .' Unable to go on she left the sentence unfinished as tears filled her eyes.

'Don't bother to turn on the waterworks, Daisy,' Vera said, guilt making her voice sound cold and hard. 'Anyway, who knows, you might enjoy yourself at your aunt's.'

'I don't want to go. Please . . . why are you having me sent away?'

'It's necessary and that's all you need to know. But I'm warning you, Daisy, keep your mouth shut. If I find out that you've been telling tales I'll make sure that you don't come home for a long, long time.'

'I won't say anything, I promise,' Daisy told her forlornly.

'Good, then we understand each other. Now off you go.'

Daisy sat quietly beside her father in the car, resigned to going to her aunt's. When they had left the house Patrick and Sean were playing in the street, and as she got into the car they took great delight in pulling faces at her, Sean pushing his nose up with his index finger, impersonating a pig as usual. Well, at least I'll be free of them for a while, she realised, taking some comfort from the thought.

They drove through London, Daisy gazing fixedly out of the

window as her father took the A3 towards Kingston. 'We'll stay on this road until we pick up the A31,' he said, finally breaking the silence.

Daisy nodded, her thoughts still on her aunt, wondering what it would be like living in the small village.

'Your auntie has had a hard time since her husband died, Daisy. She runs the business alone, with just a chap who takes the van out every day. It was a very astute of her to kit a van out as a mobile shop for outlying villages in the area.'

'How did Uncle Billy die, Daddy?'

'He had a heart attack. The poor man was only forty-three and Edna was left to bring up Lizzie on her own.' He turned his head to look at her briefly, adding, 'I hope you'll behave yourself, Daisy. It's kind of Edna to have you.'

'Will she let me help in the shop?' she asked, brightening at the idea.

'I don't know . . . perhaps.'

The journey dragged on and Daisy found herself nodding off, only waking when her father touched her knee. 'We're nearly there,' he said.

She stared at the wide expanse of undulating countryside, fields green with new growth, another with cows in, their heads down as they grazed.

Turning into a narrow road her father slowed the car to a crawl, giving her a glance as they reached a small junction – the signpost indicating left for Puddleton.

They passed a farmyard, Daisy wrinkling her nose at the smell, and then the village came into view. It consisted of a few thatched cottages, and opposite them a tiny building that her father told her was the junior school and village hall rolled into one. Then a cluster of more houses and a pub set back from the road with a wooden table and bench outside.

'There's the shop,' her father said, briefly raising one hand from the steering wheel to point at the small building.

Daisy saw a house on the corner with a Lyons ice-cream sign standing on the pavement outside. The windows were tiny, set with leaded glass, and spanning the corner was a door leading into the shop. There was ivy growing up one wall, reaching as far as the red-tiled roof and almost covering one of the upstairs windows. It looked so quaint, and exactly as she remembered it.

Her father drove into a small parking space to one side of the shop with barely enough room for them to get out of the car, and after removing her suitcases they went back to the front of the building.

As he opened the door a bell tinkled and Daisy's eyes popped at the gloomy interior, stuffed with an assortment of groceries. There was a small queue of customers at the counter and they all turned in unison to look at the newcomers.

'Hello, you two,' Edna said, smiling a greeting. 'Go through to the back and I'll be with you as soon as I can.'

Daisy saw that her aunt looked harassed as she returned to her customers, saying, 'What can I get you, Mrs Purvis?'

'I'll have a pound of those broken biscuits please, Mrs Wilkens,' she replied, pointing to a cardboard carton on the floor. 'They're a bargain and I found quite a few whole ones amongst them last week.' Then turning to watch as Daisy and her father shuffled behind the counter and went through a curtain separating the living quarters from the shop, she added, 'I see you've got your brother visiting you. Staying long, is he?'

'No, not for long. Now is there anything else I can get you, Mrs Purvis?' Edna asked, cutting off further questions.

Daisy could hear the murmur of customers' voices as she stared around the small back room, memories of her last visit returning. She recalled the narrow creaking stairs, a small bedroom far up in the eves, and the sound of a cockerel rousing her in the mornings. Unexpectedly, tears filled her eyes. Her mother had been alive then and she remembered how they had laughed together at the unaccustomed country noises.

'Put the kettle on, Henry,' Edna called, popping her head around the curtain. 'I'll be closing for lunch in a few minutes.'

Another door opened and Daisy's eyes widened as her Cousin Lizzie came into the room. She was only about five feet in height and chubby, with wispy straight brown hair. Appearing to have no neck, her wide, flat face broke into a smile as she bustled across the room.

'Hello,' she said, grasping Daisy's hand and gazing gently into her face. 'Don't be sad.'

Something twisted inside Daisy. The hand felt soft and damp, but it was Lizzie's eyes that arrested her. Sloe-shaped, they seemed to look into her soul with a warm liquid understanding. The tears that welled spilled over onto Daisy's cheeks, and Lizzie's other hand came up to tenderly brush them away. 'Don't cry. You're a good girl,' she said.

'Lizzie, leave your cousin alone. You're upsetting her,' Aunt Edna said, bustling into the room. 'Don't worry, Daisy. She won't hurt you, but she can be a bit over-affectionate at times.'

'It's all right,' Daisy protested, blinking away her tears. 'She isn't upsetting me.'

Her aunt grinned and she saw the familiar large gap between her front teeth. Edna was tall and thin like her father, and similar in colouring. 'We'll all rub along well together, Daisy. It's lovely to have you, and you can treat this like an extended holiday. Goodness, I can't believe how much you've grown,' she said, babbling away happily. 'But then I haven't seen you since your mother's funeral, and you were so upset I don't think you even realised I was there, and . . .' The smile dropped as she placed a hand over her mouth. 'Oh, I'm so sorry. I shouldn't have brought that up.'

'There's no need to apologise, Edna,' Henry said, bringing over the teapot and placing it on the table. 'Where do you keep your cups and saucers?'

Edna gulped audibly, then said hurriedly, 'I'll get them,' as she moved to a cupboard set into the wall behind her.

They all sat round the kitchen table that was covered with a pristine white linen tablecloth, a blue striped jug full of wild flowers resplendent in the centre. At first conversation was stilted, but as Daisy tucked into a large chunk of fruit cake, followed by another, her aunt burst out laughing. 'I thought it was only my Lizzie who could eat like that,' she gasped.

Lizzie, her mouth also full of cake, spluttered, and crumbs shot onto the table. 'Daisy like me. Daisy likes cake too,' she giggled.

Henry sighed. 'I'm afraid she has got rather a large appetite,' he admitted, a slight frown on his face.

'She's a growing girl, Henry. Anyway, you've given me more than enough for her keep.' She turned to look at Daisy then, asking gently, 'Do you like cooking?'

'Yes, I've had some lessons at school.'

'Well then, perhaps you'd like to help me with some of the baking?'

'I'd love to, Auntie. And may . . . may I help you in the shop too?' she asked eagerly.

'Why of course,' her aunt smiled. 'My, I can see we're all going to get along famously.'

'I must go now, Edna,' Henry said. 'Vera is still quite ill and I don't want to leave her for too long.'

'Humph. Well, you had better get yourself away then.'

He rose from his chair and moved to stand behind Daisy, resting his hand lightly on her shoulders. 'Be a good girl for your auntie,' he said gruffly. 'I'll ring you every week,' and not giving her time to rise from her chair, he almost ran out of the room.

Daisy made to follow him, but her aunt laid a detaining hand on hers. 'Let him go, love. He's upset at leaving you, and quick goodbyes are always best.'

She stared at her aunt, and seeing the understanding in her eyes, slumped with resignation.

'Let Lizzie show you your room, Daisy. Then when you've finished unpacking she can take you for a look around the village. Not that there's much to see, mind, but there are some lovely walks.'

Daisy nodded, and rising slowly to her feet, she followed her cousin out of the room.

''Lo, Mr Jackson,' Lizzie called to the old man standing by the stile, a black and white border collie lying by his feet. ''Lo Shep,' she added.

The dog came running, pink tongue lolling, ears up and alert.

Reaching Lizzie he jumped up, his paws resting on her chest as she stroked him. There was a soft whistle, and hearing the sound Shep raced back to his master. 'You've a way with animals, Lizzie,' Mr Jackson told her. 'There's not many folk that he'll go to. And who's this young lady with you?'

'My Cousin Daisy,' Lizzie told him, grinning widely. 'She's come to stay. Bye now,' she said abruptly as they walked away.

Daisy turned to look at her cousin as they ambled slowly along. Every time they came across a villager, Lizzie called out a greeting. They all responded kindly to her, many stopping to have a few words.

A woman was strolling towards them now with a basket full of vegetables in her hand. ''Lo, Mrs Cook,' Lizzie said, eyeing her large stomach. She was obviously heavily pregnant and looked tired as she shifted the basket from one hand to the other. 'Baby boy born soon,' she told her.

'Oh Lizzie. A boy! You think it's a boy?' Mrs Cook asked.

'Yes, boy,' Lizzie repeated.

'I hope you're right. Mr Cook would love a son after three daughters,' she said, delight on her face. 'Mind, I've never known you to be wrong.'

'Not wrong,' Lizzie said bluntly. 'My Cousin, Daisy,' she added, introducing her to yet another villager.

'Nice to meet you, Daisy,' Mrs Cook said, and with a small smile she moved past them, saying, 'Bye, girls.'

They turned a corner, the shop coming into view. 'Go home now?' Lizzie asked.

'Yes, all right,' Daisy agreed.

The bell above the door tinkled as they stepped inside, finding the shop empty of customers. 'Hello, you two,' Edna said. 'Did you have a nice walk?'

'Yes, thank you,' Daisy answered.

'It's gone three o'clock and we won't have many customers now, except maybe the odd one or two. Most of the villagers get their shopping in the morning while the bread and milk are still fresh. If you're not too tired perhaps you'd like to help me restock the shelves?'

'Oh, I'd love to,' Daisy said eagerly.

'Lizzie always helps with this, and now that there are two of you we'll get it done in no time.'

The next hour was a pleasant one and Daisy enjoyed collecting the boxes of tinned goods from the storeroom, stacking them neatly on the rows of wooden shelves. They chatted as they worked, her aunt gently probing about her problems at home. Daisy kept her replies down to a minimum, and after a while her aunt gave up. It was when Edna sent Lizzie off to get some jars of jam that Daisy plucked up the courage to speak.

'Aunt Edna, when we went for our walk Lizzie said some funny things to people that we met.'

'I don't doubt it, my dear,' she said, a soft smile on her face.

'Everyone seems to like her,' Daisy said, 'and she seems to just know things about them. She told one lady that her baby was going to be a boy.'

'Yes, that doesn't surprise me. It can take some getting used to at first and I don't really know how to explain it to you, except to say that Lizzie is what some people call fey. We've lived here for fifteen years now and the villagers have come to accept her strange predictions. If they're worried about anything they usually contrive to bump into Lizzie.'

'I don't understand, Aunt Edna.'

'Sorry, love, I'm not very good at explaining her behaviour, and I expect you're a bit young to understand. Lizzie doesn't do any harm to anyone, and though she's sixteen she only has the mind of a child. Strangely, though, she seems to have an innate wisdom – a sort of sensitivity to people.' Edna paused, a slight frown on her face. 'There are one or two villagers who have been cruel to her, and on occasions children too, but being busy in the shop I'm not always around to protect her.'

'I'll look after her,' Daisy offered, suddenly feeling protective of her cousin.

'That's nice of you, darling. Do you know, you're very much like your mother to look at, and you take after her in nature. She was a lovely kind person too.'

Daisy looked down and Edna, not noticing her distress, carried on speaking. 'I've been keeping Lizzie in as much as possible to avoid any trouble. It's strange really,' she mused, 'people react to me with pity when they see Lizzie, and though I'll admit I was deeply upset when she was born, I soon came to realise that I'd been given a gift. She's a wonderful girl, Daisy, full of love and affection. If you're upset she instinctively knows, and will comfort you. Lizzie has enriched my life in so many ways, and now I thank God every day for giving her to me.'

'Here, Mum, strawberry jam,' Lizzie said, coming back into the shop.

'Good girl. Now how about making a nice cup of tea? I'm sure you'll be able to manage between the two of you.'

Smiling in agreement they made their way to the back room, Daisy putting the kettle on and Lizzie, somewhat clumsily, getting out the crockery. Thankfully she didn't break any, and once the tea was made they laid a tray. Daisy carried it through to the shop, with Lizzie following behind, clutching a plate of carefully arranged biscuits.

'Oh, lovely,' Edna said in appreciation. 'Now listen, Daisy. I don't close the shop until five-thirty and then I have to prepare our dinner. We sometimes don't get to eat until about seven o'clock. In the meantime there are always cakes in the tin, and you can help yourself. As long as you don't spoil your dinner you can eat whenever you want.'

Daisy stared at her aunt in amazement. Help herself? Vera would never let her do that. Her stepmother was always trying to put her on a diet, as well as being careful of her own figure, and there were never any cakes at home. Daisy smiled; perhaps it wouldn't be so bad staying with her aunt, after all.

That night Daisy looked around the pretty bedroom she had been given under the eaves, remembering it as the one she had slept in the last time she had stayed with her aunt. There was rose-patterned wallpaper, a very old-fashioned oak dressing-table and wardrobe, and a pretty pink patchwork quilt on the bed. The room felt homely and cosy, but after the noise of London it was eerily quiet.

Turning on her side Daisy switched off the bedside lamp, surprised to find that the room was now bathed in a strange light. She looked up and saw a full moon casting a luminescent glow through the sloping window. It was this, and the unaccustomed silence that lowered her mood, emphasising her feeling of being in an alien environment. Unbidden, thoughts of her mother flooded her mind, and just as it did at home, her tummy rumbled.

Daisy tried to resist the familiar urge as she tossed and turned in the strange bed, but it was impossible. Finally she threw back the quilt, and holding her breath she crept stealthily downstairs. Quietly opening the kitchen door she was drawn like a magnet to the larder, her chubby hands reaching out for the cake tin. With a guilty glance behind her she carefully took off the lid, grabbing a handful of rock cakes.

Creeping back upstairs to her room, Daisy climbed into bed, cramming the cakes one after another into her mouth.

Chapter Sixteen

Vera watched Henry searching for a clean shirt. She had deliberately played on her supposed miscarriage, not only pretending that her nerves were bad, but also saying that she had anaemia. She had also neglected the housework, and hoped that the time was now ripe to put the next stage of her plan into action. 'I'm sorry, darling, I'm afraid I've been too tired to do any ironing,' she said with a woebegone expression.

'It doesn't matter.'

'But it does! You need clean shirts for the office and you've been wearing that one for two days now. If only I didn't feel so exhausted all the time,' she wailed, forcing tears to fill her eyes.

'Please, darling, don't upset yourself. I'm sure I can manage to iron a shirt for myself, and while I do that you can sit down and put your feet up.'

'But it isn't just the ironing, Henry, the whole house is getting so neglected. Look at it. There's dust everywhere, and it's been two weeks since I cleaned the basement flat.'

'The basement flat!' Henry exclaimed. 'Why worry about that? It's been empty for years.'

'It still needs to be kept clean or we'll be alive with vermin,' she retorted. 'Oh, if only I could have some help.'

'Perhaps we could afford a cleaner for a couple of hours a week,' Henry suggested, looking pleased with his idea.

'A couple of hours! What good would that do? This house is huge and we need someone to come in every day.'

'That would cost a lot of money, Vera.'

She sat quietly for a while, and then widened her eyes as

though struck by an idea. 'Henry, I know what we could do! You said yourself the basement flat has been empty for years. Why don't we let it rent-free in return for daily help in the house?'

'What! Have strangers living downstairs? No, I don't think so,' he said coldly.

'Don't just dismiss my idea, Henry. The flat has its own entrance and we could keep the internal door locked.'

'I know that, but the answer is still no, Vera.'

She wailed loudly. 'See, you don't care about me. I lost my baby because of your daughter, and it's made me so ill. God, you've no idea how much work is involved in keeping this house clean. I can't carry on, I really can't!'

'Calm down, darling!' Henry cried, rushing to her side.

'No, I won't calm down. Surely it wouldn't do any harm to have a woman living in the basement. I would make sure she has good references.'

Vera could see the worry lines creasing Henry's brow as he looked at her, and pushing home her advantage she groaned, holding her hands to her forehead.

'All right, Vera. Perhaps it could work,' he said, as though unable to bear her distress. 'But you must ensure the tenancy is on a monthly basis or we could be stuck with someone down there for years.'

A surge of relief flooded through her. Thank God Henry was such a soft idiot, and with a smile of gratitude, she said, 'Leave it to me, darling. I'll get the perfect tenant and I'm sure there will be loads of applicants. After all, a rent-free flat isn't something to be sniffed at.'

'I hardly think we can call two small rooms and kitchenette a flat, Vera. And though it has a toilet outside the back door, there's no bathroom. I can't see you getting many applicants.'

'Oh, I think we will. It's still a good offer, Henry, and lots of people cope without a bathroom. You told me that Molly Carson manages with just a tin bath for the whole family.'

'Yes, that's true,' he said, rising to his feet. 'Very well, dear, I'll leave it to you to find a suitable cleaner-cum-tenant. Now, I'll just go and iron a shirt, and after I've done that, would you like a cup of tea?'

'Yes, please,' she said, restraining herself from clapping her hands with delight. Oh, it was wonderful! All she had to do now was to get in touch with Betty, and her cousin could move in within the week.

'Henry, this is Betty Clarke. Our new tenant.'

Henry looked up, his eyes widening. Folding his newspaper hastily he rose to his feet, hand outstretched. 'Er . . . how do you do,' he spluttered, obviously trying to regain his composure.

''Ello,' Betty said shortly, taking his hand and shaking it briefly.

Vera hid a smile. She had decided to just present Betty to him as a fait accompli, giving him no chance to argue. 'Betty has a fourteen-month-old son called George. He's a lovely child and she's agreed to do the cleaning every day, including the washing and ironing, in return for the basement flat. Isn't that wonderful?'

'A child?' Henry squeaked.

'Yes, and he's delightful. Betty is a widow and said the offer of rent-free accommodation is a godsend. I'm satisfied with her references and she moved in this afternoon.'

'B . . . but there's only one bedroom, and . . .' he began.

'Oh, that isn't a problem. Mrs Clarke said that her son George sleeps in the same room as her, and she's satisfied with the accommodation. I'm so happy, Henry. Now that I'm going to have so much help my health is sure to improve, and I know you're as delighted as I am,' she enthused.

'Well, yes,' he stammered, his expression reflecting his bewilderment.

'Right, come along, Betty. Now that you have settled in I'll show you your duties,' Vera said, urging her cousin out of the room, and as soon as they were back in the basement, out of earshot, they dissolved into giggles.

'Blimey, what a twit,' Betty gasped, 'and you seem to 'ave him wrapped round your little finger. I can see now why you've kept your posh accent. He talks like he's got a plum in his mouth, don't he?'

'Yes, he does, and yes, I have kept up my elocution. I don't know why you don't do the same.'

'Nah, I put it on a bit in the club, but I can't keep it up like you.'

George began to whimper, but when Vera rushed into the bedroom she found he was still asleep. She stood gazing down at him, her eyes alight with happiness. Oh, it was wonderful. Every day now she would be able to see him, to hold him. Her son . . . her beautiful son.

'I couldn't bring many clothes, Vera. It was too risky,' Betty said, coming to stand beside her.

'Don't worry, we're about the same size and I'll sort you out some things. George can manage with what you brought for a week or so, and then we'll have to risk going to the High Street to buy him some outfits.'

'I'm still scared, Vera,' Betty said. 'Lennie will be back from the racetrack by now and will have realised that George is missing. He's gonna go mad.'

'Stop worrying, Betty,' Vera said, taking her cousin's arm and leading her out of the bedroom. 'Lennie hasn't got any influence around here, and without the police in his pocket he hasn't got the resources to find us.'

'Will it take long to . . . you know . . . do what you're gonna do to Henry?'

'I don't know for sure how long it will take, and then I'll have to wait for the insurance to come through. I could sell this house too and that should raise enough to set us up for years.'

'Christ, Vera, that could take ages. Ain't he got any cash?'

'I don't know for sure, but once he's out of the way I'll find out. Mind you, I can't rush it too much, and it might be a good idea if you get to know Molly Carson next door. She's a nosy old cow and we may need to allay her suspicions. You could strike up a friendship with her, lay it on thick that I'm a bad employer — she'd love to hear that. Then when Henry becomes ill you can plant the seed. Tell her that he's got an upset stomach, gastro-enteritis, or something like that.'

'Yeah, all right. It shouldn't be too difficult to get chatting to her.'

'Right, I had better get back upstairs or Henry will wonder what's keeping me. I'll see you in the morning.'

As Vera closed the internal door behind her, she closed her eyes momentarily. What she intended to do was so dangerous, and she wondered if she really had the nerve to carry it out. Yet what choice did she have? George meant everything to her and she would do anything to assure his safety. She had to get him away, far away. So far that Lennie would never be able to find them.

Chapter Seventeen

After six weeks in Puddleton, Daisy was happier than she had been for a long time. She was growing very fond of her aunt, who was becoming like a second mother to her. Edna treated her like a grown-up, yet still showered her with love and affection. Being away from Vera was wonderful, and now when her father rang she no longer begged to go home. Her father said Vera was still ill, but Daisy didn't care. She hated her stepmother, hated her lies.

She trekked along the lane, and seeing one of her favourite birds, Daisy halted. The jay was perched on a branch, the bright blue stripe on his wing shining, and with his head cocked he seemed to be looking at her. Daisy smiled and for a moment the two studied each other, before the jay suddenly took flight.

It had been her first day at school, and though she was nervous at first, some of the girls in her class had been friendly. They were fascinated to hear that she came from London and wanted to hear all about it, so during playtime she had been surrounded.

She hadn't expected to be in Puddleton long enough to go to a new school, but as the weeks passed her aunt had become concerned about her education. Edna had rung her father, and after discussing it with him, it had been agreed that she should temporarily enrol at the secondary school in the next village.

Daisy's tummy rumbled and she was glad that she was now over halfway home. Her nightly raids on the cake tin had stopped after only three weeks, the craving for food suddenly disappearing. However, it was a long walk and she was now puffing with exertion. Her thoughts turned to Lizzie and she smiled. At first she had found her cousin's constant cuddles overwhelming, but now she enjoyed the closeness they shared. Lizzie was still an enigma at times, saying such strange things, but on the whole she was childlike and rather like an exuberant puppy.

At last the shop came into view and picking up her pace, Daisy hurried to the door, hearing the familiar tinkle of the bell as she pushed it open. 'Hello Auntie, hello Lizzie,' she called in greeting.

'Hello, love. Was school all right, did you enjoy it?' Edna asked.

'Yes, it was fine. I'll just grab a quick snack and then I'll tell you all about it.'

'Right, and in the meantime I had best get on,' Edna said, climbing back onto the ladder. 'I'm just dusting these top shelves while we're quiet.'

'Down, Mum! Get down,' Lizzie suddenly cried.

'In a minute, love, I've nearly finished,' she told her, stretching out her arm to the far end of the shelf.

'*Down! Get down!*' Lizzie insisted, her voice loud.

Daisy saw the fear on her cousin's face and rushed forward. 'Please, Auntie, do as Lizzie says,' she urged, just as there was a cracking sound.

The rung Edna was standing on snapped, and with lightning reactions, Daisy was able to grab her aunt as she toppled over, still clinging onto the ladder. Clutched together they seemed to sway for a few seconds before her aunt's feet touched the floor, but as she let go of the ladder it crashed against the counter, narrowly missing a tray of eggs.

Gasping, Edna struggled to regain her equilibrium. 'Thanks, Daisy,' she finally managed to say, her face ashen.

'Don't thank me, it was Lizzie. She seemed to know that something was wrong,' Daisy reminded her.

'Yes, you're right,' Edna said, turning to give her daughter a cuddle.

'Vera fall too,' Lizzie said.

Daisy looked at her cousin with astonishment. How did she

know that Vera had fallen down the stairs? 'Yes, that's right, Lizzie. But how did you . . .'

'Vera fall again,' she interrupted.

Daisy was about to question Lizzie, but Edna, rubbing her forehead said, 'Would you mind making a cup of tea, love? I feel a bit shaken up.'

'No, of course not, and when it's made you can have a rest. Lizzie and I can manage the shop.'

'Oh, I don't know about that,' she said doubtfully.

'Honestly, we'll be fine, and anyway you won't be far away if we need help.'

'All right then, I must admit I could do with a sit-down. But don't try to use the bacon slicer or the cheese wire. If a customer wants either, then give me a call.'

'I will, Auntie,' Daisy assured her.

Whilst making the tea Daisy quickly ate a slice of bread and jam. Then calling her aunt to the back room, she took her place behind the counter. 'Mum not well,' Lizzie said, a slight frown on her usually cheerful face.

'She'll be all right. I think that fall shook her up a bit and she just needs a little rest.'

'She not well,' Lizzie repeated.

Daisy heaved a sigh. When Lizzie got a bee in her bonnet she would go on and on about it, and sometimes it was impossible to make her understand. Deciding it might be better to divert her mind, she suggested that they polish the counter, making a game of it as they took an end each to see who could finish first. They only had two customers during the following hour, one wanting just a jar of honey, the other buying a drum of Vim and a bar of Sunlight soap.

With relief Daisy turned the shop sign to Closed. One of the jobs her aunt had given her after closing each day was to count the takings, saying it would help her with arithmetic. She emptied the till, carefully counting the pound and ten-shilling notes before entering the amount in her aunt's ledger. Then came the change. Coppers, threepenny pieces, sixpences and shillings, all these went into separate bags, followed by two-shilling pieces and half-crowns. It was quite time-consuming, and while she did this Lizzie somewhat haphazardly swept the floor. When at last they were able to make their way to the back room she was surprised to find her aunt fast asleep in a chair.

'Mum not well,' Lizzie said again as they gazed at her.

'She'll be all right,' Daisy told her reassuringly. 'Your mum's just a bit tired, that's all. Shall we prepare the dinner and give her a nice surprise?'

'Tell Mum to see Dr Davies,' Lizzie said, ignoring her question.

Daisy stared at her cousin. Why had she suggested that? Was she sensing something? Turning, she studied her aunt as she lay sleeping, noticing for the first time how thin and pale she looked. Perhaps there really was something wrong and it wasn't just the fall. 'Listen, love, my dad's coming down on Sunday. He'll know if your mum should see the doctor. I'll tell him that we're worried about her.'

In seconds she found herself wrapped in her cousin's huge arms as she kissed her over and over again on her cheek. 'Yes, Daisy,' she said, a smile of relief evident on her face.

'Right, now get off me and let's get the dinner on,' Daisy gently admonished, extracting herself from Lizzie's arms.

There was a snort, then a snuffle as Edna awoke, looking confused. 'Oh dear, I must have nodded off,' she said, running a hand through her hair. 'Goodness, it that the time? I must see to the shop.'

'It's all right, Auntie, I've closed up and seen to the till. We were just going to start the dinner,' Daisy told her.

Edna smiled with delight. 'Bless you. What good girls you are and I still find it hard to believe that you're only thirteen, Daisy. You seem to have matured, and you're different from the nervous child who arrived looking so shy and distressed.'

'I'll be fourteen in just over two months, Auntie, and I love staying here with you.'

'Good, I'm glad you're happy,' Edna said, rising to her feet. 'Now I had better get a move on. Shall we have some nice pork sausages with our veg?'

'Yes, please,' Lizzie answered, a wide grin on her face.

Daisy watched the scene as her aunt bustled around, lifting her large frying pan onto the range, and putting in a generous knob of lard. Yes, she thought, I am happy here. Happier than I've been in a long time. No more being put in a cupboard, no more slaps, and if it wasn't for missing my dad, I wish I could stay here for ever.

The next few days passed quickly, and though it was the first week in June, Sunday dawned chilly and wet. Daisy threw back the quilt, reluctantly leaving the warmth of her bed. After a quick wash she went downstairs to the kitchen, a blast of lovely warm air hitting her as she entered the room. Her aunt was already up and the range door was open with a goodly fire glowing inside.

'Hello, love. You're up with the lark,' Edna said in greeting.

Daisy glanced at the clock, surprised to see that it was only seven o'clock. 'I didn't realise it was so early.'

'I expect you're excited that your dad's coming down today. You must miss him,' Edna observed. Then running a hand over her forehead she pulled out a chair and flopped onto it, her face pale.

'Are you all right, Auntie?'

'I've got a bit of a tummy ache, but it's nothing to worry about, love.'

Daisy bit her lip. Perhaps her aunt was having her monthlies and she knew how painful the first day could be, but too embarrassed to ask she said instead, 'Would you like me to make you a cup of tea?'

'Yes, please. The kettle has just boiled,' Edna replied, turning her head as the kitchen door opened again and Lizzie came in. 'Morning, darling, another early bird. I don't know what's got into you girls today.'

'Heard you,' Lizzie said abruptly. 'When Uncle Henry coming?'

'I shouldn't think he'll arrive until about eleven,' Edna told her daughter.

Daisy placed a cup of tea in front of her aunt, whilst studying her drawn face. Surely her dad would see that something was wrong? 'Do you want a cup of tea too, Lizzie?' she asked.

'Yes please, and porridge.'

'It isn't made yet. Let me drink my tea and I'll put it on,' Edna told her.

'I'll make it, Auntie. Just tell me how to do it as I go along,' Daisy offered.

'Well, if you're sure you don't mind, get the Quaker Oats out of the cupboard and measure out two cups of porridge into a saucepan.'

Daisy followed her aunt's instructions, adding milk and then stirring the porridge with a wooden spoon, her eyes anxious as she watched the mixture thicken. 'I think it's ready now. Would you fetch the bowls for me, Lizzie,' she urged.

They all sat round the table eating appreciatively. It had turned out just right and Daisy smiled with delight as her aunt tucked in, glad to see that she was emptying her bowl, and wondering if that was a good sign. After all, if she was really ill she wouldn't want to eat, would she?

'That was lovely, Daisy. Now off you go and get ready for your dad. Put your best dress on, and there's a pair of clean white socks in your drawer. You too, Lizzie, I want to see you looking nice as well.'

'I'll wash up the breakfast things first,' Daisy insisted.

'No, I'm all right, love. My tummy is a lot better now.'

'Well, if you're sure,' she answered, studying her aunt's face again, and thinking that she did have a bit more colour in her cheeks now.

'Dad, Dad!' Daisy cried, throwing her arms around him.

His face stretched as he gazed at her. 'My goodness! I'm sure you've grown an inch.'

'Henry, sit down and I'll make you a cup of tea,' Edna said.

'Thanks, love, I must say I could do with one. Now tell me – has Daisy been behaving herself?'

'Of course she has. She's been wonderful.'

'Good, I'm glad to hear it.' Turning to look at his daughter he then said, 'I'm pleased that you've settled down.'

Daisy could see the sadness in her father's eyes and said reassuringly, 'I'm fine, Dad, and though I miss you, I love staying with Aunt Edna.'

'Well, that's all right, then,' he said.

'How's Vera, Dad?'

'I'm afraid she's still not well.' He paused, pinching his bottom lip between his fingers before saying, 'Listen, Daisy, I've got something to tell you. You see, Vera couldn't manage all the housework on her own, it was just too much for her. Anyway, we've let the basement flat to a lady with a little boy and in return she's doing the cleaning for us. I hope it doesn't upset you.'

'But why should it?'

'Vera said you might feel that you've been pushed out.'

Daisy frowned, wondering why Vera would think that. A dreadful suspicion filled her mind. 'What is this lady's name, Dad, and her little boy's?'

'Betty Clarke, and her son's name is George.'

Daisy gasped audibly, trying to cover her dismay by lowering her head. So Betty had moved into the basement flat now, Georgie too, and her dad obviously didn't know who they were.

'What's the matter?' he asked. 'You've gone very quiet.'

'Er, nothing, I'm just a bit surprised, that's all.'

'George is Vera's baby,' Lizzie suddenly said, breaking into their conversation.

'No, he isn't,' Daisy said quickly, feeling her heart thumping in her chest. Her father mustn't find out the truth. If he did, Vera would blame her, and then she would carry out her threat. 'Lizzie's just a bit confused, Dad.'

'No, my dear. George isn't Vera's baby,' he said, smiling across at Lizzie.

'George is Vera's baby,' she insisted.

Daisy saw the confusion on her aunt's face. In panic she jumped up, knocking over her glass of milk. 'Oh sorry,' she gasped. 'I'll get a cloth.'

Luckily, in the haste to clear up the mess, the conversation was forgotten, and they went on to talk of other things. A little later Edna suggested that Daisy should go out for a walk with Henry. 'Spend some time together on your own,' she urged.

'Daisy, I can't take you home yet and you may have to stay here for at least another month. Vera is still finding it hard to come to terms with your behaviour, and not only that, she is still suffering from the miscarriage.'

As they climbed over a stile Henry frowned. He too was finding it hard to accept that Vera had lost the baby. It had been wonderful when she had announced her pregnancy, and he had been so looking forward to having another child. It should have brought them all together, but instead Daisy had become difficult. Was it his fault? Had she felt pushed out? He turned to look at his daughter as her voice suddenly broke into his thoughts.

'It's OK, Dad, I don't mind staying in Puddleton. Aunt Edna's lovely, but do you think she looks all right?'

'What do you mean?'

'Lizzie's worried about her, and she does seem to have lost weight.'

'I can't say that I noticed. Edna looks the same to me.'

'No, Dad, she's thinner and she looks very pale too.'

'Has she seen the doctor?'

'I don't think so. Do you think you could have a word with her?'

'Yes, all right, but I'm sure it's nothing to worry about. Leave it with me and I'll have a quiet word with her when we get back.'

'Thanks, Dad.'

'Daisy, I didn't intend to bring this up again, but I still find it difficult to understand why you were so jealous of Vera having a baby, so much so that you pushed her down the stairs. Hearing how concerned you are about your aunt makes me realise how out of character it was.'

Daisy hung her head as she walked beside him. 'I was happy about the baby, really I was. It was just an accident, Dad.'

Henry paused for a moment and gazed at his daughter sadly. Before bringing Daisy to Puddleton, she had admitted to pushing

Vera, so why now had she reverted to saying it was an accident? Perhaps she couldn't face what she had done.

As they continued their walk Henry felt Daisy's hand creeping into his and after a moment's hesitation he clasped it. Poor Daisy – she had been through so much in such a short time. She had lost her mother, and her whole world had changed overnight. Then with less than a year to adjust he had married Vera. Henry stared at the distant horizon. At the time, getting married had seemed the right thing to do. He thought that Daisy needed a mother to care for her, and Vera seemed the perfect choice. Now in retrospect he wondered if the pregnancy had come too quickly and it was just too much for his daughter to accept.

Well, there was no baby now and he sighed heavily, realising that somehow they had to put it all behind them. 'Daisy, when you come home we all need to make a fresh start, and you must try to get on with your stepmother.'

'I'll try . . . I promise,' Daisy told him.

'Good,' he said shortly. 'Now come on, let's climb to the top of that hill. Edna said there's a lovely view.'

The next hour was a pleasant one. The early rain had cleared, and the promise of summer was in the air. As they made their way back to the shop Daisy gazed at the countryside. The trees varied from pale to dark green, fresh with new growth, the leaves gleaming wetly as though gently kissed by the sun's warmth. 'Isn't it pretty, Dad?' she said, smiling in wonder at Nature's palette.

'Yes, it's lovely,' he answered, reaching out to grasp her hand.

Daisy looked up at him, enjoying the feeling of closeness. It was strange to think that there was a little boy living in the house and she wondered how he felt about it. 'Dad, what do you think of George?' she asked quietly.

'By the time I come home from work Betty is back down in the basement, so I don't see much of him. Why do you ask?'

'Oh, no reason,' she said hastily.

'Hmm, to be honest Molly sees more of him than anyone. Vera

told me that Betty has struck up a friendship with her and she is often next door. Apparently Frankie loves playing with George.'

Daisy was puzzled. It seemed a bit odd that Betty had made friends with Molly; after all, Vera couldn't stand her. She shook her head, unable to make sense of it all. Why was Vera hiding the fact that George was her son? And why was her Cousin Betty looking after him?

Glancing at her dad she was suddenly overwhelmed with guilt. Vera was lying to him. It didn't seem right and she should tell him the truth. Daisy thought about the day when she had found out that George was Vera's son, suddenly realising that it was then that her stepmother had changed. She had become so cruel, with threats and punishment coming daily.

Daisy's tormented thoughts were broken as they arrived back at the shop. She felt her father squeezing her hand reassuringly as they went in, where almost immediately he began to gently question Edna about her health.

'No, I'm fine,' she protested. 'I think I pulled a muscle when I lifted a heavy box in the stockroom, but it's better now.'

'Are you sure that's all it is, Edna?' he asked.

'Positive,' she said bluntly. 'Now, what shall we have for lunch? Do you fancy a nice shepherds pie, Henry?'

Daisy heaved a sigh of relief – a pulled muscle, that was all. She glanced at Lizzie, expecting her to be happier too, but instead she was still looking at her mother with a frown on her face.

'You not well, Mum,' she said.

'Now Lizzie, I'm fine, so stop worrying, there's a good girl,' Edna cajoled.

'George Vera's baby,' Lizzie suddenly said again, ignoring her mother as she looked at her uncle.

'No, he isn't!' Daisy said, her voice betraying her agitation. Aunt Edna was giving her a funny look again, and she knew that her suspicions were aroused. She had to divert the conversation somehow, but what about when her dad went home? What if Edna started asking questions?

Chapter Eighteen

'Hello, Betty. Come on in,' Molly invited.

'Thanks,' she gasped, puffing out her cheeks.

'You look worn out. Is that one piling more work onto you?'

'Mrs Bacon's a bleedin' slave driver, Molly. Nothing is ever done to her satisfaction. There's just no pleasing the woman.'

Molly clicked her tongue with disgust. 'Why don't you have a word with her husband? Tell him that she's giving you too much to do.'

'Nah, I can't do that. He ain't been well these last few days and the poor bloke looks as white as a sheet.'

'Oh, what's the matter with him?'

Betty bent over, scooping George up and onto her lap before saying, 'I dunno, some sort of bug I think. Anyway, Molly, thanks for looking after Georgie for me. I don't know how I'd 'ave coped without you. I usually take him with me when I go up to do the housework, and I must admit that's the one thing she's good about. But with Mr Bacon being at home 'cos he's ill, and her not wanting him disturbed – I didn't know what to do. The miserable cow still insisted she wanted the housework done. "You'll just 'ave to find someone to look after him," she said. Just like that – as if I could conjure up someone from thin air!'

'I don't mind having him, Betty. 'Tis no trouble and he's company for Frank.'

'Yeah, I can see he likes being round here,' she said, laughing as Georgie struggled to get back onto the floor. Frankie was playing with a pile of brightly painted bricks that Paddy had carved for him, and she let Georgie join him.

Molly bustled around making a cup of tea, while Betty supervised the children. Not that they needed much watching. They were taking great delight in trying to pile the bricks up, only for the other one to knock them down, resulting in fits of giggles.

Betty's thoughts drifted. The plan seemed to be working out well. Vera had started to put minute amounts of rat poison into Henry's porridge each morning, and intended to slowly increase the dose. The seed that he wasn't well had been planted with Molly now, and when Henry went to the doctor's yesterday, he had been diagnosed as having a tummy bug. Christ, she hoped Vera knew what she was doing! How she had found out that she could slowly poison Henry without being discovered was a mystery to her.

The young woman shivered with the enormity of what Vera was going to do. God, if her cousin got caught, what then? And what if she herself was implicated? Betty's stomach lurched at the thought. Sometimes she thought she was crazy, going along with Vera's plans – but what choice did she have now? She had taken George, and though she felt sorry for Henry and a part of her wanted to stop this madness, Lennie Talbot was a mad bastard and would kill them both if he caught up with them.

Of course it was guilt too that had made her agree to help Vera. It was she who had suggested that they both get jobs in Lennie's club as hostesses. It had seemed so glamorous at first, wearing wonderful cocktail dresses provided by Lennie, and so easy to persuade the customers to buy them expensive champagne. Then later being invited to his lavish parties and meeting posh, wealthy blokes. How naïve they had been. How bleedin' stupid not to have realised that eventually Lennie's girls were expected to sleep with his rich clients. Betty had thought Vera lucky at first because she had caught Lennie's eye. No sleeping with clients for *her*. Instead she became his exclusive property.

A cup was suddenly placed in front of her and Betty was so deep in thought that she jumped. 'Wake up, you're miles away,' Molly said. 'Drink your tea and it'll perk you up,'

'Thanks, love. I won't stay long. I'm sure you've had enough of Georgie by now.'

'No, he's an angel compared to my little divil,' Molly protested, yet smiling fondly at her son.

Betty picked up her tea, taking an appreciative sip. 'Do you know, Molly, I can't believe that I've been living next door for nearly eight weeks now.'

'Yes, the time has gone quickly. But tell me – does Vera ever talk about Daisy, Henry's daughter?'

'No – well, at least, not to me.'

'Poor Daisy,' Molly mused. 'It doesn't seem right that she's stuck down there in the back of beyond. The girl's being treated like an outcast.'

Not wanting this turn in conversation to go any further Betty gulped the last of her tea and rose to her feet. 'I had best be off, Molly. I've done all Mrs Bacon's washing, but I've still got me own to do.'

'Do you want me to have George again in the morning?'

'If Mr Bacon is still at home. But are you sure you don't mind?'

Molly smiled broadly. 'No, of course not – and how many times have I to tell you?'

Betty returned her smile before picking Georgie up. 'If I'm not around by ten o'clock in the morning, you'll know that Mr Bacon has gone to work. If that's the case I'll see you after I've finished me chores. Bye for now,' she chirped.

'Did Molly swallow it?' Vera asked later that evening, having sneaked quietly down to the basement when her husband was asleep.

'Yeah, she thinks Henry's got some sort of bug, and when I see her tomorrow I'll show concern that he's worse.'

'Good. Well done, Betty. Not much longer now and it will all be over.'

'Molly mentioned his daughter Daisy today. What are you gonna do about her?'

'Nothing, she can stay with her aunt. I'm his wife and his next-of-kin, so Henry's estate will all come to me. Daisy isn't entitled to anything.'

'I dunno about that, Vera. If he's made a will that could change everything.'

'Do you think I'm stupid, Betty? I've already pumped him about that, and though Henry's been talking about it, he hasn't got round to it yet.'

'All right, keep your hair on,' Betty said, and to change the subject she added, 'Georgie really does need some new clothes Vera.'

'In that case we'll have to risk going to the High Street. The market might be the best place. It'll be packed and we can disguise our appearance.'

Betty shivered. So far, by keeping to Fitzwilliam Street and the local shops she had felt safe in Clapham, but now they were going to venture further afield and her heart thumped in her chest with fear.

Chapter Nineteen

Plonking her laundry into the battered pushchair and covering it with an old sheet, Ada Tucker pushed it into the yard. The wheels squeaked loudly and for the umpteenth time she reminded herself that they needed oiling. I'll do it later, she decided, shrugging her shoulders.

Returning to the kitchen and despite the warm weather, Ada threw on her old grey coat. She then stuffed her purse into the pocket and left the house to take her laundry to the wash baths as she did every Monday morning.

Shoving the pushchair through the back gate Ada soon reached Falcon Road, making for Battersea High Street. As she hurried through the market, the stalls flanking her on each side, she smiled widely at the banter thrown at her by the costermongers.

'Blimey, what's this? I think I can hear a mouse.'

'Nah, Billy. That ain't a mouse. It's Stirling Moss with his new racing car.'

'Well, it must 'ave broken down then – 'cos he don't usually push it.'

'Shuddup, you silly sods,' Ada called. 'I don't know why you 'ave to take the micky out of me pushchair. There ain't nothing wrong with it.'

'Sorry, love, no offence. Show us your baby then. 'Cos if it ain't your wheels you must 'ave a right squeaky kid in there.'

'What! You must be joking. One look at yer ugly mug and it'll start squalling,' Ada laughed, and reaching the end of the market she headed for Shuttleworth Road, anxious to get to the baths before a queue began to form.

Puffing with exertion she paid at the entrance, and taking her ticket made her way through to the machine rooms, pleased to see her usual cronies clustered around the large washers. 'Wotcher, Flo. How are you?' she asked one of them, a small round woman in a faded crossover pinny.

'Not too bad, Ada. Me rheumatism's playing me up a bit though.'

'Yeah, I know what you mean. Still, mustn't grumble,' Ada, ever-optimistic, told her.

'Are you coming to the Railway Arms after you've done that lot?' Flo asked.

'Can a duck swim?' Ada grinned, smacking her lips at the thought of a nice glass of sweet stout.

The wash-house grew busier, the hot and steamy atmosphere cloying as Ada took her washing from the huge machine. She ran it through the mangles, and then as she shoved it into the dryers, her tummy rumbled loudly. 'Flo, I'm gonna 'ave a plate of pie and mash at Maggie Brown's in the High Street, before I come to the pub. Do you fancy some?' she called.

'Nah. I'm not hungry, Ada.'

'All right, I'll see you later,' she said, folding her clean sheets and putting them back onto the pushchair.

'Christ, Ada! Ain't it about time you oiled them bleedin' wheels?' someone shouted as she pushed her pram to the exit. 'I can hear you coming for miles.'

Blimey, not again, Ada thought, and with a sigh she shouted back, 'Yeah, I'll do them later,' determined to get the oilcan out when she went home.

Ada stood at the counter, watching greedily as thick green parsley liquor was ladled over her plate of pie and mash. 'Chuck in a portion of stewed eels, love,' she urged the skinny girl in the big overall.

Placing her bowl on the marble-topped table, Ada shuffled onto the bench, reaching out for the bottle of savoury vinegar, thick with strips of dried chillies and black peppers. After shaking on a generous helping and digging into her pie with a dessertspoon, she lifted it to her mouth in salivating anticipation.

'Where is she, Ada?' a voice growled.

Her heart sank and she hunched low on the bench. 'I dunno, Lennie,' she told him.

'Don't give me that. She's yer daughter,' he scowled, sitting opposite.

He looks ridiculous in here, Ada couldn't help thinking, nervously taking in his appearance. Lennie Talbot was wearing a black pinstripe suit, white shirt, and wide flashy tie with a huge Windsor knot. Both his large hands were splayed on the table, sporting huge gold rings on several fingers, two of them sovereigns. Flash git, Ada thought.

'I ain't seen Vera for years, Lennie. Not since she took up with you,' Ada told him.

'I don't believe you. Now I'll ask you again, where is she?' Reaching into his inside pocket he pulled out a cigarette case and after lighting up he blew a cloud of smoke into her face, his eyes cold and menacing.

Ada looked down, avoiding his gaze; her appetite gone as her stomach lurched. 'I dunno where Vera is,' she repeated. And it was true. She had no idea where her daughter was.

Christ, what an almighty row they'd had when Vera started working in Lennie's club. It had made Ada sick with nerves, and though she had begged and pleaded, her daughter had refused to pack the job in. Then her worst nightmare had been realised when Vera had turned up with a bun in the oven, saying it was Lennie's baby she was carrying. Ada had screamed and shouted at her, telling her to get rid of it, and suggesting old Peggy Green across the road would abort it for ten quid. But Vera was a stubborn little madam and refused to listen. Finally, with no other choice, she had told her the truth about Lennie Talbot, and with a look of sheer horror Vera had run out of the house. Ada closed her eyes now against the memory. It was the last time she had set eyes on her daughter.

'I've had a few of my boys watching you, Ada, but so far you ain't led me to her. Now it's up to you, gel. Tell me what I want to know – or I'll get the boys to do more than just watch you,' he threatened.

Ada blanched, her hands shaking as she laid her spoon down. 'I'm telling you the truth, Lennie. When Vera took up with you and got herself pregnant we had an almighty row. I told her to get rid of it but she wouldn't listen, and . . .' Her voice trailed off as her eyes widened with fear. Christ, me and my big mouth, she thought, Lennie will probably take that as an insult.

His hard, button-black eyes narrowed and Ada cowered. However, ignoring her remark he spoke with a chilling whisper. 'Vera's got my boy, Ada. I'm sure of it. Now I want him back, and if she don't give him to me I'll take it out on you. Do I make myself clear?'

'Lennie, if you've been 'aving me watched you must know that she didn't even turn up for her dad's funeral.'

He grinned sardonically. 'Oh, I know she didn't show, Ada, but that don't prove nothing. Vera hated her father – according to her he was a right bastard, and you don't look like a grieving widow.'

'Yeah . . . well, I can't deny that, and I can't say I'm sorry that me husband's dead.' And Davy Tucker was more of a bastard than Lennie realised, she thought. 'You're wasting yer time quizzing me. If I knew where Vera was I'd tell you.'

He cocked his head to one side, his dark hair, thick with Brylcreem, not moving out of place as he studied her. 'All right, I'll give you the benefit of the doubt for now. But if I don't find Vera soon, someone will 'ave to pay. This is my manor and I ain't allowing anyone to make a monkey out of me. I've got my reputation to think of.'

Ada kept her head lowered, relieved when Lennie stood up. 'If you hear from Vera get in touch with me at the club,' he growled before striding out of the pie and mash shop, collecting one of his gorillas who had been standing guard at the door.

Glancing around, Ada saw other customers staring at her and there wasn't a sound to be heard. Everyone seemed to be holding their breath. Until suddenly a voice said in a loud whisper, 'Christ, Lennie Talbot! Thank God he's gone.'

Now, unable to face the food in front of her, Ada scrambled from the bench, deciding that what she needed was a drink. She pushed her pram to the Railway Arms, and scurrying into the snug she saw her cronies at their usual table.

'What's up, Ada?' Lily asked. 'You look like you've seen a ghost.'

'Lennie Talbot cornered me in the pie and mash shop.'

'Bleedin' hell! What did he want?'

'He's looking for Vera,' Ada told her, adding, 'give me a glass of Mackesons, Bob,' as she moved towards the bar.

'Are you sure you don't want a drop of brandy?' the landlord asked. 'I couldn't help hearing what you said. Blimey, Lennie Talbot. You don't want to get mixed up with him.'

'I ain't!' Ada snapped. 'And I can't afford a brandy. Do you think I'm made of money?'

'All right, there's no need to take it out on me,' Bob retorted, putting a small glass to the optic behind him. 'Here, have this one on the house. You look as though you need it,' he said, placing it on the counter.

'Thanks, Bob, and I'm sorry. I didn't mean to snap, but I'm a bit shook up.' Ada lifted the glass to her lips, drowning the brandy in one gulp, gasping as the spirit hit her throat. Her voice a rasp, she croaked, 'That was good of you, Bob – just what the doctor ordered. I'll 'ave me glass of stout now, please.'

The landlord nodded an acknowledgement and after paying for her drink Ada went to sit with her friends.

'What did you tell Lennie?' Flo asked.

Ada carefully poured her stout, watching as the rich dark liquid filled the glass. 'I told him the truth. I don't know where Vera is, and that's that.' Lifting the glass to her lips she took a long swig of the sweet stout, before wiping the back of her hand across her mouth. 'Luverly,' she sighed, trying to sound flippant.

'What made your Vera take up with the likes of Lennie Talbot in the first place?' Lily wanted to know

'She didn't – it was just a job in his club at first. My Vera was always a bit of a flighty piece and I think she was attracted to the glamour. Lennie bought her nice clothes, jewellery, and she enjoyed working as a hostess in his club.'

'Huh, hostess!' Flo exclaimed.

'Yeah, hostess!' Ada snapped. 'What are you implying, Flo?'

'Nothing, nothing,' she placated, casting a meaningful look towards Lily.

Tipping the last of the stout into her glass, Ada said, 'Vera told me that all she had to do was to get blokes to buy her drinks, champagne and such, and she got a commission on how much they bought. She was doing all right the last time I saw her,' she lied, 'but that was a while ago, before we fell out.'

'Why did you fall out with her?' Flo asked.

'That's my business,' Ada blustered, 'but for one thing I didn't want her getting mixed up with that hooligan. Vera wouldn't listen to me – told me to keep my nose out of it. She used to come to visit, dressed up to the nines, talking like she had a plum in her gob and acting all high and mighty. One day she turned up with a black eye and tried to tell me that she'd walked into a door. She must think I'm a right mug to believe that. After all, I was married to Davy Tucker for nearly forty years.'

'Cor yeah, you've sported a few black eyes yerself over the years. Ada. But I expect Vera had to learn to talk proper for all those posh geezers going into Lennie's club,' Flo observed, adding with a wide toothless grin, 'Vera was always a right cracker to look at.'

'Lennie's mother must be turning in her grave with the way he's turned out,' Lily mused. 'Lena Talbot idolised him and she had a hard time bringing him up on her own when her husband buggered off. Here, Ada, didn't they use to live next door to you until Lena fell pregnant with Lennie?'

'Yeah, they did,' she said, and desperate to change the subject she blurted out, 'Christ, Flo, why don't yer wear your bloomin' dentures?'

'I can't stand the bloody things, Ada. Anyway, what does it matter? I ain't likely to go looking for blokes at my age.'

'You wouldn't look so old if you'd put your teeth in. You're sixty-nine, not ninety-nine.'

'Nah, I ain't wearing them, so put a cork in it, will you,' she admonished. Then to Ada's annoyance she turned the subject back to Vera, saying, 'I heard on the grapevine that your Vera and Lennie had a kid. Is that right, Ada?'

'I dunno,' she lied. 'I told you, I ain't seen my gel for ages.'

Looking sceptical, Flo said, 'Well, if she's left Lennie, he ain't gonna stand for it, and if Vera ain't in Soho now, I wonder where she's hiding. Ain't you got *any* idea, Ada?'

'No, and I don't want to know. Now shut up and let's talk about something else!'

'All right, keep your hair on,' Flo grumbled.

Ada grimaced. If Lennie didn't find Vera he would carry out his threat and take it out on her. Shivering, she wondered if she should put out a few feelers, perhaps try a few of Vera's old mates to see if they had heard from her.

Christ, with Lennie threatening her Ada wished she could do a runner too. How much longer would it be before the Council moved her? The house she lived in now had been condemned and she was to be given alternative accommodation. It would be smashing to see the back of her ground-floor flat. Huh, flat, she thought – two rooms with a yard and outside loo. Surely they would offer her something better than that? After all, Flo and Lily had already been re-housed – in one-bedroom flats on the new estate near the High Street. She shifted in her chair, suddenly realising that even if the Council moved her tomorrow, it wouldn't help. Lennie had snitches all over the Borough and would soon track her down. Yet why couldn't he find Vera? It must mean that her daughter was miles and miles away!

Chapter Twenty

'God, I feel so ill, Vera. Will you ring the doctor again and ask him to call?'

'Yes, darling, but he might not be able to come today.'

'I've been ill for so long now, and I'm worried about Daisy. It's been ages since I last went to see her and it really is about time she came home. She'll be fourteen next week and it doesn't seem right that she's still with Edna.'

'Henry, I can't cope with Daisy while you're ill. Have you forgotten what she did?' Vera wailed, forcing tears into her eyes.

'No, I haven't forgotten, but Daisy can't stay in Puddleton indefinitely.'

'Please, can't we leave her with your sister until you recover?'

'The last time I saw the doctor he said that if this new medication doesn't help, he would send me to hospital for some tests. I think he suspects that I might have an ulcer. Well, I certainly don't feel any better. In fact, I feel worse. Perhaps if you can get him to call he'll arrange for my referral to hospital.'

Vera's heart jolted. Henry mustn't be sent for tests . . . it would give the game away! That meant it would have to be done today before he saw the doctor again. Oh God, could she go through with it? But even if she could, she didn't have enough rat poison! 'I must go shopping, Henry,' she said hurriedly, 'but I'll ring the doctor before I go.'

'Thank you, dear.'

'I'll be back as soon as I can. Will you be all right?' she asked solicitously.

'Yes. I think I'll have a little doze while you're out.'

Closing the door softly behind her, Vera walked slowly downstairs. Her thoughts were racing, churning over all the possibilities. She was only using small amounts of poison, and it was taking longer than anticipated, but she had been too frightened to rush it.

Reaching the hall she paused, a thought crossing her mind. Maybe the doctor talking about tests could be turned to her advantage. He was a proper old duffer, and she always acted like a helpless little woman when she saw him. With any luck, if she played the part of a grieving widow, the doctor would concentrate more on her than on the cause of Henry's death. If that didn't work she could use this new weapon, saying hysterically that her husband should have been sent to the hospital earlier. That would put the wind up the soppy old sod, and he was sure to want to issue the death certificate as quickly as possible.

Perhaps things were going her way at last, she thought as she went down to the basement. George was sitting on the hearthrug playing with his toys, and she smiled at him affectionately. Since living here they had become close, though it still rankled that she couldn't tell him she was his mummy.

He looked up, giving her a heart-stopping smile that stiffened Vera's resolve. The sooner they got away the better! 'Betty, I must go to the shops,' she told her cousin. 'Do you want to come with me?'

'Yeah, all right, but give me a few minutes to disguise myself like the last time.'

'Since I've dyed your hair all you need to do is to wear some sunglasses and that should be enough,' Vera said as she picked George up and gave him a quick cuddle.

Betty scratched her head and scowling she said, 'I hate this red colour, it makes me look awful. It took some explaining to Molly too. Her face was a picture when she saw it and I had to tell her it came out wrong.'

'For goodness sake stop moaning. Once we get away you can go back to your old colour. Now come on – get a move on,' she said impatiently.

'Can you carry Georgie while I lug his pushchair up the steps?'

'Of course I can,' she said, planting a kiss on his cheek. He reached out to touch her face, at that moment looking so much like his father that Vera's stomach felt like it had turned a somersault. He was impossible to disguise and it was a terrible risk taking him out, but there was no choice. He had to come with them.

They were soon outside, Georgie looking cute in his cotton shorts and shirt. He hated his pushchair now and wanted to walk everywhere, but despite his struggles they managed to strap him in. Vera smiled – George as usual was clutching the piece of striped knitting that she had abandoned. He had been attracted to the colours and now used it as a comfort blanket, refusing to be parted from it.

As they neared the end of the street, Vera said quietly, 'I've got to finish Henry off today, and I haven't got enough rat poison. To allay any suspicions we had better not go back to the same shop. It will be safer if we go to that one over by the market.'

'Oh Vera, I'm scared!' Betty cried, her face strained. 'What if you don't get away with it?'

'Shush, keep your voice down! Anyway, I don't know what *you've* got to be scared about. I've told you before that you won't be implicated,' Vera said as they turned onto the High Street.

After crossing the busy main road they made for the railway bridge, which they would have to go over to get to the market on the other side. On reaching the steep flight of stone stairs Vera stooped down to release George from the pushchair.

'If you're gonna let him walk, hold on tight to his hand. These stairs are bleedin' dodgy,' Betty warned.

'Do you think I don't know how to keep my son safe?' Vera snapped.

'Don't get yer knickers in a twist, love. It's just that I'm a bit over-protective and I opened me gob without thinking,' Betty placated.

Vera's smile was strained. 'Sorry, Betty – I'm a mass of nerves today. But then with what I've got to do, it's hardly surprising.'

'Please Vera, don't talk about it any more. I'm shaking enough as it is, and I don't know how you've got the guts to do it.

'I'm not looking forward to it, but what choice have I got?' Vera said, gripping her son's hand, and as they ascended the stairs she watched each step that he took. Georgie stumbled and Vera quickly steadied him. He smiled up at her mischievously and her heart swelled with love – he was so beautiful. It was as they neared the top of the stairs that Betty gasped loudly, and Vera looked up.

'Hello, Vera,' Lennie Talbot said.

She froze momentarily in shock, staring up at the cold, menacing face. 'Lennie!' she cried in fear as his eyes now travelled to Georgie.

'Run, Betty! Run!' Vera screamed, scooping George up into her arms and veering sideways in an attempt to pass Lennie and the thug at his side.

'Oh no, you don't,' he growled, and moving swiftly he blocked her path, ensuring that she was trapped. 'I've been here every week since one of me snitches said they'd seen you in the market, and it's paid off at last.' With a menacing look on his face he turned to Betty. 'I trusted you with my son, you bitch, and I'll make you pay for running off with him. And as for the pair of you dyeing your hair, did you really think it would fool anyone? My snitch followed you, but lost you in the crowd on the other side of the bridge.'

Vera could feel her legs shaking like jelly. What could she do? How could she get George away?

'Hello, son,' Lennie said softly, leaning towards George with a smile on his face. 'You're coming home with your daddy.'

'No! No! You can't do that. You can't take him away!' Vera shouted in panic, clutching George closer to her chest.

'Oh yes, I can,' Lennie growled, reaching out to grab George.

'Leave him – let him go! Oh help, somebody help! Betty, for God's sake – stop him!' Vera cried hysterically as she and Lennie grappled together.

Betty's eyes were wide as she stood paralysed, her face stiff with fear as she clutched the pushchair.

Vera struggled desperately, fighting to hold on to George as she twisted her body sideways in an attempt to loosen Lennie's hands.

'You bitch! Let go of him!' he spat.

'No! Leave him alone!'

Betty suddenly came to life and moved to help, but Lennie's thug blocked her path. He was built like a tank and as she kicked out at him, fighting to reach Vera's side, he grabbed her roughly around the waist. 'Let me go, you bastard!' she cried, unable to do anything against his brute strength.

Vera felt as though she was trapped in a nightmare. Betty yelling – Georgie screaming, his face red and his arms waving in protest as Lennie tugged at him. *Oh God, help me! Please, help me!* Vera thought frantically as she felt herself weakening.

She made one last effort, pulling back from Lennie as hard as she could. But it was no good. He violently snatched George from her arms, leaving her off-balance and toppling on the brink of the stairs. The last thing Vera saw as she tumbled backwards was the sight of her son in Lennie's arms.

Chapter Twenty-One

The buzz of voices, a light penetrating her closed lids and the smell of disinfectant stinging her nostrils . . . Where am I? Vera thought as she slowly opened her eyes.

'Ah, I see you're awake, Mrs Bacon,' a soft voice said.

She turned her head to see a nurse sitting beside her. Hospital, she was in hospital! Then she remembered – in a flash it all came back. Oh God, Lennie! He had taken George. She had to get up – had to get her baby back! Desperately Vera struggled to move – only to find it impossible.

She felt strange, weak, and as she tried to move again the wail that issued from her mouth caused the nurse to start in her chair. 'My legs! I can't move my legs!' she screamed.

'Now then, Mrs Bacon, calm down, please,' the nurse urged, adding as she bustled out of the small side ward, 'I'll just get the doctor to come and have a word with you.'

Vera listened to the doctor's voice, turning her head away as he told her she was lucky to be alive. 'Mrs Bacon, it's too early to say how you will be affected by the injuries to your spine, but in the meantime you must try to lie as still as possible. I'm waiting for the X-ray results, and perhaps we will be able to tell you more then.'

Days passed in a blur. Vera was vaguely aware that Betty visited her and, looking pale but partially recovered, Henry too. But by now she had retreated into darkness. The nurses tried to feed her but she turned her head away. She didn't want to eat – she just wanted to die. Paralysed – she was paralysed from the waist down, the doctor had told her.

More time passed and they sent a psychiatrist to see her, but Vera refused to talk. 'You have lots to live for,' he said, the bloody idiot! She was crippled and she'd lost Georgie, the light of her life. Lennie would never give him back, and without him her life had no meaning.

'Come on, Vera, snap out of it,' Betty cajoled.

She turned her face to the wall, refusing to look at her cousin.

'Look, you've been stuck in here for over three weeks now and the doctors 'ave said you can come home soon. Isn't that something to look forward to?' Betty urged. 'And don't worry, I'll stay to look after you.'

Through dry lips Vera whispered one word. 'Georgie?'

'I've tried, honestly I have, but it's no good. The club's closed and there's no sign of Lennie. I've asked around but nobody seems to know anything, or if they do they ain't talking. You've got to face it, love. He's gone, and could be anywhere.'

As Vera took in Betty's words a dam seemed to burst inside of her. Tears spurted from her eyes and she was wracked by uncontrollable sobs.

'That's it, Vera, let it all out,' Betty whispered, patting the back of her hand ineffectually. 'You ain't got to worry about Henry. Blimey, when you was first brought in he was frantic, and though he still looks ill, it's amazing how quickly he recovered when that stuff you was giving him left his system. Mind you, with all the cups of tea we drank between us I ain't surprised. Christ, it must have washed it all out,' she said, laughing softly. 'Henry doesn't know anything, love. He thinks your fall was an accident. Lennie didn't hang about when you took that tumble and when the ambulance come he was long gone. And surprise, surprise, no witnesses to the accident came forward. Henry didn't even think to ask about Georgie for days 'cos he was so worried about you, and when he did ask, I told him that my mum was looking after him for the time being.'

At the sound of her son's name, Vera's sobs increased. Her face was awash as a nurse came into the room.

'Oh good,' she said, a smile on her face. 'She's broken down at last. I'll go and get the doctor.'

Lennie Talbot was close to losing his temper. The bloody kid was crying again. He had done everything to keep him happy, flooding his room with toys and games, but all to no avail.

'Angie, get in here!' he shouted, raking his hands through his hair.

'Yeah? What now?' his girlfriend said belligerently, sashaying into the room.

'For Christ's sake, you're a woman, can't you think of something to shut this kid up?'

'I've tried, but he don't wanna know. I think he wants Betty.'

'Bet . . . Bet,' George wailed. 'Want Bet!'

'Well, you can't 'ave her!' Lennie shouted back, making the small boy scream even louder.

'You shouldn't yell at him like that. You're frightening him and just making him worse,' Angie snapped.

'Well, do something then, sort him out!'

'Now look, Lennie, he's not my kid and he ain't my responsibility. I didn't expect to 'ave to take this on when I moved in with you, and it ain't fair. You should get a bleedin' nursemaid or something.'

'Don't swear in front of my son! You sound like a bloody fishwife!' Lennie bawled, his face red with temper. 'How many times 'ave I told you to speak properly. Christ, can't you show a bit of class?'

'Like Vera did, is that what you mean?' she retaliated. 'Well, it ain't just me. You swear in front of him too. I ain't bloody Vera, and you'll just 'ave to accept me the way I am.'

Too late Angie realised her mistake, and as Lennie's face took on a look of evil she backed away as he advanced towards her. His voice full of menace, he hissed, 'Get out, you useless slapper. There's plenty more tarts where you came from, and I can soon replace you. Now go on – get out!'

'No, please, I'm sorry, Lennie!'

Raising his hand he clouted her hard across the face, watching with pleasure the bright red imprint that formed. 'Get your things packed and go, or you'll get more of the same,' he threatened, enjoying the fear on her face.

Angie backed away, and as the door slammed behind her Lennie became aware of George screaming and sobbing in terror. Stooping down he snatched his son up into his arms, ineffectually patting his back as the child squirmed and squalled to be put down again.

Now what? he thought, struggling to calm his temper. What had Angie suggested? Oh yeah, a nursemaid. The daft cow! Since when did people have nursemaids nowadays? As George's cries changed to soft sobs Lennie sat down, perching him on his lap. God, if only his mother Lena was still alive, she'd have known how to deal with this little nipper. Lena would have loved the kid to death, her first and only grandchild.

As George finally quietened, Lennie found his thoughts drifting back to his own childhood. He had no memories of his father, and when questioned, his mother just told him that he'd run off while she was still pregnant. Over the years he had tried again and again to find out why, but she remained tight-lipped, refusing to talk about it.

Lennie could remember the poverty. The secondhand clothes, the hunger, and year in year out, his hate for the man who'd deserted them had grown. At school he had been teased unmercifully for not having a dad, and many times the word 'bastard' had been brandished. His face hardened and he ground his teeth, remembering how he'd had to fight to survive. But he had shown them, hadn't he – shown them all, until eventually nobody dared to challenge him.

Having cried himself to sleep, George slumped against his chest and Lennie's arms automatically enfolded his son as his thoughts continued to drift. Yes, he'd won, and instead of being bullied he had become feared, and with this knowledge came power.

God, if only his mother had lived to see how far he had come! She had been wonderful and he would never forget how hard she struggled to bring him up. His mother was the only woman he had ever loved. The rest, he soon discovered, were just tarts –

and realising that, he had used them. From small beginnings, just running a few girls, he had built an empire; an empire based on fear. No one had the nerve to cross him now, he thought with a grim smile. He'd seen to that.

As George moved on his lap Lennie's thoughts returned to the present, and the problem he had with the child. He desperately needed someone to look after him – someone he could trust. Thinking about Angie, he decided it couldn't be another one of his tarts. What did they know about kids? Nothing! All they knew was how to please men. Betty had been a tart too, but as she was related to Vera he had thought she could be trusted with George. It had been a mistake, one of the few he had made, but he shouldn't be surprised. That's what happened when you trusted women. Well, Betty would pay, but in his own time and he would savour the thought of how nervous she would be. Yes, he might wait a year before he had his revenge, but one day, when she was least expecting it, he would sort her out. Women, bloody women. Other than his mother, they had all let him down.

Nevertheless he needed someone now, someone with experience who would know how to deal with the child. He stiffened then, struck by a thought. That's it! He could hire a nanny. Of course, she would have to come from a respectable agency. After all, he wanted the best for his boy. Looking down at his son, Lennie's face softened. 'Don't you worry, mate, I'll get you the best nanny money can buy.'

George looked sleepily up at him, and as if finding reassurance in his father's face, he reached up and touched his cheek. For the first time in his life Lennie's heart turned over and he felt a surge of love, along with an overwhelming feeling of protection. 'Your daddy's gonna look after you, and I'll never let anyone take you away from me again. Yes, we'll be fine, you and me,' and remembering his own father's desertion, he added fiercely, 'and I'll never leave you, son. Never.'

Chapter Twenty-Two

'Get out! I said get out!' Vera screamed, reaching for a glass on her bedside table and aiming it at Betty's head.

She ducked and it missed her by inches, smashing into the wall and scattering shards all over the carpet. 'Now look, I ain't taking much more of this. It's been six months now and I'm fed up with it. It ain't my bleedin' fault you're a cripple,' Betty shouted, before putting her hand over her mouth and gasping, 'Oh, I'm sorry. I shouldn't 'ave said that, but you're enough to try the patience of a saint.'

'Yes, you've said it, haven't you! I'm a cripple!' Vera yelled.

'Look, the doctor said you don't 'ave to stay in bed and Henry arranged for this wheelchair to be delivered. It was his idea, not mine, but it's me that has to bear the brunt of your tantrums, ain't it.'

'Get it out of my sight then. I'm not getting into it and that's that.'

'All right, I'll shove it into the hall,' Betty told her. 'But I'm warning you, Vera, don't you aim anything else at me. I've had just about as much as I can take for one day.' She grabbed the back of the wheelchair, thrusting it out of the room, her mouth drooping despondently. I can't take any more, she thought.

At first, Betty had stayed out of pity for Vera, but now she was sure that something had happened to her cousin's mind. Vera had changed so much and now seemed tinged with madness. There had been months of verbal abuse, months of being used as a punchbag every time she washed and changed her, and now she was at the end of her tether. Yes, Henry was paying her well, but she was sick to death of it. Day in, day out, listening to Vera ranting and raving was enough to drive anyone up the pole.

I'll tell him I'm leaving when he comes home, Betty thought. He can find someone else to look after her and that's that, she decided, her head wagging. Of course Henry wouldn't believe her if she told him why. Vera was all sweetness and light when he was around and was the same when the district nurse called to give her physiotherapy. But as soon as they were alone she became impossible again. Oh, what does it matter? Betty thought, as she headed for the basement to pack her bags. The sooner I get out of here the better.

'But, Betty, you can't leave! Who will look after her?' Henry exclaimed, a look of horror on his face.

'I dunno – you'll just 'ave to find someone else.'

'Please, Betty, won't you reconsider? Perhaps I could manage to pay you a little more. You know Vera won't stand for anyone else looking after her.'

'Nah, it ain't the money. I've just had enough of being a nursemaid. I ain't suited to it, and I've made up me mind to go.'

'Is it because of your son Georgie? I know he's still with your mother and it must be very hard for you, only seeing him in the evenings.'

'It ain't that. It's as I told you – I don't like looking after your wife and I want to leave.'

He slumped, defeated by the tone of her voice. 'Very well, but will you at least stay until I can find a replacement for you?' Henry held his breath, an appeal in his eyes as he looked at her.

'Oh, all right, I suppose so,' she said, adding brusquely, 'but just until Monday. I'm going then whether you've got a replacement or not.'

'Thank you,' he said, watching Betty as she left the room. What had caused this? Why this sudden determination to leave? Surely it wasn't due to Vera . . . Oh, he knew his wife could be a bit short-tempered at times, but after what she had been through it was hardly surprising. Despite losing the use of her legs she wasn't over-demanding and was grateful for everything that was done for her.

Frowning, he swung his foot impatiently. Betty's duties weren't that onerous. Yes, she had to do some housework and cooking, but he helped as much as possible. Other than washing Vera and attending to her needs, there was little else asked of her.

Betty didn't have to run up- and downstairs because Vera now slept in the sitting room, and to give his wife some stimulus, Henry had had a television set installed. Vera watched it avidly, hardly bothering with the radio now, and when not watching the TV she was content with a book or the newspaper.

For goodness sake, Henry thought, what little there was for Betty to do – even Daisy could manage. Daisy! Yes, Daisy, he thought, jumping up and pacing the room. He could bring her home! What a fool – why hadn't he thought of his daughter before? She only had one more term to do at school before leaving when she was fifteen. Surely it wouldn't hurt if she left a few months early? Yes, this was the answer, and he was certain she would be thrilled to come home.

Henry almost ran from the room in his eagerness to talk to Vera. Would she agree to it? Originally his daughter was only supposed to stay in Puddleton for a short time, just until Vera got over the loss of their baby. But then he had become ill, followed by the accident, and time after time her return had been put off. My God, he thought, counting up the months, Daisy had been with Edna for eleven months now. In that time, she had had her fourteenth birthday, and had also spent Christmas with his sister. Now it was March, he thought, and two years since Judith had died. Where had the time gone?

'Vera, we've got a bit of a problem,' he said as he sat down on the side of the bed. 'I'm afraid Betty wants to leave us.'

'What! Leave . . . Betty wants to leave? No, she can't. Tell her I want to speak to her.'

'It would be a waste of time, my dear. She has made up her mind to go.'

'But who will look after me?' Vera cried.

'We could bring Daisy home. She's been away for far too long now.'

'Oh Henry, I couldn't bear to have Daisy looking after me. Have you forgotten what she did?'

'No, of course not, but she's changed, darling. She's almost grown up now and nothing like the girl you remember. She's lost all her puppy fat and seems so mature. When I go to see her she always asks about you, and I really do think it's time that we all put the past behind us. Think about it, darling. If you won't allow Daisy to look after you I'll have to engage a private nurse.'

Vera slumped back on her pillow, her eyes closed while Henry sat quietly beside her. After some moments she finally opened her eyes again, and in a resigned voice said, 'Very well, bring her home.'

Henry almost ran from the room and finding Betty in the kitchen, he said excitedly, 'I'm going to bring Daisy home. I'll go down to Puddleton in the morning to fetch her and I'm sure she'll be happy to look after Vera.'

'Hmm, if you say so,' Betty answered, with an edge of sarcasm in her voice. 'Well, in that case I needn't wait till Monday. I'll be off as soon as you get back.'

'I don't understand why you are acting like this, Betty. What has happened to upset you?'

'It don't matter, and you wouldn't believe me anyway. All I will say is that I feel sorry for your daughter if she's got to look after Vera.'

Henry was puzzled by Betty's enigmatic answer. What wouldn't he believe? However, with his mind on bringing Daisy home he let her comments pass, and said, 'My daughter won't mind, Betty. She'll be thrilled to come home. After all, she's been away for such a long time. Now if you'll excuse me I think I'll go and give her a ring to break the good news.'

'Yeah, well – good luck,' he heard Betty murmur as he left the room, and was slightly puzzled by the sceptical tone in her voice.

'Hello, Edna, it's Henry,' he said as his sister answered the phone.

'Yes, I think I know your voice, my dear,' she chuckled. 'How are you and how is Vera?'

'I'm fine and Vera is the same. That's what I'm ringing to talk to you about. You see, I need to bring Daisy back to London.'

'What! But wouldn't it be better to leave her with me until the end of term?'

'I'm afraid that won't be possible. Betty is leaving us, and I need Daisy home to look after Vera.'

'Don't be ridiculous, Henry. Only a few days ago Daisy was talking about her ambitions for when she leaves school; she said that she'd like to go on to college to take a secretarial course. For goodness sake – you can't ask her to act as Vera's nursemaid! Daisy needs a life of her own.'

Henry bristled. 'I think I can be the judge of that, Edna. Anyway, she will have a life of her own. I'm only talking about while I'm at work. I'll see to Vera myself in the evenings, and at weekends.'

'And what if Daisy doesn't want to look after her stepmother, Henry? Aren't you going to take her wishes into consideration?'

'Of course I am. I wouldn't force my daughter to do something that she doesn't want. Now would you please bring her to the telephone,' he said shortly, annoyed by his sister's attitude. Tapping his foot impatiently, Henry waited with the receiver to his ear.

'Hello, Daddy.'

'Hello, my dear. How are you?'

'I'm fine. Are you coming down to see us on Sunday?'

'Perhaps before that, darling. It all depends on you.'

'Me! What do you mean?'

'I've got a bit of a problem, Daisy, and it's something I want to talk to you about. I know this will come like a bolt out of the blue for you, but I wouldn't ask you if I had any other choice. As you know, Vera is unable to walk now, and I'm sure I've told you that she spends all of her time in bed, just reading or watching the television. Betty, the lady that started as our cleaner, has been looking after her, but has given in her notice. This leaves me in an awful fix, Daisy, and that's why I'm ringing. Do you think you could come home to look after Vera, just during the day? I'll see to her in the evenings and at weekends.'

'But what about school?' she exclaimed.

'I've thought about that, and I'm sure that in the circumstances it wouldn't hurt if you left now. Poor Vera is a cripple, Daisy, and I know she would hate to have a stranger looking after her. So what do you say, darling? It would be lovely to have you back here with us.'

He paused, waiting for his daughter to speak, and after what felt like minutes she responded, her voice quiet, 'All right, Daddy, I'll do as you ask.'

'Oh, that's wonderful, wonderful!' he cried. 'I'll be down to collect you as early as possible tomorrow. Goodbye, dear, I'll see you then.'

'Bye, Daddy,' he heard her say before he replaced the receiver.

Daisy returned to her aunt's kitchen, her gaze running round the room and her feelings mixed. Yes, a part of her wanted to go home – well, sort of. But she would miss her aunt and Lizzie so much, as well as the friends she had made at school.

'What did you say to your father?' Edna asked.

'I said I'd go back to London to look after Vera.'

'Oh, Daisy, are you sure? Goodness, girl, I thought you wanted to make a career for yourself. What about your plans to go to college?'

'My dad needs me, Auntie, and perhaps I'll be able to pick up my education later.'

'I don't think you realise what you're taking on. It won't be easy acting as a nursemaid, and what about all the cleaning and cooking too? It's a huge house, Daisy.'

'I'll manage, and I'm sure Dad will help. I enjoy cooking and you've taught me some wonderful recipes – it might be fun trying them out on my dad and Vera.'

Daisy watched as her aunt stood up abruptly, her lips compressed as she went over to the sink. 'Well, I think it's absolutely ridiculous,' she said. 'Your father must be out of his mind expecting you to take on the responsibility of looking after your stepmother.'

Seeing her distress Daisy crossed the room, and placing an arm around her aunt's shoulders she said, 'Honestly, I don't mind. Really I don't.'

Edna sniffed, and only her choked voice revealed her feelings as she whispered brokenly, 'Oh Daisy, I . . . I don't know how we're going to break this to Lizzie. She's grown so fond of you.'

'Perhaps it might be better if I tell her.'

'Yes, all right,' her aunt agreed. 'Why not just get it over with as soon as possible. She should be out of the bath by now.'

'I'll go up upstairs now and talk to her,' Daisy said, and as she left the room she heard her aunt sob, a strangled sound from the back of her throat. Mounting the stairs, her own eyes filled with tears, and on reaching the bathroom door she fought to bring herself under control before breaking the news to Lizzie.

'No! You no leave!' Lizzie cried as she flung her arms around Daisy.

'I have to go, darling. Vera needs me to look after her.'

Sobs wracked Lizzie's body, and tears began to stream down her cheeks. 'Want you to stay. Me love you, Daisy.'

'Oh Lizzie,' she said brokenly, her arms tightening around her cousin.

Daisy lost track of time as she stood holding Lizzie, finding her own tears joining those of her cousin. During her stay in Puddleton she had come to love both her aunt and Lizzie so much, finding their warm love and affection a soothing balm after her unhappiness at home with Vera. Yet hearing the appeal in her father's voice she had agreed to return to London without stopping to think about how hard it would be. It was too late now to change her mind, but what about when she got there? What would she find?

In the morning, after a sleepless night, Daisy carried her suitcases downstairs. She had tossed and turned for hours, not only upset about Lizzie's reaction to her news, but by fear when her thoughts turned to Vera. No, she finally admitted, she didn't want to go home to look after her stepmother, but what choice did she have? Her father had sounded so desperate, and how could she let him down?

Leaving her cases in the hall Daisy went into the kitchen, seeing her aunt sitting at the table, her eyes red as though she had been crying.

'Are you all packed?' Edna asked.

'Yes, all done,' she told her, a break in her voice.

'Oh Daisy, I'm going to miss you so much.'

'I'm going to miss you too. It's been wonderful staying here with you and Lizzie.'

'Are you sure you know what you're doing, love? It's not too late to change your mind.'

'Yes, I'm sure,' Daisy said, with eyes lowered to hide her real feelings.

Lizzie came into the room then, her face wet with tears. 'Saw your cases,' she cried, running forward and flinging her arms around Daisy. 'No go – no go!' she sobbed.

'Oh Lizzie, please don't cry,' Daisy begged. 'I've got to go, but I'm sure I'll be able to come down to visit you soon.'

'No, won't visit,' she said.

Daisy wanted to argue, to tell her cousin that she would come to Puddleton to visit them, and as often as possible – but instead she bit her lip. Lizzie's words had made her shiver. Was she making another prediction?

'Come on,' Edna said. 'I'll make us some breakfast. I don't suppose it will be much longer before your father arrives, Daisy.'

On a sob, Lizzie cried, 'Porridge, Mum.'

Daisy's eyes met those of her aunt and they laughed, though it sounded strained and false. 'You and your porridge, Lizzie,' Edna said. 'Now let go of Daisy and sit yourself down.'

Daisy forced a smile, grateful that Edna was trying to bring a touch of normality to the scene.

After breakfast Daisy helped her aunt to clear up, all the time struggling to hold back her tears – and shortly afterwards they heard a knock at the door.

'That's probably your father – he must have left home at the crack of dawn. Go and let him in, love,' Edna said, her voice breaking.

Daisy, finding herself unable to speak too, just gave a quick nod as she hurried out.

The goodbyes were emotional, and when Daisy finally pulled herself out of Lizzie's arms to climb into the car, her aunt pushed a small packet into her hands.

'Something to remember us by,' she said, her voice choking.

Daisy had bitten her bottom lip so hard in an effort to stem her tears, that it felt swollen and bruised. She pulled the car door shut, and as her father drove away she craned her neck for a last glimpse of her aunt and Lizzie. They were both still standing on the pavement – waving sadly.

They weren't far into the journey when Daisy began to open the brown paper package. It was flat and felt like a book, but as she peeled back the wrapping a picture was revealed.

Daisy gasped as she stared at a beautiful watercolour painting of the shop: the ivy clinging to the walls, the leaded windows, all in wonderful proportions.

Her father took his eyes off the road momentarily to glance at it, saying, 'One of Edna's efforts, I see. She was always very good at art. I know my parents had high hopes for her, but then she married your uncle and gave up her chance to study at college.'

'I didn't know Aunt Edna could paint. She never said. I wonder when this was done?'

'Oh, some while ago, I should think. Edna never had much time for herself once Lizzie was born.'

'Yes, I think you're right – the ivy is only halfway up the wall. It's a beautiful picture, Dad, and I'm going to write and thank her as soon as we get home.' Then, recalling her father's words, she added, 'It's awful that both yours and Mum's parents are dead. I can't even remember them.'

'I know, darling, life can be tragic sometimes. I'm not surprised that you can't remember them. After all, both my mother and father died when you were only a toddler. Your mother's parents were killed in a bombing raid during the war, and after that she went to live with her aunt. In fact, it was in the house we live in now, and it was left to her when the aunt died.' Henry turned to glance at Daisy again before saying, 'Let's get off this sad subject. How did you enjoy your stay in Puddleton?'

'Oh, it was wonderful, Dad,' and feeling a lump forming in her throat Daisy gulped, realising again how much she would miss her aunt and Lizzie. Closing her eyes she recalled her cousin's words. *No*, Lizzie had said, *you won't come back*. But why had she said that? What could possibly stop her from going to Puddleton again?

Chapter Twenty-Three

As Daisy stepped into the living room she stared with amazement at her stepmother. It couldn't be Vera! Her once shiny blonde hair was now mostly dark, and the remnants of the golden colour looked frizzy and broken where it fell lankly onto her shoulders. Her face was pale, haggard, and devoid of the make-up she always wore. There was something else; something Daisy couldn't put her finger on – a sort of desperation in Vera's eyes.

However, when she spoke her stepmother's voice was dripping with the old sarcasm. 'Well, look at you, Daisy. All that awful puppy fat gone at last.'

'Yes, I've lost weight,' she said quietly, and though Daisy's heart sank at Vera's tone, she was unable to quell the feeling of deep pity that arose as she returned her gaze. Oh, the poor woman, how awful for her to be paralysed.

Did Vera see it in her eyes? Daisy didn't know, but her stepmother's features hardened, and her eyes narrowed. She glanced quickly at the door before saying with a venomous hiss, 'Just because I'm stuck in this bed, it doesn't mean that you can start blabbing to your father. I can still tell him the truth. So think on that, miss.'

Before Daisy could form an answer her father stepped into the room, smiling as he said, 'Well, what do you think, Vera? Doesn't Daisy look wonderful?'

'Yes, Henry. She looks quiet grown up, and so pretty now that she's lost weight. It's lovely to have you home again, my dear.'

Daisy's jaw dropped, amazed that anyone's demeanour could

change so rapidly. Vera now looked soft, even vulnerable and her voice was honeyed.

'Why don't you go up and unpack, darling,' her father suggested. 'I'll put the kettle on and we can all have a nice cup of tea.'

'Yes, go and sort yourself out, Daisy,' Vera said with a sweet smile. 'I'm sure you'll find your room just as you left it.'

Bewildered, Daisy left the room, and picking up a suitcase in each hand she climbed the stairs. Vera was right, her bedroom was unchanged, with only a slight musty smell in the air.

Unwrapping her aunt's picture, Daisy propped it on the mantelpiece, gazing at it sadly before glancing down and noticing that the basket of dried flowers in the small Victorian grate were faded and dusty. Turning desolately she made her way to the window and stared down at the street below, finding the view claustrophobic after the wide open spaces of Hampshire. A young man was crossing the road towards her, and her heart skipped. It was Liam, Molly's eldest son, looking even more handsome than when she had last seen him. What would he say when he saw how much she had changed?

She followed his movements until he disappeared from view next door, and then turning quickly she picked up a suitcase. Heaving it onto her bed she began to rifle inside, determined to find something really nice to wear before popping next door to see Molly.

'Well, don't you look nice,' Vera said sweetly when Daisy returned downstairs, wearing her favourite skirt and pale blue twin-set. She had brushed her hair until it shone and it fell softly onto her shoulders.

'I like your hair like that, Daisy, it suits you wearing it longer,' her stepmother said, her voice still sickly sweet.

Henry was sitting on the side of the bed and he now stood up, his smile warm. 'Yes, you look lovely, dear. I had better make a fresh pot of tea because this one has gone cold.'

'No, it's all right, Dad. I thought I'd pop next door to see Molly.'

'But you've only just got home! Surely it can wait until tomorrow?'

'I won't be long, Dad. Just a few minutes. It's been ages since I've seen Molly,' she appealed.

'Oh, all right then,' Henry said grumpily. 'I suppose it won't hurt, and in the meantime I'll get dinner on.'

'I'll give you a hand as soon as I come back,' Daisy promised. 'I really won't be long, honestly.'

'My God! Is it really you?' Molly exclaimed as she opened the door, her eyes shining with pleasure. 'Daisy, you look wonderful.'

She grinned. Molly hadn't changed at all, and still wore what looked like the same old grey skirt with her petticoat hanging below it as usual. Stepping into the kitchen, Daisy's heart missed a beat. *He* was there, sitting at the table, and there was an imperceptible widening of his emerald-green eyes as he looked at her. 'Hello, Liam,' she said softly, feeling a blush rising.

'Well, would you believe it? It's Daisy Bacon,' he said, his grin revealing beautiful straight white teeth. 'So you're back from the sticks and looking all grown up.'

Liam then looked her slowly up and down and Daisy lowered her head self-consciously, unused to this expression in his eyes.

'That's enough of that, Liam,' Molly snapped. 'Put your eyes back in your head and leave Daisy and me alone to have a crack. Anyway, hadn't you better get ready to see Sandra? I thought the two of you were going dancing.'

'There's no harm in looking, Mammy,' he said, laughing as he left the room.

Molly shook her head, unable to help smiling. 'He'd charm the birds off the trees, that one. He and Sandra are talking about getting engaged and I can tell you I'll be glad to see him settled down.'

Daisy's heart sank. So he was still with Sandra Reynolds. She slowly sat down, berating herself for being such a fool. What chance did she have with someone like Liam?

'Are you glad to be home, darlin'?' Molly asked, breaking into her thoughts.

'Yes, but I'm going to miss my aunt and cousin,' she answered. 'I had to come home though, Molly. Dad needs me to look after Vera.'

'I know – Betty told me she was leaving, though she refused to say why. There's something fishy about it if you ask me. I haven't seen her today – has she gone yet?'

'Oh, I don't know, Molly. I came straight round here after I unpacked.'

'Betty said she was going as soon as you returned, but I expected her to pop round to say goodbye. We became friends after she moved in.'

'Yes, my father told me.'

'Mind you, things changed when your stepmother had her accident. I hardly saw Betty after that, and I'll tell you something else. I never see her little boy George either. She said that her mother's looking after him, but how could she part with him like that? 'Tis all very odd,' Molly added darkly, shaking her head.

Before Daisy could answer there was a commotion outside. The door flew open with a flourish as Sean and Patrick came in, laughing together, only to stop short, both their mouths agape when they saw her.

'I must go,' Daisy said hurriedly. 'I told Dad I'd only be a few minutes. Perhaps I'll see you again tomorrow.'

'It's never Daisy Bacon!' Sean said, staring at her in wonderment.

'Blimey,' Patrick spluttered. 'She's gone all thin.'

'Shut up you two,' Molly told them. 'Yes, pop round tomorrow, Daisy. 'Tis lovely to have you home again, and don't let that one make you do too much. She wore poor Betty out. Stand up to Vera from the start or she'll make your life a misery.'

Daisy nodded, and with her face still pink with embarrassment she left quickly. Patrick hadn't changed much, she thought. Sean neither – except that he looked taller. He was six months older than she was, so he must have left school by now, and she wondered momentarily what sort of job he had.

However, she soon forgot about Sean as she stepped indoors, her mind now on Betty. Crossing the hall she opened the internal door to the basement, calling, 'Hello, hello! Are you there?'

A face appeared at the bottom of the stairs, looking up at her. 'Yeah, what do you want?' Betty snapped.

'Er . . . I was just checking to see if you had left. You see, I've just come back from Molly's and she mentioned that she hadn't seen you today.'

'Christ, she's a nosy old cow. I'm just off, kid, so see yer.'

'Wait,' Daisy called as Betty's head disappeared from view. 'Aren't you coming up to say goodbye to Vera and my father?'

Her face appeared again. 'You must be joking,' she said, wagging her finger as she added, 'You be careful, love. I don't think Vera's right in the head.'

'Wha . . . what do you mean?'

'Just watch out, that's all I'm going to say. Now as I said, I'm off.'

Despite calling out again, the woman didn't reappear, and as Daisy slowly closed the door her brow furrowed. What did Betty mean? And why was she leaving without saying goodbye to anyone?

Chapter Twenty-Four

Daisy stood at the kitchen sink, gripping the edge, her knuckles white as she took deep breaths in an endeavour to calm down. She closed her eyes, looking back over the past five months, and wondered how much longer she could go on living like this.

When she had first come back from Aunt Edna's it hadn't been too bad. Vera had been changeable – moody and sometimes aggressive – but there were times when she actually seemed grateful for Daisy's help. Yet gradually things had worsened, and lately looking after her stepmother had become a living hell. As soon as Henry left for work in the morning, Vera changed like a chameleon. She became vicious and impossible, and remained like that all day until he came home again.

And now that's the pattern of my life, Daisy thought, still breathing deeply as she clung to the sink. Days of watching the clock, waiting for her father to return from work, and as soon as he did, seeing Vera reverting to sweetness and light for a few hours.

Daisy's mouth set in a determined line. Things had to change! She couldn't stand much more, and when Dad came home she was going to tell him that she wanted to go to night school. Last week had been her fifteenth birthday and it should have been a milestone – a time for making choices about what career she wanted. Instead she was stuck here looking after Vera, with nothing to look forward to except more of the same. She had to do something, had to make some changes, or what sort of future did she have? Daisy stiffened her shoulders. There was a shorthand and typing course starting at night school and she intended to enrol. If she could learn these skills, it might lead to a job in an office. Of course, it wouldn't give her the same qualifications as the secretarial course that she had planned to take at college, but it was better than nothing.

Maybe if she could earn a decent wage it would enable her to leave home. Oh, it would be heaven to find a place of her own. A place away from Vera!

'Daisy, come here!' her stepmother yelled.

Let her wait, Daisy thought. Let her wait – and grinding her teeth she plunged her hands into the sink, attacking the pile of washing-up with vigour.

'Daisy, didn't you hear me? I said come here!'

Sighing, she wiped her hands on the tea towel, knowing that she wouldn't get any peace until she went to see what Vera wanted.

'What do you want now?' Daisy asked, unable to keep the exasperation out of her voice.

'I've dropped my wool,' Vera said petulantly.

Daisy clenched her teeth, biting back a retort as she crossed to the side of the bed. Bending down she picked up the wool, winding it up again before passing it to Vera. She then turned to leave, halting as her stepmother spoke again.

'Where are you going? I want to talk to you.'

'I'm going back to finish the washing up, Vera. Then I've got to put the sheets in the copper to soak.'

'Leave it for a minute and sit down. I've been thinking, and there's something I want you to do for me.'

Perching on the edge of a seat, Daisy waited for the next of Vera's demands.

'I want you to take a message to my mother.'

Daisy blinked. It was the first time she had ever heard Vera mention her family. 'Your mother! I didn't know you had a mother! Why do you want me to take a message to her?'

'Of course I've got a mother, you silly girl. I want you to take a message to her because it would be pointless writing a letter. She can't read.'

'Can't read!' Daisy gasped.

'Not everyone has had a cushy life like you, miss. My mother never had the chance to go to school and she was sent out to work as a skivvy when she was only twelve years old. Things were a lot different when she was a child, and she had a dreadfully hard life.'

Daisy frowned – how awful for Vera's mother. 'Do you want me to ask her to visit you?' she enquired.

'Yes, but not when your father's at home. Make sure you tell her to call during the day, and ask her to find out if Lennie Talbot is back in the area. I don't know, but I've got a sort of feeling that he might be. If he is, I'm going to try to get George back from him.'

'But I thought Betty had him?'

'Don't be stupid, girl. If George was with Betty she'd have brought him to see me.'

Daisy lowered her eyes, thinking guiltily that she had been so wrapped up in her own unhappiness that she hadn't given Vera's son a thought. 'But I don't understand. Who's this Lennie Talbot? And why is George with him?'

'Lennie is my son's father, and he stole him from me. Now don't ask me any more questions because it's none of your business. All you need to know is that George is my son and I want him back.'

'But what about my father? What will you tell him?'

'Oh, I don't know,' Vera cried. 'I haven't thought that far ahead. God, you have no idea of the torture I've been through, and I miss my son so much. He's nearly two and a half years old now and I lie here day after day seeing his little face in my mind. I wonder what he looks like now, wonder if he's happy. Oh, you've no idea . . . no idea . . .'

As Vera's voice trailed off, Daisy found herself feeling sorry for her stepmother. Was this why she was so impossible? 'Listen,' she urged 'don't you think you should just be honest with my father and tell him all about it? I'm sure if he knew he would help you to get George back.'

'No, there's no point in saying anything to him yet. If I find out that Lennie is back in London, I'll speak to Henry then. It will take legal action to get my son back, and I haven't any money of my own to pay for it. But one step at a time. First I need you to go to my mother's house with my message.'

'All right, I'll go tomorrow,' Daisy told her, amazed when Vera gave her a sweet smile.

When Daisy went back to the kitchen she completed her chores with Vera's predicament playing in her mind. Eventually though, her thoughts drifted to Molly. She still saw her neighbour regularly, popping next door for an hour or so a few evenings a week. It was a welcome break to get out of the house for a while, and away from Vera. Sometimes if she was lucky, Liam would be in, and at that thought Daisy chastised herself. Stop it! Stop dreaming! Liam doesn't want you. He's getting engaged to Sandra soon, and Molly is already starting to talk about the wedding.

Oh, if only I looked like her, Daisy thought. Sandra was tall and willowy, her figure perfect. No wonder Liam was smitten. She looked down at her own body, saw the rolls of fat that were forming again, and shook her head despairingly. Though Vera was unable to punish her physically now, other than the occasional slap when she wasn't quick enough to keep out of harm's reach, her stepmother had a wicked tongue.

Vera constantly jeered at her, saying she was useless and undermining everything she did. Daisy's appearance attracted criticism too, with Vera constantly carping that her hair looked awful, or her clothes were too tight, going on and on until her confidence was destroyed.

Night after night Daisy would lie in bed feeling miserable and lonely, trying to fight the urge to raid the cake tin. When she was unhappy her stomach felt so empty and the urge to eat overwhelmed her, keeping her awake. Sometimes midnight found her sneaking downstairs, seeking comfort by eating the supply of coconut or queens cakes that she now baked twice a week.

The afternoon passed quickly and Vera was surprisingly undemanding for a change. They talked again about Vera's mother, and Daisy found herself looking forward to the trip the next day. It came as a surprise to find out that Ada Tucker only lived in Battersea, and she wondered how the two women had lost touch. After all, Battersea was only a bus ride away.

When her father came home from work, Daisy was so engrossed with thoughts of the visit that the talk she intended to have with him about night school went completely out of her mind.

At two o'clock in the morning the sound of the telephone ringing awoke Daisy. At first she thought she was dreaming, but hearing her father going downstairs she reached out to switch on the bedside light. Swinging her legs over the side of the bed and grabbing her dressing-gown, Daisy was unable to think who would be calling them at that time, and found a knot of anxiety forming in her stomach.

She had just reached the bottom stair as her father replaced the receiver, and as he turned she saw that his face was white with shock. 'What is it, Dad?'

'I'm afraid your aunt has been taken ill. Come into the dining room, dear. I don't want to disturb Vera.'

'I don't think there's much chance of that. Those sleeping pills she takes seem to knock her right out. What's wrong with Aunt Edna?'

Henry walked to her side, and taking her hand he drew her down onto the stairs where he sat with his arm around her shoulder. 'Edna has been taken to hospital. That was Mrs Purvis on the telephone. Apparently Lizzie knocking frantically on her door awoke her at midnight. It seems your aunt was in a lot of pain and her cries disturbed Lizzie.'

'Oh, she must be frantic, Daddy.'

'Mrs Purvis is looking after her for now, but I'll have to drive down there first thing in the morning.'

'Can I come with you?'

'No, darling. I'm sorry, but we can't leave Vera on her own. Don't worry, I'll ring you as soon as I have any news.'

Disappointed, Daisy hung her head. She knew her father was right, Vera couldn't be left, but she felt a surge of resentment that she had to stay to look after her. She wanted to go with her father, to be with Lizzie and her aunt. With a small sigh, she said, 'All right, Dad.'

'Good girl. Now go back to bed and try to get some sleep.'

Daisy nodded, and treading back upstairs to her room she prayed that her aunt would be all right.

Chapter Twenty-Five

Daisy stared at the almost deserted street. Most of the houses had the windows boarded up and were obviously empty, but a few were still occupied and in the most appalling state of disrepair. She walked slowly along, endeavouring to see the numbers on the battered front doors, and on reaching number fifteen she was relieved to see that it was still occupied. White net curtains covered the downstairs window, and the doorstep looked freshly scrubbed, incongruous against the squalor of the empty house next door.

Daisy hadn't wanted to come and had begged Vera to wait until another day. 'What if Dad rings with news about Aunt Edna and I'm not here to answer the phone?' she had argued. But Vera refused to listen. She had insisted that it was only a short journey to Battersea; and that she could be there and back before her father even arrived in Puddleton.

So here she was, standing outside the front door and taking a deep breath before she raised her hand to the knocker.

'Mrs Tucker?' Daisy asked nervously, staring at the short and very thin woman who stood in front of her. This couldn't be Vera's mother! There was absolutely no resemblance between them. Vera was tall, and had been glamorous, so how could this tiny little woman be her mother?

'Yeah, that's me, ducks.'

'I . . . I've got a message for you from your daughter.'

'My Vera!' Ada Tucker exclaimed, her face blanching. 'Is this some sort of trick? Did Lennie Talbot send you?'

'Trick? I don't understand what you mean. Vera sent me to see you.'

Mrs Tucker's eyes narrowed as she leaned forward and peered at Daisy. 'Who are you then?' she asked.

'I'm Vera's stepdaughter. My name is Daisy Bacon.'

'Stepdaughter!' she exclaimed. 'You're her stepdaughter! Well, I never. You'd better come in then,' she added, after glancing quickly up and down the street.

Following Mrs Tucker down a narrow passage Daisy was surprised to find that she was walking on bare floorboards, with just a few sheets of newspaper covering them in parts. They stepped into a tiny back room and Daisy was appalled at the poverty she saw. She had thought her old friend Susan Watson's home sparse, but it was a palace compared to this. There was just a threadbare fireside chair standing to one side of the small hearth, and in the centre of the room a battered wooden table with two chairs tucked beneath. In one corner she could see a chipped, but clean kitchen sink, and in the other a grey enamel gas cooker that looked absolutely ancient. There were no ornaments on the mantelpiece, no pictures hanging on the walls, and just a piece of faded brown material stretched on wire across the small window.

'Now then,' Mrs Tucker said, pulling out a chair and indicating that Daisy should sit down, 'what's this all about? I didn't know Vera had married, let alone that she had a stepdaughter.'

'Vera's had an accident, Mrs Tucker. She can't walk now, and that's why she sent me to see you.'

'An accident . . . she can't walk!' Ada cried, her face turning pale. 'My gawd, I can't take this in. I've been looking for me daughter for ages – ever since Lennie Talbot came to see me.'

'That's why Vera wants to see you. She wants to know if he's moved back to this area.'

'Moved back? I don't know what you mean, ducks. As far as I know, Lennie's never been away. I know he shut his club down, 'cos apparently the Old Bill raided him once too often. But there's been talk that he's opened a new one, just on the outskirts of London – Croydon way, I think. It's supposed to be real classy with a dance-floor and all. Anyway, why does my Vera want to know where he is? I'd 'ave thought she would wanna stay well away from him.'

'He's got her son, George, and she wants him back.'

'Blimey, love, this is all news to me. Lennie told me that Vera had the boy, and as I said, I've been trying to find her for ages.' Ada pursed her lips. 'I've been worrying myself sick about Lennie putting his gorillas on to me – and all for nothing.'

Daisy stared at Vera's mother, her expression perplexed. 'Is he a bad man then, Mrs Tucker?'

'Bad! He's more than bad. Lennie Talbot is a right nasty piece of work. There are rumours that a few of the new buildings in the area have got Lennie's enemies in the foundations, and knowing what he's like, it wouldn't surprise me. Ain't my Vera told yer about him?'

'No, she hasn't. I've been away, you see. After the accident, Vera's Cousin Betty looked after her, but she left recently so I was brought home to take her place.'

Daisy was surprised to see Mrs Tucker's lips tighten with annoyance. 'You're telling me that Betty knew all about this? My God, the little bitch! I only saw her last week and she never said a word. Wait till I get me hands on her.'

Daisy glanced at her watch, and calculating that her father would reach Puddleton in about an hour, she said, 'Mrs Tucker, I really must go now. Would you come back with me to see Vera?'

'What – now? Well, I suppose so, but I'll 'ave to put on me best bib and tucker first. Can you give me five minutes?'

'Yes, of course,' Daisy assured her.

'Will it take us long to get to your place?'

'Oh no, it's not far. We live in Clapham on the north side, close to the Common.'

'Well, stone the crows! I thought Vera would be miles away.' Mrs Tucker grinned then, revealing a row of broken and brown front teeth. 'My daughter always was a sly one. Who'd 'ave thought of looking for her in the next Borough? I bet Lennie was flabbergasted when he found out where she was, and I don't suppose he was too happy that she made a monkey out of him.'

Ada stood up then, adding, 'Right, I'll just change me dress and I'll be with you. Make yourself at home, ducks.'

Daisy watched Mrs Tucker as she left the room, finding that she liked Vera's mother. There was something down-to-earth and honest about her, and in spite of her obvious poverty she appeared cheerful and kind. Why had Vera hidden her background and pretended that she came from the middle classes? Was she ashamed of her roots?

'I'm ready, gel. Let's be off,' Mrs Tucker chirped, returning to the room.

It was strange sitting beside Vera's mother on the bus. Mrs Tucker talked non-stop, asking questions about her daughter, and as Daisy wasn't sure how much Vera would want her to know, she answered them vaguely. When their eyes met, Daisy could see that the woman was suspicious as she tried to probe deeper.

It was a relief when they arrived at their destination, and after alighting from the bus Daisy walked as quickly as possible, puffing heavily, and too breathless to answer any more questions.

'Cor, slow down,' Mrs Tucker gasped. 'It's too hot for rushing around, and I ain't no spring chicken.'

'I'm sorry, but I'm anxious to get home. You see, I'm expecting an important telephone call from my father,' Daisy panted, glancing anxiously at her watch before slowing her pace imperceptibly, relieved when they turned into Fitzwilliam Street.

She noticed that Mrs Tucker's eyes widened as she gazed at the house, and though they weren't wealthy, Daisy realised that in comparison to her own home, it must look like a palace. 'Please, come in,' Daisy urged, leading her up the steps and opening the front door.

'Hello, Mum,' Vera said shortly as Daisy ushered Mrs Tucker into the room. With a brief glance in Daisy's direction, she then ordered, 'Go and make us a cup of tea.'

'Has my father rung?'

'No, not yet,' Vera snapped.

'Still short-tempered, I see,' Mrs Tucker said, staring at her daughter propped up in the bed.

'Wouldn't you be, if you were stuck like this, unable to walk?' Daisy heard Vera reply waspishly as she left the room.

Leaving the sitting-room door ajar Daisy could hear the slight murmur of voices as she laid the tea tray, and putting a doily on a plate, she added a selection of cakes. She then carried the tray along the hall, and on reaching the door pushed it further open with her hips. Entering the room, Daisy was surprised to hear that Vera and Mrs Tucker's voices were raised and angry as they glared at each other. Unsure of what to do she stood just inside the room, listening to the argument. It became more and more heated, with the two women so intent on each other that they seemed unaware of Daisy's presence.

'Christ, Mum! When you told me about Lennie I was horrified. You should have told me before and then I wouldn't have got into this mess.'

'I tried to stop you working in his club, Vera, but you wouldn't listen. And I can't believe you actually went ahead and had his kid. And what's more, how could you carry on sleeping with him after what I told you? It's disgusting!'

'I *didn't* carry on sleeping with him! Bloody hell, Mum, what do you take me for? Just the thought of it made me feel sick. But I needed money; I couldn't support a baby on thin air. All through the pregnancy I feigned illness, and I can tell you I got a few clouts at first – until one of Lennie's new girls caught his eye. After that he left me alone. All he cared about was the baby I was carrying. I was like a flipping brood mare, but by then I had found out where the safe was, and was watching for a chance to learn the combination number.'

'Bleedin' hell, Vera! Surely you didn't intend to rob him?'

'Yes, I did, Mum. I planned to have the baby, and then once I'd got the money I would be able to go abroad.'

'So what went wrong?' Ada asked.

Vera laughed derisively. 'After all that – the safe was empty.'

'So what happened then?'

'He chucked me out! I wouldn't sleep with him so he chucked me out!'

'All right, he got rid of you, but you've only been in the next Borough, so why didn't you come to yer dad's funeral?'

'Funeral! I didn't know he was dead. Anyway, even if I had known I wouldn't have come – how could I? After I got Georgie back, Lennie was looking for me and I had to lay low. I'll tell you something else, Mum: I don't give a damn that Dad's dead!'

'Well, I ain't surprised to hear you say that, but the funeral was awful. I felt like a laughing stock when everyone kept asking me where you were. I was the only one in the car and you should've been beside me. It was horrible with the entire street gawking at me.'

Vera laughed then, manic laughter that sent a chill down Daisy's spine. 'Worried about the neighbours . . . after all you told me . . . you were worried about the neighbours. Oh, you're priceless, Mum.'

'Er, I've brought the tea,' Daisy interrupted nervously.

'Put it down and get out!' Vera snapped, the laughter dying abruptly in her throat.

Daisy hurriedly put the tray onto a side table and left the room, the argument starting up again before she closed the door. She glanced at the telephone on the hall table. Ring, Dad, please ring, she thought, her mind not on the strange conversation she had heard between Vera and her mother – but on her beloved Aunt Edna.

Chapter Twenty-Six

It was seven in the evening before her father rang, and by then Daisy's nerves were at screaming pitch. Mrs Tucker had left after only an hour or so, her lips tight as she was shown out. 'She's still a proper madam,' had been her only comment as she stomped out of the street door.

The rest of the day had been taken up with Vera's demands; she was petulant and snappy, refusing to talk about what had happened with her mother. 'Just leave me alone, I need to think,' was all she would say.

Daisy had done so willingly, and then her father's phone call had left her reeling. He was bringing Lizzie home with him for a while. It seemed that Aunt Edna would be in hospital for some time and Lizzie was inconsolable, continuously asking why Daisy wasn't there. His voice sounded tired, and there was something else in his tone that she couldn't put her finger on.

For the next few hours Daisy tried to keep busy, and she was now making up a bed for Lizzie in the spare room. Tucking the last blanket into place, she stood up, rubbing the small of her back. Vera could be so cruel and she was worried about her stepmother's reaction to having Lizzie in the house. However, the thoughts were driven from her mind when she heard the front door opening, and with a last quick glance around the room she flew downstairs.

When Daisy took in Lizzie's appearance, her face crumbled in distress. Her cousin looked white-faced and exhausted, and she only showed signs of animation when their eyes met. 'Daisy!' she sobbed, rushing across the hall. 'My mummy's ill, Daisy. I told you.'

'Don't cry, darling,' she begged. 'Your mum will be all right,' and trying to bolster her cousin, she added, 'The hospital will make her well again.'

'No! Not get better,' Lizzie wailed.

Daisy, looking at her father over her cousin's shoulder, saw his distress too. She widened her eyes, a question in them, but he shook his head slowly and her heart sank.

Henry then drew in a deep gulp of air, saying, 'Let's get Lizzie settled. It's been a long day and she's worn out.'

'Yes, all right, Dad,' Daisy agreed, seeing the lines of tiredness etched on his face. 'I expect you're both hungry,' she added, trying to keep her voice light. 'Would you like a sandwich and a glass of milk, Lizzie?'

'No. Want my mummy, Daisy.'

'I know, love, but you'll be all right with us until she gets better. Why don't you come upstairs and I'll show you where you're going to sleep. Have you brought Maisy with you?' she asked, knowing that Lizzie couldn't sleep without her doll.

Lizzie nodded, pointing to a bag, her rag doll just visible peeping out of the top.

Daisy was struck by an idea, and smiling she said, 'Well, Maisy might be hungry. Shall I make a sandwich for her?'

At last a glimmer of a smile showed on Lizzie's face. 'Yes, sandwich for Maisy,' she agreed.

It had taken Daisy ages to get her cousin settled and by then it was nearly midnight. She hadn't taken Lizzie in to see Vera, deciding that it could wait until the morning. Now all she wanted was sleep too, but she had to talk to her father before she went to bed. How would she be able to rest without knowing what was happening to her aunt? Judging by her father's expression, Edna's illness must be serious and Daisy quailed as she took a seat opposite him in the dining room.

'Is Lizzie settled at last?' he asked quietly.

'Yes, and I gave Vera her sleeping pill half an hour ago. Dad, please tell me what's wrong with Aunt Edna.'

His face was shadowed in the dim light from the standard lamp, but even that couldn't hide his distress at her question. 'It's serious, Daisy, and the prognosis is terminal.'

'Terminal!' she cried, her voice coming out in a squeak. 'Does that mean she's going to die?'

'I'm afraid so, darling. Your aunt has cancer. There might have been a chance if they had caught it earlier. Unfortunately, by the time her condition was diagnosed it had spread too far.'

Daisy was suddenly overwhelmed with guilt. Lizzie had tried to tell her, tried to warn her that her mother was ill. Oh God, she should have insisted that Edna went to the doctor, but instead she had listened to her excuses. And now – now it was too late. 'Dad, it's my fault,' she gasped.

'No, Daisy, of course it isn't your fault,' he said, standing up and moving to her side where she felt his hand on her shoulder.

'But Dad, when Lizzie told me that Aunt Edna was ill I should have listened to her. Oh, I know that she said it was just a pulled muscle, but I should have realised it was more than that.'

'Daisy, don't you remember speaking to me about your aunt's illness? I dismissed it too, don't forget. We talked about this when I visited Edna in hospital today. She recognised that her symptoms were the same as our mother's, and had watched our mother die. I don't think she realised that they might have been able to help her if she had sought medical attention earlier.'

'Oh, Aunt Edna,' Daisy whimpered.

'I know, it's dreadful isn't it, but you mustn't blame yourself. Your aunt admitted that she covered it up and took painkillers several times a day without your knowledge. Her one concern now is for Lizzie, and who will look after her.'

'But we will surely?'

'Yes, we will, and I told Edna that. She was so relieved, Daisy, but are you sure you can cope? You've got Vera to care for, and now Lizzie too. I don't want to over-burden you.'

'I'll be fine, Dad. Lizzie isn't much trouble; she's just a bit too clingy at times, that's all. But what about Vera? How will she feel about Lizzie living with us? She might be unkind to her.'

'Of course she won't be unkind, Daisy. What on earth makes you think that? I know she can be difficult at times, but she's in a lot of pain and discomfort. Don't worry, I'm sure Vera will do all she can to comfort your cousin.'

Daisy hung her head. Her father was blind to Vera's faults; she was all sweetness and light when he was around. She sighed deeply, too tired to think clearly. 'Will you take me to see Aunt Edna soon, Dad?'

'If we can find someone to keep an eye on Vera I'll take both you and Lizzie next weekend. Now I think you should get yourself off to bed, dear. You look worn out.'

Daisy's worst fears were realised the next morning. Her father was in a hurry to leave for work, having urgent shipping documents to prepare, and just swallowed a cup of tea before rushing out. Lizzie, still fractious and asking for her mother, clung to Daisy, getting under her feet as she tried to clear the breakfast-table.

But it had to be faced, and now was as good a time as any. Sucking in her breath, Daisy said nervously, 'Come on, Lizzie, I'll take you in to meet Vera.'

Holding her cousin's hand, Daisy took her into the living room. Vera was sitting up in bed reading the morning newspaper, but as she saw them her eyes travelled slowly up and down Lizzie's body. Then, with an expression of derision on her face, she said, 'Get that thing out of my room.'

'Where your baby?' Lizzie asked innocently.

Daisy cringed; it was the worst thing she could have asked. 'She doesn't understand, Vera,' she said quickly.

Vera's voice was deceptively calm as she spoke, but her face was set in anger as she stared at Daisy, completely ignoring Lizzie. 'Now you listen to me, girl, and I won't tell you again. Your cousin may be staying with us, and your father has told me it might be permanent, but keep her out of my room. Or else!'

'No stay here!' Lizzie cried, her eyes wide with distress. 'Want my mum . . . want my mum, Daisy.'

'For goodness sake, just look at her. She's like a bloody jelly baby!' Vera cried. 'And you aren't far behind her, Daisy. You're getting more like a lump of lard every day. Now get out of my room. Looking at the pair of you makes me sick!'

Seeing Lizzie's stricken face, something snapped inside Daisy. 'Shut up, Vera! You can say what you like to me, but I'm not standing for you hurting my cousin. Don't you realise that she's like a child, and just as innocent. She's desperately worried about her mother and is missing her. Can't you understand that and show a bit of compassion for once?'

'No shout, Daisy,' Lizzie begged. 'Lady sad . . . leave lady!' she cried.

Daisy gave in to Lizzie, and throwing Vera a look of disgust, she grabbed her cousin's hand again. Quivering with anger, she ushered Lizzie out of the room, but they had only just reached the kitchen when Vera started shouting, 'Daisy! Come back here!'

Pushing Lizzie onto a kitchen chair, she urged, 'Stay here and don't move – I won't be a minute,' and with her lips compressed she rushed back to the sitting room. 'I can't leave Lizzie on her own for long, Vera, so if you want me to do anything for you then you'll have to accept that she comes in here with me.'

'Don't get on your high horse with me, madam. You're forgetting yourself, aren't you!' Vera snapped. Then inhaling deeply, she slumped back onto her pillow. 'I don't see why your cousin has to live with us, and I intend to have a talk with your father when he comes home. He will understand that my needs are greater than hers and that I mustn't be neglected. I'm sure when I explain things to him he'll see the sense of sending Lizzie into a care home.'

'No! Oh no, you can't ask him to do that! Please Vera, I'll be able to cope.'

'You've just said that she can't be left on her own, and I certainly don't want to have to look at her, she turns my stomach. Putting Lizzie in a home is the only answer, and don't you dare try to intervene, my girl. If you do . . . well, I don't have to tell you what I'll do in return.'

Daisy stared at Vera, her heart pounding in her chest, and all her pent-up feelings were evident in her voice as she shouted, 'I *hate* you – do you know that? I hate you, and I wish you were dead!' Then, rushing from the room and into the kitchen, Daisy found that she was unable to stop herself from bursting into tears.

'No cry,' Lizzie begged as she heaved herself out of the chair.

Daisy found herself enfolded in her cousin's arms and gave into her emotions. She had tried to be strong – tried to protect Lizzie. Yet all she had done was to make matters worse, and now Vera was going to persuade her father to put Lizzie into a home. What can I do? she thought desperately. Oh, what can I do?

At last a glimmer of an idea began to form. Maybe there was a chance – a slim one, but it might work. Gently disengaging herself from Lizzie's arms she drew in ragged breaths, struggling to regain her composure. Her cousin looked white with worry, eyes full of tears too as she stared back at her. 'You all right, Daisy?' she asked.

'Yes, don't worry, everything is going to be fine. Now sit down again, Lizzie. I'm just going back to see Vera for a few minutes, and after that you and I can bake a nice fruitcake. Would you like that?' she asked, trying to make her voice sound light.

'Yes, make cake, Daisy,' she enthused, a small smile in evidence at the thought of her favourite food.

After seeing that her cousin was settled again, Daisy went back to the sitting room, opening the door purposefully.

'What do you want?' Vera snapped. 'I didn't call you.'

Her stance stiff, Daisy faced Vera. 'My father doesn't know about Lennie Talbot, or that you have a child, and what do you think his reaction would be if he found out?'

Vera's face tightened. 'I don't know, but what is this leading to, miss?'

Daisy clenched her hands together in an effort to stop them shaking. 'Well, if you try to persuade him to put Lizzie in a home, I'll tell him about Lennie and George.'

To her surprise Vera burst out laughing. 'Oh, you're priceless, Daisy. You're actually trying to blackmail me.'

Her laughter grew, sounding manic again, and Daisy began to tremble. Was her stepmother mad? Was she losing her mind?

Then, without warning the laughter died abruptly and with a sneer Vera said, 'If you tell your father about Lennie – I'll tell him you caused your mother's death.'

They stared at each other, the atmosphere charged, and after some minutes it was Vera who spoke again. 'Look, this is ridiculous. Seeing that it means so much to you I won't tell him to have that idiot put away. But keep her out of my room as much as possible.'

Daisy stared at Vera in amazement. She had backed down! She had actually backed down. It was unbelievable! Her stepmother's mood changes were mercurial, and if anything, that frightened Daisy more than ever. 'Thank you, Vera, and I'll do my best to do as you ask,' she said warily, her breath leaving her body in a rush.

'Right, that's sorted then. Now if you don't mind, I would like to finish reading the paper in peace.'

Vera watched as the door closed behind Daisy. Once she had been able to control her stepdaughter, but she had grown up now and was becoming assertive. It had been a shock when Daisy had turned on her like that, shouting her demands, and it made Vera realise that in future she must be careful not to push her too far.

Vera chewed worriedly on her bottom lip, deciding that she had better moderate her behaviour in future. Daisy had looked close to breaking point and Henry mustn't find out about George yet. She had to handle the situation carefully – to plan how she was going to break it to him. It would be a disaster if Daisy told him and something that must be avoided at all cost.

Flopping back onto her pillows, her thoughts drifted back to a time when she had been close to breaking down too, and now the memories haunted her. Why hadn't her mother told her about Lennie Talbot before? Why did she wait until she was pregnant and it was too late? She had stormed out of Ada's house, dreading going back to Lennie, the thought of having to look at him making her stomach turn. For hours she had wandered aimlessly, deep in thought. She couldn't face an abortion. Yet what choice was there?

She was near exhaustion, her feet throbbing painfully, when at last she came to a decision – choosing to take a chance and have the baby, this decision somewhat influenced by memories of one of the girls at the club who had been to a backstreet abortionist, afterwards developing an infection that had nearly killed her.

But what could she do for money? Remembering her own childhood and the poverty her mother had struggled against, Vera was determined to do better for her child. It was then that she had decided to go back to Lennie, and to somehow get into his safe before running away with Georgie.

Shaking off the memories Vera sighed heavily, wondering if her mother had carried out her instructions yet. She had told her to find Lennie's address, and once that was accomplished she would need not only Henry's help, but Daisy's too if she wanted to get Georgie back. Yes, Vera thought, even more reason to moderate her behaviour towards the girl. At a custodial hearing the judge would want to know that Georgie would be living in a stable home and that he would be well cared for. If she could prove that, Vera was sure the court would grant her custody. After all, who in their right mind would leave the child with Lennie Talbot? No, it was unthinkable.

Chapter Twenty-Seven

In Battersea Ada Tucker was staring at the envelope the postman had delivered. It was brown and looked official, but other than that she had no idea who had sent it. She frowned, wondering who she could ask to read it for her. At one time it had always been Mrs Green in the upstairs flat, but both she and her husband had been re-housed months ago. There was always Flo or Lily, but no, they were a right pair of gossips and she didn't want them knowing her business. Ada peered at the envelope again, her brow drawn in thought.

There was a sudden pop as the gas went out under the kettle, and sighing Ada dropped the envelope onto the table while she went to find a shilling for the meter. It was as she was feeding the coin into the slot that a thought struck her. Dr Freeman – she could nip down to the surgery and ask him to read it. He had been her GP for over twenty-five years and there wasn't much he didn't know about her circumstances. He already knew she couldn't read, and over the years had patiently explained the instructions on any medication he'd prescribed.

Her mind made up, Ada gulped a quick cup of tea before heading for the surgery.

There were only four people in the waiting room, and after taking a seat Ada grabbed a magazine, pretending to read as she avidly gazed at the pictures.

The buzzer sounded and a large man rose to take his turn. As Ada lifted her head she smiled at the woman sitting opposite, who smiled back saying, 'You go in after me to see the doctor. I was the last one to arrive.' Ada nodded gratefully in acknowledgement.

At last, she thought, when her turn finally came, fingering the letter in her pocket as she went in. 'Hello, Doctor,' she said, taking a seat at the side of his desk.

'Well, Mrs Tucker,' he said, peering at her over the top of his narrow glasses, grey, bushy eyebrows raised. 'It's been some time since you've come to see me. What's the problem?'

Ada pulled out the envelope. 'This came today and I wondered if you'd tell me what it says,' and despite the fact that he knew her circumstances, her face grew hot. Bloody hell, she thought, what if it was something awful, an unpaid bill or something? No, don't be daft, she told herself, straightening in the chair. She had never owed a penny to anyone, and no matter how hard things had been her rent was paid on the dot, even if it meant taking on some extra charring jobs. It was something her mother had instilled in her from a young age. 'Never get into debt,' she said. 'Never buy anything unless you've got the money to pay for it. It's easy to get into debt, my girl,' she warned, 'but hell to get out of.'

'Now then, Mrs Tucker, there's no need to be embarrassed. Many of my older patients have never had the opportunity to learn to read, and of course I'll tell you what this says,' the doctor said, placing a paper-knife under the flap and slitting open the envelope.

Ada watched anxiously as he scanned the contents, relieved to see a smile on his face. 'It's good news. The Council are offering you a new flat and it's about time, too. You must be one of the last ones in your street.'

'Yeah, I am. But do they say where the flat is?'

'Yes, it's in Battersea Park Road. To view it you just have to go to the Council Offices and pick up the key.'

'Doctor, will you read out the address of the flat for me so I can memorise it?'

Ada listened carefully, already planning to take either Flo or Lily with her when she went to see it. 'Thanks, Doctor,' she said, grinning with delight. Oh, it would be smashing to get out of the dump she was in now. She stood up, eager now to get the key.

'You do realise that you will have to sign on with a new doctor, Mrs Tucker. I'm afraid you'll be just out of my catchment area in Battersea Park Road,' he told her.

'Oh no,' Ada said with dismay.

'Now then, it's not the end of the world. You've only been to see me once in the past two years.'

'Yeah, but better the devil you know,' she told him, grinning cheekily.

'Go on – off you go,' he said, grinning back.

Ada went straight to the Council Offices, leaving with the keys clutched tightly in her hand. It was as she reached the corner of the High Street that a black Jaguar car passed and she caught a glimpse of Lennie Talbot in the back.

A surge of guilt made her lower her head. Vera had asked her to find out where he lived, but she had done nothing. She couldn't get involved, she just couldn't. Lennie's threats still terrified her, and if he found out she was poking her nose into his business, well, what he might do to her just didn't bear thinking about. She had assuaged her guilt by telling herself that her daughter wasn't fit to look after George. After all, she was a cripple now.

Ada was saddened by Vera's plight, but unable to forget how nasty she had been. Instead of asking for help, her daughter had demanded it, without thought of what Lennie would do if he found out. Christ, the girl must be mad to think she had any chance of getting her son back again. You just didn't mess with the likes of Lennie Talbot, not if you wanted to stay alive. She shivered then, praying that Vera would give up on the insane idea.

As Ada made her way to Lily's, her thoughts were still on her daughter, thinking about how hard and cruel she had become. More like her father than me, she realised suddenly. What would Vera say when she realised that she hadn't followed her instructions? Bloody hell, she'd go mad!

It was as she reached Lily's front door that the thought struck

Ada, and she slumped with relief. She wouldn't go to see Vera again. No, she'd stay out of her life. After all, the girl had only bothered to get in touch when she wanted to use her to find Lennie. For years she'd had no idea where her daughter was, and it still smarted that she hadn't come to Davy's funeral. All right, she may have hated her father, and with good reason, but she should have come to support her mother.

Relieved that she had found a way out of her dilemma, Ada straightened her shoulders. She was moving now, and if Vera sent the kid again she would find the house empty – and it would serve her right.

Yet even as Ada rang Lily's doorbell she felt a twinge of guilt. Bleedin' hell, what sort of mother am I? she thought, shaking her head ruefully. But then what sort of a daughter was Vera – expecting her to get involved in her daft scheme. The girl must be mad! Lennie would kill them both!

Lennie Talbot looked around his club, smiling with satisfaction. The roulette and blackjack tables were doing well and there was a buzz of excitement in the room. He eyed his hostesses, pleased to see they were well-groomed, noticing the new girl as she sashayed across the room. He scowled, finding that she reminded him of Vera with her hair piled on top of her head in an intricate arrangement. Her black cocktail dress clung to her figure, and tarted up she looked real classy. He had made sure she was a virgin as his client had specially requested a young one, and Lennie was sure he would be very pleased with this sixteen year old.

He glanced at his watch then made for the stairs to his top-floor private apartment. George would probably be asleep, but he liked to check in on him. So far the nanny he'd employed was doing a good job and he was pleased with his son's progress. Nancy Barker made sure that George talked well and articulately, his voice echoing the well-modulated tones of his nanny. Mind you, Lennie thought with a shake of his head, it hadn't been easy, and it had taken his son a long time to settle down after he had got him back from Vera. He had heard that she had been crippled in the process and smiled in satisfaction. It was no more than the bitch deserved and there was no worry now that she would try to snatch George back again.

Unlocking the door to his private quarters he made his way to his son's bedroom, his hard face softening as he looked down at him. George had his favourite teddy bear tucked in the bed, but when he saw the scruffy piece of cloth in his hand Lennie frowned. He was sure his boy was happy, and had everything that he could possibly want. A playroom filled with toys, from a train set to his favourite, a large rocking horse. So why did he still cling on to that rotten piece of knitting?

Turning swiftly now and without bothering to knock, he strode into the adjoining room. 'Nancy, he's still got that bloody security blanket. How many times have I got to tell you to take it away? He ain't a baby and it's about time he stopped chewing on it.'

Startled, Nancy jumped to her feet, her knitting falling onto the floor. 'I've tried to take it from him, Mr Talbot, but he goes into a tantrum.'

'Well, that's not good enough. I don't want my son turning into a bloody pansy and next time I see him it had better be without that piece of cloth.'

'Perhaps you could take it from him?'

'I employ you to look after my son and you are well-paid to do so. Are you telling me that you have no control over him?'

'No, of course not.'

'Right – well, see that you do as I ask.' Without waiting for her reply he walked out, and making his way to his own private sitting room, he picked up a decanter and poured himself a whisky. After downing the drink in one he sat down, relishing the peace and quiet, his thoughts still on his son. George had given his life new meaning, and he was determined that the boy would want for nothing. He had already taken steps to secure his future financially, but as his holdings grew Lennie knew that the time had come when he should make a will. His solicitor had been badgering him for ages, but he balked against it time and time again. It was a stupid superstition and he knew it, yet somehow the thought of making a will made him shudder. Standing up abruptly he poured another drink, deciding that it wouldn't hurt to leave making a will for a little while longer.

Making his way back downstairs to the club, Lennie was just in time to see his special client arriving. This man was in Parliament and tipped to be given a senior position in the next government re-shuffle. Yes, Lennie thought, he could turn out to be very useful.

'Gerald, how are you?' he asked, taking the man's arm. 'I think you're going to like what I've got for you this evening.'

The man smiled, and snapping his fingers Lennie beckoned one of the girls to take his hat and coat. Then, leading him into the gaming room his eyes searched for the new girl. 'Go and sit down, Gerald, and I'll call you shortly.'

Licking his lips in anticipation the man took a seat, a hostess appearing immediately to take his order.

Lennie saw Jacqueline close by, and after pointing out Gerald, he urged her into the hall. 'That man is important. Take him to one of the bedrooms in the annexe and see that you make him happy.'

The girl's eyes widened, her panic evident as she cried, 'No, no, I can't do that! You said that my job was to be a hostess.'

'Yeah, that's right – and my hostesses are paid to ensure that my clients get what they want.'

'No, please, I don't want to!'

'If you don't want your pretty little face ruined you'll do as I say. Don't tell me you didn't know what to expect when I employed you. You may be a virgin, but you ain't stupid.'

'I didn't know, honest I didn't. Please, don't make me do it!'

Lennie's smile was menacing, and glancing quickly behind him he beckoned one of his minders to his side. 'Joe, take her to one of our special rooms, and if she gives you any trouble, give her a slap.'

'Yes, boss,' he said. Grabbing the girl, and with his hand over her mouth to stifle her cries, he dragged her effortlessly away.

Lennie grinned. Gerald wouldn't mind if she resisted. In fact, he would enjoy it. Yes, he thought as he went to fetch his client, the girl was the perfect choice.

Chapter Twenty-Eight

On Thursday evening Daisy's head was throbbing. She hadn't realised how hard it would be to look after Lizzie. Still missing her mother, her cousin was fractious most of the time, and only happy when she was eating. All day she trailed behind her, constantly asking to go back to Puddleton, and no matter how many times Daisy tried to placate her, it didn't help. Still, Daisy thought, at least a sort of truce had been called with Vera. She ignored Lizzie whenever she was in the room, showing her disapproval with a tight-lipped expression. But at least her stepmother wasn't making any more cruel remarks, and strangely, Lizzie showed no fear of her.

In fact, Daisy was finding the change in Vera puzzling. Instead of reverting to her usual nasty and carping ways, she was actually being pleasant most of the time. Of course there were moments when she snapped impatiently, but now she always apologised afterwards, explaining that not only was she in pain, but she also found it frustrating to be so confined. And that was true, Daisy realised, unable to imagine how awful it must be to have lost the use of your legs.

As Daisy cleared the table, with Lizzie following behind her as usual, she suddenly found that the walls seemed to be closing in on her. The only time she was out of the house was when she went shopping, and now it began to feel like a prison. With a start Daisy realised that she hadn't been to see Molly all week. Deciding to go next door as soon as the washing-up was done, she popped her head around the sitting room door. 'I'm going round to see Molly. Do you mind, Dad?'

'No, of course not, and why don't you take Lizzie with you?'

Daisy sighed. It would have been nice to have some time on her own, but realising that Lizzie would probably play up if she tried to leave her, she resigned herself to taking her cousin along.

'Well, 'tis Daisy, come on in,' Molly invited. 'And who's this with you?'

Daisy introduced Lizzie, whispering quickly in Molly's ear to explain why she was staying with them. Molly tutted sadly, standing aside to usher them into the kitchen.

Daisy's face flamed when she saw Liam sitting at the table. God, he was gorgeous. 'Hello, Liam,' she croaked.

'Hello,' he said briefly, then returned his attention to the newspaper spread out on the table in front of him.

'He bad man,' Lizzie said.

'No, you mustn't say things like that,' Daisy admonished, shocked by her cousin's words.

'But he is,' Lizzie insisted, wagging her head.

'Shush,' Daisy hissed, pushing her onto a chair. 'Now sit there like a good girl.'

'I *is* a good girl,' Lizzie said indignantly, and if she hadn't been so embarrassed, Daisy might have smiled at the expression on her face. As it was, she looked at Molly warily.

'Well, she's a strange one,' Molly said, her face puzzled. 'I wonder what made her say that?'

'I don't know, but I'm sure she didn't mean it. How are things?' Daisy added quickly when she saw Lizzie about to speak again.

'Oh, all right, except that one's broken up with Sandra,' she said, nodding her head towards Liam. ''Tis a shame – I liked the girl.'

'Don't go on about it, Mam,' Liam complained, just as there was a cry from upstairs.

'Excuse me, Daisy, but that sounds like Francis. I'll be back in a minute,' Molly said as she bustled out of the room.

Finding herself staring at Liam, Daisy's face reddened again when he looked up, his eyes travelling over her body, before he spoke. 'When you first came back from the country I could have really fancied you, Daisy. Now look at you. What have you done to yourself, putting all that weight back on?'

'No talk to him, Daisy, he bad man. We go home now!' Lizzie cried.

'It's all right, we'll be going soon,' she placated, wondering what on earth was wrong with her cousin.

'What's the matter with her? Why does she keep saying that?' Liam asked, his voice stiff with annoyance.

'I don't know. I'm sorry,' Daisy apologised.

'Well, I'm off out. She's giving me the creeps,' he snapped.

'Lizzie, don't talk about Liam like that. It isn't nice,' she told Lizzie as soon as they were alone, alarmed to see tears forming in her cousin's eyes.

'But he bad man,' she insisted again.

'Now that's enough,' Daisy admonished quickly as she heard Molly coming downstairs.

'I've got Francis settled again,' she said, puffing heavily as she entered the room. 'Would you like a cup of tea, girls?'

'Not for me thanks,' Daisy told her. 'What about you, Lizzie? Would you like something to drink?'

'No, not want,' she said sulkily, much to Daisy's chagrin. She had never seen Lizzie acting like this before and was puzzled by her behaviour.

'She seems upset, Daisy. What's wrong with her?' Molly asked.

'I don't know, but maybe she's nervous of being in a strange place,' she offered doubtfully.

The door opened and Liam hurried in again. 'Sandra's heading down the street. Tell her I'm not in if she calls,' he told his mother.

'I'm not telling lies for you, son. I don't know what went on between the two of you, but you must sort it out for yourself.'

'Oh, for God's sake, Mam! I don't want another row,' he begged.

'He bad man,' Lizzie cried again, her eyes wide as she gazed at Liam.

'Why do you keep saying that?' Molly asked her sharply.

'He bad, bad!' Lizzie insisted.

'Daisy, I'm sorry, but will you take her home. My Liam isn't bad, and I know she's not quite the ticket, but I'm fed up with hearing it.'

'Oh Molly, I'm so sorry,' Daisy said, and taking Lizzie's hand, she urged, 'Come on, we're going home now. Say goodbye.'

Lizzie rose to her feet, and ignoring Daisy's instructions she edged warily around Liam as they went out of the door.

'Bye Molly, bye Liam, and I'm so sorry,' Daisy said again. 'I'll pop round to see you again soon.'

'You know you can come to see me at any time, Daisy, but I'd rather you left that one at home in future,' Molly told her, watching as they climbed the basement steps.

Daisy nodded, stricken by her cousin's behaviour. Molly was fiercely proud of Liam, and though she might rebuke him herself, she wouldn't let anyone else say a word against him. He was Molly's firstborn and, Daisy suspected, her favourite. 'Come on,' she said sharply to Lizzie, dragging her indoors.

Her cousin's behaviour then had her gasping in disbelief. She ran into the sitting room, throwing her arms around Vera. 'Daisy cross with me,' she cried.

Even more astounding was Vera's response. Instead of throwing the girl off with disgust, her arms tightened around Lizzie, and in a soothing voice she said, 'There, there, it's all right, darling.'

Daisy gawked; her jaw dropping as Lizzie eased herself onto the bed beside Vera, laying her head on her shoulder – and what was more, Vera was allowing it!

Her father came into the room then, smiling at the scene. 'Oh, it's lovely to see you two getting on so well,' he said, completely in ignorance of how Vera had behaved with Lizzie prior to this.

'The poor child is missing her mother and she just wants a bit of comfort, Henry,' Vera told him, smiling softly as she raised a hand and began to stroke Lizzie's hair.

'Vera, I must go to Hampshire on Sunday to see Edna, and Lizzie can come with me. It might just settle her down. Now the thing is, Daisy wants to come too, so would you allow me to ask Molly to look after you for the day?'

'No, I'm not having that woman in my house, Henry. You know I can't stand her. She's a slut and a gossip.'

'Vera, why do you keep saying things like that? It isn't true. Molly is a good and kind woman.'

'No be cross – no shout,' Lizzie pleaded, her head lifting off Vera's shoulder.

'I'm sorry, darling,' Vera soothed, and Daisy's eyes widened again.

'Henry, you know I can't bear to have strangers looking after me,' she now said, sniffing pathetically. 'Oh God, I'm just a burden to everyone, a burden!'

'Of course you aren't, darling. But if not Molly, who can we ask? I've been tearing my hair out all week trying to think of a solution.'

By the look in Vera's eyes as she turned to her, Daisy guessed what was coming.

'Please, Daisy, won't you stay with me?' she begged.

'But I want to see my aunt,' she protested. And it was on the tip of her tongue to suggest Vera's mother.

'But there isn't anyone else,' Vera cried.

Daisy closed her eyes. Oh what's the use, she thought. Vera would get her way in the end, she always did. 'All right, I'll stay.'

'Oh, thank you, darling,' she said. 'I'm sorry to be such a nuisance.'

Vera did sound genuinely grateful, Daisy thought, turning to leave the room – but if there was nobody else to look after her, how on earth was she going to get the chance to see Aunt Edna? 'I'll make us all a drink,' she said distantly, still smarting with disappointment, and surprised that Lizzie didn't rise to follow her.

The next morning Daisy went quietly downstairs to see to Vera. When she entered the sitting room she was surprised to find Lizzie already in there, happily sitting beside the bed. What had caused this complete turnaround? Yes, she had been annoyed with

Lizzie for her remarks about Liam, but surely her cousin wasn't still upset about that? Yet as their eyes met, Daisy could see that her cousin was wary of her. 'Hello, what would you like for breakfast?' she asked brightly.

'Porridge,' Lizzie said, suddenly smiling, and Daisy sighed with relief.

'That's a good idea, I'll have porridge too,' Vera said. 'Now then, Lizzie,' she added, 'you will have to move out of the way for a little while. Daisy has to help me in the mornings.'

Lizzie moved without a murmur, and as Daisy began to help Vera onto her commode she was worried that this was another of her stepmother's games. Could she trust her with her cousin?

'Go to toilet too, Daisy?' Lizzie suddenly cried, pointing to the commode.

'No, darling, you can't use this. Why don't you go upstairs to the bathroom,' Daisy urged.

'The poor girl, I can't help feeling sorry for her,' Vera remarked as soon as Lizzie left the room. 'I miss my son, and every single day he is constantly in my thoughts. Lizzie is just a child really, and is missing her mother.'

'Yes, she is,' Daisy answered, unable to help blurting out, 'Please, Vera, don't hurt her.'

'Hurt her! Why should I do that?' she answered, her face showing what looked like genuine amazement. 'All right, I know I was a bit funny with Lizzie at first. She's the only retarded person I've ever had to deal with, and I must admit I was a bit nervous of her. I didn't know what to expect, Daisy, and I thought she would have a mental illness. But I think I understand now. Lizzie is just a child in a woman's body.'

'Yes, that's right,' Daisy murmured, wondering if she should mention her cousin's strange insights, and after a few moments' thought, she said, 'There's something you should know, Vera. You see, Lizzie is a bit fey. It doesn't happen all the time, but there are occasions when she seems to know in advance when something is going to happen.'

'Really!' Vera said, her voice sharp. 'What sort of things has Lizzie seen?'

'Oh well, let me think. There was one time in Puddleton when she told a lady who was pregnant that she was going to have a boy. It's things like that.'

'What else has she predicted?'

'Lizzie knew her mother was ill, and somehow knows it's serious. That's why she's so upset.'

'I wonder if she could tell me if I'll get Georgie back?'

'She can't do it if you ask her to. It just seems to happen on odd occasions.'

'I see,' Vera mused. 'Hmm . . . well, I could still try asking her, I suppose.'

'No, it won't work and you'll just confuse her,' Daisy insisted.

Vera sighed. 'I'm sorry you can't go with your father tomorrow and I know you're disappointed. But listen, I've been thinking. It's too short notice to do anything about tomorrow, but you could pop down to my mother's again while your father's away and maybe arrange for her to look after me next week.'

'But how will you explain that to my father?'

'I've decided to tell him about my mother this evening. I just hope he'll understand.'

'Are you going to tell him about George and Lennie too?'

'No, Daisy, I think it would be too much all at once. It would be better to break it to him one step at a time. Your father is going to be awfully shocked, and I must admit I'm a bit nervous of his reaction.'

Lizzie came back into the room then, and with a small shake of her head to indicate that the conversation was over, Vera said, 'I like to be left alone while I use the commode, Lizzie. You can come back in here later.'

Daisy left the room too and as she went to the kitchen with Lizzie trotting behind her, she found her thoughts turning to her father. What would his reaction be to Vera's confessions? It seemed unlikely that he would mind that Vera had hidden her background from him. He wasn't a snob, and would probably welcome her mother into the family. However, if the time came when Vera decided to tell him about Lennie Talbot and George, that would be another matter.

When they were alone after dinner that evening, Vera said hesitantly, 'Henry, I need to tell you something . . . and . . . and I hope you'll understand.'

'You sound very serious, dear,' he said, rising to switch off the television.

'Well, I must admit I'm a bit nervous about what I'm going to confess.'

'Confess! Goodness, my dear — that sound ominous.'

Drawing in her breath and eyeing her husband warily, Vera said, 'Do you remember when we first met, and I told you that I had no family?'

'Of course I do. You told me that your parents were killed during the war.'

'Well,' she said hesitantly. 'Umm . . . that's not strictly true.'

'Not strictly true? What do you mean?'

'Oh Henry,' Vera cried dramatically before continuing. She had rehearsed this in her mind and prayed she would get it right. 'I fell in love with you almost at first sight. You were so refined, polite and well-mannered.'

'I love you too, darling,' Henry said, 'but I don't understand. What has this got to do with your parents?'

Vera forced tears into her eyes, and with a pitiful expression she said, 'I lied about my background, Henry. I was desperate and didn't want to lose you. You see, my father wasn't a solicitor, and I wasn't born in Surrey.'

'Vera, your background doesn't mean anything to me. Surely you know that?'

'Yes, I know that now. But when I first met you I had no idea how you would react to the truth. I was afraid, Henry.'

'Silly girl,' he said, smiling indulgently and grasping her hand where it rested on top of the eiderdown.

Vera drew in a deep breath again. So far so good, she thought, before ploughing on, 'My family comes from Battersea, and though it's true that my father's dead, my mother is still alive. He was a builder's labourer and my mother is a charwoman.' There was silence then as she kept her head humbly lowered, waiting with bated breath for Henry's reaction.

'I suppose I can understand why you felt you couldn't tell me this when we first met, Vera. Though God knows it wouldn't have mattered. But why have you waited until now to tell me the truth?'

'The longer I left it, the harder it became. I know the one thing you abhor is lies, Henry, and I didn't want to lose you,' she whispered, her eyes pools of liquid as she now looked up. 'I'm afraid there's more, darling. You see, my father was a brute of a man and both my mother and I suffered terribly at his hands. We lived in dreadful hardship, most of his money being spent on gambling. He was addicted to horse racing, but unfortunately rarely picked a winner. My mother kept us going by taking on charring jobs, sometimes starting as early as five in the morning to clean offices before the staff arrived.'

'How awful for her, and you, Vera,' he said sympathetically.

'One day I just couldn't take it any more, Henry. I upped and left home, and rarely went back.'

'Well, that's understandable, my dear.'

Vera heaved a sigh of relief. It was going better than she had hoped. 'I didn't see much of my mother after that, Henry, and feel so guilty about it. I wasn't living close by and was struggling to support myself. But that's no excuse really. The truth is that I just didn't want to see my father again. When he died I didn't go to his funeral because it would have felt hypocritical,' she lied, her eyes wide. 'Eventually, when I went to visit my mother, we had an awful row about it. I didn't realise how much it would mean to her, and she said she would never forgive me.' Vera shook her head sadly. 'I'm afraid I didn't see her again after that. Foolish pride, I suppose, and perhaps stubbornness. Yet now, lying here day after day, I've had time to think about it and I'd like to get in touch with her again, Henry. Perhaps invite her here to see if we can make a fresh start. Would you mind, darling?' she finished, on a rush, holding her breath in anticipation.

'Oh darling, of course I wouldn't mind. How could you think that I would?'

Vera closed her eyes, relief flooding through her. 'Thank you, and thank you for being so understanding. I'm sorry I lied to you, really I am. Can you forgive me?'

'Of course I forgive you. It sounds like you had a dreadful childhood. Yes, invite your mother here, Vera. I'd love to meet her.'

Chapter Twenty-Nine

On Sunday morning Daisy waved to her father and Lizzie as they drove off, still disappointed that she wasn't going with them. She remained on the doorstep until the car turned the corner, then was surprised to hear Molly's voice.

'Hello, Daisy. How are you?'

She turned her head swiftly. 'I'm all right, thanks.'

'I've been hoping to see you. 'Tis sorry I am for the way I behaved on Thursday. It just unnerved me, the way your cousin went on and on about Liam.'

Daisy shook her head, her expression perplexed. 'Lizzie isn't usually like that – I don't know what came over her. The only thing I can think of is that she's upset about her mother and is unsettled at the moment.'

'That's as maybe, but I still don't understand why she kept saying that Liam's a bad boy.'

Daisy struggled to think of an explanation. 'My cousin is a bit strange, Molly. Her mother calls her fey. Do you remember when Liam came back in when he saw Sandra and asked you to lie for him – maybe Lizzie sensed that it was going to happen.'

'Oh, I didn't realise she was off with the fairies! Well, that explains it then. I must admit that Liam has treated Sandra badly, and the poor girl is obviously heartbroken.'

'Has he told you why he broke up with her?'

'He said he wasn't ready to get married, and all the talk of weddings made him realise that. 'Tis a shame because it would have been nice to see him settled.' Molly sighed, then changed the subject. 'I saw your dadda driving off with Lizzie. Are they off to see your auntie?'

'Yes, they'll be back this evening.'

'Well, when you get the chance, will you pop round to see me?'

'Of course I will. If not this evening, then tomorrow.'

'That's grand, Daisy. Now I had best get on. Standing here chatting won't buy the baby a bonnet.'

'Bye, Molly,' Daisy sang out, turning to go indoors when she heard Vera calling.

Vera looked eagerly at Daisy as she went into the sitting room, and with a wide smile she said, 'I had a long talk with your father last night. He knows about my mother now and is happy for her to visit me. Are you ready to go?'

'Yes. Is there anything you want before I leave?'

'No, I'll be fine for an hour or two.'

'Right, I'll be off then.'

'Daisy . . . er . . . thanks.'

She looked at her stepmother in surprise. Was it possible for someone to change so much, so quickly?

The question was still distracting Daisy as she sat on the bus to Battersea. Memories of Vera's cruelty were still vivid, so what had caused this sudden mercurial change? Why was she being so nice?

Reaching her destination Daisy walked down Ingrave Street, her eyes widening as she stared at number fifteen. It was boarded up! Scanning each side of the road she looked desperately for a house that was still occupied, but they were all empty, the street deserted and litter-strewn. For a while Daisy stood uncertainly, not knowing what to do. Mrs Tucker must have moved away — but where had she gone?

With no other option Daisy had to return home, and as she walked into the sitting room, Vera greeted her brightly.

'Hello, I didn't expect you back so soon. Have you brought my mother with you?'

'Er . . . no. She's gone.'

'Gone! What do you mean, gone?'

'The house was empty, boarded up.'

'But when . . . where . . . did you find out?' Vera spluttered.

'I couldn't. The whole street was deserted and there was nobody there to ask.'

'But I don't understand. My mother wouldn't have just moved away without telling me.'

Daisy shook her head helplessly; her expression was sympathetic, but she was unable to think of anything to say.

Vera pushed at the bedclothes impatiently. 'Oh, this is ridiculous, there must be a way to find out where she is.' Her face suddenly lit up. 'I know, the Council have probably rehoused her and we can ask them for her new address. Go and give them a ring, Daisy.'

'But it's Sunday and there won't be anyone there. I'll ring them first thing in the morning,' Daisy placated.

Vera's body stiffened, her eyes narrowing, and seeing the signs that a tantrum might be imminent, Daisy was anxious to get out of the room. 'I'll go and make us a cup of tea,' she said quickly.

For the next two hours Daisy busied herself doing housework, and wary of Vera's mood, she avoided her as much as possible. She was dusting the dining room when the telephone rang, and hurried into the hall to answer it.

'Daisy, it's me,' her father said.

'Oh, hello. How's Auntie Edna?'

'She's very ill, and I'm afraid we won't be coming home today. Mrs Purvis is putting us up for the night and I'll ring you again if there's any more news.'

'Why aren't you staying above the shop, Dad?'

'Because I don't know if I'll be able to cope with Lizzie. She'll need someone to comfort her . . . a woman.'

'Dad, does that mean . . .' Daisy choked, unable to ask the question.

'Yes, I'm afraid so, dear. We can't leave with the end so near.'

Daisy clutched the handset, her eyes filling with tears. Aunt Edna was going to die and she hadn't had a chance to see her. She was unable to stop the tide of resentment that surged through her. If Vera hadn't been so selfish – if she had let Molly look after her, just for one day – she would have been able to see her aunt.

'Daisy, Daisy, are you still there?'

'What? Yes, sorry. Oh, Dad . . .' she sobbed.

'Listen, darling, I need you to be strong. Lizzie is going to need a lot of support and I'll have a lot to do down here. There's the shop and . . . ' His voice trailed off.

Daisy fought to pull herself together, and finally managed to say, 'Don't worry, Dad, I'll be all right.'

'Thanks, darling. Now I must go. Give my love to Vera.'

Daisy, frozen with shock, was still clutching the receiver to her ear when she realised that she was listening to the dialling tone. She stared at the telephone, bewildered, her mind refusing to function as she made her way to the kitchen. Her movements were slow, automatic, as she made a drink and carried it through to Vera.

'I've been thinking, Daisy, and I want you to go back to Battersea. One of my mum's friends, Lily Morris, will know where she is. Come on, don't just stand there. Get a move on!'

'That was my father on the telephone. He said that my aunt is very ill and that he won't be able to come home yet.'

'For goodness sake, girl, what's the matter with you? Put that tray down before you drop it. Didn't you hear what I said? I want you to go back to Battersea!'

Vera's words penetrated Daisy's mind at last, and she felt a surge of rage building up inside. 'No, I'm not going! I must be here in case my father rings again,' she shouted, slamming the tray down so hard that the cups jumped in their saucers and milk splashed over the side of the jug.

'What do you mean, you're not going? You'll do as I say!'

'No, Vera, I've just told you. My aunt is dying – *dying!*' she yelled. 'But you don't care, do you? All you care about is yourself, and if it wasn't for you I could be with her now!'

'How dare you speak to me like that! You're forgetting yourself, miss. If you don't do as I say I'll tell your father about the accident.'

'Tell him then! I'm sick of your threats and I don't care any more! Do you hear me? I don't care!' Daisy screamed, losing all control as she ran blindly out of the room, and the house.

She found herself at Molly's door, tears pouring down her cheeks as she hammered on the knocker.

'Daisy, what is it? What's wrong, darlin'?' asked Molly anxiously, seeing the girl in such a state on her doorstep.

'My . . . my aunt,' she gasped, unable to speak coherently.

'Come inside,' Molly urged, grasping Daisy's arm and guiding her into the kitchen. 'Youse lot, get yourselves out,' she hissed at her husband and sons.

Paddy rose immediately to his feet, his expression concerned. 'Come on, boys,' he urged, swinging Frankie up into his arms and ushering Sean and Patrick before him as they went upstairs.

'Sit down, love,' Molly told her.

As Daisy collapsed onto a chair, her sobs filling the room, Molly sat next to her, wisely saying nothing until the girl was able to bring herself under control.

Hiccuping now, she said, 'I'm sorry.'

'Has that Vera been upsetting you again?' Molly asked.

Wiping her eyes, Daisy croaked, 'It's my aunt. She's dying, Molly, and I never got the chance to see her again.'

'Ah, darlin', no wonder you're upset.'

'I could have gone with my father if Vera had let someone else look after her, but she wouldn't stand for it. Oh Molly, I hate her!'

'No, don't say that. 'Tis terrible to feel hate. It can be such a destructive emotion and can eat you up inside.'

'But you don't know what she's like, Molly. She's cruel – evil.'

'Evil!' Molly said, her voice high with shock. 'What do you mean? Why is she evil?'

Daisy bit her trembling lip. God, she had nearly let the cat out of the bag. 'Don't take any notice of me, Molly, I'm just upset. Please ignore what I said.'

'How can I ignore it? Look, I've had my suspicions for a long time about that woman. Why don't you tell me what's going on? I promise I'll keep it to myself.'

With her head lowered Daisy wondered if she dare confide in Molly. How would she react if she told her the truth? Yet somehow Daisy knew that she had to unburden herself to someone. She felt as though she was losing her mind, her hate so strong that she wanted to kill Vera. It was an awful feeling and it was tearing her apart.

'Come on, me darlin', talk to me,' Molly encouraged.

'Vera knows that I killed my mother,' Daisy blurted out, her heart thudding against her ribs. 'I have to do everything she wants or she'll tell my father about the accident. Oh Molly, he would hate me if he found out!'

'Killed your mother? Don't be silly, of course you didn't!'

'I *did*, Molly. I was playing in the road and my mum told me time and time again not to do that. She saw the car coming and threw me out of its path, and . . . and . . . it hit her instead. My mother died because I disobeyed her.'

'Listen to me, Daisy. It was just an accident – a terrible accident.'

'No, it wasn't. Vera saw what happened, and it's right what she says. If I hadn't been playing in the road, my mother would still be alive.'

'Oh Daisy, 'twas the car that killed your mother – not you. It was going too fast, and your mother never had a chance.'

Daisy lifted her head, scrubbing her face with a hankie. 'But Vera insists that it was my fault, and I can remember my father saying he would kill the person responsible for my mother's death.'

Molly seemed to jump out of her chair. 'Paddy, Paddy! Come down here!' she yelled, rushing to the bottom of the stairs.

'No! Please don't tell him!' Daisy begged.

'I'm not standing for this. Begod I'm not! That woman should be shot for doing this to you,' Molly cried indignantly.

'What is it?' Paddy asked, stepping into the room.

'Paddy, I want you to stay here with Daisy. I'm going next door,' Molly snapped. 'That one needs sorting out.'

'No! Please, Molly, please don't go to see her!' Daisy cried, her voice rising to near hysteria.

'Will someone tell me what's going on?' Paddy shouted above her screams.

Molly's stance was ramrod straight as she stood with her hands on her hips. 'Do you know what Vera's been saying, Paddy? She's been accusing Daisy of killing Judith.'

'No!' he exclaimed.

'Yes, Paddy. And she's been making the girl's life hell.'

'All right, Molly,' he placated, 'I know you're upset, but come and sit down, love. We need to talk this through.' Grasping his wife's arm he led her back to the table. 'It's Daisy's father you need to talk to. He needs to know what's going on.'

'No! You can't tell my dad!' Daisy cried.

'Now, now,' Paddy said softly, his calm voice beginning to penetrate her hysteria, 'we won't do anything without your agreement, Daisy. Sit down too and we'll have a good old crack – I'm sure between us we can work something out.'

There were two problems, Paddy concluded, after hearing what had been happening. Firmly and patiently he was able to convince Daisy that she hadn't killed her mother. He told her that six weeks after the accident the police had caught the driver of the car. 'Your father went to court when the case came up, Daisy, and he heard the young man being prosecuted for dangerous driving.'

'I . . . I didn't know. Why wasn't I told?' Daisy cried.

'You were still in shock, and I expect your father didn't want to remind you of the accident. He knows how it happened, Daisy, and he doesn't blame you. He never has. Most of the children in this street play in the road, darlin', my boys included. If the car hadn't been speeding, and the driver was paying attention, it would never have happened.'

Daisy stared with wide eyes at Paddy, and finally his words sank in. She cried then. Sobbed out her pain and relief. Finally, when she managed to pull herself together, they began to talk again.

The next problem was her Aunt Edna, and hearing how desperately Daisy wanted to see her, Paddy came up with a solution for that too. He was going round to see Vera and intended to make arrangements for Molly to look after her. Then, with that sorted out, there was no reason why Daisy couldn't go by train to Puddleton. He had grinned then, saying that at least the nearest station was one that Dr Beeching hadn't shut down.

'But Vera will never agree to it,' Daisy told him tearfully.

'Oh, when I've had a word in her ear, I think you'll find that she will.'

'You don't understand, Paddy,' Daisy insisted. 'Vera won't let anyone else look after her.'

'You leave that one to me. Now, stay here until I get back,' he ordered, walking out of the door with a wave of his arm, and leaving both Daisy and Molly sitting mouths agape at the table.

'You had better get yourselves around there,' Paddy said, returning after about fifteen minutes. 'I'm afraid I found Vera in a bit of a state, and her bed needs changing. But don't worry, she knows what's what now,' he said cryptically, refusing to say anything else.

Daisy and Molly rushed next door, finding a very subdued Vera. They changed her sheets, and to Daisy's surprise she made no complaint about Molly being there.

'I'll be looking after you while Daisy goes to see her aunt,' Molly said abruptly, her expression showing that she wouldn't stand for any arguments.

'I know,' Vera whispered, 'but can I have a private word with Daisy, please?'

'Yes, but you had better not upset her. I'll go and put these sheets in soak,' Molly said, wrinkling her nose, and with a wink at Daisy she left the room.

Vera waited until the door had closed, then gulping, she said, 'I . . . I'm sorry, Daisy. Please don't tell your father.'

'Why shouldn't I?' she said belligerently, her resentment still burning inside.

'He's going to be upset enough about your aunt and I don't think he could cope with it at the moment. Look, I know I've been awful to you, but I promise I'll be different in future. Won't you give me another chance?'

Daisy, her eyes unblinkered now, saw the craftiness in her stepmother's eyes. Vera wasn't worried about her father – she was just worried about herself and what his reaction would be. But in some ways Vera was right. Her father *was* going to be upset about Aunt Edna. 'All right, I won't tell him,' she said, and after a pause couldn't resist adding, 'Yet.'

It was all a mad rush after that. Daisy rang Clapham Junction station and found out that there was a train leaving for Puddleton in an hour. Throwing some clothes into a bag she kissed Molly goodbye and made a dash for the bus stop, catching a number forty-five almost immediately. *Please let me get there in time*, Daisy prayed as she rushed into the station.

She made it; just as the Puddleton connection pulled in, and with relief flopped breathlessly onto a seat in the Ladies Only compartment.

Chapter Thirty

After the initial rush Daisy found the journey intimidating, this being her first time on a train. It was also the first time she had travelled such a long distance alone. She peered at every station sign as the train pulled in, terrified she would miss her stop, and by the time she reached Puddleton her head was splitting. It was already six o'clock, and checking her purse she hoped she had enough money for a taxi to the hospital, having no idea which bus to catch.

Thankfully Daisy managed to get a cab, almost throwing her fare at the driver before rushing into the small cottage hospital. Enquiring at the desk she was directed to the ward, finding her father and Lizzie sitting by her aunt's bed, their faces drawn with exhaustion.

'Daisy! What on earth are you doing here?' her father spluttered.

'It's all right, Dad. Molly's looking after Vera. I had to come, I just had to,' she told him, approaching the bottom of the bed tentatively. No, that couldn't be her Aunt Edna! She looked so thin and haggard, like an old, old lady. 'Oh Dad,' she gasped, feeling tears brimming in her eyes. 'How is she?'

'Not good, I'm afraid, and you shouldn't have come, Daisy. It would have been better if you remembered her the way she was the last time you saw her.'

'But I had to see her, Dad. I wanted to thank her again for being so kind to me. I . . . I . . . love her,' she cried, the tears now cascading unchecked down her cheeks.

She felt a hand in hers, soft and clammy. 'Mum not well, Daisy.'

Seeing her cousin's distress Daisy took in great gulps of air, fighting to pull herself together. 'I know, darling,' she croaked, gently pushing Lizzie back towards her chair. Then, dashing her hand across her wet face, she walked around to the opposite side of the bed and gazed down at her aunt. 'Will I be able to talk to her, Dad?'

'I doubt it, darling. She's been unconscious since just after we arrived this morning.'

There was a soft groan, and without hesitation Daisy reached out to grasp her aunt's hand where it lay on top of the blankets. 'It's me, Auntie Edna. It's Daisy.'

There was no response, not even a slight movement from her aunt's fingers. 'Why is she groaning, Dad? Is she in pain?'

'No, I don't think so. It isn't long since she was given more medication. Look Daisy, now that you're here, why don't you take Lizzie down to the canteen for something to eat? She hasn't had anything since this morning.'

'But I've only just arrived and I don't want to leave Aunt Edna yet. You take her, Dad. It looks like you could both do with a break.'

Henry let out his breath on a long sigh and running his hand distractedly through his hair, he said, 'All right, maybe it would do us good to get out of the ward for a little while. Come on, Lizzie.'

'No. Stay with Mummy,' she said, shaking her head emphatically.

'Go with my dad and get something to eat, Lizzie. Maybe they'll have some nice cakes in the canteen,' Daisy urged, knowing that if anything would make Lizzie move, it would be the thought of food.

'Yes, cake,' she said, standing up. 'Get some for my mum too.'

Daisy saw her father's smile that looked more like a grimace of pain as he stood up. 'Well done,' he whispered. 'I haven't been able to prise her away from her mother. We won't be long.'

She nodded distantly, gazing at her aunt. Edna's breath was ragged and Daisy found herself inhaling and exhaling in time, almost as if she could will her aunt to keep breathing. 'Aunt Edna, can you hear me?' she asked.

Again there was no response, and as a nurse came to her side Daisy looked up, startled when she spoke. 'I couldn't help overhearing what you said. They say that even patients in a deep coma may be able to hear you – even if they don't respond. Keep talking to her,' the nurse advised before smiling gently, her face full of compassion as she moved away.

Leaning over the bed, and praying that the nurse was right, Daisy began to speak. 'Aunt Edna, thank you so much for taking me in, and for your kindness. You became like a mother to me . . . do you know that? Please don't worry about Lizzie. I promise that I'll always look after her. Oh Auntie, I love you so much,' she sobbed.

The nurse came back to her side. 'I'm sorry, my dear, the doctor wants to look at Mrs Wilkens. Would you mind waiting outside for a few minutes,' she said, whilst drawing the curtains around the bed.

Daisy scrubbed the tears from her cheeks again, and after a last quick glance at her aunt she left the ward to stand in the corridor. Looking back through the small window in the door she could see the drapes around her aunt's bed moving, and feet visible below. There seemed to be some sort of panic when a nurse suddenly threw the curtain aside, and rushing to the other side of the ward she grabbed a trolley, wheeling it back to the bed. For a split second Daisy could see a doctor leaning over her aunt, then the curtain fell back in place and everything was again hidden from view. Another doctor suddenly dashed along the corridor, thrusting Daisy hastily aside as he pushed through the ward doors. In the confusion she didn't hear her father and Lizzie until they were standing beside her.

'Got fruitcake for my mum. Her favourite,' Lizzie said.

Daisy's father must have seen the distress on her face because he asked urgently, 'What is it?'

'I don't know, Dad. But another doctor just went behind the

curtain so there's two of them with Aunt Edna now,' she told him worriedly.

Telling her to stay with Lizzie, Henry rushed into the ward. But on pulling back the drapes he was almost immediately ushered out again. With his face creased in anguish a nurse escorted him back to the corridor.

'Please wait in Sister's office,' she told them, gesturing to a room, her sympathetic smile encompassing them all. 'The doctor will come to see you shortly.'

'Did you see Aunt Edna? Is she all right, Dad?' Daisy asked, her voice coming out in a squeak.

'I . . . I think . . .' he gasped, unable to continue.

Lizzie made to run out of the room, surprising them with her perception as she yelled, 'Mum, Mum! No die, Mum!'

They managed to grab her, but Lizzie fought wildly, only ceasing her struggles when the door opened and two doctors came in. She stared at them, and before they said a word she began to cry, heart-wrenching sobs that made the hair on the back of Daisy's neck stand on end. 'Mummy dead!' she wailed.

It took them ages to calm Lizzie down, but they were now on their way to stay with Mrs Purvis for the night, reeling with tiredness. She took one look at their faces and ushered them in, fussing over them like a mother hen.

Daisy felt numb and everything had a touch of unreality about it. The lovely bone china tea set that Mrs Purvis carried in on a tray, the sandwiches laid out on a plate, she stared at them without comprehension. A cup was placed in her hand, but it didn't occur to her to drink from it, until Mrs Purvis gently admonished, 'Come on, my dear, drink your tea, and try to eat something.'

'What? Yes,' she murmured, absentmindedly lifting the cup and taking a sip. What were they doing here? Why weren't they at the shop? *Oh, Auntie, Auntie*, her mind cried. *You can't be dead, you can't!*

The room seemed to dim, the cup tilting and hot tea spilling onto her lap. Distantly Daisy heard a voice saying, 'I think she's in some kind of shock, Mr Bacon.'

'Daisy! Are you all right?'

Hearing the concern in her father's voice, she broke. Her shoulders heaved, and shaking with sobs, she gasped, 'Oh Dad, I was too late. She . . . she . . . didn't even know I was there.'

The sound of her cousin crying loudly finally penetrated Daisy's mind, and she realised how selfish she was being. Poor Lizzie had lost her mother and would need all their help to come to terms with her death. Instead of comforting her cousin, she was wrapped up in her own misery. Raising a hand Daisy quickly wiped her face and then crossed the room to kneel beside Lizzie.

When at last her cousin had calmed down again, Daisy saw that her eyelids were drooping with exhaustion. Her father must have noticed too because he suddenly said, 'It's gone eleven and I think we should all go to bed. We'll go home first thing in the morning and . . . oh dear, I should have rung Molly to see if she would mind staying overnight with Vera.'

'There's no need to worry, Dad. Molly knew it was unlikely that I'd be back, and she'd already volunteered to do that before I left.'

'It's kind of her, but I'm worried about Vera. She won't be happy with Molly looking after her. How on earth did you manage to pull that off?'

'Er . . . um . . . when we asked her again, she agreed.'

'That was very nice of her, Daisy. I know how much she hates to be looked after by strangers.'

'Molly isn't a stranger, Dad,' she told him indignantly.

'She is to Vera. They've hardly spoken to each other.'

'That isn't Molly's fault!'

'I didn't say it was, Daisy. What's the matter with you? Why are you acting like this?'

She lowered her eyes, berating herself. Her dad was already upset and now she was adding to his unhappiness. When she heard him defending Vera, part of her wanted to tell him, to blurt out the truth, but not now. She couldn't do it now. 'I'm sorry, Dad.'

'It's all right, darling, we're all distraught and not thinking straight. I'll have to come back to Puddleton almost immediately; there's the funeral to arrange, and I'll have to see your aunt's solicitor about the shop.'

'What will happen to it, Dad?'

'I don't know, though I expect it will have to be sold. It depends what instructions Edna has left in her will.' He yawned then, just as Mrs Purvis came back into the room.

'Goodness me,' she said, 'you all look worn out. Come on, girls, I'll show you where you'll both be sleeping. Mr Bacon, you're in the same room as before.'

'Thank you. You've been very kind,' he told her.

Daisy took Lizzie's hand, following Mrs Purvis upstairs. She led them into a room, a high, double brass bed almost filling the space. 'There you are, girls. I hope you don't mind sleeping together.'

'No, it's fine. Thank you, Mrs Purvis.'

'Bless you, love, you both look tired and it's no wonder. Poor Mrs Wilkens. She was a lovely woman and will be sorely missed in the village. What will happen to the shop now? And what about Lizzie?'

Daisy lowered her eyes. Mrs Purvis was being so kind looking after them like this, but she was a gossip and there was an avid gleam of interest in her eyes as she asked the questions. 'I'm not sure about the shop,' she answered guardedly, 'but Lizzie will come to live with us.'

'Oh, that's all right then, and what about—'

'Go home, go to shop,' Lizzie suddenly cried, her eyes beginning to fill with tears again.

'Shush, don't cry, darling,' Daisy soothed. Then turning to Mrs Purvis, she added, 'Thank you again, but I think I had better get Lizzie settled now.'

'Yes, of course. Goodnight, my dear, and if you need anything, just give me a shout.'

'We'll be fine,' Daisy assured her, relieved when she left the room.

Wearily she undressed, encouraging Lizzie to do the same. Her cousin was subdued, obviously exhausted from crying, and once in bed, snuggled close to her. It was a warm sultry night and Lizzie was wet with perspiration, so much so that Daisy had to fight the urge she felt to push her away. Thankfully her cousin fell asleep almost immediately, and moving carefully Daisy was able to ease a distance between them.

She lay staring up at the ceiling, and not wanting to disturb Lizzie she had to fight the tears that filled her eyes. Despite her exhaustion Daisy found herself unable to sleep as her thoughts were jumping from one thing to another. Thinking about her aunt was too painful and she found herself dwelling on Vera instead. Wondering what would happen when they returned home.

Chapter Thirty-One

Vera grabbed the rail that was suspended from the ceiling over the bed, and pulled herself up. She was desperately worried about her future, and despite taking a pill last night, sleep had been elusive. Vera knew that when Henry discovered how she had treated his daughter, he would never forgive her. It was just a matter of time before it all came into the open – and then what?

She ground her teeth with frustration. Christ, everything had gone wrong, and all her plans lay in ruins. If she weren't a cripple she would be out of this bloody house like a shot. *Oh Georgie, Georgie*, she agonised. *How can I get you back now?*

Vera watched as Molly came into the room, and sensing her anger she eyed her warily, nervously waiting for it to erupt. They had hardly spoken since yesterday, and Molly mostly attended to her needs without comment. She was a strong woman and lifted her effortlessly onto the commode when necessary. Vera had expected to be embarrassed at a stranger doing this, but Molly had a matter-of-fact attitude and left the room as quickly as possible.

When Henry rang last night, Molly had passed on his message, abruptly saying that Henry's sister had died, and that he would be back the next day.

Vera shivered, wondering how long it would be before Daisy opened her mouth. Yet even if she could persuade the girl to keep quiet, there was still Molly Carson and her husband Paddy to worry about.

Clenching the rail her shoulders began to ache unbearably, and it felt like her arms were being pulled from their sockets. It was agonising and she wouldn't be able to hold on for much longer, but dreaded asking Molly for help. Her stepdaughter always made sure she was in a sitting position every morning and only now was Vera realising how much she missed Daisy's help. 'Mrs Carson, would you mind piling my pillows up behind me so I can let go of this rail?' she asked desperately, feeling perspiration beading her brow.

Molly's lips tightened, but she put down the bowl of water she was carrying and did as she asked, pummelling the pillows vigorously and heaping them high.

Vera let go of the rail, sinking back with relief. 'Thank you,' she gasped, guessing that Molly wished it were her she was pummelling and not the pillows. Vera then allowed herself to be washed and changed, submitting to the woman's administrations without complaint.

Molly turned her one way and then the other, clicking her tongue with impatience. 'I don't know why you can't use a wheelchair. 'Tis difficult to change the bed with you in it,' she complained.

Vera said nothing. She felt helpless, trapped, and when Henry came home it would be even worse – a time bomb, just waiting to go off. How would she be able to stand it? For the first time in years Vera longed for her mother and tears filled her eyes. *Oh Mum, Mum,* she thought. *Where are you?*

It was only when Molly left the room that her words began to sink in. Wheelchair! Yes, there was a wheelchair – and if she could get to the phone she would be able to ring the Council to ask for her mother's new address. Vera waited impatiently for Molly to come back, her eyes on the door, willing it to open and saying hurriedly as soon as the woman returned, 'I've been thinking about what you said, Mrs Carson. I do have a wheelchair, and it's in the cupboard in the hall. Would you get it for me, please?'

'You've got one? Why didn't you say so before?'

'I've never used it.'

Molly threw her a look of disgust before leaving the room, her mouth set in a thin line, and only minutes later she was back, wheeling the chair through the door. Placing it by the side of the bed and throwing back the bedcovers, Molly said, 'Wrap your arms around my neck, 'twill make it easier.'

Vera did as she was asked, finding that the chair felt strange at first, but determined to use it she said, 'Would you take me into the hall, please? I want to use the telephone.'

Without comment Molly grabbed the back of the chair and pushed it through the door, leaving Vera to make her call while she bustled back to the kitchen. Vera glanced round, sensing that though the woman was out of sight, she was still hovering, waiting to listen to her conversation. Smiling grimly she lifted the receiver and spoke to the operator.

It didn't take long for her to be put through.

'What do you mean, you can't tell me her new address?' she cried, listening as she was told it wasn't Council policy to reveal confidential information.

'But it isn't confidential. She's my mother!' she told them indignantly.

Yes, she was told, but nevertheless they could not give out her address. They suggested that she write to her mother, care of the Council Offices, and they would forward her letter.

That was when Vera became hysterical. 'Write! How can I write to her? She can't bloody read!' she screamed down the phone.

But it was hopeless. No matter how much she cried and cajoled they refused to help. Defeated, Vera slammed down the receiver, tears of frustration streaming down her face.

The chair moved, and without saying a word Molly pushed her back into the sitting room. 'What do you want for your breakfast?' she asked curtly.

'Nothing, I'm not hungry.'

'Please yourself,' Molly said, and without further comment, she stalked out again. For what felt like hours Vera sat in the chair, slumped in defeat, but a quick glance at the clock showed her that only forty minutes had passed. Yet again her thoughts turned to her mother and she shook her head in despair. She glanced at her bed, finding herself glad to be out of it, and rebuked herself for being so stupid. At least in a wheelchair she had a modicum of freedom, and once she had learned how to manoeuvre herself around, there would be no need to be trapped in this one room.

Write, she thought again in disgust. Write, the Council had said. But wait – maybe it could work! If she wrote a short note, asking her mum to visit urgently, surely Ada would ask someone to read it to her? Yes, why didn't she think of that before?

Molly came back in then, duster in hand, and began to tidy the room, straightening the bed while wearing a grim expression. Why doesn't the bloody woman speak her mind? Vera thought. Why doesn't she just spit it out and get it over with?

Molly threw her a sour look, her mouth puckered as though she was sucking a lemon, and Vera glared back at her, fed up with being intimidated by this fat slut from next door. One day I'll make them pay – I'll make them all pay for this humiliation, she thought defiantly. 'Mrs Carson, I want a pad and pen,' she said. 'I've got a letter to write.'

'I'm not your lackey, get it yourself,' Molly snapped. 'You're not helpless, and 'tis about time you tried to do more for yourself instead of making Daisy wait on you hand and foot. Mind you, that won't last much longer,' she added darkly.

Just then there was a flurry of noise in the hall and the door flew open. 'Vera, what are you doing out of bed? Are you all right?' Henry asked.

'I'm fine. Molly got the chair out of the cupboard for me.'

He turned to Molly, surprise evident on his face, saying, 'Thank you so much for looking after her.'

''Twas no trouble, Henry, and I'm so sorry to hear about your sister.' Then walking across the room she laid a hand on his arm, adding, 'If you don't need me now, I'll be off home. But I'd like to speak to you in private when you can spare the time.'

'Is something wrong, Molly?' he asked.

'Yes, but 'tis nothing that can't be put right, and—'

Vera stiffened, hurriedly blurting out, 'You can go now, Mrs

Carson. I'm sure your family will be glad to have you back home.'

Molly's neck seemed to stretch, her head rising as though on a stalk. She glared angrily at Vera, obviously annoyed at being interrupted. 'As I was saying, Henry. Yes, there *is* something wrong. You see, I think you should know . . .' Then Molly stopped speaking abruptly. Her eyes softened, and as though she could see something in Henry's expression, her neck sank back like a tortoise into its shell. 'Look, don't worry about it now', she said. 'You've just lost your sister and I can see that you're worn out.'

'Yes, I must admit that I am. But I'll be round to see you as soon as I can, Molly, and thanks again for all you've done,' Henry said.

With a tight smile Molly left the room, and as soon as the door closed behind her Henry turned, his expression perplexed. 'Do you know what's wrong with her, Vera? She seems to have a bee in her bonnet about something.'

'No, I don't, but tell me, how is Lizzie?' Vera asked hastily, trying to divert his mind.

'The poor girl is in an awful state. She's going to need a lot of love and sympathy, Vera, and I will need to go back to Puddleton tomorrow. Will you be all right?' he asked anxiously.

'Yes, don't worry, I'll be fine. I'm angry with myself for not using this chair before, and it will make such a difference, Henry. I'll be able to wheel myself around, and even eat with you in the dining room again.'

The door opened and with a flurry Lizzie came in, rushing across to Vera where she sat by the window. 'My mummy dead,' she cried.

'Oh dear! Come here, darling,' Vera urged, holding out her arms.

Lizzie was about to fall to her knees beside the chair, but something checked her and she frowned at Vera. 'You going away,' she said bluntly.

'Of course I'm not going away. How can I? Don't be silly, my dear. Now come on, give me a cuddle.'

'No. No cuddle,' she said, and as Daisy joined them she ran across to her.

As Daisy held her cousin in her arms, Vera stared at the scene. She had dismissed what Lizzie said, but now wished she had questioned her further. Why had the girl said she was going – and going where? Was Lizzie making one of the predictions Daisy had spoken about? Determined to ask her, she called, 'Lizzie, come back over here, darling.'

Lizzie burrowed closer to Daisy, saying belligerently, 'No, don't want to.'

'Don't be silly – now come here at once!' Vera said impatiently.

'Leave her alone. Can't you see that she's upset?' Daisy said, her expression angry as she led Lizzie from the room.

Vera turned to look at Henry then, and seeing the puzzled expression on his face she said quickly, 'Oh dear, I think I've upset them both. I'm afraid I'm in rather a lot of pain this morning and it's making me rather short-tempered.'

Her husband rushed to her side, looking at her sympathetically. 'Don't worry, darling, I'm sure Daisy will understand. Would you like me to get your tablets?'

'Yes, and would you get me a drink of water?'

Henry rushed to do her bidding, and after tipping two pills into her hand, he went to the kitchen to fill her decanter.

Vera found herself trembling as the door closed behind him. Why hadn't she guarded her tongue? She had upset Daisy already and it was imperative that she kept on the girl's good side. Annoyed with herself, she knew that she would have to put things right between them. Sighing heavily Vera closed her eyes, praying that Daisy would keep her mouth shut until then.

Chapter Thirty-Two

Vera's nerves were on edge until Henry left for Puddleton again the next morning. She hadn't had a chance to talk alone with Daisy, but could already see an unbelievable change in her attitude. There was no fear in her stepdaughter's eyes now, and a defiant tilt to her head when she attended to her needs. She would have to speak to Daisy soon. Somehow she had to ensure the girl's silence, and the only way Vera could think of to do that would be to gain her sympathy.

Waiting until Daisy had helped her into the wheelchair and pushed her into the dining room, Vera grasped her stepdaughter's hand, saying quietly, 'I am truly sorry for the way I've treated you, my dear.'

'I should think so too. The way you punished me as a child was bad enough, and then you lied to get me sent to my aunt's. But worse was the blackmail.' She shuddered. 'For years I believed I was responsible for my mother's death, and you encouraged that belief. Why? Why did you do it?'

Vera hung her head. What could she say? She had to give the girl some sort of reason, and floundering she said, 'I realise I've been awful to you, but I think it's a result of my upbringing. I had a terrible childhood, Daisy, and we were unbelievably poor. You see, I . . . I was jealous of the way your father showered you with love. My father was a cruel man, who thought nothing of using me as a punchbag.' She lowered her eyes for a moment before looking up and saying contritely, 'Oh, I realise that's no excuse, but I really am so terribly sorry. Please, dear, can't we make a fresh start and put it all behind us?'

'No, I don't think we can. What you did is unforgivable,' Daisy snapped.

Vera nipped her lower lip between her teeth. She had been hoping that Daisy would soften, not only so she would keep her mouth shut, but also because she wanted her to go back to Battersea to find her mother's old friends. It would be quicker than writing and surely one of them would know where she had gone?

'Had my wash, Daisy,' Lizzie said as she came into the room.

'Good girl, come and sit down.'

'No, I eat in kitchen,' she cried, bustling out of the room again.

'Vera, I have to go to Lizzie. I really don't know what's the matter with her and she's never refused to eat in here before.'

Hiding her annoyance that Lizzie had broken into their conversation, Vera tried to look concerned as she said, 'It's to be expected really. After all, the poor girl's just lost her mother.'

Yet as Vera watched Daisy hurrying from the room, she couldn't help wondering about the look she had seen on Lizzie's face when their eyes met. She looked sulky, belligerent, and no longer ran to her for comfort. What was wrong with the girl?

'Lizzie, what's the matter? Has Vera upset you?' Daisy asked as she went into the kitchen.

'She go away,' Lizzie said cryptically.

'Vera isn't going anywhere, darling.'

'She is. Me no want her to go.'

Daisy shook her head. Poor Lizzie, she had just lost her mother and now she had somehow got it into her head that Vera was leaving too.

'Not hungry,' Lizzie suddenly said. 'Hot . . . I hot.'

Turning sharply Daisy looked at her cousin, noticing for the first time that her cheeks were flushed. Placing her hand across Lizzie's forehead, she was surprised at how warm she felt. 'I think you had better go back to bed, darling,' she said anxiously.

Without argument, Lizzie nodded, ambling slowly from the room.

Daisy followed behind, and once upstairs, helped her cousin into bed. Should she phone the doctor? she wondered. Vera started calling, and after a last glance at Lizzie, who appeared to be falling asleep, Daisy returned downstairs. 'What do you want?' she asked as she went into the dining room.

'I know I've got no right to ask you, Daisy. But please, would you go to Battersea for me?'

'No, I can't. Lizzie is ill and I may have to call the doctor.'

'She looked all right to me. It's probably nothing much, just a tummy upset or something, and I'm sure it won't hurt to leave her for an hour or so. Honestly, Daisy, I wouldn't ask you to go if it wasn't important. Can't you imagine how awful it is for me, not knowing where my mother is? I must find her, I must,' Vera begged.

Though Daisy hated her stepmother, she couldn't help feeling a surge of pity when she saw the desperation in her eyes. 'I really can't leave Lizzie,' she said, 'but when she's better I'll go to Battersea for you. Now do you want me to take you back to your room before I go upstairs again?'

'No, don't bother,' Vera said. 'I can at least try writing to my mother – maybe she'll get someone to read the letter to her. Would it be too much to ask that you post it for me?'

'Yes, of course I'll post it. Give me a shout when it's ready.'

As soon as the door closed behind Daisy, Vera's look became venomous. The little bitch, surely she could have left Lizzie for an hour or two? She grasped the metal rims around the edge of the wheels and struggled to manoeuvre the chair across the room. It took a little practice and she was perspiring by the time she reached the bureau, but felt triumphant at her achievement. There was usually writing paper and envelopes on top, but finding none Vera impatiently pulled at the desk lid, surprised to find it open. Rifling inside she took a sheet of writing paper, and began to compose her letter.

When it was finished Vera put it into an envelope, idly looking at the sheaves of bills and papers stuffed into the various compartments. A long white document caught her eye; one she was sure hadn't been in there before her accident. With a quick glance at the door she untied the ribbon and opened it, gently unfurling the thick parchment paper. Henry's will, she thought excitedly.

Her pleasure was shortlived however, when she read the contents. Other than making adequate provisions for her care, Henry's whole estate had been left to Daisy. Vera checked the date, her eyes narrowing. It had been drawn up a couple of months after the accident, and seeing that, her blood boiled. The bastard! How could he do this to her? God, she wished she had been successful in poisoning him now. Men – they were all the same – rotten through and through. First her father, then Lennie, and now Henry.

Lizzie's condition worsened and by late afternoon she was coughing and wheezing painfully. She refused all food and drank little, and when Daisy felt her forehead again she was alarmed at how hot it felt. In a panic she called the surgery, and it was a disgruntled Dr Taylor who arrived an hour later.

However, after examining Lizzie he pursed his lips and with a grave look said, 'She's got a nasty chest infection, and will need careful watching to make sure it doesn't develop into pneumonia.' Taking a pad out of his case he wrote a prescription for penicillin. 'Get this filled as soon as possible, and call the surgery again if there's no sign of improvement after forty-eight hours.'

After seeing the doctor out Daisy ran a hand over the perspiration on her face. The hot sunny day had changed, the air sultry as heavy clouds gathered. Lizzie finally fell asleep and knowing that this might be her last chance to get to the chemist, Daisy ran downstairs again, rushing into the dining room, 'Vera, I've got to go out, but I'll be as quick as I can. I just hope Lizzie doesn't wake up before I get back.'

'All right, but would you post this letter and get me some cigarettes?'

Daisy had to wait twenty minutes for the prescription to be filled. She then hurried to the tobacconist, hearing distant thunder as she left the shop. Within minutes the sky burst, heavy rain bouncing wildly on the pavement, and by the time she arrived back at Fitzwilliam Street she looked like a drowned rat. Her hair was plastered to her forehead, and her thin summer dress clung wetly to her body as she turned the corner, horrified when she bumped heavily into Liam.

'Whoops, easy there!' he cried, wrapping his arms round her. Daisy jumped back, her face flushing as she mumbled an apology. Liam's smile was mocking as he took in her appearance, and wishing the ground would open up and swallow her, she dodged past him, almost running the rest of the way home.

The telephone was ringing as Daisy rushed indoors and stumbling across the hall she quickly lifted the receiver, gasping, 'Hello.'

'Hello, Daisy,' her father answered. 'I'm afraid I won't be back for a couple of days.'

'Oh Dad! Can't you come back sooner than that?'

'Why! What's the matter? Is it Vera?' he exclaimed.

'No, she's all right. It's Lizzie,' Daisy told him, going on to explain her cousin's condition.

There was a long drawn-out sigh before her father responded. 'Listen, dear, I would come back earlier if I could, but there is so much to do here. I've made arrangements with an undertaker to transport Edna to a funeral parlour in Clapham; it will be much easier to hold her funeral in London than for all of us to travel back to Puddleton again. I've also seen her solicitor, and your aunt's will stipulates that the shop should be sold, with the first option going to her van driver. He's agreed to buy it, so that means I will have to do an inventory and stock-taking.'

Daisy held the phone to her ear, her thoughts racing. Lizzie would need care, and Vera still needed attention. How on earth could she manage on her own?

'Daisy, are you there?'

'Sorry, Dad, but I just don't know how I'm going to cope.'

'Darling, I'm sure you'll manage splendidly. If you get stuck you could ask Molly to give you a hand. I'm sure she wouldn't mind, and I promise I'll be back as soon as I can.'

'All right, Dad,' she said, trying to hide her dismay.

'Good girl. Give my love to Vera and I'll see you soon.'

'Yes, I will. Goodbye,' she said, slowly replacing the receiver.

Darting briefly into the sitting room, she almost threw the packet of cigarettes at Vera, and then ran upstairs to check on her cousin. Thankfully Lizzie was still asleep, and grabbing a towel, Daisy dried herself off. Then, with barely time to draw breath she hurried back downstairs again and into the kitchen. Would there be enough time to prepare something to eat before Lizzie woke, she worried, checking in the refrigerator for something quick and easy to prepare. Vera had asked when dinner would be ready over an hour ago, but she hadn't even started it yet. Deciding to make an omelette Daisy broke some eggs into a bowl and whipped them frantically. If she served it with some grilled tomatoes and thick slices of bread and butter, perhaps it would be enough to satisfy her stepmother.

Unable to face food herself, she carried the meal through to Vera. 'Dad just rang to say he won't be back for a couple of days,' Daisy told her. 'Lizzie is so ill, and I don't think I can manage on my own. My father suggested that I ask Molly to give me a hand.'

'No, don't do that,' Vera said quickly. 'If you just help me into bed at night, and then back into the wheelchair in the morning, I'll be fine. That will only leave my toiletries to attend to, and who knows, I might even be able to help out in the kitchen now. I could do things like peeling the potatoes and preparing the vegetables. I know that you must concentrate your energies on Lizzie and I won't be demanding, I promise.'

Daisy gawked at Vera, unable to believe her ears. 'Well . . . er . . . all right,' she stammered. 'Is there anything else you want before I go back upstairs?'

'No, I'm fine – you go and look after poor Lizzie.'

Shaking her head slowly in wonderment, Daisy left the room, returning to sit by her cousin's side.

Vera smiled as the door closed. Lizzie's illness had come at just the right time and before Henry returned, with any luck, she would have Daisy eating out of her hand.

Finishing her meal she manoeuvred her chair around, deciding to see if she could manage to wheel herself into the kitchen. At first she hadn't liked her door being left open, but soon realised that there was little choice if she wanted to wheel herself in and out of the room. Panting, Vera pushed herself into the hall, finding that negotiating the narrow space beside the stairs and then turning round into the kitchen door, was more difficult than she'd anticipated.

When at last she managed to get into the room it took her some minutes to regain her breath, and now Vera's gaze encompassed the cupboards. The bottom ones presented no problem, but it would be impossible to reach the higher ones. Pushing herself over to the sink she found that it was too high, and washing-up would be impossible. Still, at least she would be able to prepare simple food, and hopefully that would please her stepdaughter.

Lizzie was delirious, thrashing about and rambling incoherently during the night. Daisy bathed her cousin's forehead as she tossed and turned, hearing her calling for her mother over and over again. Daisy's heart went out to her; she too had lost her mother and knew how devastating it was.

When Lizzie finally settled, Daisy flopped back in the chair, exhausted, yet fighting to stay awake. Her thoughts drifted to Vera, amazed at how sweet she had been. She hadn't called her once during the evening, and when she went down to help her into bed her stepmother seemed genuinely concerned about Lizzie.

Time passed slowly and despite her efforts Daisy found herself dozing on and off, jerked awake every few minutes when Lizzie rambled. Her cousin's body was bathed in perspiration and the sheets needed changing, but not wanting to disturb her any more than necessary, Daisy decided to wait until morning.

Finally dawn crept over the horizon, and if she hadn't been so tired Daisy might have appreciated the beauty of the sky as its crimson glow reflected on the rooftops. Standing up stiffly she gazed down at Lizzie, seeing that at last her cousin was sleeping peacefully.

Softly leaving the room she padded downstairs and, careful not to make any noise, she put the kettle on, licking her parched lips in anticipation of a nice hot cup of tea. But on opening the fridge to get the milk, Daisy's heart sank. It was off, and she wrinkled her nose at the sour smell. God, now what? she thought tiredly, realising that it would be impossible to go shopping.

Pulling out a kitchen chair she slumped onto it. She had only had about an hour's sleep and her thoughts were fuddled, her eyes bleary. Molly! Yes, Molly. She would get some shopping for them. Glancing at the clock Daisy saw that it was far too early to disturb her neighbour, and was surprised to hear Vera calling.

Heaving a sigh she stood up, stiffly making her way to the sitting room, saying as she entered, 'You're awake early.'

'I took my pill at nine-thirty, and was asleep by ten o'clock. How's Lizzie this morning?'

'She had a dreadful night, and was delirious most of the time,' Daisy told her. 'I'm afraid I can't make you a drink yet, Vera. The milk has soured.'

'Never mind. I'll be happy with a glass of orange juice for now if we've got any.'

Nodding tiredly Daisy made her way back to the kitchen, and after pouring two glasses of juice she gulped one down herself before carrying the other, almost zombie-like, to the sitting room.

'Daisy, you look worn out, dear,' Vera said, sounding concerned as she reached out to take her drink. 'If Lizzie is resting quietly now, why don't you try to get a couple of hours' sleep while you've got the chance. Don't worry yourself about me. If you just see to my toilet needs before you go, I'll be fine.'

Smiling gratefully Daisy completed the tasks, and then went back upstairs. However, on opening Lizzie's door to see if she was still resting quietly, she found her cousin rambling again, tossing and turning, the sheets a tangled mess. Daisy realised that sleep would have to wait. Lizzie couldn't be left in that state and the bed would have to be changed.

Struggling, with Lizzie thrashing against her, Daisy was finally able to remove the damp bottom sheet, but it seemed to take ages before she was able to change all of the bedding.

Her cousin looked awful, and too nervous to leave her, Daisy once again settled herself in a chair beside the bed. She dozed fitfully until nine o'clock, and then seeing that Lizzie had settled again she decided to make a dash round to Molly's.

Splashing water onto her face and dragging a comb quickly through her hair, she rushed out of the house, running down Molly's basement steps.

Daisy's eyes widened when Liam opened the door, and babbling, she gasped, 'I . . . I need to see Molly.'

'She's gone to the school. Apparently Patrick has been up to mischief and Mam's got to see the headmaster,' he said, suddenly frowning as he took in her appearance. 'Is something wrong, Daisy?'

'My cousin's very ill and I can't leave her. I was going to ask your mum if she could get some shopping for me.'

'What do you need? I'll get it for you,' Liam said.

'Oh, would you? It's just milk and bread I need most urgently.'

'Right, go on home and I'll be back with it in a jiffy,' he said.

True to his word, there was a knock on the door only twenty minutes later, and as Daisy went to open it she found her head was swimming. She felt so hot and had difficulty focusing on Liam.

'You look awful. Have you had any sleep at all?' he asked.

'Not really, just the odd few minutes here and there.'

'Well, you're not fit to look after your cousin at the moment, that's for sure,' he said, scratching his head. 'Look, I've got the day off today, and I could sit with her while you get a couple of hour's sleep.'

'But are you sure . . .' She tried to go on but her brain refused to function.

With a smile of reassurance, Liam said, 'I'm sure I'll be able to cope with her for a while.'

'Who's that, Daisy?' Vera shouted.

'It's Liam – Molly's son,' she told her, crossing tiredly to the sitting-room door. 'He went to get some milk for us.'

'Oh, that was kind of him. Can I have a cup of tea now if it's not too much trouble?'

'Yes, of course,' Daisy mumbled.

'Show me where your cousin is first,' Liam said quietly.

In a fog she led him upstairs, and going into Lizzie's room was relieved to find her cousin still asleep. The room began to spin and Daisy clutched onto the bedpost.

'Go to bed,' she heard Liam say, his voice seeming to come from a distance. 'Do you hear me, Daisy? Go to bed . . . I'll see to them both for a while.'

'Tea, Vera wanted tea,' she croaked.

'Go – I'll see to it,' he ordered.

Daisy stumbled through the doorway, and reaching her own room she slumped across the bed, almost immediately falling asleep.

Liam stared at Lizzie, wondering what on earth had made him volunteer to look after her. Annoyed with himself, he made his way downstairs to the kitchen. It didn't take him long to find the necessities for making a cup of tea, and his task completed, he carried it through to Vera.

She smiled sweetly at him and Liam found himself studying her, his head on one side. Christ, he thought, she must have been a right beauty in her time, but now she looked a bit of a mess. How did Henry Bacon put up with living with a cripple? What about sex? Was it possible now? He would have loved to ask the question, finding himself titillated by the thought of making love to a woman who could only lie helpless beneath him, unable to fight back. One of the reasons he had broken up with Sandra was because she kept trying to take the initiative and her boldness turned him off. He knew she found his resistance surprising, but he told her he wanted to wait until they were married.

Liam liked his women passive so he could dominate them, and as he stared at Vera the thought of making love to her excited him. Feeling himself hardening he flushed, leaving the room hastily and telling her to call him if she needed anything.

Two hours later Daisy woke up with a start, and after glancing at the clock she jumped hastily off the bed, finding that for a moment the room seemed to spin. Hurrying into Lizzie's room she was relieved to see Liam sitting by her side, reading a newspaper.

'Hello, feeling better now?' he asked.

'Yes, and thank you. Has she been any trouble?'

'No, she's been asleep all the time. If you can cope now I'd better be off. Mam will be wondering where I am.'

'Liam, thank you so much for your help,' Daisy said again.

''Twas nothing. I expect my mam will call round when she knows what a fix you're in. Bye now,' he said, giving her a cheeky little wink that made Daisy's heart leap in her chest.

She watched him running down the stairs, then turned back to her cousin. Lizzie's face appeared awfully flushed, but at least she seemed to be sleeping peacefully. Was she over the worst, Daisy wondered as she made her way downstairs and into Vera's room.

'You still look awful!' Vera exclaimed as Daisy walked in. 'It was nice of Liam to keep an eye on Lizzie while you got some sleep, but it doesn't look to have done you much good. He popped down once saying that Lizzie was delirious for a while, but then she eventually settled.'

'Oh, he didn't tell me that,' Daisy said weakly.

'Come here and let me feel your forehead,' Vera said.

As Daisy leaned down in front of her, Vera placed a hand across her brow, her voice high as she said, 'Goodness, you feel like you're burning up! I think you're coming down with a fever, too. It must have been that soaking you got yesterday. You had better take a couple of aspirin before it gets any worse.'

Daisy nodded tiredly. 'I'll take some in a minute, but first I'll get you up. You must be sick of lying in bed by now.'

'Thank you, but after that I think you should try to get some rest. I can make myself a sandwich if I get hungry so you don't have to worry about me.'

'Are you sure?'

'Of course I am.'

Daisy had helped Vera onto her commode and then into her wheelchair, when she heard a shout from upstairs. 'Go, my dear. I'll be fine,' Vera urged.

Giving her stepmother a grateful smile, Daisy went back upstairs to find her cousin struggling to sit up. 'There, there, darling,' she soothed, endeavouring to get her settled. 'Lie down, it's all right.'

'Bad man. Bad man!' Lizzie cried, her head beginning to thrash from side to side.

Daisy frowned. Was her cousin talking about Liam again? Had she woken up at some point and seen him? When she finally managed to get Lizzie settled Daisy went to the bathroom, and finding some aspirin in the medicine cabinet she swallowed them hurriedly. Fever or not, somehow she had to carry on, and fighting her exhaustion she returned to sit by her cousin's side.

Two days had now passed and with little sleep for forty-eight hours, Daisy was at breaking point. Molly hadn't been round and at first Daisy had been surprised – until Liam called with a message to say that Frankie was ill too. When Molly undressed him she had found him covered in a rash that turned out to be measles. Liam had offered to help again, but Daisy had to decline his offer. Lizzie had been awake when she brought him into the bedroom, and her cousin had immediately become hysterical, screaming at him to go away. 'He a bad man, a bad man!' she cried over and over again. Liam's face had flamed as he hurried out, and Daisy had been mortified by Lizzie's behaviour. She had no idea why her cousin reacted like that every time she saw him, and gentle questioning hadn't helped. Lizzie refused to answer and after a bout of crying, she had fallen back to sleep.

Now, at one o'clock, Daisy was sitting by Lizzie again, her head throbbing despite the pills she had taken again that morning. She didn't hear her father arrive and jumped when she heard his voice, turning to see him standing in the doorway. 'Oh Dad, thank goodness you're back,' she said.

'You look awful, Daisy,' he said, his concern evident. 'How is Lizzie?'

'I think she's over the worst and she feels a lot cooler this morning.'

'Vera said you've been absolutely marvellous. Why didn't you phone me again? I would have come home if I had known you were ill too,' he gently cajoled.

'You said you had a lot to do, Dad, and I didn't like to bother you.'

'Well, I'm here now so go to bed, Daisy. I can take over.'

'Yes, all right. Did you get everything sorted out in Puddleton?'

'The sale of the shop still has to be completed, but that's about all. Oh, and your aunt has left you a little something in her will, Daisy.'

'Did she? That was nice of her.'

'You're to have a hundred pounds from her estate. She also appointed me as Lizzie's guardian and trustee, with provisions for her keep. The rest, amounting to many thousands of pounds, goes to Lizzie, with instructions for investments. Your aunt was a very clever and astute woman, Daisy.'

Her mind groggy, Daisy was unable to take it in. So much money, it was unbelievable. 'I don't think you'll need to do much for Lizzie for a while, Dad. She's sound asleep, but if she wakes up, are you sure you can manage?'

'Of course I can. Now off you go – you look like you're dropping on your feet. If you're no better in the morning I'll give the doctor a ring.'

'I'm better than I was, Dad, and once I've had some sleep I'll be fine.'

'We'll see – now go!' he urged.

Daisy climbed onto her bed, too tired to undress. Her thoughts seemed to be all jumbled, running from one thing into the other. She was thrilled that her aunt had left her so much money, but as yet unable to even think about what she would do with it. Vera had been wonderful, and Daisy still found it confusing. She was undemanding, and more self-sufficient now that she could wheel herself into the kitchen. Of course, she could only manage to prepare cold food like sandwiches and salad, but Vera had done this without complaint. Maybe her stepmother *was* trying to make amends, Daisy thought. Her eyelids grew heavy, and as she fell into an exhausted sleep, she wondered if they really could make a fresh start.

Chapter Thirty-Three

By the time her mother's funeral had been arranged, Lizzie had recovered sufficiently to attend. Yet it was a different Lizzie that Daisy observed as she saw her cousin staring listlessly out of the window. She had been up for two days now, but was dreadfully subdued and hardly spoke.

Her father came into the room and Daisy nodded her head towards Lizzie, indicating her concern.

Henry followed her gaze, his own forehead creasing, and taking his daughter's arm he led her into the hall, out of earshot. 'Don't look so worried,' he said softly. 'It's her mother's funeral today and she's bound to be upset.'

'I thought that at first, Dad, but I don't think Lizzie even knows what a funeral is. Yes, she's upset about Aunt Edna, but I'm sure there's something else worrying her.'

'She's been dreadfully ill, Daisy, and is still quite weak. Give her time, my dear. Lizzie has had a lot to adjust to.'

'Yes, maybe you're right,' she answered hopefully, adding, 'Is Vera ready?'

'Nearly, and I'm so proud of her. I could hardly believe it when she said she wanted to come to the funeral, and it will be the first time she's been out of the house since the accident. I know she hates the thought of people staring at her, yet she still insisted on attending.'

Daisy had to admit that her stepmother had been marvellous lately, and she was like a totally different woman. Earlier she had washed and styled Vera's hair, cutting off the last of the blonde tips and curling it under so that it fell gently onto her shoulders.

Her stepmother had been so delighted with it, that she had actually given her a cuddle. Daisy smiled now, recalling the delight Vera had shown with the black skirt that she had managed to find for her in Arding & Hobbs. Ankle-length, it completely covered her poor withered legs, and now that she had started to apply her make-up again, Vera was looking a lot more like her old self.

Daisy had almost decided not to tell her father about what had happened in the past. After all, Vera did seem genuinely sorry for all the awful things she had done.

Molly had wanted to tell him soon after he had returned from Puddleton, and it had taken a lot of persuasion to keep her quiet. It was Paddy who had stayed her hand, telling her that it was for Daisy to decide. Of course Molly had got into a huff, and still pressed her to tell her father at every opportunity, but Daisy just couldn't make up her mind to do it. Her father was still grieving, and it would only cause him further hurt and unhappiness. No, every time Daisy envisaged his reaction, she just couldn't face it.

The hearse would be here shortly, so returning to the dining room Daisy urged Lizzie into her jacket, and then gave her a quick hug. The funeral would be sparsely attended; just the four of them. Yet if it had been held in Puddleton the whole village would have turned out. Oh, Aunt Edna, she thought, and fearful of upsetting her cousin, Daisy struggled to quell her tears.

'It's time to go,' Henry called.

Leading Lizzie into the hall, Daisy watched her father carrying Vera down the outside steps. The undertaker opened the door of the large black car and Henry placed Vera gently inside.

Holding her cousin's hand Daisy then led her to the car. 'Get in, Lizzie,' she said and climbing in beside her cousin she averted her eyes from the hearse carrying her aunt's coffin.

It was the last week in September, with an Indian summer, and as Daisy looked out of the window she choked back a sob. How could the sky be so blue? How could the sun shine today? It should be raining . . . pouring . . . the sky crying just as she was. She saw both Molly and Paddy standing on the pavement, Paddy with his cap in his hand and head lowered in respect. Then the car moved slowly off. It seemed to crawl along at a snail's pace and Daisy wondered why, until she realised that the undertaker was walking in front of the hearse, leading it slowly down the road.

The atmosphere was sombre, yet as she brushed the tears from her cheeks Daisy suddenly heard Lizzie chuckle. In the silence of the car it sounded awful, obscene, and she turned sharply to see what her cousin was giggling at. A small boy was grinning at them through the window. Unreasonably, Daisy felt angry. How could anyone be laughing, or even smiling? Her aunt was dead! Her lovely, and kind, Aunt Edna.

Memories flooded back then, memories of her own mother's funeral, but then Lizzie suddenly lost interest in the boy and tuned to gaze at her. Looking down quickly, Daisy endeavoured to hide her feelings, but Lizzie grasped her chin, raising her face until their eyes met. Then, her head cocked to one side, and with a puzzled expression, she asked, 'What matter, Daisy?'

Grabbing her cousin's hand, Daisy felt a surge of guilt – just as she had in Puddleton. She was doing it again, focusing on herself instead of her cousin. Lizzie, poor Lizzie, had no idea that this was her mother's funeral, and instead of being wrapped in her own grief, she should be trying to help her cousin.

The funeral procession reached the end of the street and the car stopped momentarily. Daisy saw the undertaker take off his top hat before climbing into the front of the hearse, and then their speed picked up – until they reached the crematorium.

It was so quick! How could it be so quick? There was a hymn, and a prayer. Then words from the vicar that made Daisy shiver. '*Ashes to ashes. Dust to dust.*' Was that it? Was that all her aunt was going to be? Dust!

Then there was the sound of plaintive music as the curtains slowly closed, and Daisy had a last glimpse of the beautiful white lilies in the form of a cross lying on top of her aunt's coffin. She closed her eyes, thinking they looked repugnant. How could anything look beautiful today? Oh God, do You exist? And if You do – how could You let this happen?

She felt a soft nudge, and with a strained smile her father

indicated that they should leave the chapel. They filed out and for a while looked at the various floral tributes laid out on the grass, most sent from Puddleton. Daisy leaned forward and touched a beautiful pink rose, recognising it as one of her aunt's favourite flowers. Her father, seeing her action, plucked it from the wreath. With a sad smile he handed it to her, saying, 'Perhaps you could press it in your Bible.'

Then they were on their way home again. Lizzie was obviously bewildered, but seemed to have finally grasped what had happened. She sobbed all the way back, crying out for her mother; glancing at Vera, Daisy was surprised to see that she was crying too.

Subdued, they got out of the car, her father again carrying Vera, while Daisy lugged the wheelchair indoors. She felt tired and emotionally drained, but Lizzie was in an awful state and needed comfort. Like her, she had lost her mother, and Daisy knew exactly how that felt as she held her cousin in her arms.

Vera felt exhilarated. It had been wonderful to get out of the house and she found herself surprisingly unaffected by the stares of bystanders in the street. She was too enthralled to care as she breathed fresh air, felt a soft breeze against her cheeks, and looked up to see an azure blue sky. Then, as they slowly passed Clapham Common, she had gazed at wide stretches of grass and majestic oak trees, rich in foliage that was just beginning to turn gold. It had been uplifting, wondrous, and she felt like a child seeing the world through fresh eyes. Never again, she vowed, would she allow herself to be confined to the house.

Henry touched her shoulder as he wheeled her into the sitting room and Vera gazed at her bed with distaste. What a fool I've been, she thought.

'Would you like something to drink, darling?' he asked.

'Yes, a cold drink would be nice,' she told him, relieved when he left the room. She needed to think, to plan. Still unsure of Daisy, she lived in fear of her opening her mouth and was sick of pussyfooting around her, pretending to be all sweetness and light. She had even managed to squeeze a tear out of her eyes when in the car on their way back from the crematorium, and Vera smiled, recalling the look of surprise and even gratitude on Daisy's face.

Henry had placed her by the window and Vera looked out at the limited view, seeing in part the tall house opposite. She had lived in that house, in one poky room, and she grimaced when she thought about her nosy landlady. At one time she had thought it would be Olive Cole who would cause her the most problems. How wrong she had been. It was Molly Carson and her husband Paddy that she now feared. Yes, Daisy had told her that she had asked them not to say anything, but how long would that last? Molly despised her and it was doubtful that she would keep her mouth shut indefinitely.

No, it was no good, she had to have a bolt-hole, somewhere she could go if the worst happened. Gripping the arms of her wheelchair, her knuckles white, Vera felt anger mounting that her mother still hadn't been in touch. If the Council had rehoused her in a big enough place there was no reason why she couldn't live with her. All right, it wouldn't be ideal, but anything was better than this!

The walls began to close in on her again and Vera felt trapped, imprisoned. *Oh Mum, Mum, where are you?* she agonised. The door opened and she struggled to pull herself together as Henry walked in, carrying a tray.

'Here you are, darling. I've brought you a sandwich too,' he told her. Then his eyes clouded as he noticed her strained expression. 'What is it? You look upset.'

'Oh Henry, I would love to be able to go out more often, but with you being at work all week it's impossible. Those steps outside are like a barrier.'

'They needn't be, Vera. I'm sure we could have a ramp built to one side.'

'A ramp! How clever of you,' she enthused, her eyes lighting up. 'Can you arrange it straight away, darling?'

'Yes. In fact, I'll do it as soon as I've finished my coffee. I'm sure I can find a few builders to give me some estimates.'

Vera beamed at Henry with genuine delight. Oh, it would be

wonderful! She would be able to go out whenever she wanted. Her smile then widened as she suddenly realised that since she had told Henry the truth about her parents, there was no reason why she couldn't ask him to drive her to Battersea to find her mother. Oh, I've been so stupid, she thought. Why didn't I have the courage to go out before?

Chapter Thirty-Four

For the umpteenth time, Ada stared at the envelope propped on the mantelpiece. She knew it was from Vera, having travelled back to see her old doctor and asking him to read it for her. He had been good about it too, even though he again insisted that she'd have to sign on with a practice in her new area.

Ada looked around her sitting room, still unable to believe her luck. Her flat was on the ground floor of a small block of eight, and as well as this spacious sitting room she had a lovely modern kitchen, two bedrooms and wonder of wonder, her own bathroom. She could have a bath whenever she wanted and had stared in amazement at the Ascot providing all the hot water she needed. No more trips to the public baths once a week, no more going outside in all weathers to use the toilet.

She grinned to herself. Two bedrooms, that had been a nice surprise. Apparently the Council still had Vera registered as living at home, and Ada certainly hadn't enlightened them. Sighing with pleasure now she looked at her furniture. It had been her mate Lily who told her she could get a grant, and she had been quick to apply for one. The woman who had called to make an assessment of her circumstances had difficulty in hiding her surprise when she had seen her few belongings, and a grant hadn't been long in arriving. It wasn't a great deal, but by shopping around and trawling the secondhand shops Ada had got everything she needed, and after her old home she now felt she was living a life of luxury.

The fashion now was for light modern furniture, young couples showing no interest in old dark mahogany, or wartime utility pieces. Because of this she had found some nice stuff, and once again Ada gazed around with delight at the bargains she had found.

Her eyes strayed back to the mantelpiece and she felt a surge of guilt. Vera wanted to see her, and urgently, but she had ignored the message. It was obvious what the girl wanted – Lennie's address – and there was no way she was going to supply her with that information. But what if it was something else? What if Vera was ill?

Ada had made sure that she covered her tracks well, only telling Flo and Lily her new address. Reminding both her friends of Lennie's threats, she had warned them not to pass on her whereabouts to anyone. They hadn't heard that Lennie had called off the search for Vera – and until they did – she could be assured that they would keep their mouths shut.

So far, they both said, nobody had made any enquiries, and Ada had started to relax. If Vera sent that kid to Ingrave Street it wouldn't do her any good. Everyone had been rehoused and the street was empty. All the houses in the area were going to be demolished soon, and she had heard that a huge new estate was going to be built in their place. Tall tower blocks, some as high as fifteen floors, Flo had told her.

Levering herself to her feet Ada went into the kitchen to put the kettle on. Jack would be up soon and looking for a cup of tea. Jack Talbot – who'd have thought *he* would turn up after all these years? It had been a shock to see him, and strange really that he had arrived on the day she was moving. He had been standing gazing at the empty house next door, and at first she hadn't recognised him. Tall and gaunt, with his cap pulled low over his forehead, Ada had stared at him with suspicion until he turned to look at her. She had recoiled in shock at first, but seeing how ill he looked, this had soon turned to sympathy. Christ, I must be getting soft, she thought, as she poured boiling water into the teapot, because finding that he had travelled to London from the West Country and had nowhere to stay, she had offered to put him up.

Now weeks later he was still here, sleeping in her spare room, and as yet he hadn't said why he was back in London.

'Morning, Ada,' he said, making her jump, hot water spilling onto the draining board.

'Christ, Jack! You gave me a fright – I didn't hear you getting up.'

'Sorry, I didn't mean to startle you.'

'Well, come on in and sit yerself down,' she told him. 'What do you fancy for your breakfast? I've got a couple of slices of black pudding with a nice fried egg or two.'

'Yeah, great,' he said, pulling out a kitchen chair and sitting down.

Ada gave him a cup of tea, and then taking a frying pan out of the cupboard she dropped in a generous knob of lard, watching as it slowly melted. With her back towards him she then took the plunge, asking, 'Why 'ave you come back to London, Jack?'

Hearing his quick intake of breath and the rattle of his cup as he replaced it in the saucer, she turned quickly to look at him, but he lowered his head, avoiding her eyes.

'Sorry, forget I asked. It ain't none of my business,' Ada said hurriedly.

It was quiet then as she prepared their breakfast, and Ada's thoughts drifted. She could remember when Jack and Lena Talbot had moved next door to them in Ingrave Street. God, how she had envied Lena! Unlike her husband, Jack was a good man, and he had a fruit and vegetable stall down Northcote Road Market. Times were hard then, but even so he managed to make a good living and Lena didn't have to go out charring at the crack of dawn. Eventually though, she had struck up a friendship with Lena, and though she knew that Jack Talbot wasn't overly keen on her husband, the two couples began to go down to the pub together on a Saturday night.

Now, piling the man's breakfast onto a plate, she said, 'I know things went wrong, but before that we had some good times, didn't we? Do you remember when we all spent Christmas together? We had a right laugh.'

'Yeah, I remember, but that was before I found out what a

bastard your husband was,' he replied darkly. 'Why did you stay with him, Ada?'

'What choice did I 'ave? I had my Vera to think about and where could I 'ave gone?'

Jack sighed heavily. 'I couldn't stick it with Lena. But now I wish I'd let the cat out of the bag before I buggered off – at least then me name wouldn't have been ruined. Christ, Ada, I've heard how Lennie has turned out and he's a bad lot. The name Talbot used to be respected in Battersea and my family had a stall down the market for generations.'

'Yeah, I know you did. Well, until you scarpered that is,' Ada said. Then placing a hand over her mouth in horror, she gasped, 'Gawd, I'm sorry, Jack. I shouldn't 'ave said that.'

'No, it's all right. Yeah, I know I did a runner, but do you blame me?'

'Of course not. You had good reason, and it was me that persuaded you to keep quiet. We was such a tight-knit little community in them days, Jack, and can you imagine the scandal it would 'ave caused?'

'I know, and I did keep quiet, didn't I? But not any more, not after what Lennie's reputation has done to me name.'

'Eat your breakfast, it's going cold,' Ada urged. But as she picked up her own knife and fork his words sunk in, and her face stretched with horror. 'No, no, you can't say anything! Not now – not after all these years! Lennie idolised his mother, and if you destroy his illusions he'd go mad. God, you've no idea what he's like.'

'Yes, I have. Over the years I've kept in touch with a few of me old mates in the Borough. Don't you see, Ada, I want my name cleared before it's too late.'

'Too late? What do you mean, too late?'

Jack pushed the food around on his plate, before saying, 'I ain't got long to live, Ada – nine months at the most. Nah, don't get upset,' he added, seeing tears flooding her eyes. 'I've had a good innings, and now all I want to do is to set the record straight while I've still got time.'

'Oh Jack, I'm frightened. Lennie Talbot is a mad bastard, and you don't know what you're doing.'

'You ain't got nothing to be frightened about. He won't hurt you – why should he?'

Gulping with distress she placed her hand over his. 'Jack, there's something you should know,' and as Ada told him, she saw his face blanch.

Chapter Thirty-Five

'I'm sorry that we couldn't find anyone to tell us where your mother is, Vera. Those friends of hers you mentioned must have moved too. The whole area looks like it's being developed.'

'Thank you for taking me, Henry. I know how hard it must be for you to carry me up and down the steps, but it'll be easier once the ramp is finished. And yes, you're right, the whole area looks like a huge building site. Though I'm surprised the landlord of the Railway Arms couldn't tell us where my mother has moved to. It was her local pub for years.'

'Perhaps we could try the Council again?'

'No, it's pointless. You heard how adamant they were and how they repeated what they told me over the phone. I have to write to her via their offices and they'll forward the letter.' Vera shook her head dolefully. 'I've done just that, and written to her twice now.'

'Maybe she'll be in touch soon, darling,' Henry said, distressed to see Vera so unhappy. Yet it wasn't just Vera – he was worried about Lizzie too. She was still very subdued, and though he knew she was still grieving for Edna, he felt there was more to it than that.

Henry rose to his feet. Now that Lizzie had gone to bed, he decided to have a word with Daisy. Maybe she knew what the problem was with her cousin. Vera had settled back to watch the television, so after giving her a quick smile, he left the room.

'Daisy, do you know what's worrying Lizzie? She's hardly said a word for nearly two months now and I've noticed that she seems to avoid me,' he asked, stepping into the dining room.

'No, I'm as puzzled as you are, Dad. She seems to have been acting strangely since just before Aunt Edna's funeral.'

'Well, she did lose her mother, and I suppose that could account for her behaviour. Yet why does she shy away from me?'

Daisy frowned. It wasn't only her father that Lizzie avoided — it was all men. When they went shopping she veered away from them as though frightened. She had tried to talk to her about it, but her cousin refused to answer and just shook her head stubbornly.

They had fallen back into their old routine now, with Lizzie trailing behind her most of the time. It wasn't just her father she avoided in the house — she was sulky with Vera too. What would happen when the ramp was finished? Vera was so excited at the prospect of being taken out and talked endlessly about it. Yet if Lizzie refused to go with them, it would be impossible. After all, she couldn't leave her cousin on her own.

'You're the only one she talks to, Daisy, and things can't go on like this. We need to find out what's wrong with her.'

'Maybe I should take her to the doctor's, Dad. She's hardly eating, and lately I've noticed that she's sometimes sick in the mornings.'

'Is she? Why didn't you tell me before?'

'Because once she's been sick, she seems fine again.'

Daisy saw a look of horror pass over her father's face before he turned swiftly away, his back towards her as he strode across the room to gaze out of the window. 'Oh God. Oh God,' she heard him mumble.

Seeing his agitation she ran to his side, clutching his arm. 'What is it, Dad?'

He turned, his eyes stricken. 'Daisy, has Lizzie been on her own with anyone recently? I mean anyone of the opposite sex.'

'No, of course not. She never goes out on her own.'

His shoulders slumped and he sighed heavily, his relief evident as he said, 'I must be wrong then and it must be something else. Yes, take her to see the doctor, Daisy.'

*

The following morning Daisy took Lizzie to the surgery. She had been sick again soon after getting up, and once again refused to eat.

They sat in the waiting room, other patients staring at Lizzie as she hummed softly to herself whilst turning the pages of a comic.

Daisy felt a surge of protection. Why did people have to stare like that, as if her cousin was some sort of circus freak? She glared at them angrily, and most lowered their heads with embarrassment. Yet one lady instead of looking away smiled at her sympathetically, and that was almost as bad. Daisy wanted to shout at them – to tell them all that Lizzie was a wonderful person. That she was kind, caring, and loving, and not some sort of monster to be gawked at.

As if sensing her feelings Lizzie reached out and grasped her hand, dropping the comic in the process. 'What matter, Daisy?' she asked, her face full of concern.

'Nothing, darling, I'm fine,' she told her, reaching down to pick up the comic from the floor. Inhaling deeply to calm herself she turned a few pages, pointing out pictures of Desperate Dan holding a huge pie. Lizzie giggled, and shortly afterwards, it was their turn to see the doctor. Daisy stood up, and ignoring the other patients she took Lizzie's hand, leading her into the surgery.

'Miss Bacon, I would like to see your father,' Dr Taylor told her after examining Lizzie.

'My father! But why?' Daisy asked, worried by the expression on his face.

'There's something I need to discuss with him and it's most urgent. Would you ask him to see me as soon as possible, please.'

'Can't you tell me what's wrong with Lizzie?'

He smiled gently 'No, I'm afraid not. Your father is her guardian.'

'But I don't understand.'

'No, I don't expect you do, my dear. Now take your cousin home and please pass on my message,' he said shortly.

The next day Daisy stared at her father as he came in, hoping to gain reassurance from his expression. 'We need to talk,' he said abruptly, his face grim, 'but not in front of Lizzie.'

'She's asleep, Dad. She always seems tired lately.'

'Right, come on then. Vera needs to hear this too.'

Daisy followed her father into the sitting room where they found Vera looking out of the window, watching the builders at work. 'Hello you two,' she said brightly. 'The ramp's nearly finished, isn't it wonderful?' The smile dropped from her face when she saw Henry's expression. 'Goodness, you look awfully upset. What is it, dear?'

'It's Lizzie. I've got some awful news.'

'What did the doctor say? Surely it's nothing serious?'

'She's pregnant,' he blurted out.

'No, Dad. No, she can't be!' Daisy exclaimed.

'I'm afraid she is. Now the question is – who is the father?'

'Dad, it's impossible. I've told you, she doesn't go out on her own.'

'It isn't an Immaculate Conception, Daisy,' he snapped. 'If Lizzie doesn't go out alone then it has to be someone who's been in the house.'

'How far along is she, Henry?' Vera asked.

'About two months.'

Daisy closed her eyes, rapidly thinking back. She felt sick, dreadfully sick, and bile rose in her throat. No! It couldn't have been him! With her hand over her mouth she fled the room, just making it to the bathroom in time.

Afterwards, as Daisy splashed cold water onto her face, she knew she should rejoin her father and Vera. Yet at the thought of telling them, she trembled.

'Are you all right?' she heard her father call.

'Yes, I'm just coming.' Slowly making her way back downstairs she entered the sitting room, and immediately noticed the strange look that Vera gave her, one that was almost calculating.

'Yes, Daisy, I can see by your face that you've worked it out too,' she said, adding as she swivelled her chair to look at Henry, 'You had better sit down, my dear. This is going to be another shock for you, I'm afraid.'

'Why? Do you know who the father is, Vera?' he asked sharply.

'I think so. Do you remember when you went to Puddleton to sort out your sister's estate?'

'Yes, of course I do, but what is this leading to?'

'Well, you'll also recall that Lizzie was ill at the time, and poor Daisy had a fever too. She hardly had any sleep for days and . . .'

'Yes, yes, I remember,' he said impatiently. 'For goodness sake get to the point, Vera. What has this got to do with Lizzie's pregnancy?'

'If you hadn't interrupted me so rudely, Henry, you would have found that I was just coming to that. Now as I said, Daisy was exhausted, and when she couldn't go to the shops, Molly's son Liam kindly went for us. He also offered to sit with Lizzie for a while to enable Daisy to get a few hours' sleep and—'

'You're not suggesting that he . . .' Henry blurted out, shaking his head in bewilderment as he cried, 'No! I just don't believe it!'

'It has to be him, Henry. He's the only man who's been alone with Lizzie,' Vera insisted.

'Daisy, is this true?'

She hung her head, still feeling nauseous. Sex was still largely a mystery to her. Yes, she knew a little about it because Molly had told her a few things when she had started her periods. But other than that, all she had heard was playground talk, girls giggling, whispering in corners. 'It's true that Liam was alone with Lizzie,' she finally managed to say.

'My God, it's disgusting! How could he?' Henry ground out, his teeth clenched in anger. 'Right, I'm going round to see him. He's not getting away with this.'

'I'll come with you, Dad.'

'No, you won't. You'll stay here with Vera,' he ordered, marching swiftly out of the room.

'No! Begod no! How dare you accuse my son of such a thing?' Molly said indignantly.

'He's the only man who's been alone with her. It has to be him.'

'You're mad! You've lost your mind. Liam wouldn't touch that . . . that . . . thing!'

Henry's face reddened. 'Molly, how dare you call my niece a *thing*! God, I can't believe you actually said that.'

'All right, I'm sorry, but what do you expect when you come round here making false accusations against my son?'

'It is not a false accusation, Molly. Liam's the only one who had the opportunity. Now, I'll ask you again. Where is he?'

'Henry, you're mad! You're off your head, and I'm not letting you near my son!'

'Where is he? *Tell me where he is*!'

'No! Now get out of my house, Henry Bacon!'

'I'm not going anywhere until I've spoken to him, Molly, and if you're so sure that Liam's innocent – let's hear him deny it.'

'Why you . . . you . . .' Molly spluttered as she marched to the bottom of the stairs. 'Liam, come down here!' she yelled.

'Yes, what is it, Mam?' he asked as he clattered downstairs and into the kitchen.

'Go on then, Henry. Go on – ask him!' Molly shouted.

'Did you take advantage of Lizzie?' Henry spat, staring at him with distaste.

Liam's face flooded with colour. 'No, of course not. What do you take me for?' he cried.

'You were alone with her for a few hours, and you're the only one that had the opportunity. Now I'll ask you again. Did you touch my niece?'

'No, I bloody didn't. Mam – tell him!' he yelled.

'Right, you heard my son. Now get out!'

'He can deny it all he likes, Molly, but take a look at his face. The truth is written all over it!'

To Henry's utter astonishment he saw Molly advancing across the room towards him. Her face was suffused with anger and spittle sprayed from her mouth as she screamed, 'I said get out, Henry! Do you hear me? Get out!' and throwing back her arm she slapped him hard across the face.

'All right, I'm going, but you haven't heard the last of this,' Henry told her, rubbing his stinging cheek. Then, throwing a look of disgust at Liam, he cried, 'Lizzie is pregnant! Do you hear me? She's pregnant, and it's *your* child, no matter how much you try to deny it!'

'I didn't touch her . . . I didn't!' Liam protested loudly.

'My God, you disgust me! You're an animal!' Henry roared as he strode out of the door. 'I'll be back. What you did to Lizzie amounts to rape, and the police will want to talk to you.'

'God, the man must be mad!' Molly cried, her face livid as the door slammed behind Henry. 'To accuse you of such a dreadful thing.'

Liam just stared at her, his face still flaming, and at his expression she felt her stomach lurch as a dreadful suspicion began to fill her. 'No, Liam! No! Tell me it isn't true!'

He didn't answer, his head lowering as he avoided her eyes. It couldn't be true, Molly thought frantically. Liam wouldn't touch that poor retarded girl. 'Answer me, son!' she demanded.

Without a word he ran from the room, his footsteps pounding up the stairs, and feeling faint with shock Molly almost fell onto a chair. She gasped, huge shudders shaking her body. Then leaning forward she laid her arms full length across the table as though in supplication. Her head went down, the wood hard and cold against her forehead as she began to sob, 'No, please God, no! Oh Liam, Liam! Mary, Mother of Jesus, help me! Please help me.'

Liam searched his own room and then his mother's, frantically looking for a suitcase. The police, Henry Bacon was going to report it to the police, and he was desperate to get away before they came to question him. Finding a battered old case under his mother's bed he hastily began to throw his belongings inside, his thoughts in turmoil.

God, it wasn't his fault; he just hadn't been able to stop himself when he saw Lizzie lying helpless in bed. It had started with Vera . . . and he remembered how he'd imagined making love to her. Embarrassed that his excitement might be showing, he had rushed back upstairs. But then, sitting beside Lizzie, instead of calming down, his lust had reached fever pitch. He had squirmed in the chair, touching himself as she gazed at her. He had to have her! Had to have relief – and mindlessly he climbed onto the bed.

Thinking about it now, Liam found his excitement mounting again. Helpless, Lizzie had been helpless as he held his hand over her mouth. He pictured that other girl again – the one who had laughed at him. Lizzie didn't laugh. No, all he saw in her eyes was fear. And he loved it. Loved the feeling of power.

Slamming the suitcase shut, Liam's thoughts went back to that day during the school summer holidays when he was fourteen. He had gone to his friend's house, but his sister Dora had opened the door, saying he was out. With a warm smile she had invited him in to wait, and like a mug, he'd agreed.

Dora was seventeen, and alone in the house she had flirted shamelessly with him. She was brazen – exciting – as she led him up to her bedroom. His eyes wide, and his mouth dry, Liam had watched as she slowly and provocatively undressed, seeing a girl in just her bra and panties for the first time. God, he had nearly burst with excitement. She had reached out, pulling him onto the bed, and now he closed his eyes in shame at the memory . . .

Undoing his trousers, Dora's hand had slipped inside, and with a knowing smile she had grasped him. It was too much, he couldn't hold it – couldn't restrain himself, and at her touch he exploded, panting as he lay beside her, his face red with shame.

Dora had laughed at his embarrassment, but it hadn't ended there. 'My,' she had said, 'you'll have to do better than that if you want to please a girl.' Slowly she had begun to arouse him again, and as she stripped off her bra and panties he felt himself reaching fever pitch.

Dora teased him, played with him, until at last, when he didn't think he could stand much more, she had pulled him on top of her. Fumbling, he had tried to enter her, his inexperience making him clumsy. Tutting with impatience she had taken over, and as soon as he felt her closing around him he had exploded again, unable to restrain himself.

Dora went mad then. She screamed and shouted that he was useless. He was less than a man, she yelled, and would never be able to satisfy a woman. He had dressed hastily while she continued to belittle him, and the last thing he heard as he fled the room, was the sound of her hysterical laughter.

Shaking off the painful memory, Liam pulled his suitcase off the bed, and holding it clasped in his hand he looked around the room. Where could he go? What would he do for money? Women – bloody women – he hated them! Dora had opened his eyes, and he saw them for what they were. They were all the same. Tarts – they were all tarts!

After his encounter with Dora he had never had the nerve to try it on with another girl, unable to stand the thought of being laughed at again. It had been all right with Sandra for a while, but once they got engaged she had started to become brazen too, just like Dora. God, it made him sick the way she threw herself at him.

As Liam came downstairs and stepped into the kitchen, Molly saw the suitcase in his hand. Jumping to her feet she frantically grasped his arm. 'No, son, don't leave home – please, don't go!'

'I've got to, Mam. You heard what Mr Bacon said – he's going to the police.'

'But where will you go?'

'I don't know, but I've got to get away.'

'Why did you do it, Liam? What possessed you?'

'Please, Mam, I can't talk to you about it,' he told her, his face flaming.

'Oh son, I can't believe it of you, and to make that poor girl pregnant.'

He closed his eyes against the pain in his mother's face, only able to whisper, 'I'm sorry.'

'You could go to my sister in Donegal. You'll be safe there.'

Ireland! Why hadn't he thought of that? He watched his mother now as she scuttled over to the old dresser. Opening a drawer she rifled inside and then pulled out a dented tobacco tin. 'Here, take this,' she said, thrusting it into his hand.

'What is it?' he asked, puzzled. He pulled off the lid, gasping when he saw the wad of notes and loose silver stuffed inside.

'It's fifty pounds, Liam. I've been saving a little every week for years. It's my nest egg.'

'But I can't take this, Mammy!'

'Yes, you can. You have to get away, and I see that now. Go to your Aunt Kathleen, she'll take care of you until you can get on your feet again.' Reaching out, Molly pulled him into her arms, her voice a choked whisper as she said, 'Write to me, son. Promise you'll write to me.'

'Yes, I promise,' he answered, pulling himself out of her arms, and without looking back he almost ran out of the door.

'Oh Liam, Liam!' he heard his mother wail before the door slammed shut.

Chapter Thirty-Six

'But, Dad. Why has she got to have an abortion?'

'There's no other choice.'

'For goodness sake, Daisy, think about it,' Vera intervened. 'How could Lizzie manage to look after a baby? She's just a child herself.'

'Yes, I understand that, but couldn't we look after the baby?'

'No, definitely not,' and seeing his daughter's expression Henry's voice softened. 'Listen, darling, Dr Taylor doesn't think that Lizzie is mentally able to continue with the pregnancy.'

'But . . .'

'Daisy, I'm sure this is the right decision,' he interrupted. 'We're to take her to the hospital on Tuesday morning, and I can tell you it hasn't been easy to arrange. Two doctors had to sign the consent form with all the grounds presented before an abortion would be allowed. Not only Lizzie's weak health, but her mental condition was taken into consideration, along with the fact that she had been raped.' He ground his teeth. 'I'm still sorry in some ways that I didn't put the police onto Liam. He deserves to be punished for what he did.'

'Molly's still in a dreadful state, Dad. She's heartbroken about it and is so ashamed of him.'

'I know. It was courageous of her to come to see me, and though I told her not to blame herself, she's still wracked with guilt. It was seeing the state she was in, and the effect it would have had on Lizzie if she was questioned by the police, that stopped me reporting Liam to the police.'

'Molly feels that she must have been a bad mother, and nothing

I can say will convince her differently. Paddy's no help either – it's knocked the stuffing out of him too.'

'Time is a great healer,' Vera said flippantly, using the age-old adage. 'Have you explained things to Lizzie, Henry?'

'No, I'm afraid not. How do I explain something like this to her? She doesn't even understand that she's pregnant.'

'Would you like me to talk to her?' Vera asked.

'Would you, darling?'

'Of course, but does Lizzie need to know the truth? Can't we just tell her that she's having a little operation?'

'Yes, good idea. In fact, it might be better if it comes from Daisy. Lizzie trusts her above any of us.'

Daisy had gently told Lizzie that the doctor had found a little thing wrong with her and that was why she was being sick all the time. However, trying to make her understand the concepts of an operation proved impossible, but she trustingly held Daisy's hand as they took her to the hospital.

The worst part had been leaving her. Lizzie had cried pitifully, but the ward sister was strict and insisted they had to go, her mouth set as she reminded them that they would only be able to see Lizzie during visiting hours.

It had been awful walking out of the long and clinical ward. Seeing Lizzie's look of terror when she glanced back at her, Daisy had turned on her heels, running back to the bed and enfolding her in her arms – until the ward sister had bustled to their side again, saying sharply that she had to leave.

'Don't worry, I'll keep an eye on her, love,' the women in the next bed said, and seeing her kindly smile, Daisy felt a little reassured. Yet her mind was still in turmoil as she left the hospital. Oh, if only they could have kept the baby. She would have looked after it, loved it, and feeling her eyes filling with tears, Daisy wondered why life was so cruel.

That evening they returned, relieved to see that Lizzie looked much happier. As promised, the lady in the next bed had befriended her, and Daisy smiled to see their easy interaction. It was unusual to see someone in a rapport with Lizzie so quickly, but the lady whispered that her sister had a daughter just like Lizzie, though a little younger.

Lizzie was to have her operation the next morning and Daisy bit her lip painfully as she sat beside her cousin. Once again she thought how awful it was that the tiny life inside Lizzie was going to be destroyed – was it a boy or a girl? She tried to dispel the awful image of the operation from her mind, her thoughts turning to Liam. God, how could he have done such a thing? And how could she have ever thought herself in love with him? Yes, he was good-looking, with his wonderful deep green eyes and perfect smile, but all that just disguised a monster.

She was startled when she heard the bell signalling that visiting time was over, but this time Lizzie didn't become upset as they left. She smiled at them so innocently and happily as they left the ward, that it brought tears to Daisy's eyes.

'Daisy, now that the ramp is finished, would you mind taking me out?' Vera asked hesitantly the next morning.

'But Daddy said I shouldn't attempt to use the ramp until he had checked that I could manage it.'

'Oh, it can't be that difficult, Daisy. Please, my dear, I don't think I can bear to sit here all morning worrying about Lizzie. The walls feel like they're closing in on me, and I thought a little walk might take our mind off of it.'

Daisy bit her lip. She too was feeling the strain, and like Vera she needed to get out of the house for a while. After a moment's hesitation she said, 'All right, I don't suppose the ramp can be that hard to use.'

'Of course it won't. And, Daisy, before we go there's something else I've been meaning to say to you. Thank you for not telling your father about the way that I treated you. It's more than I deserve.'

'Let's just forget it, Vera. The past is the past, and we said we'd make a new start.'

'I know, but I still wanted to tell you how much I appreciate you giving me a second chance.'

Daisy smiled, and walking behind the chair she pushed Vera into the hall. Opening the front door she looked at the ramp nervously. Spanning six steps it looked awfully steep and bracing herself she tentatively moved the wheelchair over the edge. It was harder than expected, and Daisy clung onto the handles, her face stretched with fear as she tried to control the speed. 'Grab the wheel rims, Vera!' she shouted as she hung on tightly, pulling back with all her might.

Vera, ignoring her instruction, cried out, her arms thrust out in front of her in terror. They were almost at the bottom of the ramp now, with Vera's weight and the huge wheels making it impossible for Daisy to slow the momentum. She had to stop the chair somehow, she thought frantically, or they would end up in the road!

Her strength was ebbing and just as she opened her mouth to yell, the chair came to an abrupt halt. Daisy's eyes were wide with shock, and as they alighted on their rescuer she cried, 'Oh, thank you. Thank you, Sean!'

'Sure 'tis nothing,' he said flippantly, sounding so much like Molly with her Irish brogue that it made Daisy smile, especially as she knew he had been born and bred in London.

'That was our first attempt,' Daisy confessed, 'and it was harder than I expected.'

Vera smiled charmingly at Sean. 'Well done, young man. I think you averted what could have been a nasty accident.'

'That's all right, glad to have helped,' he answered, adding as he looked at Daisy, 'Can you manage now?'

'Yes, thanks to you.'

'I . . . er . . . I've been wanting a word with you. I want to apologise for what Liam did.'

'There's no need for you to apologise, Sean. It wasn't your fault.'

'I know, but we're all so ashamed, Daisy. And for him to run off like that. How is she – your cousin, I mean?'

'She's having a termination this morning.'

'God, I didn't know. Have you told my mother?'

'No, we haven't,' Vera told him shortly, breaking into their conversation.

'But don't you think you should? Surely she's got a right to know?'

Embarrassed by Vera's bluntness, Daisy said, 'Sean, I'm sorry, but my cousin only has the mind of a child and her health isn't strong. It was all arranged so quickly and it didn't occur to me to tell your mother.'

'That Liam,' Sean spat, shaking his head with disgust.

'Can we go now?' Vera said impatiently.

Daisy nodded distantly, thinking that Sean was so different now from the boy who had teased and bullied her just a couple of years ago. She had hardly seen him since coming back from Puddleton. Molly had told her that he had a job working night shifts as a machine minder at a local printers, and spent most of his spare time at the boxing club. What happened to Lizzie hadn't been his fault, and it was nice of him to apologise.

'Bye,' she whispered, giving him a small smile before turning to wheel Vera along the road, determined now to see Molly later on. She wasn't to blame either, and though both she and her father had tried to reassure the woman, so far it hadn't helped. Molly had lost the twinkle in her eyes and cried incessantly whenever she went to see her. Sean was right though, Daisy thought guiltily. She should have told Molly that Lizzie was having the baby aborted today.

At two o'clock Daisy stepped nervously into the ward, her eyes lighting up when she saw Lizzie sitting up in bed. She looked a little pale and tired, but there was a smile on her face as she approached the bed. ''Lo, Daisy,' she said.

'Hello, darling, how are you?' she asked, bending down to kiss her on the cheek.

'I all right. Isn't I, Kate?'

'Yeah, of course you are, darling,' her neighbour answered, adding as she beamed at Daisy, 'She's a good kid, and woke up almost as soon as she was brought back to the ward.'

Daisy heaved a sigh of relief, and pulling out a chair she sat down by Lizzie's side. 'You'll be coming home soon,' she told her, taking her hand.

'Kate come too?'

Disconcerted and smiling ruefully, Daisy said, 'No, dear, Kate has her own home to go to.'

'Come see me?' Lizzie appealed, turning to look at her new friend.

'Course I will, ducks.' Gingerly throwing her legs over the side of the bed, Kate came to sit next to Daisy, asking when she was settled, 'Would it be all right if I came to visit Lizzie?'

'Er . . . well, yes I suppose so.'

'Bless you, don't look so worried. I won't intrude if it would cause any problems.'

Daisy smiled at Kate, liking her more and more. She seemed to have such a warm, motherly nature, and it was easy to see why Lizzie had taken to her. 'No, it won't be a problem, please come,' she invited.

They went on to exchange addresses, surprised to find that they only lived a few streets apart. Kate went on to say that since her sister had moved to Devon she didn't have any family living close by. Daisy could sense her loneliness and her heart went out to her. Glancing at Lizzie she was surprised to see that while they had been talking, her cousin had fallen asleep.

'She reminds me so much of my niece, Judy,' Kate said, a soft smile on her face as she too looked at Lizzie. 'She's going to be fine though and was only down in theatre for a short time. What did she come in for?'

Daisy felt her face flooding with colour and she quickly averting her eyes, stammering, 'She . . . she . . .' unable to think of an excuse.

'It's all right. By the look on your face I can guess,' Kate told her, patting her gently on the shoulder. 'But how on earth did it happen?'

'She was raped,' Daisy told her, adding as she felt a lump rising in her throat, 'and if you don't mind, and I'd rather not talk about it.'

'Sorry, it's none of my business. The poor kid though – did she know that she was pregnant?'

'No, we thought it better not to tell her. Lizzie has such a low mental age, and I don't think she would have understood.'

'I'm sure you made the right decision, though what sort of bloke could do that to her doesn't bear thinking about. Now, are you sure it will be all right for me to visit Lizzie when you take her home?'

'Yes, of course,' Daisy answered, going on to explain about Vera.

'Gawd, you've got your hands full for such a young'un!' Kate exclaimed.

They chatted for a while longer, then seeing that Lizzie was still asleep, Daisy got up to leave. 'I'll be back later with my father,' she told Kate.

'Righto, ducks, I'll see you again then. And don't worry, I'll watch out for her.'

Smiling her thanks, Daisy left the ward, hoping Vera and her father wouldn't object to Kate paying them a visit.

As she left the hospital grounds and began to walk home, Daisy was surprised to see Sean strolling along on the other side of the street, his head down against the biting wind and hands stuffed into his pockets. He lifted his head to glance across the street and seeing her he rushed to her side.

'Have you been to see Lizzie?' he asked immediately.

'Yes, and she seems fine.'

'I told Mam and she's a bit upset.'

'Perhaps I should pop in to see her now. Vera should be all right for another half an hour or so.'

Sean frowned. 'I know all about your stepmother, Daisy. In our small flat it's difficult not to hear things when my mam and dad are talking. How do you put up with it?'

'Oh, it's not so bad now.'

They had reached his house and Sean stepped to one side, allowing Daisy to go down to the basement ahead of him.

'Oh, so you've come to see me at last,' Molly said sharply, 'I suppose you had better come in.'

As Daisy walked into the kitchen, Molly told Sean to go upstairs. 'Why, Mam? Why have I got to leave?' he asked.

'I want to talk to Daisy in private,' she snapped.

Throwing her a sympathetic glance, Sean left the room, and as soon as he was out of sight Molly glared at her angrily. 'Don't you think I had a right to know that Lizzie was having the baby aborted?'

'I . . . I'm sorry, Molly, I didn't think. It all happened so quickly, you see.'

'Well, youse lot seem to have forgotten that despite everything, it was still my grandchild,' she cried before tears flooded her eyes.

'Oh Molly, please don't cry! Lizzie *had* to have an abortion. She wasn't mentally capable or strong enough to continue with the pregnancy.'

'I know, Sean told me, and I expect you think I'm being silly. It's just that I don't believe in abortions. 'Tis a sin against God to take an innocent life.'

'We didn't have any choice,' Daisy told her again, and walking to her side she put an arm around Molly's shoulder. 'Please, try to understand that it was the only thing we could do.'

It was quiet then and only Molly's snuffles filled the silence. Finally she wiped her eyes, saying, 'I'm sorry, Daisy, I suppose I've no right to be angry, or to take it out on you. It's all been such a shock, and I still feel so deeply ashamed about what Liam did to the poor girl.'

'Have you heard from him?'

'No, not a word,' she sobbed, 'and his father doesn't *want* to hear from him. Paddy said that as far as he's concerned, Liam is no longer his son.'

Daisy patted Molly's arm ineffectually, knowing there was nothing she could say to comfort her. She felt the same as Paddy – she never wanted to set eyes on Liam again.

'He'll never be able to come home again, Daisy. As soon as he shows his face the police will arrest him.'

'No, Molly, my father didn't report Liam to the police. He felt that Lizzie wouldn't be able to cope with the questioning.'

'Why didn't he tell me?' the woman flared up again. 'God, I've been worried sick, and expecting them to catch my boy every day.'

'Molly, we've all been in such a state worrying about Lizzie and obviously our wires have crossed. I agree that my father should have told you. I assumed you knew.'

Molly pulled an old handkerchief out of her apron pocket, and after blowing her nose loudly, she said, 'I know Liam deserves to be punished, Daisy. What he did was a terrible thing. But despite everything he is still my son, and I can't help worrying about him.'

'Yes, and Liam has always been your favourite,' Sean said, surprising them as he stepped into the room, his voice hard as he added, 'But he's rotten, sick, and I agree with Dadda. I hope he never shows his face again.'

'You shut your mouth!' Molly shouted.

'I had better go,' Daisy said hurriedly as she saw Sean's face darken with anger. She had no sooner shut the door behind her than she heard the sound of raised voices. Sean's equally as loud as his mother's.

Chapter Thirty-Seven

Lizzie developed an infection that prolonged her stay in hospital, and it was now two weeks since she had had the abortion.

When Kate left a week earlier, Lizzie had been dreadfully upset, so much so that her new friend came back to the hospital every day to visit her.

During one visit Daisy asked Kate why she had been in hospital, embarrassed when Kate had gone on to describe her gynaecological problems in graphic detail. The woman then went on to tell Daisy that she was a childless widow, and had been for many years.

'Look, Daisy, look – it's Kate!' Lizzie now said, her voice high with excitement as she saw her friend walking into the ward.

''Ello, darlin,' Kate said, smiling fondly as she came to the side of the bed, leaning over to give Lizzie a kiss on the cheek. 'I hear you're going home tomorrow.'

'Yes, go home,' she told her.

''Ello, Daisy,' Kate grinned, giving her a little wink before adding, 'I like that dress on you, and it looks like you've lost a bit of weight.'

'Yes, I have, nearly half a stone. Now that I've mastered the use of the ramp I take Vera out every day. It must be the extra exercise of pushing her around in her wheelchair that has made me lose weight.'

'Well, you look very nice – sort of sophisticated.'

'Vera helped me to choose it,' Daisy told her, looking down at her new navy-blue wool dress whilst fingering the little white collar. When she tried it on, she had liked the way the semi-fitted style skimmed her hips, giving her a much slimmer outline. 'I've got a new winter coat too,' she said, indicating the coat hanging on the back of her chair, 'and as soon as Lizzie is up to it, we're going to buy her a new one as well.'

'Cor, that's nice. Ain't you a lucky girl, Lizzie?'

Lizzie nodded, and glancing at her watch Daisy said, 'Kate, I'm glad you came this afternoon as I've got to go soon. The physiotherapist is due in half an hour and I've persuaded her to teach me how to massage Vera's legs.'

'Massage her legs! Why do you want to learn how to do that?'

'Vera has a lot of pain and the physiotherapy helps, but the nurse can only come once a week. I'm hoping that if I can learn how to do a massage it will help her between visits.'

'Blimey, Daisy, how much more are you gonna take on?'

'Oh, it's not much, and it will be worth it to ease Vera's pain. Now, Lizze, I'm going, but I'll be back with my dad this evening. Then tomorrow we'll be able to take you home.'

'Kate come too?' Lizzie asked, her eyes clouding.

Disconcerted and unable to answer, Daisy was relieved when Kate came to her rescue, saying, 'Don't worry, Lizzie, I'll be popping round to see you. Now where is that book I was reading to you?'

Daisy smiled gratefully at Kate, pleased to see Lizzie happy as she settled down to listen to another chapter from *Alice in Wonderland*. She quietly left the ward, and on leaving the hospital wasn't surprised to see Sean hanging around near the entrance. He had taken to waiting for her after visiting time, and at first she had thought it was because he was concerned about Lizzie. But for the last few days she had begun to wonder if he had another motive. When he finished his night shift at the printers, Daisy knew that he slept until just after midday. Then, during his spare time in the afternoon, he went to the boxing club. Yet for over a week now he had waited for her outside, and falling into step beside her, he would walk her home.

'Hello, Daisy, you look nice,' he said, his face reddening.

'Thanks,' she said, hiding a smile at his blush.

They walked along quietly, and as she turned her head to

glance at Sean she saw him biting worriedly on his lower lip. 'Have you stopped going to the boxing club?' she asked.

'No. It's just that I . . .'

'Yes?' Daisy urged when Sean's voice trailed off.

'Will you come to the pictures on Saturday night?' he blurted out.

'What?' Daisy squeaked, her eyes widening.

'I said will you come to the pic—'

'Yes, I heard what you said, but why do you want *me* to come with you?'

'Blimey, Daisy, you don't half make it hard for a bloke. I . . . I like you, and want to take you out, that's all.'

'Take me out!' Daisy gawked at Sean, unable to believe her ears.

'Yes, take you out,' he said, grinning ruefully. 'I would have thought it was obvious by the way I've been hanging around waiting for you every day. Now, will you come to the pictures with me?'

Daisy stared at Sean in wonderment. Yes, she realised, she would like to go out with him. He was nothing like the boy who used to torment her. Instead she found him quiet and gentle, and although not handsome, he had a nice face and an infectious smile. 'Yes, I would like to go out with you,' she told him shyly, 'but I don't know if I can. You see, Lizzie is coming out of hospital tomorrow and may need looking after. Then there's Vera and . . .'

'All right, one excuse is enough,' he said, interrupting her mid-sentence.

'No, I mean it, I really would like to come out with you,' she assured him. 'It's just that I don't think I can make it this Saturday.'

'How about next week then?' he asked, relief evident on his face.

'I'll try, honestly,' she told him.

They arrived at her house and she smiled at him shyly before mounting the steps. 'See you,' she said, inserting her key into the lock.

'Yeah, see you,' Sean said, smiling back. 'And will you let me know about the pictures?'

Daisy nodded, her face still flushed as she stepped inside.

Vera watched the scene from the window, unable to hear what they were saying, but judging by the way that they looked at each other, she could guess. Well, we'll see what her father's got to say about it, she thought, sure that Henry wouldn't be happy to know his daughter was flirting with another of Molly's sons.

She saw them say goodbye, and scowling pushed herself away from the window. Yet what do I care? she thought. Sod the lot of them. Glancing around the room and with nothing else to distract her, Vera was once again plagued with memories of her son. *Oh Georgie, Georgie*. He filled her mind day and night. So much time had passed since she had seen him, and it was now becoming impossible to remain optimistic that she would ever get him back.

Georgie was all she cared about, and without him what was the point of going on? Life without her son was empty, meaningless. *Oh Mum, mum*, she moaned silently. *How could you do this to me?*

The door opened, and as Daisy stepped into the room she said, 'Are you all right, Vera?'

The woman sighed, wondering how much longer she could continue with this act. 'Yes, I'm fine,' she murmured, and feigning interest, asked, 'Did I see you chatting to Sean?'

'Yes, he's asked me to go to the pictures with him.'

'Is that wise? Surely you'd be better off having nothing more to do with that family.'

'You can't blame them all for what Liam did – and anyway, Sean is nothing like his brother.'

'And since when did you become an expert on men?' Vera asked sarcastically, but seeing Daisy's face, she said hastily, 'Sorry. I'm in a lot of pain, love, and it's making me a bit snappy.'

Vera pushed the chair towards her bed, sick to death of having to butter up to her stepdaughter. Every day was like living on a knife-edge, worrying that despite their new understanding, Daisy might tell Henry about how she had been treated. Forcing her voice to sound honeyed, she said, 'I'm sorry to be a nuisance, dear, but could you help me into bed, please.'

'Yes, of course, and the physiotherapist should be here shortly. Is there anything else I can do for you?'

Yes, drop dead, Vera thought. Christ, what was the point of living – stuck here with Henry, Daisy, and that loony. Wincing as she was helped onto the bed she asked to be left alone for a while, cringing at the sympathetic smile Daisy gave her before leaving the room.

Closing her eyes, Vera looked back on her life, seeing each decade like chapters in a book. A rotten childhood. Her violent father. Leaving home to work for Lennie. Giving birth to Georgie, and then having him snatched away from her. And the accident! The accident that had left her a helpless cripple. How much happiness had there been? Not a lot, she thought, unable to stop the negative thoughts that went around and around in her head. It would be Christmas in a few weeks, and what did she have to look forward to? Nothing!

She had no chance of ever getting Georgie back and Vera realised that now – realised that she had been living in a fantasy. Lennie would never let him go. God, she might as well be dead, and as Vera dwelt on the thought it became more and more compelling. No more pain, no more emptiness without her son. It would be easy; all she had to do was swallow her supply of sleeping pills in one go. Eyeing the bottle she saw only about six tablets left, and groaned softly, realising it would have to wait until her new prescription was filled.

She heard Daisy coming back into the room and shut her eyes quickly. With any luck the girl would think she was asleep and leave her in peace. The door closed softly and Vera sighed with relief, thinking about her stepdaughter. It was all right for her! Daisy had her whole life ahead of her, and what unhappiness had *she* known? Hardly any! Yes, she had lost her mother, but her father adored her and the girl wanted for nothing.

Bitterness filled Vera's mind – bitterness with life and all that it had thrown at her. Yes, she would end it all, end the pain and misery, and she only had to wait until she got a new supply of pills.

Chapter Thirty-Eight

Lizzie soon settled in again, pleased to be home, but she was still sulky around Vera and avoided her as much as possible. It made Daisy's life difficult as she struggled to look after them both, and there was the added worry that her stepmother had taken to spending most of her time in bed again. Even Henry hadn't been able to cheer her up and was concerned that his wife might be sinking into depression. Vera hardly ate, no matter how many tempting meals Daisy prepared, and hardly spoke unless it was absolutely necessary.

Despite her aunt's death Daisy decided to try to make Christmas special this year, hoping that somehow it might bring them all together. It was only two weeks away, and foraging in the upstairs storerooms she had unearthed a box of Christmas decorations. Memories returned . . . memories of Christmases when her mother was alive. She fingered the tinsel, baubles, and fairy lights, recalling helping her to put them on the tree. At the bottom of the box she found an angel and was unable to hold back a sob. It was one her mother had made, and though tatty now, she could remember how as a small child she had gazed at in wonderment when her father had put it on the top of the tree.

She picked up the box and returned downstairs. Kate was coming round soon and she would be pleased to see her. Her cheerful face was sometimes the only thing that brightened Daisy's day, and now she had become as close to Kate as Lizzie.

Daisy had told her father about her date with Sean, but he was so worried about Vera that he hardly listened, the nod of his head distant as he hurried back to her side.

The problem was Lizzie, and Daisy still didn't know what to do about her. The house seemed divided in two during the evenings. With Vera refusing to get out of bed, her father sat beside her in the sitting room, while she and Lizzie stayed in the dining room, mostly watching the second television that Henry had recently purchased.

Lizzie refused to sit in the same room as Vera, and no matter how many times Daisy told her that Vera wasn't leaving, she refused to believe her. So how on earth then would she be able to go out with Sean?

The doorbell rang and Daisy hurried to answer it, her heart lifting when she saw Kate beaming at her.

'Wotcher, ducks! 'Ave you got the kettle on?'

Daisy's face broke into an answering smile, and Lizzie rushed excitedly into the hall. 'Kate!' she cried, throwing herself into her friend's arms.

'Let her go so she can come inside,' Daisy said. 'Now why don't you take Kate into the sitting room, and I'll make the tea.'

When Daisy carried the tray into the room a few minutes later she saw Kate reading to Lizzie, something they both seemed to enjoy. Pouring out the tea she said, 'I need to pop out to the shops, Kate. Would you mind keeping an eye on Lizzie for me? You don't have to worry about Vera – I just looked in on her and she's asleep.'

'Of course I don't mind, and take as long as you like. If Vera wakes up I'm sure I'll be able to sort out anything she needs.'

Daisy smiled gratefully, knowing that it was true. There was something about Kate – a special quality that inspired trust. When she had first come to visit them, Daisy had nervously introduced her to Vera, and was surprised when the two women seemed to hit it off.

It was then that an idea struck. Would Kate agree? Dare she ask? Taking a deep breath Daisy said, 'I'd like to go out on Saturday night, but I can't really leave Lizzie, so I was wonder—'

'I'd be pleased to 'ave her,' Kate said, before she had time to finish her sentence. 'Why don't you bring Lizzie round to my place? It'll make a change for her, and she's always asking to see where I live.'

'Oh thanks, Kate, and I can pick her up on my way home.'

'There's no need for that. Lizzie might as well stay the night and you can fetch her on Sunday morning.'

Thanking Kate profusely, Daisy hastily put her coat on. Then, closing the street door behind her, she stood on the steps biting her bottom lip. Would she have time to pop next door? If Sean was in, she could confirm their date. But even if he wasn't, it would be nice to see Molly as she hadn't seen her since Lizzie had come out of hospital. Take your time, Kate had said, so perhaps it wouldn't hurt to pop round for a few minutes before she went to the shops.

'Daisy, come in,' Molly said, still without her welcoming smile. 'How is she? Your cousin, I mean?'

'Fine, Lizzie's fine. Are you all right now, Molly?'

'Yes, I suppose so,' she said distantly, her eyes clouded. Molly still hadn't heard from Liam, and it was tearing her apart. Daisy had good reason to hate her son, so how could she share her pain with the girl? Yet despite what Liam had done Molly still loved him desperately. Every day the same thoughts went over and over in her mind. How could he have touched Lizzie? How could he have been attracted to her? Liam was sick, he had to be, sick in his mind. Had she caused it? Had she failed him as a mother?

'Molly, what is it? What's wrong?'

She could hear the anxiety in Daisy's voice, but too choked to answer, Molly just shook her head.

'Are you upset because I'm going out with Sean?'

Molly's eyes widened. Daisy and Sean – when did that happen? 'I didn't know you and Sean were seeing each other. The lad didn't tell me.'

'We're not really. Sean just asked me to go to the pictures with him on Saturday, that's all.'

'Did he now? Well, he's a dark horse,' and as she said the words, Molly's stomach lurched. Liam had been a dark horse too.

Was Sean the same? No . . . no . . . stop it, don't think like that, she told herself.

'You look so pale, Molly. If it's upsetting you, I won't go out with him.'

Seeing the concern on the girl's face, she struggled to pull herself together. 'No, don't worry, I really don't mind you seeing Sean. I'm just a bit tired, that's all,' and hearing the sound of boots clattering down the outside steps, Molly added, 'That'll be him now.'

The front door opened and Sean stepped into the room, his eyes moving quickly from his mother to Daisy. 'Has something happened?' he asked worriedly.

'No, son. Daisy has just popped down to see me,' and forcing a smile, Molly added, 'What's this I hear about you asking her out?'

His face went bright red. 'I was going to tell you, Mam, but Daisy hasn't said yes yet.'

'I *will* be able to go out with you on Saturday, Sean,' Daisy shyly told him.

'That's great. I'll pick you up at about seven. Is that all right?'

'Yes, that's fine, but I'd better be off now as I've still got some shopping to do.'

After saying goodbye and closing the door behind Daisy, Molly turned to her son, her voice harsh as she said, 'Now you behave yourself with Daisy, me laddo. I don't want any more trouble at my door.'

Sean's body seemed to stretch and his face reddened again, this time with anger. 'How can you say that? I'm not your precious Liam – and just because he's a pervert it doesn't mean I'm tarred with the same brush!'

'Shut up! Don't talk about your brother like that,' Molly shouted, all her pent-up emotions rising to the surface as she cried, 'Get out of my sight, Sean!'

'Yes, I'll go, Mammy. After all, I'm used to it. All my life you've compared me to Liam. Liam was better at school, Liam was better at football. Liam – Liam – Liam. He's the only one of us you care about!'

'That's not true,' Molly blustered, yet realising as her son stormed upstairs that there was truth in what he said. She *had* favoured Liam above the others, she knew that now. He was her firstborn and the birth had been a difficult one. She had nearly lost him and that made him even more precious. Pulling out a chair she sat down heavily. Tears filled her eyes, and resting her arms on the table Molly laid her head down, her body once again wracked with sobs.

She felt a touch – a hand stroking her hair. 'Don't, Mammy, don't cry. I'm sorry,' Sean told her, his voice cracking with emotion.

Raising her head she grasped his hand. 'No, son, 'tis me that's sorry, sorry to the heart of me. I love you, Sean. Patrick and Francis too. Please, don't ever doubt that.'

'I know you do,' he told her. 'Mammy, listen, you must stop torturing yourself about Liam. He'll be fine, he always falls on his feet and you know that.'

She sighed heavily. Yes, what Sean said was true, but why hadn't her eldest son written?

Chapter Thirty-Nine

Ada slammed the front door and leaned against it, her breath coming in gasps. She couldn't believe it; couldn't believe what Betty had told her.

'Are you all right?' Jack Talbot asked as he stepped into the hall.

'I've just seen my niece Betty. Oh, Jack, you won't believe what she told me!'

'Come into the kitchen and I'll pour you a cuppa, and then you can tell me all about it,' he urged, walking up and taking the shopping bags out of her hands.

Ada nodded, her mind still reeling as she followed Jack along the hall. He gently guided her to a chair before placing a cup of tea in front of her, and as she picked it up Ada found she needed both hands to hold it steady before she could raise it to her lips.

'Now then, love, what has your niece been saying to get you in this state?' he asked.

Taking a gulp of the strong acrid tea that Jack favoured, Ada placed the cup back on the saucer, closing her eyes momentarily before she spoke. 'I've been looking out for Betty for ages, and today I saw her down the market. She knew all about Vera's accident and I was fuming that she hadn't told me. I started to 'ave a go at her, but I didn't get far. My God, Jack! You won't believe this, but Betty rounded on me and said some terrible things. She said that Vera's lost her mind – that she was gonna kill her husband, and it was only the accident that stopped her.'

'Now calm down, Ada, and think about it. Why would Vera kill her husband? It don't make sense.'

'That's what I said, but Betty insisted that Vera only married this bloke to get his money. She was gonna poison him, Jack! He's got his own house, some savings, and life insurance. Betty said that after Vera finished him off, she planned to use his dosh to take her son George abroad where Lennie Talbot could never find them.'

'It seems a bit far-fetched if you ask me. No, I can't believe Vera would do something like that.'

'I didn't want to believe it either, but I don't think Betty was lying. I reckon it must 'ave turned Vera's mind when I told her about Lennie. Think of what a terrible shock it must have been for her, and she must 'ave been going mad with worry during the whole of her pregnancy.'

'That bastards got a lot to pay for,' Jack said darkly.

'I know. Yet when you think about it, Jack, it didn't start with Lennie. It started with your Lena and my Davy. God, if only we hadn't kept it a secret.'

'Well, that wasn't my idea, Ada.'

'I know, you don't 'ave to rub it in. But at the time I honestly thought it was the best thing to do. Christ, my Vera was just a baby then! How was I to know that one day she'd get mixed up with Lennie Talbot?'

'You couldn't 'ave known, Ada. You didn't 'ave a crystal ball.'

'Oh Jack, I can't believe my Vera was gonna kill her husband. She was a good kid, and though she was a bit wild at times, there was no badness in her.'

'Calm down, love,' he said, reaching out to grasp her hand.

Pulling at her hair, Ada cried, 'When Vera got pregnant I *had* to tell her! What choice did I 'ave? Please, tell me that I done the right thing, Jack!'

'Of course you did, and it was her choice to 'ave the baby.' He shook his head sadly. 'The poor cow has had a rotten time of it, ain't she? First the shock of finding out about Lennie. Then getting her son back, only to have him snatched away from her again. Christ, and to top it all she had that terrible accident. No, not accident – I think that Lennie deliberately pushed her down the stairs. Gawd, Ada, when you think about it, it's a miracle the girl survived it all.'

Ada stared at Jack, guilt flooding her mind and making her feel nauseous. He was right. Vera had gone through hell, and what had she done to help her? Nothing! All she had cared about was herself – her fear of Lennie making her abandon her own daughter.

'Why don't you go to see her, Ada? Talk to the girl – find out if what Betty said is true.'

She gulped, remembering how desperate her daughter was, and her stomach fluttered with nerves. 'No, I can't go to see her. She'll ask me about Lennie again, and I daren't tell her what she wants to know.'

'What can't you tell her?'

Ada took a gulp of air. 'She wants me to find out where Lennie lives now so she can get her son back. Oh God, Jack, don't you see? If Lennie finds out that I've been meddling in his affairs he'd go mad. He . . . he'd kill us both!'

'You leave Lennie to me,' Jack said darkly. 'Now get yer coat on Ada, and go to see your daughter.'

'But what will I tell her?'

'You can tell her what she wants to know. Listen, Ada, stop worrying. I promise that Lennie will never hurt either of you again.'

'How can you promise that? You don't know what he's like – or what he's capable of.'

'Ada, for Gawd's sake, just trust me, will you?'

She looked into his eyes, and seeing something that reassured her, heaved a sigh. 'All right, I'll go, but it's already four o'clock so maybe I should leave it until tomorrow.'

'Nah, go now. You need to sort things out with your daughter and you know you won't sleep a wink tonight with it on your mind.'

'Yeah, I suppose you're right,' but at the strange expression that flitted across Jack's face she added worriedly, 'You will be here when I get back, won't you?'

'Of course I will,' he told her, his smile more like a grimace.

'I can't leave you, Jack. You're in pain, aren't you?'

'Nah, I'm all right. That stuff the doctor gave me does the trick. Now go on, off you go to see your daughter, and I'll see you later.'

Ada got off the bus and walked slowly towards the street where Vera lived, doubts creeping in that she was doing the right thing. It was all right for Jack to say she shouldn't worry, but he had no real idea of what Lennie was capable of. Giving Vera his address would be like loading a gun and waiting for it to go off.

Sighing, she turned into Fitzwilliam Street, and on reaching Vera's house she mounted the steps, taking a deep breath before nervously ringing the bell.

The door opened almost immediately, giving Ada no time to change her mind, and Daisy stood on the threshold. The girl's face at first registered surprise, but then turned into a welcoming smile.

'Oh, Vera's going to be so thrilled that you've come to see her at last,' she said, ushering her inside. 'Come in. Please, come in.'

Following Daisy into the sitting room, Ada stared at her daughter propped up in bed, thinking that she looked even worse than the last time she'd seen her. Vera was thin, and haggard, with her hair hanging in rat's tails onto her shoulders. 'Oh Vera,' Ada whispered.

Her daughter gave her such a look of scorn that she involuntarily stepped back. 'So, you've decided to come at last,' she sneered.

'I'll make you both a drink,' Daisy said, and as if to reassure Ada, she added, 'Vera hasn't been well, but now that you're here I'm sure she'll perk up.'

Ada moved towards her daughter. 'Vera, listen. I'm sorry, really I am. I was scared, you see – scared of what Lennie might do if you tried to get the boy back.'

'Yes, it was always self-preservation with you, wasn't it, Mum. You let Dad beat the shit out of us both, and what did you do? Nothing!' she spat, showing the first signs of animation.

'But he went for me more than you,' Ada protested.

'Oh, and that's supposed to make it all right, is it? He broke my arm, Mum, and you covered up for him.'

'I didn't 'ave much choice. He was me husband.'

'And what about him and Lennie's mother? You made sure that was covered up too, didn't you?' Vera laughed then, manic laughter that made the hair on the back of Ada's neck stand on end. 'Is that what's really worrying you, Mum? Are you frightened of what people will think if they find out what you've managed to hide all these years – that you stayed with a man who committed adultery with your friend and next-door neighbour?'

'Well, I'd be happier if nobody knew about it.'

'Yes, I'm sure you would. Nobody would be able to believe that you stayed with my father after he got Lena Talbot pregnant. But look what you're covering up caused, Mum. How do you think I felt when you told me – in fact, *threw* it at me – that I might give birth to a monster! Because all you cared about was your reputation – because you kept your disgusting secret – I ended up having sex with my *brother*!'

'Your *half-brother*,' Ada snapped.

'Oh, is that supposed to make a difference? God, you're priceless, Mum.'

The row became heated then, both throwing accusations at each other, their voices loud.

Henry opened the front door, frowning when he saw Daisy standing in the hall, her face white, and her eyes like saucers as she gripped a tray. At the sound of raised voices he walked across to the sitting room, but as one voice screeched loudly he pulled up short, hovering outside the door.

'Yeah, but *I* didn't try to kill me husband – unlike you, Vera! Yeah, that's shut you up, ain't it! I saw Betty down the market and she told me. She said you were trying to poison Henry so you could get his money. You would 'ave succeeded too, 'cos Betty told me how ill he was. Not only that, Betty also said that you connived to get rid of Daisy by pretending that she pushed you down the stairs! It must 'ave been God's justice when Lennie snatched your son back — 'cos instead of play-acting, you fell downstairs for real that time, didn't you!'

'Shut up!' Henry heard Vera scream, as he stepped into the room.

'Is this true?' he shouted. 'Is what I just heard true?'

The expression on Vera's face told him all he needed to know; she looked terrified, yet guilty at the same time. 'No, Henry! My mother is lying,' she gasped.

Henry turned to look at Vera's mother, seeing a short, thin woman who bore no resemblance to her daughter. 'Were you lying?' he asked shortly.

With her mouth set in a thin line Ada lowered her head, avoiding his eyes.

'No,' Henry mused, 'I don't think you are, and by saying nothing I think you're trying to protect your daughter.' Struck by his own words he turned his head, calling, 'Daisy, would you come in here, please.'

Henry watched as his daughter stepped nervously into the room, still carrying the tray. 'Put that down, I want to talk to you,' he urged, waiting until she had placed it on the table before continuing. 'Now, Daisy, I want you to think back to the time when Vera accused you of pushing her down the stairs. As far as you can remember, I'd like you to tell me exactly what happened.'

His daughter looked towards the bed, and Henry caught a glimpse of the venomous look Vera threw at her. He took Daisy by the shoulders and turned her around so that her back was towards her stepmother, and then giving her a smile of encouragement he said, 'Don't worry about Vera. Just tell me the truth.'

Daisy began to speak, hesitantly at first, describing the scene that day. As he listened to her Henry was filled with guilt. Guilt that he hadn't believed her . . . guilt that because of Vera's lies he had sent his daughter away. 'Tell me, Daisy, what do you know of Vera's child?' he asked, realising too late that his voice sounded clipped and cold.

He saw her face suffuse with colour before she threw herself into his arms. 'I'm sorry I didn't tell you, Dad. Please, don't be angry with me. I knew that Georgie was Vera's son, but I couldn't tell you, I just couldn't.'

'I'm not angry with you, Daisy,' he assured, giving her a gentle squeeze. 'I'm angry with myself for being such a fool. But why couldn't you tell me?' he added, struck by her words.

He felt her tremble in his arms, and easing her away from him he gave her another smile of reassurance. 'Don't be frightened. Just explain why you felt you couldn't tell me.'

'B . . . because Vera said that if I didn't keep my mouth shut . . .' Daisy closed her eyes at the terrible words she was about to utter – words that he been left unsaid for so very long. 'She'd tell you that I killed Mummy.' Tears poured down her face.

'She said *what*!' Henry exclaimed, finding that his voice came out in a roar. 'Of course you didn't kill your mother!'

'I know that now, Dad, but for years I believed her. It was only when Aunt Edna was dying that I found out the truth from Molly and Paddy.'

'You'd better start at the beginning and tell me everything.'

He listened with growing horror, unable to believe he'd been so blind to what his daughter had been through. Vera didn't interrupt, or try to defend herself, which pointed to her guilt. Though Henry heard the occasional gasp from her mother.

When Daisy stopped speaking, he glanced across at Vera, and seeing the animosity on her face Henry urged his daughter towards the door. 'Go into the dining room, Daisy.'

Her shoulders stiffened and a look of panic crossed her face as their eyes met. 'It's all right, Daisy. I believe what you've told me,' he said softly, and after another quick look into his eyes, she left the room.

Henry walked over to the door and closed it behind his daughter, and for a few moments there was absolute silence in the room as he gathered his thoughts. Then, his mouth set with determination; he turned to face Vera. 'What you did to my daughter is unforgivable, and is enough for me to throw you out of my house. Which, incidentally, I intend to do. However, it seems you tried to poison me too, and that is something I am sure the police will want to hear about.'

Vera laughed then, a laugh touched with hysteria. 'You can't prove it, you daft sod. There won't be anything left in your system after all this time, and as for chucking me out of your house – well, I'll be glad to go.' Her laughter died abruptly and her face contorted into a sneer. 'Do you think I want to stay with an idiot like you? No, I'll be glad that I haven't got to look at your ugly mug ever again.'

'Vera, stop it! Don't you think you've done enough damage?' Ada shouted.

'Yes, she has, but she won't be able to do any more,' Henry said, turning to look at Vera's mother. Instead of losing his temper again, he found that shock had frozen his emotions and he felt icily calm. He smiled grimly, wondering how much longer this feeling would last. 'I'll go and pack your daughter's things and you can take Vera with you when you go,' he said shortly, before abruptly leaving the room.

'Christ, Vera! What are you gonna do now?'

'I would have thought that was obvious, Mum. I'll come to live with you, of course.'

'Me! Live with *me*!' Ada exclaimed.

'Well, where else am I supposed to go?'

Ada nodded slowly. 'What goes round, comes round,' she muttered. 'All right, I suppose it's the only answer, but don't ask me how we're going to get there.'

'Don't worry, Mum, we'll sort something out. Now come on, help me into my wheelchair.'

Ada found it a terrible struggle and was terrified she would hurt her daughter. How on earth would she be able to manage to look after her? She was panting when Vera was finally in her wheelchair, and trying to catch her breath she collapsed onto a chair. Christ, what about Jack? Vera would need his bedroom, yet the poor man was so ill and she could hardly turn him out.

'We'll have to take my commode, Mum,' Vera said, breaking into her thoughts.

'Yeah, all right,' Ada answered distantly, unanswered questions still going around in her mind.

Daisy stood just inside the dinning room and found herself shaking. Thankfully she had already taken Lizzie to Kate's house so the girl wasn't there to witness these awful scenes. Vera was leaving, her father said, and she shivered then – remembering Lizzie's prediction.

It had been frightening at first when her father had called her into the sitting room; the venomous look on Vera's face had made her knees tremble. Yet it had shown that her stepmother hadn't really changed at all – it had all been an act. Daisy had been taken in, just like her father, and had believed Vera's lies about making a fresh start. Seeing her stepmother's animosity had given Daisy the courage to speak – to tell her father the truth, and to bring it all into the open at last.

She heard her father coming downstairs and stepped into the hall. He was carrying two suitcases, and placing them on the floor he grabbed Vera's coats from the rack and threw them on top. Then, seeing her standing there, he gave a small strained smile, saying, 'It might be better if you stay out of the way, Daisy.'

She nodded, but as he went into the sitting room she couldn't resist standing outside, listening to the conversation.

'Your things are packed and you can go now, Vera,' he snapped.

'And just how do you think I'm supposed to leave without any transport, Henry?'

'That isn't my problem. You can call a taxi.'

'Oh, and how am I supposed to get into it? The driver won't lift me, and I can't fly.'

'I don't care how you get to where you're going. I just want you out of my house, and now!'

'Please,' Ada intervened, 'I know it's a lot to ask, but Vera's right and we won't be able to get her into a taxi. It isn't just her wheelchair and cases, there's her commode too. Look, she's coming to stay with me, and the only way for us to get there is for you to take us in your car.'

'What! You must be mad, woman!'

'What else do you suggest then? If you want Vera to leave, you'll have to help us,' Ada said brusquely, for the first time showing some spirit.

Vera laughed. 'Yes, Henry. That's stumped you, hasn't it?'

'Please, it's the only way,' Ada urged.

There were a few moments of strained silence before Daisy heard her father's reply. His voice heavy with resolution, he said, 'Yes, all right. I suppose it is the only way to get rid of her, and anyway I will need to know where she is to file for a divorce.'

Laughter rang out then, and Vera's voice was tinged with hysteria as she spluttered, 'Divorce! That's a good one. No, you can't divorce me, Henry. You see, we aren't married.'

'What!'

'I'm still married to Lennie Talbot. I went back to using my maiden name after he chucked me out, but I'm still legally his wife.'

'No. Oh no,' Ada whimpered. 'But you can't 'ave. He's your bro . . .'

'Shut up, Mum!'

'This means you've committed bigamy, Vera,' Henry said, 'and that's against the law.'

'Do you think I care? Do you really think I'm bothered about going to prison? Without my son, my life means nothing! Prison couldn't be any worse than the hell I've had to put up with, being stuck here with you!' she spat. 'Yes – go on – report me. I don't give a damn!' Vera smirked then. 'But what about you, Henry? How will *you* feel having your name splashed all over the newspapers, and everyone finding out what a fool you've been!'

There was a deathly silence and Daisy held her breath, only to rear back when her father suddenly appeared at the door. Striding into the hall he picked up Vera's suitcases, and opening the front door he rushed down the steps, almost throwing them into the car.

When he came back in, Daisy saw the stiff expression on his face, and watched mouth agog as he went back into the sitting room. Without a word he grasped the back of the wheelchair and pushed it into the hall, ignoring Vera's gasp of pain as she was roughly jolted.

'Here! Hold on. You be careful with me daughter!' Ada protested.

'My God, woman! You're lucky I don't wring her bloody neck,' Henry muttered.

Daisy gaped at her father. It was the first time she had ever heard him swear, but seeing the dark look on his face she hung back nervously.

'Get the commode, Daisy,' he ordered.

She ran to do his bidding and carried it down the steps, with Ada following close behind.

As they reached the car, Ada grasped Daisy's arm, saying softly, 'I'm so sorry, love. I don't know what to say about the way you've been treated. It fair broke my heart to hear what my daughter did to you. Betty said she thought that Vera had lost her mind, and after listening to what's been said, I think she may be right.'

Daisy, unable to think of any reply, just nodded her head. Then, avoiding looking at Vera sitting in the front seat, she went to the rear of the car, watching as her father struggled to fit the commode into the boot.

He gave her a parody of a smile, saying, 'I'll be back soon, and don't worry. Everything is going to be all right.'

She stared as the car drove off, then climbing the steps and closing the door behind her, she leaned against it. So much had been said in the last hour that she had difficulty in untangling her jumbled thoughts. Uppermost in her mind was hearing that Vera had tried to poison her father. My God, she thought, no wonder she wanted me out of the way.

With a start came the realisation that she should be getting ready to go out with Sean. Yet how could she go? There had been such shock and despair on her father's face, and she couldn't leave him on his own.

Opening the front door again she made her way to Molly's, realising that she had no choice but to break her date with Sean.

Chapter Forty

Jack Talbot's heart went out to Vera. Especially when he saw the attitude of the bloke who had dropped her off. The man had dumped Vera in the wheelchair, leaving her surrounded with her things on the pavement as he drove away without a backward glance.

He had wheeled her inside, and had seen the look of utter dejection on her face as she stared at the living room. 'Vera, this is Jack Talbot,' Ada said, making the introduction.

She became animated then, her face lifting and showing a trace of what must have been beauty before the tragic accident. 'Jack Talbot!' she cried. 'Lennie's father? What are you doing here?'

'No, not Lennie's father, love.'

'Of course you aren't. I'm sorry.'

'Vera's going to stay with me now, Jack,' Ada told him, biting her bottom lip worriedly.

He could see the dilemma Ada was in, realising quickly that he'd be in the way. Smiling softly he said, 'Now, don't worry, gel. You've been kind enough to put me up, but it's time I moved on.'

'But where will you go?' Ada asked.

'Oh, I'll find somewhere easily enough,' he said flippantly.

'But you're ill! You can't leave here without somewhere else to stay.'

'It's all sorted,' Jack lied. Then turning to Vera, he said, 'Tell me about your son. Is that right that Lennie snatched him from you?'

The look of anguish that crossed Vera's face was terrible to see.

He listened as she told him what had happened, seeing tears form in her eyes and her hard face soften as she described Georgie.

'What's this about you and Lennie being married?' Ada asked.

The hard look immediately returned to Vera's face, and with a sneer she answered her mother, 'Yes, we're married all right. As soon as I got pregnant, Lennie insisted on it. He said there was no way he was going to stand for his kid being born a bastard.' Her face suffused with hate, she added, 'He thinks nothing of beating up his rivals, and rumours have it that he's killed a few of them. He runs prostitutes, plans robberies – doesn't take part in them, of course, he's too fly for that – but makes sure he gets a share of the haul. Yet he became all moral when I got pregnant.'

'But how could you marry him after what I told you? And it can't be legal. After all, Vera, you're his half-sist—'

Vera's burst of laughter was loud, almost manic again, and it drowned out the rest of Ada's words. 'I married him before I found out the truth, and it was too late then. As for it being legal – Jack here is down as Lennie's father on his birth certificate, so other than us, who's to know any different? Oh, what I wouldn't give to see his face if he found out,' Vera cried, through tears of mirth. 'He married his sister, and he doesn't even know it.'

She grimaced suddenly and Ada rose hastily to her feet. 'Are you in pain, love?'

'Yes a bit. Can you get my pills for me, Mum?'

Jack frowned surprised at the mercurial changes in Vera's moods. The girl obviously needed psychological help. Her mind seemed twisted, yet all he could feel as he looked at her was deep pity, and disgust that Lennie had done this to her. He rose to his feet, his resolve strengthening as he looked at the clock. Yes, there was still time. 'I'll just go and pack me things,' he said, and on reaching the bedroom, he closed the door behind him.

After shoving his belongings into a case, Jack grabbed a sheet of paper, and with his tongue sticking out of the corner of his mouth in concentration, he began to write. Scanning the note, and satisfied with the contents, he popped it into an envelope, sealed it, and wrote Ada's address on the front. All he had to do now was to post it when he left, and she would get it on Monday or Tuesday morning.

Shrugging his jacket on, he put the note into his inside pocket before returning to the living room. 'Ada, I'm off now, love. Thanks for putting me up.'

'Oh Jack, are you sure you're gonna be all right?'

'Yes, I'll be fine,' and turning to Vera he added, 'Take care of yourself, love. And listen, don't worry about Lennie. I've got a feeling your worries will be over soon.'

Jack saw the puzzled look on Vera's face, and anxious not to give the game away he turned to leave. Ada walked him to the street door where he took her arm, saying urgently, 'Listen, you're going to get a letter soon, and I want you to promise me that you'll follow the instructions in it.'

'Jack, you're frightening me. What's going on? What are you talking about?'

'There's no need to be frightened, Ada. Just promise me you'll do as the letter says.'

She scrutinised his face and he winked, trying to lighten the atmosphere.

With a small shake of her head, she said, 'All right, Jack. I can't make any sense of what yer saying, but I promise.'

'Good girl,' he said, planting a kiss on her cheek before stepping outside.

'Please, Jack, will you let me know where you are?'

'Don't worry, Ada. You'll soon find out,' he said cryptically as he walked away.

It didn't take Jack long to reach Clapham Junction; he had posted the letter and now, finding a telephone box, he went inside. Pausing before feeding some coins into the slot, he gathered his thoughts. Then, stiffening his shoulders, he dialled the number that had taken him weeks to find, all his old contacts coming in useful at last.

'The Burlington Club. How can I help you?'

Drawing in his breath, Jack said, 'I'd like to speak to Lennie Talbot.'

'I don't know if Mr Talbot is available,' the woman's tinny voice replied. 'Whom shall I say is calling?'

Jack smiled at the voice, and its attempt at a posh accent. 'Tell him it's his father.'

'Oh right, just one moment please.'

Finding a few more pennies in case his time ran out, Jack waited. Lennie had to be there, he just had to, or all his careful plans would come to nothing. Resting the receiver on his shoulder Jack fumbled for his tobacco tin, taking out a roll-up and lighting it. Inhaling deeply, the nicotine caught in his throat, causing him to cough so loudly that he only faintly heard the sound of a voice. Hurriedly placing the phone to his ear, he croaked, ''Allo, 'allo, is anyone there?'

'Yeah, what do you want?'

'Is that you, Lennie?' Jack wheezed, hastily removing the fag from the corner of his mouth.

'Yeah – and I'll ask you again. What do you want?'

'I wanna see you. I've got something of your mother's that I think she would want you to 'ave.'

'You've got a nerve, turning up after all these years with this claptrap. What could you possibly 'ave of Mum's? As far as I know, you took nothing with you when you buggered off.'

'Listen, son,' Jack cajoled, grimacing at having to put that title on Lennie, 'I ain't got long to go. Me lungs 'ave 'ad it, and I've come all the way from Devon to see you. There's something very important I've got to tell you, and there's something else that I'm sure you'll want to see. It's been on me conscience for years, and now that me number's up I'd like to set the record straight.'

'All right,' Lennie said after a pause, taking the bait as Jack had hoped. 'Come to the club.'

'Nah, I can't do that. I'm too weak to travel any further,' he lied, 'and I'm going back to Devon tonight. Look, can you meet me at Clapham Junction station? I'll be at the far end of platform five.'

There was a pause and Jack held his breath, his eyes lifting in silent prayer.

'What time's your train due?'

'In an hour, son.'

'Christ, you're cutting it a bit fine. All right, I'll be there in about forty-five minutes,' Lennie told him, before abruptly replacing the receiver.

Grinning with delight, Jack made his way to the station and after buying a platform ticket he struggled up the stairs, his breath coming in gasps. He scanned the far end of the platform where it was at its narrowest. There were only three other people in sight, and looking through the window of the waiting room he could see a couple of teenagers locked in an embrace.

So far so good, Jack thought. His timing had to be spot on, but he had studied the timetable carefully, and finding that there were regular fast trains going through platform five, it seemed the ideal choice. He spotted a bench and sat down, his lungs screaming with pain. Just over thirty minutes, that was all he had to wait now, and taking out his tobacco tin again he lit another cigarette, cupping his hand around the match as it flared.

Jack had thought long and hard about what he was going to do, sometimes feeling his resolve weakening. But he didn't have long to go now, a month or two at most before he found himself in a hospital bed, pumped full of drugs. No, he didn't fancy going like that. This was a much better way, and what was that old saying? Yes, that's it, he thought, finally remembering – I'll be killing two birds with one stone.

Drawing deeply on his cigarette he found it had gone out and tutted impatiently as he struck another match. Seeing Vera and the state she was in had finally removed all his doubts. Christ, it all went back to his wife Lena's adultery with Davy Tucker and the monster they had brought into the world. Vera was suffering as a result and it wasn't fair. The poor cow deserved a bit of happiness after what she had been through. Anyway, what he intended to do was no more than Lennie deserved, and it would stop the bastard from ruining any more lives.

When it was almost time Jack stood up and made his way to the end of the platform. He was pleased to see no one else around as he stood with his hands in his pockets, trying to look nonchalant.

Five minutes later he heard the sound of approaching footsteps, and turning sharply Jack saw a man walking towards him. From the description he'd been given, there was no mistaking that it was Lennie. It was spot on, right down to the black slicked-back hair, flashy suit and camel-hair coat. As Lennie drew closer his eyes narrowed, a question in them, and with the grimace of a smile, Jack said, 'Yeah, it's me, son.'

Looking him up and down, Lennie's face broke into a sneer. 'So you're me old man. The one that run out on me and Mum before I was born.'

Jack glanced at the clock, three minutes to go – just three minutes. God, give me the strength he prayed. 'Yeah, I ran out on you, but I ain't yer old man. You ain't fit to 'ave the name of Talbot.'

'What are you talking about?' Lennie growled, his eyes dark with menace.

Walking casually towards the edge of the platform, Jack drew a piece of paper out of his pocket. 'Read this, and it'll tell you all you need to know.'

Lennie stepped forward, snatching the paper out of his hand. The light was dim, Jack suddenly realised, panic running through him. He hadn't thought of that! Lennie wouldn't be able to see what it said! What if he walked away towards a lamp?

Just as he feared, Lennie peered at the paper, shaking his head impatiently before turning to scan the platform. Delay him! I've got to delay him, Jack thought frantically. 'I can tell you what it says,' he said quickly. 'It's a letter – a letter to David Tucker written by your mother. It was never delivered 'cos I intercepted it. You can read it yourself later, but all you need to know for now is that it proves *Tucker* is your father, not me.'

Lennie's brow creased, and hearing the fast pistons of the approaching train, Jack braced himself. It wouldn't stop – there would be no slowing down – it was the through train to Victoria.

Glancing at Lennie, Jack saw that the penny hadn't dropped yet, and he wanted to see the bastard's face when it did. There was time – just enough time! The engine driver pulled the cord, and with a hiss of steam the whistle screeched. It was coming. It was almost on top of them!

'Your precious mother was a tart, do you hear me! She was a tart! She had it off with Davy Tucker, and you're the result,' Jack yelled, throwing himself at Lennie and unbalancing them both in the process. 'And do you know what that means? Vera's your *sister*!'

There was a split second as they tumbled over the edge of the platform – a second when Jack saw a look of horror pass over Lennie's face. Then there was nothing as they both went under the heavy wheels.

Chapter Forty-One

Ada picked up the letter lying on the mat, her thoughts still on Jack. It was good of him to move out so quickly and she still felt awful about it, praying that he was telling her the truth when he insisted that he would easily find somewhere else to stay. Daily she had seen the awful pain he was in and had hardly slept on Saturday night for worrying about him, and last night hadn't been much better. And despite it being a fraught weekend, Jack had been constantly on her mind.

Vera had never let up, going on and on about Lennie's new address until Ada couldn't stand it any more. And when she had finally given in – what good had it done? She and Vera had talked and talked, until her daughter finally realised that even with Lennie's address, it wouldn't do her any good. There was no way Lennie Talbot would give up his son again.

Seeing the agony, both physical and emotional, that her daughter was suffering, tore Ada apart. Betty had said that Vera had lost her mind, yet so far Ada had seen no sign of that. All she could see was the anguish that Vera was going through.

Sighing heavily now, Ada looked at the squiggles on the front of the envelope without comprehension, and shaking her head impatiently she took it into the living room, handing it to Vera. 'Can you read it for me, love?'

Her daughter ripped the envelope open, drawing out a single sheet of paper. At first Vera's forehead was creased as she read the note, but then to Ada's surprise she burst into tears. Tears that turned into heaving sobs as the note fluttered onto the floor.

'What's wrong? What does it say?' Ada cried, hurrying to her side.

Drawing in shuddering breaths, Vera gasped, 'It's from Jack.'

'Jack! Oh my God, is it bad news? I've been so worried about him.'

'He says that by the time we read this, Lennie will be dead.'

'But I don't understand. How can Jack possibly know that?'

'Because he left here on Saturday intending to knock him off, Mum. He says he's been planning it since he arrived. But that's not all – Jack's told me how to get my Georgie back.'

Ada shook her head in confusion; none of this made any sense. 'No, I don't believe it. Jack couldn't 'ave killed Lennie. The man's dreadfully ill and he's in constant pain. There's no way he would 'ave been strong enough.'

'It doesn't take a lot of strength to shoot someone, and perhaps that's what he did?'

'Don't be daft, Vera. Where would he 'ave got a gun?'

'If you want something badly enough, and have the right contacts, there are ways to get hold of anything, Mum,' she said brusquely. Then changing the subject abruptly she said, 'Will you get my brown handbag for me? I think I saw you put it in the bottom of the wardrobe when you unpacked my things.'

'For Christ's sake, Vera! You've just told me that Jack's killed Lennie Talbot, and now you calmly tell me you want your handbag. Are you mad? Why do you want your bleedin' handbag?'

'Because I hid my marriage lines in the lining. The ones that prove I was married to Lennie.'

Ada stared at Vera, shaking her head in bewilderment, but as far as she was concerned, her daughter's handbag was unimportant as her mind flew back to Jack. Thoughts, staccato-like, jumped into her head. It couldn't be true. He couldn't have killed Lennie. But what if it was? What would happen to him? Oh, Jack. Poor Jack!

'Mum, for goodness sake! Will you go and get my bag!'

'Yeah, in a minute,' Ada mumbled, her mind still reeling.

'Mum, listen to me and I'll try to explain why it's so

important. You see, if it's true that Lennie's dead, I'll be able to claim Georgie. Jack says all I've got to do is to take my marriage lines and George's birth certificate to a solicitor. It proves that he's my son, and with Lennie out of the way there's nothing to stop me from getting him back.'

Ada stared at her daughter, seeing the joy on her face. She looked to have dropped ten years, her skin glowing, and her eyes dancing with excitement. 'Oh, Vera,' she whispered, just as there was a loud knock on the front door, startling them both.

'I wonder who that is?' Ada said nervously as she hurried to open it.

'Ada, 'ave you heard the news?' Lily cried as she unceremoniously pushed her way in. 'Lennie Talbot's dead, his old man too. Both of them fell under a train at the Junction.'

Oh God, so it *was* true, Ada thought, staring wide-eyed at her friend.

'Steady on, gel. You've gone as white as a sheet.'

Trying to gather her thoughts, Ada dragged herself to the living room, hardly hearing Lily's yell of surprise when she saw Vera.

'Mum, what's the matter?' she asked, seeing her mother's pale face.

'Lily's just confirmed it. Lennie's dead, Jack too – they both went under a train,' and fighting tears, Ada rushed into the kitchen, busying herself with putting the kettle on. She could hear her daughter talking to Lily, but took little interest, her mind still on Jack. What had possessed him to do such a thing? Yes, Lennie had tainted his name, but did that warrant killing him? He had appeared such a kind and caring man, obviously upset about Vera's plight. Was that the reason? No – surely not!

Ada shuddered. What a horrible way to die too, and what if it wasn't instantaneous? Had he suffered? Don't be stupid, woman, she berated herself. Jack was already in agony with malignant cancer, and maybe he wanted a quick death. With shaking hands she poured boiling water into the teapot, topping it with a cosy before returning to the living room.

It felt like hours before Lily went home and Ada could sense Vera's impatience. 'Mum, I'm not waiting for a solicitor to sort it all out. I'm going to Lennie's club,' she said as soon as the woman had gone.

'Oh Vera, is that wise?'

'Sod being wise, Mum. I haven't seen my son for ages and I just can't wait any longer.'

'But how are we gonna get to his club?'

'We'll get a taxi, but we'll have to find someone who can lift me in and out of it. Come on – think, Mum! Who can we ask?' Vera said urgently.

Ada wracked her brains, but came up empty. 'I don't know anyone, love,' she finally said, heaving a sigh.

Vera sat drumming her fingers on the arm of her wheelchair, but then her face suddenly became animated. 'I know who we can ask. Danny Barton – he'd do it.'

'What, Nora's lad?'

'Yes, Mum. He worked as a bouncer at the Soho club, and had a soft spot for me. He didn't realise I was Lennie's girl when he asked me out, but that didn't stop Lennie sacking him on the spot. I tried to stand up for him but that just made it worse. Yes, Danny would help me. He has good reason for hating Lennie.'

'We could give it a try, I suppose. Nora will be on her stall in the High Street, so I'll pop down there and ask her how we can get in touch with Danny.'

'So she's still flogging those cheap handbags and shoes then.'

'Yeah, she does all right too. Will you be OK while I'm gone?'

'Yes, I'll be fine for a while, but be as fast as you can, Mum. Because if we can't find Danny, we'll have to think of someone else.'

In well under an hour her mother was back, and Vera grinned with delight when she saw Danny walking into the room behind her. 'Wotcher, love. Long time no see,' he said, his eyes clouding when he saw the wheelchair. 'Gawd, there's been rumours floating around that you had a run-in with Lennie. Did he put you in that chair?'

'Yes, but he's got his comeuppance now. I suppose you've heard the news?'

'Blimey, Vera, the whole Borough seems to be talking about nothing else, and most of them are dead chuffed about it too. But what's this your mum's been telling me? She said you want to go the Burlington Club. Is that right?'

'Yes, it is, Danny. You see, well over a year ago Lennie snatched my son from me, and I want to get him back. I know it's a lot to ask, but will you help me?'

Without hesitation, he said, 'Of course I will. Though it might not be easy if Lennie's gorillas are around.'

'What can they do? George is my son, and they can't stop me from taking him.'

Ada cut in then, saying, 'I was lucky, Vera. Danny had just come back from the wholesalers. He'd been to pick up a batch of shoes for his mum.'

'Are you working for your mother now?' Vera asked.

'Blimey, you must be joking! What, work for that old battleaxe!' he said, his grin belying his words. 'No, I'm still a bouncer, and free during the day. I just help me old ma out occasionally when she wants new stock picked up.'

'Well, in that case, can you take us to the club now?' Vera asked hopefully.

'Yep. I've got me car outside, so get your coat on and we'll be off.'

'A car! No wonder you both got back so quickly,' she said.

Vera stared through the windscreen, yet hardly taking in anything of the scenery. Her heart was thumping wildly and all she could think about was Georgie. She had planned what she intended to do when they arrived at the club, but was unsure whether it would work. Glancing round at Danny, Vera recalled how easily he had picked her up to put her into the car, almost as though she weighed no more than a feather. Yes, he was strong, but if this went wrong, what chance would he have against Lennie's huge minders?

As though sensing her thoughts, Danny returned her glance. 'Don't look so worried. There's no point in getting all hot and bothered, Vera. I don't think anyone will give us any grief. With

Lennie Talbot out of the way there's no one to give any orders, and his gorillas ain't got a brain cell between them.'

'I hope you're right, Danny . . . I just hope you're right,' she breathed.

Forty minutes later they turned onto a circular drive and drew up outside the club. Vera stared in amazement at the large imposing detached house, with only a small sign on the wall betraying that it was anything other than a private dwelling.

'Are you sure this is the right place, Danny?'

'Yeah, of course I am. From what I've heard it's an exclusive and very private Members Only gambling club,' he told her, getting out of the car and removing her wheelchair from the boot. Pushing it to the side of the passenger door he leaned in, lifting Vera gently into his arms. 'Right, come on, Duchess, brace yourself.'

'Maybe you had better wait here, Mum?' Vera said, seeing her mother twisting the straps of her handbag nervously.

'No, I want to see me grandson, and just let anyone try to stop me,' she threatened.

Vera frowned. Her mother was less than five feet tall, thin as a rake, and it would only take a puff of wind to knock her over. At that moment Danny squeezed her shoulder, and drawing strength from his touch, she said, 'All right, Mum, come on then, but stay behind Danny.'

Danny tried the front door but found it locked, so he put his finger on the bell, not taking it off until the door swung open. 'Yeah, what do yer want?'

Vera stared at the pug-nosed burly man, recognising him immediately as the one who had been with Lennie when he had snatched George. 'Hello, Joe. There's no need for me to introduce myself, is there?' she said, her voice hard. Vera knew she would have to act the part if she meant to pull this off, and sneering she added, 'As Lennie's wife, I think you'll find this club is mine now, along with anything else he owns.'

'Er . . . well . . . I don't know about that.'

'Would you prefer that I got the law out here, Joe?'

'No, no,' he said quickly, holding up his hands as if to ward them off, then standing back he added, 'I suppose you'd better come in.'

'Where are the other boys, Joe?'

'Gone. They jemmied the safe and scarpered as soon as they got the news. All the girls 'ave flown the coop too.'

Girls, Vera thought. So Lennie was still up to his old tricks. Danny pushed her over the threshold and Vera stared in amazement at the opulent hall. It had Oak panelling, deep red carpet, and looking up she saw a huge crystal chandelier. There were several doors on each side and a wide curving staircase.

'Where is my son?' she demanded.

'He's upstairs with his nanny,' Joe spluttered.

Vera hid her surprise. A nanny – George had a nanny. Looking defiantly at Joe, she ordered, 'Get him!'

Without a word Joe headed for the stairs, while Danny moved to the huge double doors to their left, swinging them open. 'Well, take a look at this, Vera,' he breathed.

She turned her head, gasping when she saw the large room kitted out as a casino. There were various tables, and on one what looked like a roulette wheel. Again there was a huge chandelier suspended from the high ceiling. Bloody hell, Vera thought, Lennie must have been raking it in. She was distracted then at a sound from the staircase, and turning her head again she saw a woman descending, holding the hand of a little boy.

Vera's heart leaped. George was nearly three years old now and no longer the toddler she remembered. Could this beautiful little boy with dark shining hair really be her son? Oh, he was so lovely. As they reached the bottom of the stairs she held out her arms. 'Georgie, oh, Georgie,' she cried. 'It's me, your mummy.'

George stared at her, his eyes round, and instead of coming forward he clung onto the nanny's skirt, burying his face against her thigh.

'Come on, darling. Don't you remember me?' she urged.

He peeped at her from the corner of his eyes and said, 'Where's my daddy?'

Vera closed her eyes momentarily, then taking a deep breath, she said, 'Daddy isn't here, darling.'

'Oh, he's lovely,' Ada whispered, moving towards George, her eyes moist. ''Ello whippersnapper, and I'm your granny.'

'Just a moment, madam,' the nanny said, her expression haughty as she pushed George behind her. 'Do you have any proof of this? Since hearing of Mr Talbot's unfortunate accident we've been trying to find his relatives, but so far we haven't been successful.'

'Of course I have proof,' Vera snapped, opening her bag and pulling out her son's birth certificate, along with her marriage lines. 'You won't find any relatives of my *husband's*,' she added, emphasising the word. 'He doesn't have any.'

The woman came forward, George still clutching her skirt, and taking the documents she read them before handing them back. 'Thank you. I'm sorry to be so blunt, but this is a difficult time and I have never heard Mr Talbot mention that he had a wife. Are you divorced?'

'No, we are not. Now if you don't mind, I'd like to speak to my son.'

'I'm sorry, Mrs Talbot, but I will still need further proof of your claim before I can hand George over to you.'

Vera's eyes narrowed. She hadn't bargained on encountering anyone like this, and had only expected to deal with Lennie's minders. Glancing round the hall again, she suddenly realised that though she had been bluffing about owning the club, unless Lennie had made a will she actually did.

'Have you spoken to Mr Talbot's lawyer?'

'Yes, I have, but he wouldn't tell me anything,' the woman said.

Vera hid a smile. Old Davidson had always been cagey, especially where Lennie's business was concerned. 'He'll speak to me,' she said imperiously, and indicating the telephone, she ordered, 'Get in touch with him.'

'I'll need to get his number from the office. Wait here, George,' the woman said, turning to hurry across the hall, and into another room.

Vera leaned forward, holding out a hand appealingly towards her son, her face breaking into an expression of joy when he moved forward and shyly held it. Slowly, take it slowly, she told herself and squeezing his fingers lightly, she said, 'Hello, darling. I've missed you so much.'

'I want my daddy. Do you know where he is?'

God, what can I tell him? Vera agonised. 'I'm afraid your daddy has had to go away for a little while and that's why I'm here, darling. I've come to look after you.'

'Where has he gone?'

Vera was saved from answering when the nanny returned clutching a piece of paper. She marched straight to the telephone, and after speaking into it briefly, she held the receiver out towards Vera. 'He'd like to talk to you.'

Danny wheeled the chair across and with a lift of her shoulders Vera took the phone. Holding it close to her ear, and well aware of the others listening to the one-sided conversation, she said, 'Hello. Yes, it's me. No, I can't come to the office, you'll have to come here to the club. Right, I'll see you in about an hour. Oh, and Mr Davidson, am I right in thinking that I'm Lennie's next-of-kin? Yes, of course I realise that it's something you can't speak about on the telephone, but my husband's employees need some assurance that I have a right to be here, especially my son's nanny. Would you? Thank you so much, I'll put her back on. Yes, I'll see you later, goodbye.'

After handing the receiver back to the nanny, Vera smiled triumphantly at her mother. Then she turned her attention to Joe. His face drained of colour, and with a strangled choke he said, 'What do yer want me to do, Mrs Talbot?'

'I would have thought that was obvious. You played a part in landing me in this chair, Joe, and unless you're out of this house in thirty seconds, Danny here might just help you on your way.'

'Did I hear you right, Vera? Did you say Joe helped to put you in this wheelchair?' Danny growled, moving towards Joe, who despite his bulk was backing off gingerly.

'Leave him, Danny, he isn't worth it. Now get out, Joe!'

Within seconds the door slammed behind him, the sound

echoing in the hall. Vera's thoughts were churning as a plan began to formulate, one that would set them up for life. 'Well, I don't fancy sitting here until the solicitor arrives,' she said. 'Is there somewhere else we can wait?'

Her tone completely changed, the nanny said, 'Of course, Mrs Talbot. Please, come this way.'

They followed her along a passageway to the side of the stairs, eyes widening as she led them into a sumptuously decorated room. There were huge leather sofas, plush Chinese rugs, highly polished mahogany cabinets and side tables that gleamed in the glow from the log fire burning in the large fireplace.

'Perhaps I should introduce myself. My name is Nancy Barker. Now, can I get you something to drink?' she asked, smiling ingratiatingly.

Hearing the question, Vera pulled herself together. 'Yes, a sherry please. What about you, Mother?'

'A cup of tea would be nice,' she answered, her eyes round with wonder as she gazed around the room.

'What would you like, Danny?' Vera asked.

''Ave you got any beer, love?' he asked, eyeing Nancy appreciatively.

'Yes, of course. If you would like to make yourselves comfortable, I'll go and get the drinks.'

Vera attempted a regal nod, finding that Nancy Barker was already getting up her nose. Just who did the woman think she was, acting as if she owned the place? Well, she would soon sort *her* out!

The moment the woman had left the room, Ada exploded, 'Bleedin' Nora! This place is really something.'

'Yes, it is, Mum. And from what little the solicitor told me, I think it's mine now.'

'Oh, my God!' Ada gasped, flopping down onto one of the huge sofas.

Vera smiled. Her luck had changed at last, and as George's hand suddenly crept into hers, she felt an overwhelming surge of happiness.

When Nancy Barker returned with the tray of drinks she

placed it on a side table, and as she left the room again she made no attempt to take George with her, only saying, 'If there's anything else you need, please don't hesitate to call me.'

Vera nodded briefly and as soon as the door closed behind her, she turned to Danny, smiling widely. 'It looks like I've fallen on my feet – well, metaphorically, that is. Anyway, I've been thinking. How do you fancy working for me now?'

Danny's face stretched with surprise. 'Work for you! Well, I dunno, Vera. What sort of job are you offering me?'

'To start with I'll need a permanent driver, one who won't mind lifting me in and out of the car as you did today. Then, if I decide to keep this club, there will be lots of other things that need doing. I'll be looking for someone to run it for me, someone I can trust. So how about it, Danny?'

'You're on, Vera, but why don't you run the club yourself?'

'I'll be much too busy, and anyway this isn't a suitable environment for a child. Once I find out how much money Lennie has left, I'm going to look for a nice house. And from then on, the only job I'm interested in is being a full-time mother.' She gently pulled her son around until he was facing her, her expression full of love as she gazed at him. 'What do you think, Georgie? Would you like to live in a nice house with your mummy and Granny Tucker?'

Chapter Forty-Two

'Vera not come back,' Lizzie said as they walked to the butcher's.

'No, I don't think so,' Daisy told her.

'Not come,' Lizzie said, her face crumbling.

Daisy turned to look at her cousin, amazed that she was upset that Vera had left. She had been a terrible person, yet Lizzie had taken to her. Why hadn't her cousin sensed the truth? Vera had been bad, worse than bad, and even now Daisy was finding it hard to believe that she had tried to poison her father. Yet Lizzie had liked her! What was it that she could see in Vera?

'Go home now?' Lizzie asked.

'Soon, darling, I've just got a little more shopping to do.' As they walked along, Daisy's thoughts continued to drift. Lizzie had changed towards Vera after Aunt Edna died, and with a start she realised that was when her cousin had predicted that Vera was leaving. Was that why Lizzie became sullen and refused to be around Vera? Was she upset that she was going out of her life too?

They reached the High Street and still Daisy's thoughts were confused. Why did Lizzie sense some things, but not others?

'I go to Kate's now?' Lizzie said.

Finally realising that there were no answers to her questions, Daisy shook off her musings. Vera had gone, and that was all that mattered. She smiled at Lizzie. 'You're going to Kate's later. Now come on, let's finish the shopping.'

On their way back to Fitzwilliam Street Daisy's thoughts turned to her father. He seemed a broken man now, and she sighed, wishing there was something she could do to help him. When not at work he sat morosely in his chair, staring with unseeing eyes at the television, and though she had tried to talk to him, his replies were monosyllabic.

Arriving home, Daisy unpacked the shopping. That done, she went on to prepare the dinner while Lizzie, excited about staying with Kate, went upstairs to pack her things. 'Just put in your night clothes, toiletries and toothbrush, darling, along with some clean underwear for the morning. You won't need anything else,' Daisy called.

The vegetables ready and after putting a beef casserole into the oven, Daisy couldn't help grinning when she stood up. Lizzie was standing in the doorway clutching a large bag, with Maisie her rag doll just visible peeping out of the top.

'Go now, Daisy.'

'No, not yet, it's far too early. I'll take you to Kate's after we've had our dinner.'

Lizzie frowned, obviously disappointed. 'Go now,' she repeated.

'Not until after we've eaten,' Daisy gently admonished again. 'Now come on, show me what you've packed.'

With Lizzie holding out the bag, Daisy peeped inside, shaking her head when she saw how her cousin had just stuffed everything in. She removed the contents and folded them neatly, wondering what else she could do to distract the girl. 'Shall we pop next door to see Molly?' she asked, realising that she hadn't been next door since Vera had left.

'Hello, girls, come on in,' Molly invited, a wide smile on her face that had been absent for so long.

Daisy stepped over the threshold, Lizzie behind, wondering what had brought about this remarkable change in Molly. 'How's things?' she asked.

Molly lowered her head, but then immediately raised it again. 'I know you won't want to hear this, Daisy, but I've had a letter from my sister, and *you know who*,' she mouthed, glancing quickly at Lizzie, 'has finally arrived in Donegal. It seems he turned up one day with hardly any explanation about where he'd been, just saying something about getting his life sorted out. Anyway, he's got a job on a farm now, and Kathleen says that he's settled down well, even going to church with them on Sundays. But the most exciting thing my sister has told me is that she's seen him talking regularly to the priest.'

'A priest?'

'Yes – and don't you see what this means?' Molly cried. 'It shows that he's feeling repentance for what he did. Kathleen asked him to write to me, and do you know what his answer was? He said he had to feel clean before he contacted me. Oh, 'tis wonderful, wonderful,' she breathed, a hint of tears in her eyes, 'and who knows, he might decide to enter the priesthood. Just think about it, Daisy. My son, becoming a priest!'

Seeing Molly's happiness, Daisy couldn't help feeling pleased for her, but knowing what Liam was capable of she didn't think it likely that he would join the priesthood. Yet who was she to judge? Maybe he really had turned over a new leaf.

'What am I thinking about? Sit down, Daisy, and you too, Lizzie,' Molly urged. 'I'll make you both a drink. I've heard a little from Sean about the shenanigans you've been through, but you know what men are like. It's like pulling teeth trying to get them to talk. Now tell me all about it.'

Daisy couldn't help smiling at the avid interest showing on Molly's face, but was unsure what to say. She couldn't mention that the marriage had been bigamous, or about the poisoning. When she had asked her father if he was going to report Vera to the police he had reared up angrily, shouting that he felt enough of a fool without everyone knowing about it. Deciding to edit the explanations, she said, 'My father found out about the way Vera treated me, and how she lied to get me sent to my aunt's in Puddleton.'

'But I thought you had decided not to tell him.'

'Oh, it wasn't me. Vera's mother turned up and during a row it all came out.'

Molly shook her head. 'Well, I can't say I'm sorry. I never did like the woman, and though Paddy said 'tis all in my imagination, I used to feel her hate coming at me through the walls. So, where has she gone now?'

'To stay with her mother.'

'And how's your dadda?'

'Not too good, Molly. He hardly speaks, and is so miserable. It's terrible to see him like this, but I don't know how to help him.'

'He'll come round, Daisy. Just give him time.'

Although Lizzie had sat quietly during the whole of this conversation, her eyes going from one to the other, she now said, 'Go Kate's now?'

'Is that the woman Sean mentioned? The one I've seen calling on you lately?'

'Yes, she was in the same ward as Lizzie and they struck up a friendship. She's a lovely lady and is going to look after her tonight so I can go out with Sean.'

'Well, that's nice. But why can't Lizzie stay with your father?'

'I don't think he's up to looking after her. He's in a world of his own most of the time.'

'Ah well, 'tis to be expected, I suppose. Now where are you and Sean off to tonight?'

'To the cinema, and would you believe I've talked him into taking me to see *Gone with the Wind*. I know it's an old film, but I've never seen it.'

Molly burst out laughing. 'Begod! Sean must be smitten,' she spluttered. 'And guess what – I've got a bit of news too. Francis is starting at the nursery every afternoon, and I've got myself a little part-time job.'

'Have you? Where?'

'In the baker's shop. I'll be working from one till three every day and I start on Monday. Paddy wasn't too happy at first, but I talked him round. The extra money will come in handy, and I'm so looking forward to getting out of the house for a little while every day.'

'I'm pleased for you, and if you ever get stuck I'll always look after Frankie for you.'

'Oh, thanks, Daisy. I must admit I was a bit worried about the school holidays. I could leave him with Patrick – after all, he's thirteen now – but he's still a bit of a scallywag and I'm not sure that I can trust him.'

'I'd be pleased to have Frankie,' Daisy assured her. Then, draining her cup she stood up. 'We had better be off now, I've got a casserole in the oven that needs checking. Thanks for the tea, Molly.'

'You're welcome, darlin'.'

Lizzie rose to her feet, and taking her hand Daisy led her out, just as Patrick came clattering down the steps. 'Hello,' he said. 'I hear you're going out with Sean tonight. Who'd have thought it, eh?' he added with a wry smile.

Lizzie let out a peal of laughter and Patrick, grinning widely, poked out his tongue.

'Funny boy, Daisy. Funny boy,' she giggled.

Hearing Molly's laughter coming from behind them, Daisy heaved a sigh of relief. At least Lizzie hadn't called Patrick a bad boy, as she had Liam. Glancing quickly over her shoulder she met Molly's eyes, and as if sensing her thoughts, Molly nodded slowly and happily.

At five-thirty when her father arrived home, Daisy hurriedly dished up the dinner, and by the time he'd had a quick wash she was placing the plates on the table. Without a word he sat down, picked up his knife and fork, and began to eat.

'How were things at the office today?' Daisy asked, trying to draw her father out.

'Fine.'

'Why do you have to work on Saturdays, Dad?'

'We're busy,' he said shortly.

'I'm going out with Sean tonight and we're going to the pictures.'

His head lifted, a question in his eyes. 'What about Lizzie?'

'Kate's going to look after her, and she's staying overnight at her house.'

Nodding his head, Henry went back to his food, and for the rest of the meal, no matter how hard Daisy tried, her father hardly spoke.

Sighing, she picked up the plates, took them through to the kitchen where she quickly washed up. Time was getting on and she was anxious to get ready for her date. Throwing on her coat she called goodbye to her father, before ushering Lizzie out of the door.

It didn't take long to get to Kate's house, and Lizzie's face was wreathed with delight when she saw her friend. She went inside with hardly a backward glance, and in minutes Daisy was on her way home again.

Poking her head into the living room Daisy stared worriedly at her father as he sat gazing into the fire. He looked so desolate and her heart went out to him. Would he even remember to add more coal, she wondered. 'Dad, would you like me to stay in?'

'What? No, of course not,' he answered, lifting his head momentarily before turning back to the fire.

'All right, if you're sure,' Daisy told him, yet still feeling uncertain as she went upstairs to get ready.

After a quick bath she dressed carefully, putting on a navy-blue skirt and red sweater. Then, with one last check in the mirror she made her way back to the living room, asking as she entered, 'Do I look all right, Dad?'

Henry slowly turned round, his face so drawn that instead of looking in his early forties, he resembled a tired old man. 'Yes, you look fine,' he said, his voice distant.

Daisy ran to his side, crouching down beside his chair. 'Oh Dad, I can't leave you like this. I won't go out – I'll stay in with you.'

'Stop fussing, Daisy. I'll be perfectly all right on my own. Now go out and enjoy yourself.'

Surprised at such a long speech, Daisy rose to her feet at the sound of the doorbell. She kissed her father lightly on the top of his head. 'I won't be late,' she whispered, turning to leave.

The film held Daisy enthralled. Vivien Leigh looked beautiful in fabulous crinoline dresses, and Clark Gable so handsome with his small moustache and rakish smile. As the story unfolded she couldn't help crying, and Sean, trying to hide a smile, gave her his handkerchief.

She sighed when it came to an end, and as they stood when the National Anthem was played, she whispered, 'Oh, it was wonderful . . . wonderful!'

'Load of old tosh,' Sean said as he led her from the cinema, 'but I'm glad you enjoyed it.'

'Oh, I did,' Daisy told him, feeling her face flame as he suddenly reached out and took her hand. The film had taken her out of herself, letting her forget her worries for a short while. But now, glancing at the clock over the entrance to Arding & Hobbs department store, she pulled anxiously on Sean's hand. 'I must go home, it's late, and I hope we won't have to wait long for a bus.'

'I didn't realise that your father was strict. What time did he say you've got to be in?'

'It's not that, Sean. It's just that I'm worried about him.'

'It seems to me that you need someone to worry about *you* for a change, Daisy. From what my mother's told me it sounds like you haven't had any freedom since you left school. First you had to look after your stepmother, and now Lizzie. When do you ever have any time for yourself?'

'I've come out with you tonight, haven't I?'

'Yes, but only because you were able to find someone to look after your cousin. What if I want to take you out tomorrow night too?'

'Oh, I couldn't come out again so soon,' Daisy said worriedly.

'It's all right, don't look at me like that. As it happens, with me working nights, I only get Saturday and Sunday nights free. But what about during the week? Could I see you sometimes in the afternoons?'

'What about the boxing club?' she asked as a bus pulled up and they jumped onto the platform.

'I'd rather spend time with you,' Sean said as he took the seat beside her.

'I can't leave Lizzie on her own,' Daisy told him. 'Though I could ask Kate if she'd look after her again,' she added, brightening at the thought.

'Yes, good idea. Perhaps she wouldn't mind if we just go out for a couple of hours. We could go for a walk or something.'

'All right, I'll ask her,' Daisy told him, smiling shyly as Sean then wrapped an arm around her shoulders.

And that became the pattern of their days as spring turned to summer. Daisy continued to go out with Sean on Saturday nights, taking Lizzie to stay with Kate. Also twice a week Kate would come round at one o'clock in the afternoon, enabling Daisy to go for walks with Sean. They usually went to Clapham Common, but on the odd occasion they ventured as far as Battersea Park where Daisy loved the fountains, the Guinness Clock, and the small zoo.

It was lovely to see Lizzie so content too. She absolutely adored Kate, and seeing them together it was obvious that her feelings were reciprocated. Kate was so patient with her and would spend many hours reading to Lizzie or helping her to do simple jigsaw puzzles.

In August, on her sixteenth birthday, Daisy was thrilled when her father gave her a lovely cross on a fine gold chain. During the last few months she had seen him slowly coming out of his shell, and though still quiet, he seemed to be recovering.

Sean had give her a bottle of Coty's *L'aimant* perfume, and Lizzie, with Kate's help, had baked her a cake.

Smiling now, Daisy gazed at the ducks on the pond. The sun came out from behind a cloud, sparkling like thousands of small bright jewels on the rippling surface of the water. They were sitting on a bench under the shade of a willow tree: it had become their special place, a place where they were almost hidden from view. Leaning back she sighed, turning to look at Sean as he put an arm around her shoulders.

'Do you remember when I used to call you Porky Pig?' he asked.

'Of course I do. After all, it was only a couple of years ago. You were a horror – Patrick too.'

'I know, and I'm sorry, but we were just silly kids. I really do regret the way we behaved, especially when I came to realise what you had been through. Mind you, I certainly couldn't call you porky now. You've lost so much weight, Daisy.'

'I know, but I don't think I'll ever be really slim.'

'I like you just the way you are,' and giving her a little squeeze, he added, 'A man likes something to get hold of.'

'Oh, you're a man now, are you?' she teased.

Sean went quiet then, his eyes darkening as he gazed at her. Then suddenly he pulled her into his arms. 'Daisy,' he whispered, 'I think I'm falling in love with you. I know we're only young, but from our first date I knew you were the only girl for me.'

'Oh, Sean, I love you too,' she whispered, her heart pounding.

'Maybe next year, when you're seventeen, your father will let us get engaged,' he said.

'Oh, is this your idea of a proposal, Sean?'

'Yes, I suppose it is. Surely you don't expect me to get down on one knee?'

She laughed. 'No, and I shouldn't be surprised that you haven't. After all, you haven't got a romantic bone in your body.'

'Oh, haven't I? Just you wait, Daisy Bacon, and I might surprise you one day. But come on, you haven't answered my question. Do you think your father will allow it?'

'I don't know, Sean, but I don't see why not. We'll have been going out for a long time by then.'

'Well, in that case, I suppose I had better start saving.'

'I wish I could save too, but I don't have any money of my own, except for the hundred pounds my aunt left me in her will.'

'A hundred pounds! My goodness, I'm getting myself an heiress,' he joked. 'But doesn't your dadda give you any money for yourself?'

'No, and I don't think he's ever thought about it. I get the housekeeping every week, but that's all. If I need anything I only have to ask.'

Sean frowned. 'That doesn't seem fair, Daisy. If you were going out to work you'd be earning a wage, but instead you're stuck at home looking after Lizzie.'

'It doesn't matter. I really don't mind.'

'I know you don't, but I still think you should have a word

with your father. He could at least give you a bit of pocket money.'

'I'll think about it. Now come on, we had better get back. We've been out for two hours.'

'I wish we could spend more time together, Daisy,' Sean said as they ambled home.

'So do I, but at least we have these afternoons.'

'Maybe I should think about getting a day job, then we could spend more evenings together.'

'But I wouldn't be able to come out, Sean. I can't ask Kate because she works behind the bar at the Dog and Duck from Monday to Friday.'

His face darkened and Daisy looked at him worriedly. With Sean working nights, at least they had these afternoons, but if he changed to day work they would hardly see each other. For the first time she felt a surge of resentment, wishing that she had the freedom other girls of her age seemed to have. 'I'm sorry, Sean,' she said quietly.

'There must be something we can do,' he said impatiently.

'There isn't. Can't we just leave things the way they are?' she asked hopefully.

They turned into Fitzwilliam Street then, and as they paused outside Daisy's house, Sean answered, 'We don't seem to have much choice, do we?' Bending forward he gave her a quick kiss, before adding, 'But we can't go on like this for ever, love.'

Daisy watched Sean as he headed for his basement steps. What did he mean? Was he hinting that unless she had more freedom, they would have to stop seeing each other? No, don't be silly, she told herself. After all, he had just proposed.

Chapter Forty-Three

After a lovely summer the sun lowered in the sky and autumn foliage cloaked the trees on Clapham Common, poignantly reminding Daisy of Puddleton.

Fortunately Sean appeared to have given up on the idea of a day job, and to Daisy's relief the subject was never mentioned again.

They grew closer and closer as the months passed, and now as she finished getting ready, Daisy glanced in the mirror to check her appearance.

Her dark brown hair was below shoulder length, and she wore it parted on the side with a soft wave falling onto her forehead. Leaning closer to the mirror she applied a coat of pink lipstick, something she had taken to wearing since her father had finally agreed to give her an allowance. Not that she spent much of the pound a week he gave her, most of it going into her savings. But just occasionally she would treat herself to something frivolous, and had once purchased a pair of black patent shoes, with a narrow two-inch heel. Daisy thought they looked very glamorous, but it was Kate who had gently pointed out that they didn't suit her. Yes, she was slimmer now, but she had thick legs and wide feet, which made the shoes look incongruous, as if she had tried to stuff a quart into a pint pot. Sadly she had accepted the fact that she would never be glamorous. 'Wholesome', that was how Kate referred to her.

Oh well, Daisy shrugged, as with a last glance in the mirror she left her room. Sean always appeared happy with the way she looked, and let's face it, she couldn't make a silk purse out of a sow's ear. The reference to a pig made her giggle. Very apt, she thought, as she went into the sitting room to check on Lizzie.

Her cousin was engrossed with a jigsaw puzzle, her tongue sticking out of the corner of her mouth as she tried to fit the large wooden pieces together. She looked up as Daisy went in, and smiling, said, 'Pretty, Daisy. You pretty.'

'Thank you, kind maiden,' she joked and hearing the doorbell, hurried to answer it.

Kate stood on the doorstep, shaking the rain off her umbrella. 'Nice weather for ducks,' she quipped. 'I don't think you and Sean will be able to go far in this, Daisy.'

'I know, it's awful,' she agreed, shutting the door hastily as a sudden squall blew rain into the hall.

Only a few moments later she had to open the door again when Sean arrived, and even coming the short distance from next door, he was soaked. 'We can't go out in this, Daisy,' he gasped, running his hands over his wet face.

'No, perhaps we had better stay in,' she suggested, and taking his hand they went into the sitting room. 'We can't go out, Kate, so I'll take Sean into the dining room to play some records. Is that all right with you?'

'Well, yeah, I suppose so, but keep the door open, Daisy. Wait, now is as good a time as any. I've . . . er . . . I've got something to tell you.'

Moving further into the room, Daisy stared at Kate worriedly. Judging by her expression it was something important, so taking a seat on the sofa she indicated to Sean that he should join her.

'Look, love, it's like this,' Kate began, glancing worriedly at Lizzie. 'Not long ago I got a letter from my sister in Devon, and believe me I've given it a lot of thought. You see, the thing is — she wants me to go and live with her.'

'Kate, you're not going, are you?' Daisy asked, an edge of panic in her voice.

'Well, at first I dismissed the idea, but then my mind seemed to be made up for me. You see, Daisy, when I said no, my sister wrote again, this time telling me that she's ill and can't manage to look after Judy on her own. I've got to go, ducks. If I don't, my niece might have to go into care.'

'No go! No go!' Lizzie suddenly screamed, rushing forward and throwing herself at Kate.

'God, I've been dreading this,' the woman said, stroking Lizzie's hair as she held her. 'I don't want to leave, but she's me sister and the only family I've got. It breaks my heart to go, but I must put them first.'

'When are you going?' Daisy asked, raising her voice to be heard over Lizzie's screams.

'Next Monday, and though I hate to let you down, I've got so much packing and sorting out to do that I won't be able to 'ave Lizzie on Saturday night. I'm sorry, love.'

Daisy turned to look at Sean, relieved when he gave her a consoling smile. The rest of the afternoon was a continuing disaster as they all tried to comfort Lizzie. She was absolutely inconsolable and only when she fell asleep with tears of exhaustion, was Kate able to leave.

It was late by then and as Kate finally put her coat on, Daisy heard her father coming in. Henry walked into the sitting room, his eyes quickly moving across them all, finally settling on Lizzie, asleep on the sofa. 'Is something wrong?'

'Kate's moving to Devon, and Lizzie is very upset about it, Dad.'

'Oh, I see,' he said, his voice showing his lack of interest.

Daisy bit worriedly on her thumbnail. Her father obviously had no conception of what a disaster this was. With Kate no longer able to look after Lizzie, how could she go out with Sean?

'I've got to go,' Sean said, glancing at the clock. 'My shift starts in an hour.'

Daisy walked with him to the door, and with Kate following behind they didn't get a chance to talk. He squeezed her hand gently before leaving, saying softly, 'Don't worry, darling, we'll sort something out.'

Yes, but what? Daisy thought.

Hurriedly putting up her umbrella, Kate called, 'I'll be round to see you before I leave, Daisy.'

After closing the street door, Daisy poked her head into the sitting room and gestured to her father. When he came into the hall, she asked, 'Dad, would you mind looking after Lizzie on Saturday night so I can go out with Sean?'

'I don't think I could cope with her, Daisy. She always has a tantrum when you leave her and I don't know how to deal with it. Can't you take her with you?'

'But we want to be on our own, Dad.'

'You're only sixteen, and that's far too young to be courting seriously.'

'But you haven't said anything before, and I've been going out with Sean for ages.'

Henry's lips tightened and he said impatiently, 'Well, I meant to talk to you about it, but I just never got round to it. You should be seeing other boys at your age, not settling on the first one who asks you out.'

It was then that Daisy's temper flared. 'Oh, and when am I supposed to meet other boys? I've never had the chance to go out like other girls of my age. My life is spent looking after you and Lizzie, and anyway I don't want to meet other boys. I love Sean!'

'Love! Don't be ridiculous. You're far too young to know the meaning of the word.'

'I do love him – I do. Please, Dad, I'm only asking you to keep an eye on Lizzie once a week.'

'No, and I think you should stop seeing Sean. I repeat, you are too young to be courting.'

Daisy stared in horror at her father. Surely he didn't mean it? In desperation she yelled, 'You can't stop me seeing him, and anyway we're getting engaged next year!'

'Don't you dare shout at me! And as for you getting engaged – forget it! Now get out of my sight, and I don't want to see you again until you apologise.'

Daisy fled upstairs, unable to believe what had happened. She threw herself across the bed, tears flooding her eyes. *Oh Sean, Sean*, she cried inwardly. Surely her father couldn't stop her from seeing him?

Henry heard his daughter's bedroom door slam, and returning to the sitting room he walked across to the window, arguing inwardly with himself. She was far too young to be courting, wasn't she? *And* she had shouted at him, showing no respect for his authority. A small voice pricked his conscience – but maybe there was something in what she said about having no freedom?

No, he bristled. It wasn't true. Daisy had plenty of freedom. In fact, she had all day to do what she wanted, go out when she wanted. All right, she had to take Lizzie with her, but she loved her cousin so how could that be a hardship?

Looking out onto the wet street Henry gazed at the lamplight reflecting in the puddles. What choice did he have anyway? He had promised his sister that he would care for Lizzie, and was it his fault that Daisy was the only one who could deal with her? He had done his best. What more could he do? Anyway, Daisy was only sixteen and there would be plenty of time for boys when she was a bit older. At the moment all he asked of her was that she looked after Lizzie, and surely that wasn't too much?

The desolate weather matched his mood – a mood he had been unable to snap out of since Vera had left. God, he'd been a complete and utter fool, blind to her faults. No, you weren't, his conscience told him. You knew what she was like in the early days, but as soon as she got pregnant you chose to ignore it. You let her lead you around like a dog on a leash, believing everything she told you. And why? Because you desperately wanted a son.

Henry turned abruptly from the window, shaking his head angrily. All he wanted now was a little peace, and was that too much to ask? He didn't want to think any more, to analyse. He just wanted to forget. Switching on the television and trying to drown out his thoughts, he turned the volume up, forgetting that Lizzie was asleep on the sofa.

'Where Daisy?'

The voice startled him. 'Daisy's upstairs. Now be a good girl and watch the television until she comes down.'

'No. Want Daisy.'

'Well, go upstairs then,' Henry said impatiently, and seeing the distress on Lizzie's face as she fled the room, his conscience pricked again. He should make more of an effort with his niece, he knew that, but somehow he just didn't have the energy. It was then that he admitted the truth to himself. He didn't want Daisy going out with Sean, because he'd be stuck with looking after Lizzie. Sighing heavily he sank down in his chair. He was angry with himself, but more than that he was angry at everything that life had thrown at him. With his mouth set in a grim line, he stared fixedly at the television screen.

Daisy cuffed the tears from her face as she lay on her bed. She hadn't given her father his dinner, and Lizzie must be hungry too. Oh, Lord! She had left her downstairs! She was about to thrust her legs over the side of the bed when the door opened and her cousin scurried into the room.

'Where Kate? Where Kate?' she cried.

'She's gone home, darling. Now come on, don't get upset again.'

'Not go Devon?' Lizzie asked hopefully.

Daisy's shoulders slumped as she wondered how she could make Lizzie understand. 'Kate has to go, darling. Her sister is ill.'

'She come back?'

Daisy forced a smile. If Lizzie thought that Kate had only gone for a short while, maybe it would give her time to come to terms with it. 'Yes, perhaps she'll come back one day,' she answered. 'Now let's go downstairs. We haven't had our dinner yet.'

Lizzie sat at the kitchen table watching as Daisy prepared the food. Whilst peeling the potatoes her thoughts returned to Sean, and she pictured his face in her mind. At first she hadn't thought him handsome, but as her feelings grew she had come to love his features. Sean's every emotion reflected on his face: anger, joy, and there was the special way his eyes softened when he looked at her. Suddenly filled with defiance, Daisy's chin lifted. She didn't care what her father said! Nothing was going to stop her from seeing Sean.

But things didn't work out the way Daisy had hoped. No matter how much she begged and pleaded, her father refused to look after Lizzie on Saturday night. The only compensation being that this time he hadn't said she couldn't see Sean.

Finally, seeing their plight, Molly had stepped in and offered to look after her, but as she waited for Sean to come downstairs, Daisy stared at Lizzie with trepidation. She had followed her round to Molly's without protest; happily taking a seat at the kitchen table while Daisy sat nervously opposite.

'Lizzie, I'm leaving you with Molly for a little while,' she told her.

The girl looked about to protest, and Daisy quickly reached into her bag. 'Look, a new jigsaw puzzle for you.'

Her cousin smiled, and as she held out her hand, Daisy said, 'You can play with this, and before you know it I'll be back.' She knew it was a bribe and felt a pang of guilt, but what choice did she have?

Lizzie took the box with a wide smile and immediately began to open it, soon becoming absorbed as she tried to fit the large pieces together.

With relief Daisy saw Sean coming into the room, and hastily stood up. Smiling gratefully at Molly, she whispered, 'I think she'll be all right. Come on, Sean, let's go while she's distracted.'

They only got as far as the door when all hell broke loose. 'No! No go!' Lizzie screamed as she thrust back her chair. Jumping to her feet and catapulting across the room, she flung her arms around Daisy. 'No leave me! No leave me!'

'Calm down, Lizzie. We won't be long.'

'No! Stay with me!' she cried while Daisy gently tried to extract herself from her arms.

Her loud screams frightened Frankie, and his cries joined Lizzie's, the resulting cacophony echoing in the small room. With a look of despair Daisy tried to make herself heard above the din. 'It's no good, Sean. She won't stand for it – you can see that.'

Endeavouring to quieten Frankie, Molly shook her head despairingly. 'Daisy's right. It won't work and the pair of you will have to stay in.'

Sean's face darkened. 'This is bloody ridiculous,' he snapped.

'I'm sorry, Sean,' Daisy shouted before turning her attention back to Lizzie. Patting her cousin gently on the back, she urged, 'Come on, darling, let me go. It's all right, I won't leave you.'

At Daisy's words Lizzie's cries stopped instantly, though her breath was still coming in gasps. 'No leave?' she appealed.

'No, don't worry. I'll stay with you.'

'Well, that's it then,' Sean growled. 'We can't go out, and I don't fancy sitting in here all evening, so you might as well take her home, Daisy.'

Seeing his expression, Daisy nodded her head. It looked like it would take Sean some time to calm down, and anyway he was right, they could hardly spend the evening in Molly's kitchen – there was hardly enough room for them all to sit down. 'Yes, it may be for the best,' she agreed, and ushering Lizzie to the door her heart sank when Sean just gave her a grim smile, making no effort to escort them the short distance home.

'I'm ashamed of you, so I am,' Molly told her son as the door closed behind Daisy and Lizzie.

'Why? What have I done now?'

'My God, if you don't know, I'm not going to tell you. Except to say that you don't deserve a nice girl like Daisy.'

At his mother's words Sean's head lowered, and pulling out a chair he sat down fingering the pieces of puzzle left on the table. 'She forgot this,' he mused.

'Well, that's hardly surprising, is it? You made it pretty obvious you wanted to be rid of her.'

'No!' Sean cried, his head lifting. 'It's not Daisy I want rid of, but surely you can see how impossible it is for us? How are we ever going to see each other? And it'll be even harder now that I'm starting on day shifts next week.'

'Does Daisy know?'

'Not yet. I was going to tell her this evening, but Lizzie put paid to that.'

'Why have you changed your hours, Sean?'

'I'm fed up with working nights. When I come home after my shift I sleep all morning, then after a few hours of free time in the afternoon, it's back to work again. It drives me mad, Mammy.

It's not natural to sleep during the day and work at night. All I want is to live a normal life, and to have my evenings free.'

'I can understand that, but it will make things difficult for you and Daisy. Maybe you should have a word with Henry. He's not an unreasonable man, and 'tis about time he took a share in looking after Lizzie.'

'Don't you think Daisy hasn't tried to talk to him? He won't listen, and he seems to think that we shouldn't be courting.'

'What makes him think that?' Molly asked, her back stiffening. Did Henry Bacon think that Sean wasn't good enough for his daughter? Well, she'd have something to say about that!

'He thinks Daisy is too young.'

Molly took a seat opposite her son, annoyed with herself for jumping to conclusions. She leaned forward, and patting the back of Sean's hand, said, 'Do you know, Sean, I met your dadda when I was Daisy's age and we've been together ever since. Because of that I've been happy for the pair of you to start courting so young. But maybe Henry's got a point – neither of you have been out with anyone else.'

'I don't want anyone else. Daisy's the only girl for me.'

Molly sighed. Her heart went out to her son, but she couldn't see a way around their problems. Kate was the only other person that Lizzie would stay with, and even if Henry agreed to look after her, she doubted the girl would stand for it. Unable to think of words to console her son she continued to pat the back of his hand, wondering sadly if he and Daisy had any future together.

Chapter Forty-Four

Christmas came and went, and Daisy knew that Sean was at the end of his tether. Lizzie, still pining for Kate, had become clingy again, following Daisy around like a shadow. They hadn't had an evening out alone for over three months, and with Sean on day shifts there were no more walks on the Common in the afternoons, alone or otherwise.

On Sean's birthday, Henry, after much persuasion, finally agreed to look after Lizzie for the evening so they could go out for a meal. Daisy had dressed carefully, and when Sean called to pick her up she thought he looked wonderful in his dark suit and white shirt. But when they tried to leave it became a disaster – the same scenario all over again. Lizzie became hysterical and despite all their cajoling, she clung onto Daisy. With no other choice, once again Daisy had to give in, telling her cousin that she wouldn't leave her. But while extracting herself from Lizzie's arms, Daisy saw the expression on Sean's face, and her heart was filled with dread.

'This is ridiculous, Daisy, we can't go on like this. Can't you make Lizzie see sense?'

'Oh Sean, don't you think I've tried! It's just that she's so insecure now. First she lost her mother, and shortly after that . . . well, you know what happened with Liam. Then, just when Lizzie became close to Kate, the woman moved to Devon. How can I make you understand that Lizzie has the mind and emotions of a child? She's clinging on to the one thing that seems constant to her now – and that's me.'

'Daisy, I'm not a monster. I can see she's upset, but just how long is this going to go on for?'

'I don't know, Sean, but at least my father allows you to come round here in the evenings now.'

'Yes, but we rarely get the chance to be alone, do we? We're stuck in the sitting room watching the television with him and Lizzie, and even then nine times out of ten she plonks herself between us on the sofa.'

'I'm sorry,' Daisy choked.

'Please don't cry,' he begged, wrapping her in his arms. 'All right, we'll give it a little more time, and who knows, perhaps Lizzie will settle down again.'

Another two months went by and Daisy began to notice a change in Sean. He had rejoined the boxing club, spending more and more time with his mates, and when he did call round he seemed different, almost remote.

The last time she had seen him was four days ago and he'd only stayed for just over an hour, almost as though coming to see her had been an obligation. She should say something to him, she knew that, but dreaded a confrontation . . . dreaded what he might say.

Daisy gazed out of the window now; missing him, and wondering if he would call round this evening.

'What matter, Daisy?'

Swinging round, and seeing Lizzie's worried face, she forced a smile. 'Nothing, darling. I'm just looking out for Sean – he said he might come round.'

Catching a glimpse of herself in the mirror, Daisy grimaced. The less she saw of Sean, the more the weight had piled on again. Seeking comfort, she went back to baking and eating cakes, and though hating how she looked, she seemed unable to stop herself. She was losing Sean, and food was her only consolation.

Daisy glanced at her watch and seeing it was seven o'clock, she turned to look out of the window again. Her heart skipped a beat. He was coming! Sean was coming, and she ran to open the front door.

Her heart sank when she saw the expression on his face, and even though a part of her was expecting it, Daisy braced herself, praying she was wrong.

'Can we talk?' he asked, avoiding her eyes.

'Yes, come in.'

'No. It would be better if we talk out here.'

Daisy pulled the door partially closed, knowing it wouldn't be long before Lizzie came searching for her.

'We can't go on like this,' Sean said quietly.

'I know.'

'We talked about getting engaged, Daisy, but how could we get married when you have to spend all of your time looking after your cousin?'

'I know it would be difficult, but couldn't Lizzie come to live with us?' Daisy asked in desperation.

Sean's eyes finally met hers and she could see his distress. He slowly shook his head. 'No, I'm sorry, Daisy. What sort of marriage would that be?'

'Oh, Sean.'

'Daisy, I know I haven't been round much lately, but I just can't stand the thought of sitting in with your father and Lizzie night after night. Christ, we never spend any time together on our own and we should be able to go out and enjoy ourselves. I've tried, honestly I have, but I can't see a future for us.'

Unable to talk, her throat constricted, Daisy reached out to touch him, but he stepped quickly back.

'I'm sorry, Daisy, but it's over,' and with a desolate shake of his head, Sean turned and walked away.

Daisy fought to hold back the tears, but as hard as she tried it was impossible. She watched, agonised, praying that he would change his mind and come back. But as he disappeared from view she rushed inside, and slamming the door behind her, she flew upstairs to her bedroom.

After only a short time Lizzie opened the door, and seeing Daisy's distress she sat down on the side of the bed. Her hand came out, brushing the tears from Daisy's cheek, her eyes liquid pools of sympathy. 'No cry. No cry, Daisy.'

Unable to speak, Daisy reached out and pulled her cousin down beside her, and clutching her in her arms, she gave vent to her emotions.

'What on earth's the matter, Daisy?'

'Oh Dad,' she sobbed when she saw her father standing on the threshold of her room, 'I've broken up with Sean.'

'Perhaps it's for the best – and there are plenty more fish in the sea, you know.'

At the dismissive tone in Henry's voice Daisy's tears increased, and with a tutting sound her father went back downstairs.

She didn't know how long she lay there crying, but as her eyelids grew heavy Daisy fell into an exhausted sleep, Lizzie still clutched in her arms.

'What do you mean, you've broken up with Daisy?' Molly cried.

'I've had enough, Mammy. We never get the chance to go out together, in fact we never get more than two minutes on our own. All we ever do is sit watching the television, and nine times out of ten Lizzie sits between us.'

'But I thought you loved the girl, Sean?'

'I do, but there's no future for us. Daisy will never be free of her cousin, or her father, come to that.'

'Have you got yourself another girl then?'

'No, of course not. Now just leave it, Mammy, I don't want to talk about it any more.'

Molly, seeing her big strapping son close to tears, watched sadly as he went out again. With four sons she longed for a daughter, and when Sean had started courting Daisy, she had almost burst with happiness. Molly had loved the girl since she was a child and had watched her growing up. It would have been wonderful to have her for a daughter-in-law, but now her dreams had come to nothing.

'Why the long face?' Paddy asked as he stepped into the room.

'Oh, why is life so unfair, Paddy? Why do some people suffer so much while others sail through life without a care in the world?'

'Well, what a question. What's brought this on?'

Molly told him what had happened and with a small shake of his head, he spoke quietly. 'Do you know, I always admired Henry Bacon, and I saw him as a cut above the rest of us. Yet now I see there was nothing to admire, after all. It seems to me that he's a selfish man with no thought to the hurt he's causing his daughter.'

'That poor girl's been through so much, Paddy, and surely she deserves a bit of happiness in her life. You would expect her to be bitter with all that she's endured, but she isn't. And now that our Sean has broken up with her, I can't imagine how hurt she must be feeling.'

'I expect Sean's hurting too, Molly.'

'Oh, I know he is,' she answered impatiently. 'But he's a young man and free to go out and meet other girls – which no doubt he will.'

Paddy reached out and touched her hand. 'Daisy will be all right, Molly, and if anything, this will make her stronger. You spoke about people sailing through life without any troubles, but think about these people, Molly. They usually lack sympathy because they have no understanding of pain, and some of them are probably shallow and uncaring. Then one day, when tragedy hits them – as it inevitably will – it hits them hard and they aren't equipped to deal with it.' He shook his head, adding, 'Don't worry, darlin'. All that Daisy has suffered is moulding her into a wonderful and caring young woman, and you wait and see, she'll cope. I'm sure that one day everything will turn out all right for her.'

'Oh Paddy, where do you get your wisdom from?' Molly asked, tears filling her eyes.

''Tis just common sense,' he protested.

'I just wish we could do something to help,' she sobbed.

'I know, and maybe in time we'll be able to come up with something, but come on now, stop crying. I think I can hear Patrick coming downstairs and you don't want him to see you in this state.'

Chapter Forty-Five

Vera smiled at her son as he frolicked on the floor with Danny, relieved that she had made the decision over a year ago to offer him a job.

It had been hard at first as George had pined for his father, asking for him constantly, and it soon became apparent just how deeply and how lovingly Lennie had cared for their son.

Her thoughts drifted back to the time when she found out how much money she had inherited. When the solicitor had gone through the portfolio with her – the offshore bank accounts, the investments, the property – she had reeled with shock. Then, with hardly any time to gather her wits, Mr Davidson had gone on to explain that Lennie had set up a trust fund for George, the amount in it staggering.

Yet despite that, the early months had been difficult. Vera had kept Nancy Barker on for George's sake. He had just lost his father, and was obviously fond of his nanny, so much so that it would have been a dreadful wrench for him to lose her too. Instead Vera had gradually cut down the hours George spent with her each week. Then, six months later, Nancy had handed in her notice, saying that she felt she wasn't needed any more.

Now look at us, Vera thought. Over a year had passed, a year that should have brought her so much happiness. She hadn't sold the club – again because she didn't want to unsettle George. It had been amazing when Danny had carried her upstairs and she had seen the wonderful flat. George's playroom had been a revelation when she saw the amount of toys he had, among them a huge rocking horse, and a large train set with all the accessories laid out on the floor.

She had posted a note on the door saying that the club was closed. At first it had been a nuisance when every night vehicles had sped up the drive, the car doors banging before they drove away again, disappointed not to have gained admittance.

George's giggles now snapped Vera out of her reveries, and she found herself looking at the muscles rippling in Danny's back as he held her son effortlessly over his head. A surge of hot lust made her gasp. Yes, the doctors had told her that there was no reason why she shouldn't still enjoy sexual activity, but she had never even thought about it until Danny had come into her life. He was a wonderful man, honest, caring and kind, and her feelings for him had gradually grown, until now she had to hide them from him.

As if sensing her thoughts, Danny placed George on the floor in front of his toy cars and turned to look at her. 'Are you all right, Duchess? You're very quiet.'

'Yes, I'm fine,' Vera told him, unable to help smiling at the nickname Danny had given her.

'What time does your mum want picking up?'

'Oh, not for another hour or so. You know what she's like when she's with her old cronies.' Shaking her head she added, 'I don't think I'll ever be able to wean her away from Battersea.'

Danny grinned. 'No, I don't think you will, but she's happy enough to live here as long as she can see her mates a couple of times a week. And now you've had the conversions done, Ada loves living upstairs in her own little flat.'

Vera forced a smile. Yes, once her mother had a separate apartment she seemed happier, though it had taken a while to change these ground-floor rooms from a gambling establishment to the lovely home it was now.

'The conversion to the annexe is nearly finished too, and I think Betty will be dead chuffed.'

'I hope so,' Vera said. When realising how awful she had been to her cousin, and determined to make amends, she had sent Danny to find her. Betty's face was a picture when Vera handed her a cheque, going on to say that there would be a flat for her in the annexe if she wanted it. Vera grimaced, remembering her disgust when she had found the bedrooms, done up like tarts' boudoirs. It had seemed poetic justice to give Betty a substantial amount of money – money she had been forced to earn for Lennie by sleeping with his clients. Now, hopefully, when she moved into the annexe they could build new bridges.

'Do yer fancy going out for a drive, Duchess?'

'Er, yes, all right,' Vera said, her thoughts still on Betty.

'Penny for your thoughts, Duchess,' Danny said huskily, his voice at odds with his build as he now knelt before her.

Vera saw that look in his eyes again – a softness, even fondness. Stop it, she berated herself, it's all in your mind. What would Danny want with a cripple?

'Well, do you want to go out?' he repeated.

'Yes,' she said again, and frightened that he would see how she felt, she lowered her eyes.

'Right, I'll go and bring the car round. Coming, nipper?' he said as he stood up.

George scrambled to his feet, his toys forgotten as he ran to Danny's side, a look of hero-worship on his face as he gazed up at him.

Danny lifted Vera into the car, tucking a rug solicitously around her legs, while Georgie scrambled into the back. 'Right, off we go, nipper,' he said, climbing into the driver's side. 'Let's go and pick up your nan.'

Nearing Clapham, Vera again felt a surge of guilt, a guilt that had plagued her for so long. She didn't deserve to have so much! She didn't deserve to be happy!

She glanced over her shoulder at George, who as usual when travelling had already fallen asleep, slumped across the back seat. She had wanted her son back so badly, and at first when she thought about Henry, she had tried to use her desperation as an excuse to salve her conscience.

Yet during the past year as George slowly began to accept that she was his mother, her guilt had increased. She didn't deserve him, didn't deserve his love. Night after night now she lay in an agony of self-recrimination, her thoughts constantly turning to the time when she had been trying to poison Henry. Could she have gone through with it? Could she have killed him? Surely it was God's retribution that on the day she intended to finish Henry off, Lennie had snatched George back. Yes, she had fallen down the stairs, but she hadn't been pushed, she had lost her balance.

Unable to sleep, the constant agonising had caused her to lose weight and she had become pale and gaunt. She knew it worried both Danny and her mother, yet she was powerless to do anything about it. The way she had treated Daisy also played on her mind. God, she had been so cruel! It was as if she had become another person, a madwoman.

A sob escaped her lips, and turning sharply Danny said, 'What's the matter, Duchess?'

'Nothing, I'm all right,' she whispered.

'No you're not.' Swiftly pulling into the kerb and turning off the ignition, he moved round to study her. 'Look, Vera, I think it's about time I spoke me mind. There's something wrong, something worrying you. Can't you tell me what it is? I might be able to help.'

'No one can help me, Danny.'

'You don't know that, Vera. Come on, tell me what's troubling you.'

As she looked into Danny's eyes, the need to unburden herself became overwhelming, and unable to hold it back any longer Vera sank her head against the seat saying, 'Oh God, I'm an awful person. You see . . .'

Vera didn't look at Danny once while she told him how she had treated Henry and his daughter, unable to bear the thought of the censure she would see in his eyes. She faltered slightly before confessing about the attempted poisoning, but finally she blurted it out, her eyes brimming as she cried, 'Oh Danny, I'll never know – never know if I would have gone through with it.'

'I think when it came to the crunch you'd 'ave found you couldn't do it, Vera. Yeah, you did some rotten things, but not that. Anyway, I ain't been no angel meself, so who am I to cast stones?'

'You haven't tried to murder anyone, Danny.'

'It sounds like you were desperate, and with Lennie Talbot after you I ain't surprised. The woman you've been telling me about is nothing like the one I've come to know during the last year. It was another side of you – a side that was brought out by what you've been through.' A small smile played across his rugged features then, and with a shrug he continued, 'Yeah, I must admit I thought you were a right hard nut at first, but knowing what Lennie had done to you it was understandable.' He took her hand, his voice soft as he urged, 'Vera, listen to me. It's over now – things 'ave turned round and you've got the chance to be happy at last. Don't let Lennie ruin your life. Don't let him win, even from the grave.'

'I can't forget what I've done, Danny!'

'Vera, think about the nipper,' he said, indicating the back seat with a flick of his head. 'You're a good mother, and George loves you, but the kid's been pushed from pillar to post. Now, just when he's got a bit of stability, you're making yourself ill over things that you can't change.'

Vera closed her eyes, a groan escaping her lips. Danny didn't understand. How could she just forget it and put it all behind her? Yes, she *had* been desperate to get away from Lennie, but that was no excuse. What she had done was wrong, wicked, and nothing she could say or do could put it right.

'Vera, snap out of it. Look, the nipper's waking up and you'll upset him.'

'Mummy,' a small voice piped up from the back seat.

'Pull yourself together for his sake,' Danny whispered.

Taking great heaving breaths, Vera dashed the tears from her face. She couldn't put the past behind her, it would be impossible, and she knew that. If only there was some way she could make it up to them – but after agonising over it night after night she knew it was impossible. Neither Henry nor Daisy would ever want anything more to do with her, and anyway it was better for them that she stayed out of their lives. Yes, she had money, lots of it, but they would throw it in her face, and she wouldn't blame them.

No, the past would always be there to haunt her, but Danny was right, and somehow she had to pull herself together for George's sake. 'Oh God,' she whispered. 'Please, forgive me.'

Vera turned to look at her son and he smiled – that heart-stopping innocent smile that she loved so much. Her thoughts then turned to Lizzie, poor Lizzie who would never grow up and would always remain childlike. She too always had such an innocent smile. It was then that Vera realised what she could do. Yes, it was a salve to her conscience, but surely some good would come out of it too.

'Danny, close to Fitzwilliam road I often saw a school for Down's syndrome children. It's near the engineering factory. Do you know where I mean?'

'Yeah,'

'Would you take me there, please.'

Danny shot her a puzzled glance, but turned the car to do as she asked. It was only a short ride away and as the car slid into the kerb she said, 'Push me to the door, Danny, then leave me, please. I'll only be a few minutes.' Then turning to Georgie she added, 'Be a good boy, darling. Mummy will be back soon.'

It didn't take Vera long to find the school office, and taking her cheque book out of her bag she quickly wrote out a cheque. The woman behind the desk looked puzzled when Vera handed it to her, saying, 'I've come into a substantial amount of money, so please accept this donation to your school.'

The woman looked at the figure and her jaw dropped. Then, obviously trying to compose herself she said, 'Please, will you wait, Mrs . . . er . . . Talbot. I am sure the headmaster will want to thank you personally.'

'No, I can't stop.' Vera said as she turned her wheelchair hurriedly to leave. 'You do a marvellous job here, and I hope the donation will help.' As she moved into the playground, it was suddenly full of children – children like Lizzie who looked at her with innocent eyes.

It had been easy, Vera thought, just as it had been easy to give

Betty money, but it didn't make up for all she had done. As Danny settled her into the car then put her chair back in the boot, she saw that Georgie was looking out of the window, gazing at the children through the school railings as they smiled and waved at him.

'We can go now, Danny,' she said.

'I can guess what you've been up to, Duchess, and it was a good thing to do.'

'What, salving my conscience? Because that's all it is really. I'm still an awful person.'

Danny reached out and took her hand, squeezing it gently. 'Everyone makes mistakes, Vera. You seem to think you're all bad, but if you were you wouldn't be suffering from a guilty conscience. The fact that you recognise your mistakes and are trying to make up for them, shows me that you have more good in you than bad.'

'Oh Danny, do you really think so?'

'Yes, I do. Really bad people don't give a damn about what they've done. Now come on, you've done your best to make up for your mistakes, and it's time to put the past behind you.'

'I'll try, I really will,' she told him, his commonsense words easing her pain.

'Vera, let me look after you.'

Her head shot round, and at the look she could see in his eyes, her heart leaped. No, it couldn't be, she was imagining things. 'You do look after me, Danny. I don't know how I could manage without you.'

'Christ, I'm not much good at this,' he said. 'What I'm trying to say is that I love you, Vera. Surely you know that?'

'But . . . but I'm a cripple. I can't use my legs.'

'It ain't your legs I'm in love with – it's you. And anyway,' he added, laughing softly, 'they're only a small part of you, and there ain't nothing wrong with the rest.'

'Oh Danny,' she whispered.

He reached out and pulled her into his arms, and as his lips met hers Vera heard her son chuckle. 'Dan kissing Mummy.'

Their lips parted as they both dissolved into laughter, Vera's joy increasing when Danny turned to Georgie, ruffling his hair as he said, 'I'm going to ask your mummy to marry me. What do you think she'll say, son?'

'Yes!' Georgie piped.

Turning to look at her, his eyes full of love, Danny said huskily, 'Is he right?'

Slowly, and happily, Vera nodded.

Chapter Forty-Six

Daisy read Kate's latest letter again, and then threw it onto the desk. She hadn't had much to say this time, unlike her earlier letters that were full of descriptions of Devon. Instead she sounded rather sad, echoing Daisy's own unhappiness.

Walking back to the window she stared onto the street, wondering how much longer this pain would last.

After only a month she had seen Sean with another girl, and had thought her heart would break. Until then she had nursed a secret hope that he would come back to her, that he would knock on the door and tell her he couldn't live without her.

It didn't help that he lived next door, and Daisy found herself drawn to the window to watch out for Sean when he left for work in the mornings. Then when he was due home in the evening, she would return to her post, her heart full of longing as she watched him striding along the street.

Listlessly she glanced at her watch and saw that it was time to take Lizzie to the surgery. Just lately, her cousin's breathing had become very laboured and even the short walk to the shops left her gasping for air, the journey taking twice as long. Daisy had become sufficiently concerned to book a doctor's appointment.

'Come on, we've got to go,' Daisy told her, finding it difficult to raise enough energy to face the walk to the surgery. In fact, since breaking up with Sean she found every day an ordeal, and had to force herself to get out of bed each morning. Lizzie, sensing her unhappiness, was constantly trying to cuddle her, and though Daisy tried to be patient it was proving impossible not to push her cousin away. The resentment she felt tortured her, embittered her, and she found herself constantly thinking, *If only* . . .

It was a chilly morning as they stepped out onto the street, but by the time they arrived at the surgery Lizzie was running with perspiration, her hair sticking to her forehead. Even sitting in the waiting room her breathing was laboured and Daisy looked at her worriedly, relieved when they were called in.

The elderly doctor was patient with Lizzie and thankfully she allowed herself to be examined without fuss, only showing signs of nerves when the stethoscope was placed onto her chest. She was then weighed, the doctor sighing with exasperation when he looked at the scales.

'There's no sign of a chest infection, but this won't do, you know, and I'm not surprised that she's breathless. You really must put her on a diet. In fact,' he added, peering at Daisy over his half-moon spectacles, 'I think you could do with joining her, young lady.'

Daisy felt herself blushing deeply and lowered her face from the doctor's gaze. She knew he was right – she was almost as fat as Lizzie now.

'Now then,' the doctor said, returning to sit in his chair. 'Lizzie's breathing difficulties are a direct result of her obesity and it will eventually put too much of a strain on her heart.' Opening a drawer in his desk he rifled amongst the papers, eventually finding what he was looking for, and holding it out, he said, 'This is a diet sheet, and you must ensure that she sticks to it rigidly. I can't emphasise enough how important it is for her to lose weight.'

His manner then became dismissive as he scribbled on Lizzie's notes. 'Bring her back to see me in a month, and I hope by then to find that she's lost several pounds.'

Daisy whispered, 'Yes, Doctor,' and grabbing Lizzie's arm she ushered her out of the surgery. Diet! How would she be able to put Lizzie on a diet? Her cousin's appetite was enormous, and rapidly scanning the diet sheet Daisy grimaced. No cakes, no biscuits, no pastry – just lots of white meat and plenty of fruit and vegetables. Yet worried by the doctor saying that Lizzie's weight was causing a strain on her heart, Daisy knew that somehow she would have to ensure that her cousin kept to the new regime.

Right, let's start as we mean to go on, she thought, and on their way home she stopped at the greengrocer's, filling her bag with seasonal vegetables and fruit.

It was hard at first, but to encourage her cousin, Daisy went on the same diet. With relief she found it worked, because when Lizzie saw that Daisy had the same food on her plate, she ate what she was given, if a little reluctantly at first.

After a month they went back to see the doctor, and Daisy was gratified when he weighed Lizzie to find that amazingly her cousin had lost over half a stone.

Trying to avoid fattening foods became a torture for Daisy. Every night she tossed and turned in bed, feeling so hungry, and longing to raid the larder, her mouth salivating at the thought of food. But with no cakes or biscuits in the tins, she had to comfort herself with an apple instead.

She saw Sean with a different girl, but this one didn't last either, and a tall willowy blonde followed her almost immediately. The pain hadn't lessened, and seeing how slim this latest girl was, something pierced Daisy's heart.

Soon after that, her dieting became an obsession. Daisy would constantly look at herself in the mirror, seeing nothing but fat. She thought her hips looked huge, her legs like sausages, and her face round and chubby. It was food that had caused it, food that had destroyed her relationship with Sean. No wonder he had broken up with her, Daisy decided. After all, she looked disgusting!

Sometimes, unable to stick to the diet, Daisy's unhappiness made her binge, and then she would be filled with guilt. At these times she would rush to the bathroom, and sticking her fingers down her throat, she would make herself sick.

The months dragged by, Daisy's loneliness a deep ache within her. She spent her days looking after Lizzie, as well as cooking and vigorously cleaning the house. When she went out she didn't venture far, getting almost everything she needed from the local shops.

Now, wiping the perspiration from her forehead, Daisy carried a tray into the dining room. 'Here you are, Dad,' she said, placing his dinner on the table. It was an unusually hot June day, and Daisy thought it perfect weather for eating salad.

Henry looked with distaste at his plate. 'Not salad again.'

'It's too hot to cook, Dad. The kitchen's like an oven.'

He sighed heavily as he picked up his cutlery. 'Aren't you eating anything?'

'I had mine before you came in. Now come on, Lizzie, eat your dinner.'

'You no eat,' Lizzie protested.

'I had mine earlier!' Daisy snapped.

Henry frowned. Something in Daisy's voice penetrated his lethargy and he looked up, noticing for the first time the change in his daughter's appearance. Was she ill? She looked white, gaunt, and running his eyes over her body Henry was suddenly struck by how thin she was. The shock hit him with a jolt. He should have noticed before, but he had been blind and too wrapped up in his own misery. 'Daisy, you look awful! What's the matter with you?' he blurted out.

His daughter threw him a look of anguish before rushing from the room, the door slamming behind her. For a moment Henry stared at Lizzie as if expecting her to tell him what was wrong, but his niece just stared back at him, her mouth slack. Shoving his chair to one side he went after Daisy, finding her in her bedroom, her cries muffled as she hugged her pillow.

'Daisy, what is it, darling? Please, tell me what's wrong. Are you ill?'

She shook her head, her voice a croak as she whispered, 'No.'

'But you're so thin.'

'I'm not thin! I'm fat!' his daughter cried. 'Fat and ugly!'

Henry stared at her without comprehension, unable to make sense of her words. His worry made his voice sound sharp. 'Now stop it! Stop this crying! You're not making any sense. Of course you aren't fat, Daisy. If anything, you could do with putting on a bit of weight.'

'Just go away and leave me alone, Dad.'

He sat on the edge of the bed, ineffectually patting her hand. 'But I can't leave you in this state. Now pull yourself together, Daisy. It will upset Lizzie to see you like this.'

To his surprise, his daughter suddenly reared up, her eyes wild as she cried, 'Lizzie! Don't talk to me about Lizzie! If it wasn't for her . . .' Daisy's voice trailed off, the pain on her face awful to see. She gulped, taking in deep breaths of air in an effort to compose herself, and after a few minutes' silence, she slid her legs over the side of the bed. 'Oh, what's the point? All right, Dad, I'll come downstairs now.'

Henry was still surreptitiously studying Daisy when they returned to the dining room; angry with himself for not noticing how much she had changed. He sat picking at his salad, and taking a good look at himself, he didn't like what he saw. It was guilt that had made him shut out his daughter – she had suffered terribly at Vera's hands, and he was still unable to forgive himself for failing to protect her. And now, because of his own self-pity, she was suffering again, but with what? How could he find out?

'Are you sure you're not ill?' he asked her tentatively. 'Maybe you should see the doctor?'

'No, I'm all right,' Daisy said listlessly as she began to clear the table.

Henry's thoughts were racing as his daughter left the room, Lizzie trailing behind her as usual. If only there was someone he could speak to, someone who might be able to help. Molly! Yes, Molly – maybe she would know what had caused this change in Daisy. Rising rapidly to his feet he went into the kitchen. 'I'm just popping out for a little while,' he said. 'I'll see you later.'

His daughter didn't bother to turn her head as she plunged the dishes into the sink, just giving him an imperceptible nod. Henry ran his hands over his forehead, looking worriedly at her for a moment, before making his way next door.

'Henry!' Molly said, her voice high with surprise. 'Is something wrong?'

'I don't know, Molly, but can I talk to you?'

'Yes, of course,' she said, standing aside to usher him in.

As Henry stepped into the kitchen he saw Molly's husband sitting at the table, and with hardly a smile Paddy said, 'Hello, Henry. Come and sit down.'

Drawing out a chair he sat down quietly, and glancing around the basement he felt sweat breaking out on his forehead. The back door was open, but this did little to cool the room and it was like sitting in an oven. Both Paddy and Molly were looking at him expectantly, so taking the bull by the horns he said, 'I'm sorry to bother you both, but I know Daisy talks to you, Molly, and I wondered if you know what's wrong with her.'

'Henry, since she broke up with Sean, I hardly see the girl. Daisy was badly hurt, and I don't blame her for staying away.'

'But you must have seen her when she's been out and about.'

'Well yes, but only the odd glimpse now and then. Is it her weight that's bothering you?'

'So you've noticed. Yes, Daisy's as thin as a rake and looks so ill, yet when I questioned her she insisted that there's nothing wrong.'

Paddy broke in then, his voice unusually harsh, ''Tis unhappiness – that's her problem, and if you can't see that, you're blind. Now listen, Henry. I want you to hear what I've got to say without interruption, for it will take some telling, but 'tis time you saw the truth.'

Henry stared at Paddy, surprised by the tone of his voice. 'Truth? What truth?'

Paddy pulled out his tobacco pouch and began to roll a wafer-thin cigarette, then after a glance at his wife he began to speak. 'I've watched Daisy grow up, Henry, and I know what she's been through. First she lost her mother, and what she suffered at her stepmother's hands doesn't bear thinking about. We only found out ourselves when she came back from that place you sent her to in the country, and it broke our hearts, I can tell you. We wanted to speak to you, but Daisy wouldn't have it. No, she insisted, you were upset at losing your sister and she didn't want to burden you with any more grief.'

'I know, and I'm wracked with guilt about it, Paddy. I sent her away. I believed Vera, and now I feel a complete and utter fool.'

'It's not *you* we're talking about now, 'tis your daughter,' Paddy snapped. 'She's a young woman who out of duty came home to look after her stepmother. Then on top of that, when your sister died, Daisy had the added burden of Lizzie. The poor girl has never had a normal life. She's never had any freedom and instead she's been tied to your house. Daisy has been made old before her time.'

'But she doesn't mind, and she loves Lizzie,' Henry protested.

'Don't talk daft, man. 'Tis your fault that she and Sean broke up. Daisy begged you to help her with Lizzie so they could go out occasionally, but you wouldn't have it, would you! It was too much trouble.'

'No, that's not true, Paddy. I tried, but Lizzie won't let Daisy out of her sight.'

'That's just excuses you're making. You should have tried a bit harder to establish a relationship with Lizzie, and then you would have gained her trust.' Paddy held up his hand, forestalling Henry when he tried to speak. 'All right, it may not have happened overnight, but it would have worked eventually. If you had just made more of an effort with Lizzie, your daughter could have had a little more freedom.'

Henry lowered his head, thinking about the man's words, and suddenly filled with shame he murmured, 'Yes, you're right, Paddy, and thanks, you've given me food for thought.' Rising to his feet he went towards the door, saying as he left, 'I just hope I can find a way to make it up to Daisy.'

Henry's mind was churning as he opened his front door. There had to be something he could do, but what? He went into the dining room, and drawing out a chair he sat at his desk, his mind still searching for a solution. Absentmindedly picking up an envelope, Henry's eyes were drawn to the postmark. Drawing out the letter, he quickly scanned the contents, his eyes narrowing in thought. Could this be the answer he was looking for?

Chapter Forty-Seven

Paddy listened to Henry, pleased that the man had come to his senses at last. He seemed determined now to have everything in place by Daisy's birthday and excitedly gave him the letter to read.

'Have you spoken to Sean yet?' he asked.

'No, not yet. I wanted to be sure you could pull this off first. But don't worry, I know my boy. Sean's like an open book to me, and that blonde piece he was seeing joined the others on the scrapheap.' Paddy finished reading the letter that had arrived from Devon that morning, and handed it back to him.

'I just hope we're doing the right thing' Henry fretted. 'I know Daisy still feels the same, but how can you be sure that your son does too?'

'Henry, I'm almost certain. Yet even if I'm wrong, what you're doing will still change Daisy's life for the better.'

Henry grinned. 'I still can't believe my luck. If I hadn't found that letter from Kate, none of this would have been possible. It's not as if she wrote anything to indicate her unhappiness. It was just something about the tone . . . something I could read between the lines.'

'Well, 'tis great news. Though from what you've told me, it's going to cost you a pretty penny.'

Smiling ruefully, Henry said, 'Yes, but it'll be worth it just to see the look on Daisy's face when I tell her she's to have her own flat.' He frowned, adding, 'I'm still worried about Sean though. He might not be so keen on the idea.'

'Of course he will. Leave the lad to me, Henry, and I'll tell him all about it when he comes home.'

'I'd best be off now, Paddy. I don't want to arouse Daisy's suspicions. Will you let me know what Sean says as soon as possible?'

'Yes, of course, but if you don't want to give the game away you had better wipe that smile off your face before you go indoors.'

Paddy prayed inwardly that he hadn't given the man false hope. What if he was wrong? What if he had misread his son's feeling for Daisy? Yet thinking back to last month, he was sure he hadn't imagined the expression on Sean's face. They had been walking home together, when, drawing close to Daisy's house, the door opened and she came out, Lizzie as usual close behind. Seeing them she had turned hurriedly, scooting back inside again. It was then, as he glanced quickly at his son, that Paddy saw the look of pain etched on his features.

What Henry intended to do was amazing. Daisy would still be living in the house, but in a separate flat, and it was marvellous that she was to gain her independence at last. Impatiently tapping his fingers on the table, Paddy sighed with relief when he heard his son coming down the basement steps.

At last, he thought, and composing his features as Sean came in, he said, 'Sit down for a minute, lad. I want to talk to you.'

'Where's Ma?' the boy asked, his eyes quickly scanning the room.

'She's out in the garden with Francis.'

'What do you want to talk to me about?' Sean asked, his eyes puzzled.

As his son sat opposite him Paddy took a deep breath, deciding to plunge straight in. 'I've seen you with one girl after another lately. You pick them up, then throw them away, and it's obvious that you're not happy. Do you still care for Daisy? Is that the problem?'

Sean lowered his head. 'I don't want to talk about it, Dadda.'

'I know you don't, but I've good reason for asking. Now, tell me the truth. Do you still love the girl?'

As Sean looked up, the misery in his eyes was clear to see, and with a sigh he said, 'Yes, I do, but it's pointless. I know that somehow I've got to get over her, Dad. Maybe it's stupid to go out with other girls, but I don't know what else to do.' He smiled wryly, adding, 'I thought it would be better than drowning my sorrows with drink.'

'And has it worked, Sean?'

'No, of course not. None of them can hold a candle to Daisy. Oh, I know a couple have been pretty, and fun, but there was just something missing. They didn't have Daisy's smile, or her soft voice.' He shrugged. 'But what choice have I got, Dadda? Do you expect me to become a monk?'

Paddy smiled. So he hadn't been wrong. 'No, son, of course not. But listen, because I've got something important to tell you.'

Daisy stood gazing listlessly out of the window in the sitting room, unappreciative of the cloudless blue sky and bright sunshine that bathed the street in light. She felt tired and weak, her mind grappling with the strange buzz of activities that had been going on in the house for the last few weeks. Builders had called round, and saying that he didn't want to be disturbed, her father had been ensconced with them in the dining room. When she had questioned him he had waffled something about getting the ramp converted back to steps, but he failed to meet her eyes and her suspicions were aroused.

Twice Daisy had seen her father going next door to Molly's, but again he evaded her questions. This time his excuse was that he had been round to collect some plant cuttings that Paddy had cultivated for him. There was no doubt her father was happier these days, but what had brought about this sudden change?

She sighed heavily. It was her birthday today, but she hadn't received a single card. In fact, it hadn't even been mentioned at breakfast. Moving away from the window, Daisy shook her head. She was seventeen, and for the first time her father had forgotten her birthday. It was funny really, for she had dreaded the day.

Dreaded having to pretend that she was happy, when all the time she was crying inside. How could she forget that if she hadn't broken up with Sean, they would have been getting engaged today.

It was strange too that her father had gone out. Sunday mornings were usually leisurely for him, and he would spend hours either reading the papers or pottering about in the garden. But this morning he had risen early, and after hurriedly eating his breakfast, he had rushed out, saying he would be back at about half-past ten.

Daisy glanced at Lizzie who was busily engaged with yet another new jigsaw puzzle, a picture of a monkey gradually appearing. It was odd that her cousin hadn't sensed the strange atmosphere in the house. If anything Lizzie had changed too, and though still clingy she seemed more content lately.

Glancing at the clock Daisy saw that it was nearly twenty to eleven, and just as she turned to go back to the window there was a flurry of activity in the hall. She heard voices, laughter, and then the door flew open.

'Happy Birthday, Daisy – and look who I've brought to see you!' her father cried, standing to one side.

It was Lizzie who reacted first, while Daisy stood frozen, unable to believe her eyes.

'Kate, Kate!' she yelled, scrambling to her feet and running towards the woman who was standing in the doorway.

''Ello, ducks, give us a kiss,' Kate said, opening her arms wide, and as Lizzie flew into them she added, 'Well, Daisy, has the cat got your tongue?'

'I . . . I . . . Kate! How . . . when . . .?' she stammered, unable to believe what she was seeing.

'There's plenty of time for explanations, but right now I'm spitting feathers. It's been a long journey and I could do with a cuppa.'

'Yes . . . of course, I'll go and make one.' Her head spinning, Daisy hurried to the kitchen, grasping Kate's hand and giving it a quick squeeze as she passed.

Lizzie was still wrapped in Kate's arms, clinging on like a limpet, her face wreathed in smiles.

As she hurriedly made the tea, Daisy tried to put her scrambled thoughts into order. What was Kate doing here? Had she come for a holiday? Oh, it was lovely to see her, but how would Lizzie react when she went back to Devon? Last time, the separation had been so traumatic.

Turning with the tray in her hands she saw her father standing in the doorway, a gentle smile on his face. 'What's going on, Dad?' she asked.

'Did you think I'd forgotten your birthday, Daisy?'

'Well, yes, and it's lovely to see Kate, but how did you arrange it? And how long is she staying?'

He winked, saying enigmatically, 'Bring the tray through and you'll find out.'

As Daisy walked back into the sitting room she found that the scene hadn't changed much. Kate had moved further into the room, but Lizzie was still hugging her. 'Let Kate sit down, Lizzie,' she urged.

Placing the tea tray on the table, Daisy was bewildered by the clandestine looks that passed between her father and Kate. 'Will somebody tell me what's going on?' she begged whilst pouring the tea and passing the cups around.

'Bless her . . . she's champing at the bit. Can I tell her, Henry?'

'Yes, all right, but you had better start at the beginning.'

Kate folded her arms, lifting up her ample bosoms in the process. 'Right, well – it's like this, Daisy. I gave up my home to go and live with me sister because I was under the impression that she was ill. Huh, she was ill all right, but it wasn't serious.' Her lips pursed. 'Talk about exaggeration – the letters sounded like she was at death's door. Anyway, to cut a long story short, she soon recovered from what turned out to be a kidney infection. Christ, Daisy, she lives in the middle of nowhere, and it was more a case of loneliness than illness.' Kate sighed before continuing, 'I couldn't stick it, love. I just ain't cut out for living in the country, but what could I do? Where else could I go?' With a rueful smile, she said, 'My trouble is that I've always been impetuous. I act without thinking, and I realise now that I should have checked me sister's story out before giving up me flat. I must admit it was lovely to see me niece Judy again, but I wasn't really needed. You see, soon after I moved in, me sister went and found a day centre for Judy. I thought it might 'ave given us the opportunity to go out and about a bit, but no, me sister just wanted to spend her free time pottering about in the garden.'

Daisy stared as Kate picked up her cup and took a sip of tea, willing her to continue. At last the cup was put back in the saucer and she said, 'So when I got your dad's letter I was over the moon and—'

'Letter? What letter?' Daisy asked.

'Give us a chance, love, and I'll tell you. Your dad wrote with an offer of a position, a wonderful one too. It was like the answer to all me prayers.'

'Position? I don't understand.'

'Gawd, Daisy, you would if you'd stop interrupting,' Kate chuckled. 'Now, it's like this. I'm coming here to live, and your dad is going to convert the house into two flats. Me, Lizzie and your dad will live in one, and you'll live in the other.'

'What!'

'Blimey, I can see you're shocked, but shut your mouth or you might catch a fly.' Hitching up her bosoms again, Kate continued, 'Now as I was saying, I'm going to look after Lizzie, and I'm dead chuffed about it. I love the girl, Daisy. She's like a daughter to me and I've missed her so much.'

Daisy turned to her father. 'I can't believe it. Is this true, Dad?'

'Yes, darling. You see, I've come to realise how selfish I've been, and now with Kate looking after Lizzie you'll be free to do what you want with your life. You could perhaps go to college and take a secretarial course. I know it's something you've always wanted to do.'

Unable to take it in, questions raced around in Daisy's mind. 'But how are you going to convert the house into two flats?'

'Well, it will take a bit of time, but the builders have assured me it can be done. The basement will be a kitchen-dining room, and this floor will have a living room and bedroom, with the present kitchen converted into a bathroom. The flat upstairs will be much the same, but to make three bedrooms, the top floor that we only use for storage at the moment will also be converted.'

'But why go to all the trouble of turning the house into two flats, Dad? It will cost a fortune and I don't see why it's necessary. With Kate living in and looking after Lizzie, I'd still be able to have the freedom you talk about. Why do we have to have separate flats?'

Her father's eyes widened imperceptibly and he shot a glance of what looked like desperation at Kate, and it was she who responded. 'Well, er . . . it's like this, you see. I . . . um . . . I wanted a place of me own. It's all very well saying I could just move in here with you, but I wanted a bit of independence. Living with me sister made me realise that, and it's one of the things I insisted on before agreeing to your father's offer.'

'If my father is moving into the top flat with you and Lizzie, how is that giving you independence?'

'Your dad's out to work all day, and with you maybe starting college, he'll need someone to cook his meals.'

'But . . .'

'Look gel, it's been a long and tiring journey from Devon and me head's spinning with all these questions,' Kate protested.

Daisy was still puzzled. It all sounded a bit odd, but before she could gather her thoughts her father spoke, saying, 'Darling, go and get your glad rags on now. I'm taking you out.'

'You're taking me out? Where are we going?'

'Now that would spoil the surprise, wouldn't it? Go on, off you go and get ready.'

'But Kate's only just arrived.'

'I ain't going anywhere, ducks. I'll still be here when you come back.'

Daisy's eyes encompassed them all, seeing that it was only Lizzie who looked back at her without guile. Her father and Kate's expressions held something she couldn't put her finger on, a mixture of secretiveness and glee. 'You're up to something, I just know you are, and I wish I knew what it was,' she told them, yet smiling as she left the room.

'Put something pretty on!' her father called.

Mounting the stairs Daisy's heart felt a little lighter. It would be lovely to have Kate living with them and looking after Lizzie. And it was wonderful that at last she would be able to go to college.

But as Daisy entered the bedroom and rifled in her wardrobe, she couldn't help wishing that all this had happened six months ago. If it had, she might not have lost Sean. Daisy remembered the lovely willowy blonde he was with now, and slipping a dress over her head she felt a knot of pain in her chest. It was too late now. Sean had found someone else, and someone with whom she couldn't possibly compete.

'My, you look as pretty as a picture,' Kate said as Daisy stepped into the living room. 'But you're a bit thin, love, and I can see I'm gonna need to feed you up.'

Daisy had brushed her hair until it shone, and added a pretty slide to one side. Her blue floral dress, clinched in at the waist with a white belt, flounced out from her hips and swung as she moved. A pair of white sandals and matching handbag completed the outfit. Thin, Kate had said, yet her mirror told her otherwise and Daisy knew that Kate was just being kind.

'Come on then, let's be off. We don't want to be late,' her father said, taking her arm.

Lizzie, happily sitting beside Kate, made no protest, and just gave them a little wave as they left the room.

Stepping outside, Daisy asked, 'Where are we going, Dad?'

'You'll see,' was his enigmatic reply.

'Happy Birthday, Daisy. I'll see you later,' a voice called.

She turned her head, surprised to see Molly standing at the top of her basement steps. 'Er . . . thanks,' she answered.

Molly grinned widely, and with a little wink turned to go back downstairs.

What was going on, Daisy wondered. Why was everyone behaving so strangely?

'No, we're not going in the car,' her father said as she moved towards it, and instead he began to lead her along the street.

Daisy's bewilderment increased when they reached Clapham Common, her father leading her down a path that went towards the duck pond. No, she didn't want to take this route. There were too many painful memories, and her steps faltered.

She saw the willow tree ahead, the bench almost hidden from view, and looked down in anguish. It was their bench – their special bench – where Sean had proposed.

With a start Daisy realised that her father had drawn them to a halt. Surprised, she looked up at him, seeing an odd crooked smile on his face. He bent down and kissed her gently on the cheek, then with his hand on her back he pushed her lightly forward. 'Go on, darling,' he murmured. 'There's someone waiting to see you – someone you may soon want to share your flat with.'

Daisy looked ahead and saw a figure emerging from behind the tree – the sun turning his hair to a coppery glow. Her eyes filled with tears of joy. 'Sean – Sean,' she whispered, running forward as he held out his arms.